Elizabeth Hoyt is a *New York Times* bestselling author of historical romance. She lives in central Illinois with her husband, two children and three dogs. Elizabeth is always more than happy to receive missives from her readers. You can write to her at: P.O. Box 17134, Urbana, IL 61873.

Visit Elizabeth Hoyt online:

www.elizabethhoyt.com
www.twitter.com/elizabethhoyt
www.facebook.com/ElizabethHoytBooks

Praise for Elizabeth Hoyt:

'Hoyt uses her gift for reimagining classic fairy tale themes to create a magnificently rendered story that not only enchants but enthrals. With its mesmerising plot and unforgettable characters, *Wicked Intentions* will make readers eager for the next Maiden Lane novel'
Romantic Times

'With its lush sensuality, lusciously wrought prose and luxuriously dark plot, *Scandalous Desires* . . . is a romance to treasure'
Booklist

'Hoyt brings steamy sensuality to the slums of early 18th-century London in this engaging seriess . . . enhanced by earthy, richly detailed characterisations and deft historical touches'

Also by Elizabeth Hoyt

Maiden Lane series:

LORD *of* DARKNESS

ELIZABETH HOYT

piatkus

PIATKUS

First published in the US in 2013 by Grand Central Publishing,
A division of Hachette Book Group, Inc.
First published in Great Britain in 2013 by Piatkus

A CIP catalogue record for this book
is available from the British Library.

ISBN 978-0-7499-5816-9

Printed and bound in Great Britain by Clays Ltd, St Ives plc

Papers used by Piatkus are from well-managed forests
and other responsible sources.

MIX
Paper from
responsible sources
FSC® C104740

Piatkus
An imprint of
Little, Brown Book Group
100 Victoria Embankment
London EC4Y 0DY

An Hachette UK Company
www.hachette.co.uk

www.piatkus.co.uk

For my darling eldest, Emma.
I am so proud of you.

Acknowledgments

Once again I must thank the team of professionals who helped to put this book into your hands: my wonderful agent, Susannah Taylor; my incredibly patient editor, Amy Pierpont; and my most excellent copy editor, Carrie Andrews (all mistakes—particularly those involving *eye color*—are my own). In addition, Amy's assistant (and editor in her own right!), Lauren Plude, always knows what's going on, Diane Luger from the GCP Art Department has put together a gorgeous cover, and Nick Small and Joan Schulhafer from publicity have worked tirelessly to make sure my books are actually read.

Thank you all.

Chapter One

Have you ever heard tell of the Hellequin?...
—From *The Legend of the Hellequin*

LONDON, ENGLAND
MARCH 1740

The night Godric St. John saw his wife for the first time since their marriage two years previously, she was aiming a pistol at his head. Lady Margaret stood beside her carriage in the filthy St. Giles street, her glossy, dark curls tumbling from the velvet hood of her cloak. Her shoulders were square, both hands firmly grasped the pistol, and a murderous gleam shone in her pretty eyes. For a split second, Godric caught his breath in admiration.

In the next moment, Lady Margaret pulled the trigger.

BOOM!

The report was deafening but fortunately not fatal, as his wife was apparently an execrable shot. This did not reassure Godric as much as it should have, because Lady Margaret immediately turned and pulled a *second* pistol from her carriage.

Even the worst shots could get lucky on occasion.

But Godric hadn't the time to meditate on the odds of his wife actually murdering him tonight. He was too busy saving her ungrateful hide from the half-dozen footpads who had stopped her carriage here, in the most dangerous part of London.

Godric ducked the enormous fist coming at his head and kicked the footpad in the stomach. The man grunted but didn't go down, probably because he was as big as a draft horse. Instead, the robber began a counterclockwise circle of Godric as his compatriots—four of them, and every one quite as well fed—closed in on him.

Godric narrowed his eyes and raised his swords, a long one in his right hand, a short one in his left for defense and close fighting, and—

God's *balls*—Lady Margaret fired her second pistol at him.

The gunshot shattered the night, echoing off the decrepit buildings lining the narrow street. Godric felt a tug on his short cape as the lead ball went through the wool.

Lady Margaret swore with a startling breadth of vocabulary.

The footpad nearest Godric grinned, revealing teeth the color of week-old piss. "Don't like 'e much, now, do she?"

Not *precisely* true. Lady Margaret was trying to kill the Ghost of St. Giles. Unfortunately, she had no way of knowing that the Ghost of St. Giles happened to be her husband. The black leather mask on Godric's face hid his identity quite effectively.

For a moment, all of St. Giles seemed to hold its breath. The sixth robber still stood, both of his pistols aimed at Lady Margaret's coachman and two footmen. A female spoke in low, urgent tones from inside the carriage, no doubt trying to lure Lady Margaret back to safety. The lady herself glared from her stance beside the carriage, apparently oblivious to the fact that she might be murdered—or worse—if Godric failed to save her from the robbers. High overhead, the wan moon looked down dispassionately on the crumbling brick buildings, the broken cobblestones underfoot, and a single chandler's shop sign creaking wearily in the wind.

Godric leaped at the still-grinning footpad.

Lady Margaret might be a foolish chit for being here, and the footpad might be merely following the instincts of any feral predator who runs down the careless prey that ventures into his path, but it mattered not. Godric was the Ghost of St. Giles, protector of the weak, a predator to be feared himself, lord of St. Giles and the night, and, *damn it*, Lady Margaret's *husband*.

So Godric stabbed fast and low, impaling the footpad before his grin had time to disappear. The man grunted and began to fall as Godric elbowed another footpad advancing behind him. The man's nose shattered with a crunching sound.

Godric pulled his sword free in a splatter of scarlet and whirled, slashing at a third man. His sword opened a swath of blood diagonally across the man's cheek, and the footpad stumbled back, screaming, his hands to his face.

The remaining two attackers hesitated, which in a street fight was nearly always fatal.

Godric charged them, the sword in his right hand whistling as it swept toward one of the footpads. His strike missed, but he stabbed the short sword in his left hand deep into the thigh of the fifth footpad. The man shrieked. Both robbers backed away and then turned to flee.

Godric straightened, his chest heaving as he caught his breath and looked around. The only robber still standing was the one with the pistols.

The coachman—a thickset man of middling years with a tough, reddened face—narrowed his eyes at the robber and pulled a pistol out from under his seat.

The last footpad turned and fled without a sound.

"Shoot him," Lady Margaret snapped. Her voice trembled, but Godric had the feeling it was from rage rather than fear.

"M'lady?" The coachman looked at his mistress, confused, since the footpads were now out of sight.

But Godric knew quite well that she wasn't ordering the murder of a footpad, and suddenly something inside of him—something he'd thought dead for years—woke.

His nostrils flared as he stepped over the body of the man he'd killed for her. "No need to thank me."

He spoke in a whisper to disguise his voice, but she seemed to have no trouble hearing him.

The bloodthirsty wench actually clenched her teeth, hissing, "I wasn't about to."

"No?" He cocked his head, his smile grim. "Not even a kiss for good luck?"

Her eyes dropped to his mouth, left uncovered by the half-mask, and her upper lip curled in disgust. "I'd rather embrace an adder."

Oh, that's lovely. His smile widened. "Frightened of me, sweeting?"

He watched, fascinated, as she opened her mouth, no doubt to scorch his hide with her retort, but she was interrupted before she could speak.

"Thank you!" cried a feminine voice from inside the carriage.

Lady Margaret scowled and turned. Apparently she was close enough to see the speaker in the dark even if he couldn't. "Don't thank him! He's a murderer."

"He hasn't murdered *us*," the woman in the carriage pointed out. "Besides, it's too late. I've thanked him for both of us, so climb in the carriage and let's leave this awful place before he changes his mind."

The set of Lady Margaret's jaw reminded Godric of a little girl denied a sweet.

"She's right, you know," he whispered to her. "Believe it or not, toffs have been known to be accosted by foot-pads in this very spot."

"Megs!" hissed the female in the carriage.

Lady Margaret's glare could've scorched wood. "I shall find you again, and when I do, I intend to kill you."

She was completely in earnest, her stubborn little chin set.

He took off his large floppy hat and swept her a mocking bow. "I look forward to dying in your arms, sweeting."

Her eyes narrowed on his wicked double entendre, but her companion was muttering urgently now. Lady Margaret gave him one last look of disdain before ducking inside her carriage.

The coachman shouted to the horses, and the vehicle rumbled away.

And Godric St. John realized two things: his lady wife was apparently over her mourning—and he'd better make it back to his town house before her carriage arrived. He paused for a second, glancing at the body of the man he'd killed. Black blood wound in a sluggish trail to the channel in the middle of the lane. The man's eyes stared glassily at the indifferent heavens. Godric searched within himself, looking for some emotion...and found what he always did.

Nothing.

He whirled and darted down a narrow alley. Only now that he was moving did he notice that his right shoulder ached. He'd either damaged something in the brawl or one of the footpads had succeeded in landing a blow. No matter. Saint House was on the river, not terribly far in the usual way, but he'd get there faster by rooftop.

He was already swinging himself up onto the top of a shed when he heard it: shrill, girlish screams, coming from around the bend in the alley up ahead.

Damn it. He hadn't the time for this. Godric dropped back down to the alley and drew both his swords.

Another terrified cry.

He darted around the corner.

There were two of them, which accounted for all the noise. One was not more than five. She stood, shaking, in the middle of the reeking alley, screaming with all of her might. She could do little else because the second child had already been caught. That one was a bit older and fought with the desperate ferocity of a cornered rat, but to no avail.

The man who held the older child was three times her size and cuffed her easily on the side of the head.

The older girl crumpled to the ground while the smaller one ran to her still form.

The man bent toward the children.

"Oi!" Godric growled.

The man looked up. "What th—"

Godric laid him flat with a right haymaker to the side of the head.

He placed his sword at the man's bared throat and leaned down to whisper, "Doesn't feel very good when you're on the receiving end, does it?"

The oaf scowled, his hand rubbing the side of his head. "Now see 'ere. I 'as a right to do as I please wif me own girls."

"We're *not* your girls!"

Godric saw out of the corner of his eye that the elder chit had sat up.

"'E's not our da!"

Blood trickled from the corner of her mouth, making him snarl.

"Get on to your home," he urged in a low voice to the girls. "I'll deal with this ruffian."

"We don't 'ave a 'ome," the smaller child whimpered.

She'd barely got the words out when the elder nudged her and hissed, "Shut it!"

Godric was tired and the news that the children were homeless distracted him. That was what he told himself anyway when the rogue on the ground swept his legs out from under him.

Godric hit the cobblestones rolling. He surged to his feet, but the man was already rounding the corner at the far end of the alley.

He sighed, wincing as he straightened. He'd landed on his injured shoulder and it was not thanking him for the treat.

He glanced at the girls. "Best come with me, then."

The smaller child obediently began to rise, but the elder pulled her back down. "Don't be daft, Moll. 'E's as like to be a lassie snatcher as the other one."

Godric raised his eyebrows at the words *lassie snatcher*. He hadn't heard that name for a while. He shook his head. He hadn't time to dig into these matters now. Lady Margaret would reach his home soon, and if he wasn't there, awkward questions might arise.

"Come," he said, holding out his hand to the girls. "I'm not a lassie snatcher, and I know a nice, warm place where you can spend the night." *And many nights hereafter.*

He thought his tone gentle enough, but the elder girl's face wrinkled mutinously. "We're not going wif you."

Godric smiled pleasantly—before swooping down and scooping one child over his shoulder and the other under his arm. "Oh, yes, you are."

It wasn't that simple, of course. The elder cursed quite shockingly for a female child of such tender years, while the younger burst into tears, and they both fought like wildcats.

Five minutes later he was within sight of the Home for Unfortunate Infants and Foundling Children when he nearly dropped them both.

"Ow!" He swallowed stronger language and took a firmer grip on the elder child, who had come perilously close to unmanning him.

Grimly, Godric stalked to the back door of the St. Giles orphanage and kicked at it until a light appeared in the kitchen window.

The door swung open to reveal a tall man in rumpled shirtsleeves and breeches.

Winter Makepeace, the manager of the home, arched an eyebrow at the sight of the Ghost of St. Giles, holding two struggling, weeping girls on his doorstep.

Godric hadn't time for explanations.

"Here." He unceremoniously dumped the children on the kitchen tiles and glanced at the bemused manager. "I'd advise a firm hold—they're slipperier than greased eels."

With that, he swung shut the home's door, turned, and sprinted toward his town house.

LADY MARGARET ST. John started shaking the moment her carriage left St. Giles. The Ghost had been so large, so frighteningly deadly in his movements. When he'd advanced on her, his bloody swords gripped in his big, leather-clad hands and his eyes glinting behind his grotesque mask, it had been all she could do to hold herself still.

Megs inhaled, trying to quiet the quicksilver racing through her veins. She'd spent two years hating the man, but she'd never expected, when she finally met him, to feel so ... so ...

So *alive*.

She glanced down at the heavy pistols in her lap and then across the carriage to her dear friend and sister-in-law, Sarah St. John. "I'm sorry. That was ..."

"An idiotic idea?" Sarah arched one light brown eyebrow. Her straight-as-a-pin hair varied from mouse-brown to the lightest shade of gold and was tucked back into a sedate and very orderly knot at the back of her head.

In contrast, Megs's own dark, curly hair had mostly escaped from its pins hours ago and was now waving about her face like a tentacled sea monster.

Megs frowned. "Well, I don't know if *idiotic* is quite—"

"Addled?" Sarah supplied crisply. "Boneheaded? Daft? Foolish? Ill-advised?"

"While all of those adjectives are in part appropriate," Megs interjected primly before Sarah could continue her list—her friend's vocabulary was *quite* extensive—"I think *ill-advised* might be the most applicable. I am so sorry for putting your life in danger."

"And yours."

Megs blinked. "What?"

Sarah leaned a little forward so that her face came into the carriage lantern's light. Sarah usually had the sweet countenance of a gently reared maiden lady—which at five and twenty she was—belied only by a certain mocking humor lurking at the back of her soft brown eyes, but right now she might've been an Amazon warrior.

"*Your* life, Megs," Sarah replied. "You risked not only my life and the lives of the servants, but *your* life as well. What could possibly be important enough to venture into *St. Giles* at this time of night?"

Megs looked away from her dearest friend. Sarah had come to live with her at the St. John estate in Cheshire nearly a year after Megs's marriage to Godric, so Sarah didn't know the real reason for their hasty nuptials.

Megs shook her head, gazing out the carriage window. "I'm sorry. I just wanted to see..."

When she didn't finish the sentence, Sarah moved restlessly. "See what?"

Where Roger was murdered. Even the thought sent a shard of dull pain through her heart. She'd directed Tom the coachman to drive into St. Giles, hoping to find some lingering trace of Roger. There hadn't been, of course. He'd been long dead. Long lost to her. But she'd had a second reason to look around St. Giles: to learn more about Roger's murderer, the Ghost of St. Giles. And in that, at least, she'd succeeded. The Ghost had appeared. She hadn't been adequately prepared tonight, but next time she would be.

Next time she wouldn't let him get away.

Next time she'd blast a bullet through the Ghost of St. Giles's black heart.

"Megs?" Her friend's gentle murmur interrupted her bloody thoughts.

Megs shook her head and smiled brightly—perhaps too brightly—at her dear friend. "Never mind."

"What—"

"Goodness, are we here already?" Megs's change of subject was not subtle, but the carriage was slowing as if they'd finally arrived at their destination.

She leaned forward, peering out the window. The street was dark.

Megs frowned. "Maybe not."

Sarah crossed her arms. "What do you see?"

"We're on a narrow, winding lane and there's a tall, dark house up ahead. It looks very . . . um . . ."

"Ancient?"

Megs glanced at her companion. "Yes?"

Sarah nodded once. "That's Saint House, then. It's as old as dust, didn't you know? Didn't you see Saint House when you married my brother?"

"No." Megs pretended to be engrossed in the dim view out the window. "The wedding breakfast was at my brother's house and I left London a sennight after." And in between she'd been bedridden at her mother's house. Megs pushed the sad memory from her mind. "How old is Saint House?"

"Medieval and, as I remember, quite drafty in winter."

"Oh."

"And not in the most fashionable part of London, either," Sarah continued cheerfully. "Right on the river-bank. But that's what you get when your family came over with the Conqueror: venerable old buildings without a lick of modern style or convenience."

"I'm sure it's quite famous," Megs said, trying to be loyal. She was a St. John now after all.

"Oh, yes," Sarah said, her tone dry. "Saint House has been mentioned in more than one history. No doubt that'll comfort you when your toes turn to blocks of ice in the middle of the night."

"If it's so awful, then why did you accompany me to London?" Megs asked.

"To see the sights and shop, of course." Sarah sounded quite cheerful despite her gloomy description of Saint House. "It's been forever since I was last in London."

The carriage jerked to a halt at that moment, and Sarah began gathering her needlework basket and shawls. Oliver, the younger of the two footmen Megs had brought with them, opened the door to the carriage. He wore a white wig as part of his livery, but it didn't disguise his red eyebrows.

"Never thought we'd make it alive," Oliver muttered as he set the steps. "Was a close one with them footpads, if'n you don't mind me saying so, m'lady."

"You and Johnny were very brave," Megs said as she stepped down. She glanced up at her coachman. "And you, too, Tom."

The coachman grunted and hunched his broad shoulders. "Ye an' Miss St. John best be gettin' inside, m'lady, where 'tis safe."

"I will." Megs turned to the house and only then noticed the second carriage, already drawn up outside.

Sarah stepped down beside her. "It looks like your great-aunt Elvina arrived before us."

"Yes, it does," Megs said slowly. "But why is her carriage still outside?"

The door to the second carriage popped open as if in answer.

"Margaret!" Great-Aunt Elvina's worried face was topped by a cloud of soft gray curls intertwined with pink ribbons. Her voice was overly loud, booming off the stone buildings. Great-Aunt Elvina was rather deaf. "Margaret, the wretched butler won't let us in. We've been sitting in the courtyard for ages, and Her Grace has become quite restless."

A muffled yelp from inside the carriage emphasized the statement.

Megs turned to her husband's house. No light betrayed human habitation, but obviously *someone* was at home if a butler had earlier answered Great-Aunt Elvina's summons. She marched up to the door and lifted the great iron ring that served as knocker, letting it fall with a sharp *bang*.

Then she stepped back and looked up. The building was a hodgepodge of historical styles. The first two floors were of ancient red brick—perhaps the original building. But then some later owner had added another three stories in a paler, beige brick. Chimneys and gables sprouted here and there over the roofline, romping without any seeming pattern. On either side, low, dark wings framed the end of the street, making a de facto courtyard.

"You did write to tell Godric you were coming," Sarah murmured.

Megs bit her lip. "Ah..."

A light appearing at a narrow window immediately to the right saved her from having to admit that she hadn't notified her husband of their trip. The door opened with an ominous creaking.

A lone servant stood in the doorway, stoop-shouldered, his head topped by a flaking white wig, a single candlestick in one hand.

The man drew a slow, rattling breath. "Mr. St. John is not rec—"

"Oh, thank you," Megs said as she walked straight at the butler.

For a moment she feared the man wouldn't move. His rheumy eyes widened and then he shifted just enough so that she could glide by.

She pivoted once inside and began removing her gloves. "I am Lady Margaret St. John, Mr. St. John's wife."

The butler's shaggy eyebrows snapped down. "Wife—"

"Yes." She bestowed a smile on him and for a moment he merely goggled. "And you are ... ?"

He straightened and she realized his posture had made him look older than he really was. The man couldn't be past his midthirties. "Moulder, m'lady. The butler."

"Splendid!" Megs handed him her gloves as she glanced about the hallway. *Not* impressive. There appeared to be a veritable village of spiders living in the beamed ceiling. She spotted a candelabra on a table nearby and, taking the candle from Moulder, began lighting it. "Now, Moulder, I have my dear great-aunt waiting in the carriage outside—you may call her Miss Howard—as well as Miss St. John here, Mr. St. John's eldest little sister ... if that makes any sense at all."

Sarah grinned cheerfully as she deposited her own gloves in the bemused butler's hands. "I haven't been to London in several years. You must be new."

Moulder's mouth opened. "I—"

"We also have our three lady's maids," Megs continued, handing the candle back to the butler as he snapped his mouth shut, "four footmen between ours and my great-aunt's, and the two coachmen. Great-Aunt Elvina *would* insist on her own carriage, although I have to admit I'm not sure how we'd have all fit in only one carriage anyway."

"It would never have worked," Sarah said. "*And* your aunt snores."

Megs shrugged. "True." She turned back to the butler. "Naturally we brought Higgins the gardener and Charlie the bootblack boy because he is such a dear and because he's Higgins's nephew and rather attached to him. Oh, and Her Grace, who is in a delicate condition and appears to take only chicken livers well minced and simmered in white wine these days. Now, have you got all that?"

Moulder goggled. "Ah..."

"*Wonderful.*" Megs shot him another smile. "Where is my husband?"

Alarm seemed to break through the butler's confusion. "Mr. St. John is in the library, m'lady, but he's—"

"No, no!" Megs patted the air reassuringly. "No need to show me. I'm sure Sarah and I can find the library all by ourselves. Best you deal with my aunt's needs and see to the servants' supper—*and* Her Grace's. It was such a very long journey, you know."

She picked up the lit candelabra and marched up the stairs.

Sarah trotted up beside her, chuckling under her breath. "Luckily you've started in the right direction, at least. The library, if I remember correctly, is on the first floor, second door on the left."

"Oh, good," Megs muttered. Having once screwed her courage to this point, it would be fatal to back down now. "I'm sure you're looking forward to seeing your brother again just as much as I."

"Naturally," Sarah murmured. "But I won't be so gauche as to ruin your reunion with Godric."

Megs stopped on the first-floor landing. "What?"

"Tomorrow morning is soon enough to see my brother." Sarah smiled gently from three steps below. "I'll go help with Great-Aunt Elvina."

"Oh, but—"

Megs's feeble protest was made to the empty air. Sarah had already scampered lightly down the stairs.

Right. Library. Second door on the left.

Megs took a deep breath and turned to face the gloomy hallway. It'd been two years since she'd last seen her husband, but she remembered him—from the little she'd seen of him before their marriage—as a nice enough gentleman. Certainly not ogrelike, anyway. His brown eyes had been quite kind at their wedding ceremony. Megs squinted doubtfully as she marched down the corridor. Or were his eyes blue? Well, whatever color they'd been, his eyes had been *kind*.

Surely that much couldn't have changed in two years?

Megs grasped the doorknob to the library and quickly opened it before any last-minute second thoughts could dissuade her.

After all that, the library was something of an anticlimax.

Dim and cramped like the corridor, the room's only light came from the embers of a dying fire and a single candle by an old, overstuffed armchair. She tiptoed closer. The occupant of the ancient armchair looked . . .

Equally ancient.

He wore a burgundy banyan frayed pink at the hem and elbows. His stockinged feet, lodged in disreputable slippers, were crossed on a tufted footstool so close to the fireplace that the fabric nearest the hearth bore traces of earlier singeing. His head lolled against his shoulder, casually covered by a soft, dark green turban with a rather rakish gilt tassel hanging over his left eye. Half-moon spectacles were perched perilously on his forehead, and if it weren't for the deep snores issuing from between his lips, she might've thought Godric St. John had died.

Of old age.

Megs blinked and straightened. Surely her husband couldn't be *that* old. She had a vague notion that he was a bit older than her brother Griffin, who had arranged their marriage and who was himself three and thirty, but try as she might, she couldn't remember her husband's actual age being mentioned.

It had been the darkest hour of her existence, and, perhaps thankfully, much of it was obscured in her mind.

Megs peered anxiously down at the sleeping man. He was slack-jawed and snoring, but his eyelashes lay thick and black against his cheeks. She stared for a moment, oddly caught by the sight.

Her lips firmed. Many men married late in life and were still able to perform. The Duke of Frye had managed just last year and he was well past seventy. Surely Godric, then, could do the deed.

Thus cheered, Megs cleared her throat. Gently, of course, for he was the main reason she'd come all the way to London, and it wouldn't do to startle her husband into an apoplectic fit before he'd done his duty.

Which was, of course, to make her pregnant.

GODRIC ST. JOHN turned his snore into a snort as he pretended to wake. He opened his eyes to find his wife staring at him with a frown between her delicate brows. At their wedding, she'd been drawn and vague, her eyes never quite meeting his, even when she'd pledged herself to him until death do they part. Only hours after the ceremony, she'd taken ill at their wedding breakfast and been whisked away to the comfort of her mother and sister. A letter the next day had informed him that she'd miscarried the child that had made the hasty wedding necessary.

Grim irony.

Now she examined him with a bold, bright curiosity that made him want to check that his banyan was still tightly wrapped.

"What?" Godric started as if surprised by her presence.

She swiftly pasted on a broad, guileless smile that might as well have shouted, *I'm up to something!* "Oh, hello."

Hello? After two years' absence? Hello?

"Ah…Margaret, is it?" Godric repressed a wince. Not that he was doing much better.

"Yes!" She beamed at him as if he were a senile old man who'd had a sudden spark of reason. "I've come to visit you."

"Have you?" He sat a little straighter in the chair. "How…unexpected."

His tone might've been a trifle dry.

She darted a nervous glance at him and turned to aimlessly wander the room. "Yes, and I've brought Sarah, your sister." She inhaled and peered at a tiny medieval etching propped on the mantel. Impossible that she could make out the subject matter in the room's dimness. "Well, of course you know she's your *sister*. She's thrilled for the opportunity to shop, and see the sights, and go to the theater and perhaps an opera or even a pleasure garden, and...and..."

She'd picked up an ancient leather-bound book of Van Oosten's commentary on Catullus and now she waved it vaguely. "And..."

"Shop some more, perhaps?" Godric raised his brows. "I may not have seen Sarah for an age, but I do remember her fondness for shopping."

"Quite." She looked somewhat subdued as she thumbed the crumbling pages of the book.

"And you?"

"What?"

"Why have you come to London?" he inquired.

Van Oosten exploded in her hands.

"Oh!" She dropped to her knees and frantically began gathering the fragile pages. "Oh, I'm so sorry!"

Godric repressed a sigh as he watched her. Half the pages were disintegrating as fast as she picked them up. That particular tome had cost him five guineas at Warwick and Sons and was, as far as he knew, the last of its kind. "No matter. The book was in need of rebinding anyway."

"Was it?" She looked dubiously at the pages in her hands before gently laying the mess in his lap. "Well, that's a relief, isn't it?"

Her face was tilted up toward his, her brown eyes large and somehow pleading, and she'd forgotten to take her hands away again. They lay, quite circumspectly, on top of the remains of the book in his lap, but something about her position, kneeling beside him, made him catch his breath. A strange, ethereal feeling squeezed his chest, even as a thoroughly rude and earthly one warmed his loins. *Good Lord.* That *was inconvenient.*

He cleared his throat. "Margaret?"

She blinked slowly, almost seductively. *Idiot.* She must be sleepy. That was why her eyelids looked so heavy and languid. Was it even possible to blink seductively?

"Yes?"

"How long do you plan to stay in London?"

"Oh..." She lowered her head as she fumbled with the demolished book. Presumably she meant to gather the papers together, but all she succeeded in doing was crumbling them further. "Oh, well, there's so much to do here, isn't there? And...and I have several dear, *dear* friends to call on—"

"Margaret—"

She jumped to her feet, still holding Van Oosten's battered back cover. "It simply wouldn't do to snub anyone." She aimed a brilliant smile somewhere over his right shoulder.

"Margaret."

She yawned widely. "Do forgive me. I'm afraid the trip has quite fatigued me. Oh, Daniels"—she turned in what looked like relief as a petite lady's maid appeared at the doorway—"is my room readied?"

The maid curtsied even as her gaze darted about the library curiously. "Yes, my lady. As ready as ever it can be tonight anyway. You'll never credit the cobwebs we—"

"Yes, well, I'm sure it's fine." Lady Margaret whirled and nodded at him. "Good night, er…husband. I'll see you on the morrow, shall I?"

And she darted from the room, the back cover of poor Van Oosten still held captive.

The maid closed the door behind her.

Godric eyed the solid oak of his library door. The room without her spinning, brilliant presence seemed all of a sudden hollow and tomblike. Strange. He'd always thought his library a comfortable place before.

Godric shook his head irritably. *What is she about? Why has she come to London?*

Theirs had been a marriage of convenience—at least on her part. She'd needed a name for the babe in her belly. It'd been a marriage of blackmail via her ass of a brother, Griffin, on his part, for Godric had not fathered the child. Indeed, he'd never spoken to Lady Margaret before the day of their wedding. Afterward, when she'd retired to his neglected country estate, he'd resumed his life—such as it was—in London.

For a year there'd been no communication at all, save for the odd secondhand bit of information from his stepmother or one of his half sisters. Then, suddenly, a letter out of the blue, from Lady Margaret herself, asking if he would mind if she cut down the overgrown grapevine in the garden. What overgrown grapevine? He hadn't seen Laurelwood Manor, the house on his Cheshire estate, since the early years of his marriage to his beloved Clara. He'd written back and told her politely but tersely that she could do as she wished with the grapevine and anything else she had the mind to in the garden.

That should've been the end to it, but his stranger bride

had continued to write him once or twice a month for the last year. Long, chatty letters about the garden; the eldest of his half sisters, Sarah, who had come to live with Margaret; the travails of repairing and redecorating the rather decrepit house; and the petty arguments and gossip from the nearby village. He hadn't known quite how to respond to such a flurry of information, so in general he simply hadn't. But as the months had gone by, he'd become oddly taken with her missives. Finding one of her letters beside his morning coffee gave him a feeling of lightness. He'd even been impatient when her letter was a day or two late.

Well. He *had* been living alone and lonely for years now.

But the small delight of a letter was a far cry from the lady herself invading his domain.

"Never seen the like, I haven't," Moulder muttered as he entered the library, shutting the door behind him. "Might as well've been a traveling fair, the bunch o' them."

"What are you talking about?" Godric asked as he stood and doffed the banyan.

Underneath he still wore the Ghost's motley. It'd been a near thing. Both carriages had been drawn up outside his house when he'd slunk in the back. Godric had heard Moulder trying to hold off the occupants even as he'd run up the hidden back stairs that led from his study to the library. Saint House was so old it had a myriad of secret passages and hidey-holes—a boon to his Ghostly activities. He'd reached the library, pulled off his boots, thrown his swords, cape, and mask behind one of the bookshelves, and had just tugged the soft turban onto his head and wound the banyan about his waist when he'd heard the doorknob turn.

It'd been close—*too* damn close.

"M'lady and all she brought with her." Moulder waved both hands as if to encompass a multitude.

Godric arched an eyebrow. "Ladies do usually travel with maids and such."

"'Tisn't just *such*," Moulder muttered as he helped Godric from the Ghost's tunic. In addition to his other vague duties, Moulder served as valet when needed. "There's a gardener and bootblack boy and a snorty sort o' dog that belongs to Lady Margaret's great-aunt, and *she's* here too."

Godric squinted, trying to work through that sentence. "The dog or the aunt?"

"Both." Moulder shook out the Ghost's tunic, eyeing it for tears and stains. A sly expression crossed his face just before he glanced up innocently at Godric. "'Tis a pity, though."

"What?" Godric asked as he stripped the Ghost's leggings off and donned his nightshirt.

"Won't be able to go out gallivanting at all hours o' the night now, will you?" Moulder said as he folded the tunic and leggings. He shook his head sorrowfully. "Right shame, but there 'tis. Your days as the Ghost are over, I'm feared, now that your missus has arrived to live with you."

"I suppose you'd be right"—he took off the silly turban and ran a hand over his tightly cropped hair—"if Lady Margaret were actually going to live with me permanently."

Moulder looked doubtful. "She sure brought enough people and luggage to take up residence."

"No matter. I don't intend to give up being the Ghost of St. Giles. Which means"—Godric strode to the door—"my wife and all her accouterments will be gone by next week at the outside."

And when she was gone, Godric promised himself, he could go back to his business of saving the poor of St. Giles and forget that Lady Margaret had ever disrupted his lonely life.

Chapter Two

*Now mind me well: the Hellequin is the Devil's right-hand
man. He roams the world, mounted on a great black horse,
in search of the wicked dead and those who die unshriven.
And when the Hellequin finds them, he drags their souls
to hell. His companions are tiny imps, naked, scarlet,
and ugly. Their names are Despair, Grief, and Loss.
The Hellequin himself is as black as night and his
heart—what is left of it—is nothing but a lump
of hard coal....*
—From *The Legend of the Hellequin*

Godric woke the next morning to the sounds of feminine
voices in the room next to his. He lay in bed, blinking for
a moment, thinking how *foreign* it was to hear activity
from that direction.

He slept in the ancient master's bedroom, of course,
and the mistress of the house had the connecting room.
But Clara had occupied the rooms for only the first year
or two of their marriage. After that, the disease that had
eventually eaten away at her body had begun to grow. The
doctors had recommended complete quiet, so Clara had
been moved to the old nursery a floor above. There she
had suffered for nine long years before she'd died.

Godric shook his head and climbed from his bed, his bare feet hitting the cold floor. Such maudlin thoughts wouldn't bring Clara back. If they could, she would've sprung alive, dancing and free from her terrible pain, thousands of times in the years since her death.

He dressed swiftly, in a simple brown suit and gray wig, and left his room while the female voices were still chattering indistinctly next door. The realization that Lady Margaret had slept so close to him sent a frisson along his nerves. It wasn't that he ran from such signs of life, but it was only natural to be unused to the presence of others—*female* others—in his gloomy old house.

Godric descended the stairs to the lower level. Normally he broke his fast at a coffeehouse, both to hear the latest news and because the meals at his own home were somewhat erratic. Today, however, he squared his shoulders and ventured into the little-used dining room at the back of the house.

Only to find it occupied.

"Sarah."

For a disconcerting second, he hadn't recognized her, this self-possessed lady, dressed in a sedate dove-gray costume. How many years had it been since he'd last seen her?

She turned at her name, and her calm face lit with a smile of welcome. His chest warmed and it caught him off guard. They'd never been close—he was a full dozen years older than she—and he'd not even known that he'd missed her.

Apparently he had.

"Godric!"

She rose, moving around the long, battered table where she'd been seated alone. She hugged him, swift and hard, her touch a shock to his frame. He'd been in solitude so very long.

She moved back before he could remember to respond and eyed him with disconcertingly perceptive brown eyes. "How are you?"

"Fine." He shrugged and turned away. After nearly three years, he was used to the concerned looks, the gentle inquiries, especially from women. Sadly, though, he hadn't become any more comfortable with them. "Have you already eaten?"

"As of yet, I haven't seen anything to eat," she observed drily. "Your man, Moulder, promised me breakfast and then disappeared. That was nearly half an hour ago."

"Ah." He wished he could feign surprise, but the fact was he wasn't even sure there *was* anything edible in the house. "Er... perhaps we should decamp to an inn or—"

Moulder burst through the door, carrying a heavy tray. "Here we are, then."

He thumped the tray down in the center of the table and stepped back in pride.

Godric examined the tray. A teapot stood in the center with one cup. Beside it were a half-dozen or so burned pieces of toast, a pot of butter, and five eggs on a plate. Hopefully they'd been boiled.

Godric arched an eyebrow at his manservant. "Cook is... er... indisposed, I perceive."

Moulder snorted. "Cook is gone. And so is that nice wheel o' cheese, the silver saltcellar, and half the plate. Didn't seem too happy when he heard last night that we had so many guests."

"Just as well, I'm afraid, considering the unfortunate way he handled a joint."

"He was overfamiliar with your wine stock, too, if you don't mind me saying so, sir," Moulder said. "I'll go see if we have any more teacups, shall I?"

"Thank you, Moulder." Godric waited until the butler left the room before turning to his sister. "I apologize for the paucity of my table."

He held out a chair for her.

"Please don't worry," Sarah said as she sat. "We did descend on you without any notice."

She reached for the teapot.

"Mmm," Godric murmured as he lowered himself to a chair across from her. "I wondered about that."

"I was under the impression that Megs had written to you." His sister lifted an eyebrow at him.

He merely shook his head as he took a piece of toast.

"I wonder why she didn't tell you of our arrival?" she asked softly as she buttered her own toast. "We'd planned the trip for weeks. Do you think she was fearful that you'd turn her away?"

He nearly choked on his toast. "I wouldn't do that. Whatever gave you the notion?"

She shrugged elegant shoulders. "You've been separated since your marriage. You hardly write her or me. Or, for that matter, Mama, Charlotte, or Jane."

Godric's lips firmed. He was on cordial terms with his stepmother and younger half sisters, but they'd never been especially close. "Ours wasn't a love match."

"Obviously." Sarah took a cautious nibble of her toast. "Mama worries for you, you know. As do I."

He poured her tea without answering. What could he say? *Oh, I'm all right. Lost the love of my life, don't you know, but the pain's quite bearable, considering.* To pretend that he was whole, that rising every day wasn't a chore, became exhausting. Why did they ask, anyway? Couldn't they see that he was so broken nothing would fix him?

"Godric?" Her voice was gentle.

He made the corners of his mouth twitch upward as he pushed the cup of tea across the table to her. "How are my stepmother and sisters?"

She pursed her lips as if she wanted to prod him more, but in the end she took a sip of tea instead. "Mama is well. She's in the midst of preparations for Jane's coming-out. They plan to stay with Mama's bosom-bow, Lady Hartford, for the season in the fall."

"Ah." Godric felt a twinge of relief that his stepmother didn't want to stay at Saint House. Guilt followed immediately thereafter: he should've been aware that his youngest half sister was old enough to make her debut into society. Gads! He remembered Jane as a freckle-faced schoolgirl running about with a hoop and stick. "And how is Charlotte?"

Sarah cast her eyes heavenward. "Fascinating all the young men of Upper Hornsfield."

"Are there many eligible young men in Upper Hornsfield?"

"Not as many as in Lower Hornsfield, of course, but between the new curate and the local squire's sons, she has a fair coterie of young men. I'm not sure she even knows that wherever she goes, she's followed by longing male eyes."

The thought of little Charlotte—whom he'd last seen arguing with Jane rather heatedly over a piece of fig tart—becoming a rural femme fatale made Godric smile.

The door to the dining room opened at that moment and he looked up.

Straight into the eyes of his wife, poised in the doorway like Boudicca about to storm some poor, unsuspecting Roman general's camp.

MEGS HALTED ON the threshold to the dining room, taking a deep breath. Godric looked different somehow than the man she remembered from just last night. Perhaps it was simply the daylight. Or it might be the fact that he was properly dressed in a well-cut but somewhat worn acorn-brown suit.

Or maybe it was the tiny smile still lingering on his face. It smoothed the lines of care and grief on his forehead and about his gray eyes, and drew attention to a mouth that was wide and full, bracketed by two deep indents. For a moment her gaze lingered on that mouth, wondering what it might feel like on her own....

"Good morning." He rose politely.

She blinked, hastily looking up. She'd decided last night—quite logically!—to wait until the morning to begin her planned seduction. Who would expect to jump straight into bed with one's stranger-husband after a two-year absence, after all? But now it was morning, so...

Right. Seducing the husband.

Her silence had caused his smile to fade entirely, and his eyes were narrowed as he waited for her response. He looked altogether formidable.

Baby.

Megs squared her shoulders. "Good morning!"

Her smile might've been a trifle too wide as she strove to cover her lapse.

Sarah, who'd turned at her entrance, arched an eyebrow.

Godric rounded the table and pulled out a chair for her next to Sarah. "I hope you slept well?"

The room had been damp, dusty, and smelled of mildew. "Yes, very well."

He glanced at her dubiously.

She walked toward him—and then around the table to the chair next to his vacant one.

"I'd like to sit here, if you don't mind," she said throatily, lowering her eyelashes in what she hoped was a seductive manner. "Close to you."

He cocked his head to the side, his expression inscrutable. "Do you have a cold?"

Sarah choked on her tea.

Drat! It'd been so long since she'd done anything like flirting. Megs shot an irritated glance at her sister-in-law, repressing the urge to stick out her tongue.

"As you wish." Godric was suddenly beside her, and she nearly started at his rasping voice in her ear. Good Lord, the man could move quietly.

"Thank you." She sank into the chair, aware of his presence behind her, looming large and intimidating, and then he returned to his own seat.

Megs bit her lip, glancing at him from the corner of her eye. Should she rub against his leg under the table? But his profile was so very ... grave. It seemed a bit like goosing the Archbishop of Canterbury.

And then she caught sight of breakfast and her dismal seduction attempt abruptly fled her mind.

Megs squinted at the plate in the middle of the table. It held a few burned fragments of toast and some hard-boiled eggs. She scanned the room but saw no other signs of nourishment.

"Would you care for some toast?" Sarah murmured across from her.

"Oh, thank you." Megs widened her eyes in question at her.

"It appears the cook did a runner, as Oliver would say." Sarah shrugged infinitesimally as she pushed the plate over. "I believe that Moulder is searching for another tea-cup for the tea right now, but in the meantime, do feel free to have a sip of mine."

"Er…" Megs was saved from having to reply by the dining room door being flung open.

"My dears!" Great-Aunt Elvina swept into the room. "You'll not credit the ghastly room I slept in last night. Her Grace was quite overcome by the dust and spent the night wheezing horribly."

Godric had risen at Great-Aunt Elvina's entrance and now he cleared his throat. "Her Grace?"

A small but very rotund fawn pug waddled into the room, glanced perfunctorily at Great-Aunt Elvina, and plopped down onto the rug, rolling immediately to her side. She lay there, panting pathetically, her distended belly rising and falling.

Her Grace's flair for the dramatic was almost as well honed as her mistress's.

"This is Her Grace," Megs hurried to explain to her husband, adding perhaps unnecessarily, "She's in an interesting way."

"Indeed," Godric murmured. "Is the … er … Her Grace quite well? She looks rather worried."

"Pugs always look worried," Great-Aunt Elvina pronounced loudly. Her ability to hear came and went with disconcerting irregularity. "She could do with a dish of warm milk with perhaps a spoonful of sherry in it."

Godric blinked. "Ah...I do apologize, but I don't believe we have any milk on the premises. As for the sherry..."

"None o' that neither," Moulder said with dour satisfaction as he entered the room behind Great-Aunt Elvina. In his arms he carried an array of mismatched teacups.

"Quite," Godric murmured. "Perhaps if I'd been informed in *advance* of your arrival..."

"Oh, no need to apologize," Megs said quickly.

He turned and narrowed his eyes at her. This close she could see the small lines fanning from the corners of his eyes in an altogether alluring way, which made no sense because why would crow's-feet be alluring?

Megs shook herself mentally and continued. "After all, your house hasn't had a feminine hand managing it in quite some time. I expect once we employ a new cook and some scullery maids—"

"And a housekeeper and upstairs maids," Sarah put in.

"Not to mention some footmen," Great-Aunt Elvina muttered. "Big, strong ones."

"Well, we did bring Oliver and Johnny and your two footmen," Megs pointed out.

"They can't be expected to do all the heavy lifting required to clean this place," Great-Aunt Elvina said with a frown. "Have you *seen* the upper floors?"

"Er..." Megs hadn't in fact explored the upper floors, but if the condition of the rooms they'd slept in last night were any indication..."Best we hire at least half a dozen strapping lads."

"I doubt I'll need a veritable army to run Saint House,"

her husband said in a dry tone, "especially after you all leave, which will, I'm sure, be *soon*."

"What?" barked Great-Aunt Elvina, cupping her hand behind her ear.

Megs held up a finger to interrupt because a thought had occurred to her. She addressed Moulder. "Surely you have *some* help running the house?"

"There was a couple o' strong lads and some maids, but they left awhile back, one by one, like, and we just never hired others." Moulder cast his eyes up as if to address the spiders lurking in the cobwebs dangling from the ceiling. "Did have a girl name o' Tilly, m'lady, but she got in the family way 'bout a month back—*not* my fault."

All eyes swung toward Godric.

He raised his brows in what looked like mild exasperation. "Nor mine."

Thank goodness. Megs returned her gaze to Moulder, very aware of her husband glowering at her shoulder.

The butler shrugged. "Tilly up and left not long after. Think she was chasin' the butcher's apprentice. Maybe *he* was the father. Or it might've been the tinker what used to come 'round the kitchen door."

For a moment there was silence as they all contemplated the mystery of Tilly's baby's paternity.

Then Godric cleared his throat. "How *long*, exactly, were you planning on staying in London, Margaret?"

Megs smiled brilliantly, even though she'd never really liked her full name—especially when it was drawled in a gravelly voice that seemed somehow ominous—for she really didn't want to answer the question. "Oh, I don't like to make plans. It's so much more fun to simply let matters take their own course, don't you think?"

"Actually I don't—"

Good Lord, the man was persistent! She turned hastily to Moulder. "Then you've been managing the house all by yourself?"

Moulder's great shaggy brows knit, causing a myriad of wrinkles to form in his forehead and around his hangdog eyes. He was the very picture of martyrdom. "I have, m'lady. You have no idea the work—the terrible job 'tis!—to keep up a house such as this. Why, me health is much the worse for it."

Godric muttered something, the only words of which Megs caught were "laying it on thick."

She ignored her husband. "I really must thank you, Moulder, for taking care of Mr. St. John so loyally, despite the toil involved."

Moulder blushed. "Aw, it weren't nothin', m'lady."

Godric snorted loudly.

Megs hastily said, "Yes, well, I'm sure now that I'm in residence, we'll have the house in order in no time."

"And *exactly* how long will it take to—" Godric began.

"Oh, look at the time!" Megs said, squinting at a small clock on the fireplace mantel. It was hard to tell if it still ran, but no matter. "We must be going or we'll be late to the meeting of the Ladies' Syndicate for the Benefit of the Home for Unfortunate Infants and Foundling Children."

Sarah looked interested. "At the orphanage in St. Giles you told us about?"

Megs nodded.

Great-Aunt Elvina glanced up from trying to tempt Her Grace with a bit of toast. "What is it?"

"The Ladies' *Syndicate* meeting at the *orphanage*," Megs said in a sort of muted shout. "It's time we *go* there."

"Good," Great-Aunt Elvina pronounced, stooping to pick up Her Grace. "With any luck, they'll have some tea and refreshments at the meeting."

"That's settled, then."

Megs finally turned to look at her husband. His face was rather stern and she was suddenly aware that he'd been watching her.

He glanced away now, though. "I suppose you'll all return for supper, then."

His tone was lifeless, nearly bored.

Something inside her rebelled. He'd taken her invasion into his home and their plans to hire new servants and clean up his ratty old house without turning a hair.

She wanted to see him turn a hair.

And, more importantly, she reminded herself: *baby*. "Oh, no," she purred, "I expect you'll see us again in ten minutes."

He turned slowly back to her, his eyes narrowed. "I beg your pardon?"

She opened her eyes wide. "You *are* coming with us, aren't you?"

"I believe it's a *ladies'* syndicate," he said, but there was a whisper of uncertainty in his tone.

"I'd like your company." She let the tip of her tongue nudge the corner of her mouth.

And there—finally!—she saw it. His gaze flickered oh so briefly to her mouth.

Megs had to bite back a grin as he said with surly suspicion, "If you wish."

GODRIC SAT IN the carriage watching Lady Margaret with what he very much feared was a brooding air. He wasn't entirely certain how he'd come to be here. Usually at this time of day he'd be at his favorite coffeehouse engrossed in newspapers or barricaded in his study perusing his latest classical tome. Except that wasn't quite right. It'd been weeks since he'd lingered at Basham's Coffeehouse and longer still since he'd found the energy to read his favorite books.

More often he'd found himself simply staring at the damp walls of his study.

And yet today his whirlwind of a wife had persuaded him to accompany her on a social call.

He narrowed his eyes. If he weren't a man of reason and learning, he might suspect some type of sorcery. His wife sat across from him, talking animatedly with her great-aunt next to her and Sarah, who was beside Godric. Lady Margaret was very careful to avoid his eye as she kept up a running stream of chatter about London and the history of this ladies' syndicate.

His wife's cheeks were lightly flushed with her excitement, making her dark eyes sparkle. A curling strand of hair had already escaped her coiffure and now bobbed seductively against her temple, as if to tempt some unwary male to try to contain it.

Godric pressed his lips together and faced the window.

Perhaps his wife had a lover.

The thought was not a pleasant one, but why else would such a vivacious girl seek his company except that she had a secret lover in London? It hadn't occurred to him before that his absent wife might take a lover, but after all, was it such a strange thought? She was no virgin and he'd never attempted to consummate their marriage. Just because he was resigned to a solitary, celibate life didn't mean *she* was. Lady Margaret was a young, beautiful woman. A woman of high spirits, if this morning was anything to go by. Such a lady might even have more than one lover.

But no. Godric's sense of logic broke through his melancholy thoughts. If she had a lover, surely he would reside near Godric's country estate. After all, Lady Margaret had left Laurelwood Manor only a few times in the last two years—and then only to visit her family. She must have some other reason for suddenly descending on him.

"Here we are at last," his wife exclaimed.

Godric glanced out the window and saw that the carriage was indeed drawing up outside the Home for Unfortunate Infants and Foundling Children. The building was only a couple of years old, a clean, neat edifice several stories high and taking up most of Maiden Lane. The bright brick stood out, fresh and new, against the other, older and destitute buildings in St. Giles.

Godric waited until Lady Margaret's footman had set the step and then jumped down to help the ladies. Great-Aunt Elvina rose precariously. The lady was at least seventy, and although she disdained the use of a cane, Godric had noticed that she was at times unsteady on her feet. She held her pregnant pug in her arms, and Godric swiftly realized he would have to do the gentlemanly thing.

"If I might take Her Grace," he enunciated into her ear.

The elderly lady shot him a grateful glance. "Thank you, Mr. St. John."

Godric gingerly took the warm, panting little body, pretending not to notice when the animal drooled on his sleeve. He held out his free hand to Great-Aunt Elvina.

The lady descended, then frowned, glancing around.

"What a very disreputable area this is." She brightened. "Won't dear Lady Cambridge be scandalized when I write her about it!"

Still holding the pug, Godric helped Sarah out and then took Lady Margaret's hand, warm, trembling, and alive, in his. She kept her gaze lowered as she stepped from the carriage, the curl of hair bobbing gently against her face. The scent of something sweet lingered in the air. She made a show of shaking out her skirts when she stood on the cobblestones.

Damn it, she wasn't looking at him. On impulse, he reached out and took that wayward tendril between thumb and forefinger, firmly tucking it behind her ear.

She glanced up, her lips parted, so near he could see the swirls of gold in her pretty brown eyes, and he suddenly identified her scent: orange blossoms.

Her voice was breathless when she spoke. "Thank you."

His jaw flexed. "Not at all."

Godric turned and mounted the steps to the home, knocking briskly.

The door was opened almost at once by a butler who looked haughty enough to be attending a royal palace rather than an orphanage in St. Giles.

Godric nodded to the man as he entered. "My wife and her friends are here for the Ladies' Syndicate meeting. I wonder if Makepeace is about?"

"Certainly, sir," the butler intoned. He took hats and gloves from the ladies as they entered in a flurry of skirts and chatter behind Godric. "I'll fetch Mr. Makepeace."

"No need, Butterman." Winter Makepeace appeared in a doorway farther down the hall. He wore his usual black, although the cut of his clothes had improved noticeably since his marriage to the former Lady Beckinhall. "Good morning, St. John. Ladies."

"Oh, Mr. Makepeace." Lady Margaret caught his hand, smiling brightly, and Godric frowned, feeling a flicker of jealousy—which was completely ridiculous. His wife seemed to smile at *everyone* brightly. "May I present my sister-in-law and my dear great-aunt?"

Introductions were made. Makepeace inclined his head gravely to each lady rather than making the more usual sweeping bow, but neither Sarah nor Great-Aunt Elvina seemed at all put out.

The manager of the home turned to Godric and the panting pug in his arms, his eyes lit with a gentle amusement. "Who is your companion?"

"Her Grace," Godric said curtly.

Makepeace blinked. "I beg your pardon?"

Godric began to shake his head when a small white terrier came barreling down the hallway. The animal was making a sound rather like a bumblebee, but on sight of Her Grace, the terrier erupted into hysterical barking.

Her Grace yipped back—very shrilly—while both Lady Margaret and Sarah made futile shushing noises, and if Godric wasn't mistaken, Great-Aunt Elvina aimed a surreptitious kick at the terrier.

Makepeace stepped to the side, opened a door into the sitting room, and cocked an eyebrow. Godric nodded and in a few brisk movements deposited the pug back in Great-Aunt Elvina's arms and ushered the three ladies into the sitting room where the meeting was being held.

Makepeace shut the door so swiftly the terrier nearly lost her nose. He glanced at Godric. "This way."

The home's manager turned toward the staircase at the

back of the hall. "Really, that was most inhospitable of you, Dodo."

The terrier, trotting adoringly by his side, tilted her head, perking up one ear as if listening attentively.

"You're quite lucky I don't lock you up in the root cellar." Makepeace's voice was calm and reasoned as he chided the dog.

Godric cleared his throat. "Does, er, Dodo always attack visitors?"

"No." Makepeace shot Godric a sardonic look. "Only canine visitors receive that welcome."

"Ah."

"Two new girls came to our home last night," Makepeace continued as he mounted the wide marble staircase, his tone bone-dry. "Deposited here by the notorious Ghost of St. Giles."

"Indeed?"

Makepeace flashed him an intelligent glance. "I thought you might like to meet our newest inmates."

"Naturally." At least his trip to the home wasn't without purpose.

"Here we are," Makepeace said, holding open a door to one of the classrooms.

A glance inside showed rows of girls sitting on benches, dutifully copying something down on their slates. At the far end of one of the rows sat Moll and her elder sister, their heads together. Godric was glad to see them whispering to one another. Chatting seemed to be a uniquely feminine sign of happiness—Lady Margaret talking with the other ladies in the carriage flashed through his mind—and he hoped it meant the girls would settle happily at the home.

"Moll and Janet McNab," Makepeace said in a low

voice. "Moll is too young for this class, but we thought it best not to separate the sisters in their first few days here." He closed the door and strolled farther along the deserted hall. All the children appeared to be at lessons behind the closed doors. "The girls are orphans. Janet has told me that their father was a night-soil man who met an unfortunate end when one of the mounds of...er...dirt on the outskirts of London fell and buried him."

Godric winced. "How awful."

"Quite." Makepeace paused at the end of the corridor. There were two chairs here, arranged beneath a window, but he made no move to sit. "It seems the McNab sisters were on the streets for nearly a fortnight before they ran afoul of the lassie snatchers."

"Lassie snatchers," Godric repeated softly. "I seem to remember that name being bandied about St. Giles awhile back. You dealt with them, didn't you?"

Makepeace glanced cautiously down the hall before lowering his voice. "Two years ago, the lassie snatchers kidnapped girls off the streets of St. Giles."

Godric raised his brows. "Why?"

"To make lace stockings in an illegal workshop," Makepeace said grimly. "The girls were made to work long hours with very little food and with frequent beatings. And they weren't paid."

"But the lassie snatchers were stopped."

Makepeace nodded his head curtly. "I stopped them. Found the workshop and cut off the head of the snake—an aristocrat by the name of Seymour. I haven't heard of them since."

Godric narrowed his eyes. "But?"

"But I've heard disturbing rumors in the last few

weeks." Makepeace frowned. "Girls disappearing off the streets of St. Giles. Gossip about a hidden workshop manned by little girls. And worse: my wife has found evidence of the lace silk stockings they make being hawked to the upper crust of aristocratic society."

Isabel Makepeace was still a formidable force in society, despite her marriage to the manager of an orphanage.

Godric said, "Did you kill the wrong man?"

"No." Makepeace's look was grim. "Seymour was quite proud of his crime, believe me. He boasted of it before I ended his life. Either someone else has started up an entirely different operation or—"

"Or Seymour wasn't the only one in the original business," Godric murmured.

"Either way, someone must find out who is behind the lassie snatchers and stop them. I'm out of the business since my marriage." Makepeace paused delicately. "I assume that you're still operating. Although, with your wife now in town—"

"She won't be for long," Godric said crisply.

Makepeace arched an eyebrow but was far too discreet to inquire further.

Godric's lips thinned. "What about the other?"

Makepeace shook his head. "He hunts only one thing in St. Giles; you know that. He's been monomaniacal for years now."

Godric nodded. They were all loners, but the third of their bizarre trilogy was near obsessive. He would be no help in this matter.

"It's up to you alone, I'm afraid," Makepeace said.

"Very well." Godric thought a moment. "If Seymour did have a partner, do you have any idea who it might be?"

"It could be anyone, but were I you, I'd begin with Seymour's friends: Viscount d'Arque and the Earl of Kershaw. All three were as thick as thieves before Seymour's death." Makepeace paused and looked at him intently. "But, St. John?"

Godric raised his brows.

Makepeace's face was grim. "You also need to find this workshop. Last time, some of the girls nearly didn't make it out alive."

Chapter Three

One moonless night, the Hellequin came upon the soul of a young man lying in the crossroads, dying in the arms of his beloved. The woman was lovely, her face both innocent and good, and for a moment the Hellequin paused, staring at her. There are those who whisper that the Hellequin was not always in the Devil's service. Once, they say, the Hellequin was a man like any other. If this tale is true, perhaps the girl's face sparked some human memory, wandering lost, deep in the Hellequin's mind....
—From *The Legend of the Hellequin*

Megs perched on a settee in the home's cozy sitting room and sipped from her dish of tea as she glanced around at the other ladies in the Syndicate. The membership hadn't changed, it seemed, in her absence. Her sister-in-law, Lady Hero Reading, one of the two founding members, sat beside her on the settee, her hair nearly the same color as the fireplace flames. Next to Hero was her younger sister, Lady Phoebe Batten, a pleasant girl with a plump figure who smiled rather vaguely at nothing in particular.

Megs knit her brows in worry. The girl's eyesight had been very poor when last she'd seen her—had Phoebe gone entirely blind in the intervening years? Beside

Phoebe was Lady Penelope Chadwicke, rumored to be one of the wealthiest heiresses in England—and with her pansy-purple eyes and black hair, certainly one of the most beautiful. Lady Penelope was nearly always accompanied by her lady's companion, Miss Artemis Greaves, a retiring but pleasant lady. On the far side of Miss Greaves was the other founding patroness, the daunting, silver-haired Lady Caire. Next to Lady Caire sat her daughter-in-law, Temperance Huntington, Lady Caire, and next to Temperance was her brother's wife, the former Lady Beckinhall—Isabel Makepeace.

The membership may not've changed, but there were other differences since last she'd attended a meeting. This room, for instance. When last Megs had seen it, the sitting room had been clean and neat but far from homey. Now, thanks to what she suspected was the new Mrs. Makepeace's intervention, the room boasted a lovely landscape over the fireplace and a series of amusing knickknacks on the mantel: an odd little green and white Chinese bowl, a gilt clock held aloft by cupids, and a blue statuette of a stork and what appeared to be a salamander.

Megs squinted. Surely it couldn't be a salamander?

"I'm so glad that you decided to come back to town, sister, dear," Lady Hero interrupted her thoughts. Hero had acquired the rather sweet habit of calling Megs *sister* since marrying Megs's brother Griffin.

"Did you miss me at the meetings?" Megs asked lightly.

"Yes, of course." Hero gave her a faintly chiding look. "But you know Griffin has missed you, and I have as well. We don't see you nearly as much as I'd like."

Megs wrinkled her nose, feeling guilty, and reached for

a biscuit from the plate sitting on the table beside her. "I'm sorry. I did mean to come up for Christmas, but the weather was so bad...." She trailed off. Her excuse sounded weak even to her own ears. It was just that ever since Griffin had intervened on her behalf with Godric—had found a way to save her from her own folly—she hadn't known how to face him. Wasn't even sure what she could say.

Hero folded her hands in her lap. "All that matters is that you're here now. Have you seen Thomas and Lavinia yet?"

"Er..." Megs took a hasty sip of tea.

Hero's eyes narrowed. "Thomas *does* know you're in town?"

Actually, Megs hadn't informed her eldest brother—otherwise known as the Marquess of Mandeville—of her arrival.

Hero, with her usual quiet perception, seemed to realize that Megs hadn't told *anyone* of her trip. But instead of badgering Megs with questions, she merely sighed. "Well, your visit will be a fine excuse to have everyone over for dinner. And perhaps you can come early to see my sweet William. He's bigger than Annalise now, you know."

And Hero nodded to one of the other changes in the room.

Petite Annalise Huntington, the daughter of Temperance and Lord Caire, clung to the edge of a low table as she carefully, but very determinedly, tiptoed toward Her Grace. The pug was under Great-Aunt Elvina's chair and keeping a wary eye out for the toddler. Annalise was a year and a half now and wore a lace-trimmed white gown and sash, her delicate dark hair ornamented by a single blue bow.

She was about the same age Megs's baby would've been—had he lived.

Megs blinked and swallowed down the old, bitter grief. When she'd first miscarried—and lost her last link to Roger—she'd thought she'd not survive. How could a body endure so much pain, so many tears, and live on? But it seemed that grief really couldn't kill a person. She *had* lived. Had healed from the physical trauma of the miscarriage. Had risen from her sickbed, had—slowly— taken an interest in the things and people around her. Had, in time, even smiled and laughed.

But she hadn't forgotten the loss. The almost physical ache to feel a babe in her arms.

Megs inhaled, steadying herself. She hadn't seen her brother's son since he was a week old—a visit she'd cut short after only three days. It had simply been too torturous for her.

"Does William still have such bright red hair?" she asked wistfully.

Hero chuckled. William had been born with carrot-red hair. "No, it's begun to darken. I think Griffin is disappointed. He claims he wanted an heir with hair as red as mine." She touched a finger to her own fiery locks.

Megs felt her lips curve in a smile. "I'm looking forward to seeing my nephew again."

And she meant it—she'd lost too much time with William already because of the pain it had caused her to see the happy, healthy baby.

"I'm glad," Hero said simply, but there was a wealth of understanding in her eyes. She was one of the few people who knew the true reason for Megs's hasty wedding.

There was a smatter of laughter as Annalise reached

Her Grace only to have the pug get up and flee. Megs was glad of the distraction to look away from her sister-in-law's too-perceptive eyes.

Her Grace circled the room, panting, before taking refuge under Megs's chair.

Annalise stared at the dog, her face beginning to crumple. Temperance bent toward her daughter, but the elder Lady Caire was faster. "There, there, darling. Have another biscuit."

Temperance said nothing, but Megs caught her rolling her eyes as the elegant, silver-haired older lady gave the baby the offering.

Temperance blushed slightly when she saw that Megs was watching and leaned over to whisper, "She spoils her terribly."

"A grandmama's prerogative," Lady Caire said, apparently having heard. "Now, then. I wonder if we might discuss the apprenticeship of the girls of the home." She glanced at Megs. "The number of children at the home has increased in the last year. Presently we have . . ."

"Four and fifty children," Isabel Makepeace supplied the number. "Two new girls were brought in just last night."

Lady Caire nodded. "Thank you, Mrs. Makepeace. We are pleased that the home is able to help so many children now, but it seems that we have had some difficulties in placing the children—particularly the girls—properly."

"But surely there is no lack of maidservant positions in London," Lady Penelope said.

"Actually, there is," Temperance replied. "At least maidservant positions in respectable houses where the girls are treated properly and given some type of training."

Isabel leaned forward to pour some more tea in her dish. "Just last week we took back a girl whose position proved to be unfortunate."

Megs raised her eyebrows. "Unfortunate?"

"The mistress of the house saw fit to beat the girl with a hairbrush," Lady Caire said grimly.

"Oh." Megs felt horror sweep through her, and then an idea. "But I'm in need of maidservants."

The rest of the ladies looked at her.

"Indeed?" Lady Caire asked.

"Oh, yes," Sarah said, joining the conversation for the first time. "It seems my brother has been reduced to one manservant at Saint House."

"Good Lord." Temperance frowned worriedly. "I'm sure Caire has no idea that Mr. St. John was in such straits."

"Well, the straits weren't financial." Sarah sent her an ironic glance. "Godric can certainly afford any number of servants—he simply didn't bother to hire new ones."

"Eh?" Great-Aunt Elvina leaned toward Sarah.

Sarah turned toward her and said distinctly, "I doubt it occurred to my brother that he needed more servants."

"Men are absentminded in such matters." Great-Aunt Elvina shook her head disapprovingly.

"Quite," Lady Caire said. "But having been appraised of his—and your—difficulties, Lady Margaret, we will naturally help. I'm sure we have several girls ready to be apprenticed out?" She glanced at Isabel.

"At least four," Isabel said. "But they are all under the age of twelve and will need strict supervision and tutelage as to their duties."

"As to that," Lady Caire said, "I can recommend a house-keeper of very good repute, manners, and intelligence."

"Thank you." Megs had always thought Lady Caire a bit austere, but it seemed she could be kind as well. And Megs *was* very grateful. In one swoop she already had a housekeeper and maids for Saint House.

Lady Caire inclined her head. "I'll send her around this evening if that suits you?"

"Oh, yes." Megs felt a touch at her knee and looked down.

Annalise had one hand braced on her lap as she squatted to look under the chair Megs sat on. From beneath came a faint whine.

Her Grace had been discovered.

Annalise chortled and for a moment glanced up at Megs, tiny, perfect teeth showing in a delighted grin. And Megs's breath froze in her throat. *This.* This was what she wanted with all her soul, all her heart. A baby of her own.

Last night her courage had failed her, but she wouldn't let that happen tonight.

Tonight she would seduce her husband.

BUT HOW, EXACTLY, did one go about seducing a husband one hardly knew? That was the question Megs pondered all that afternoon and evening as she set about ordering Saint House. This morning's efforts had been...less than successful. Perhaps she should alert him somehow? Send a note perhaps? *Dear sir, I would be much obliged if you would consent to consummate our marriage. Yours very truly, your wife.*

"If that would agree with you, my lady?"

Megs started, looking up into the serious dark eyes of her new housekeeper, Mrs. Crumb. They were in the dining room, which, apparently, was one of the few rooms in Saint House that Mrs. Crumb considered habitable at the moment. "Er, yes? I'm sorry, I didn't quite catch that last bit."

Mrs. Crumb was too well trained—nearly terrifyingly so—to indicate in any way that she was repeating herself. "If it agrees with you, my lady, I shall take the responsibility of finding and hiring a new cook. I've found in the past that great care should be taken with the employment of cooks. Staff run so much better when well fed."

Mrs. Crumb gazed at Megs with a deferential yet determined air. She was something of a surprise. Not that Megs doubted in any way that Mrs. Crumb was an exceptional housekeeper—within minutes of entering Saint House, she'd set the girls from the orphanage to cleaning, sweeping, and ordering, and she'd so cowed Mr. Moulder that he'd not even questioned the housekeeper when she'd instructed him to throw out any edibles still left in what, apparently, was a quite filthy kitchen. Tall for a woman and with a bearing that would have done a general proud, Mrs. Crumb had black hair neatly tucked beneath a white cap and dark eyes that seemed to compel obedience in both little girls and grown footmen. But— and here was the surprising part—the woman couldn't be over the age of five and twenty. Megs would love to ask her how, exactly, she'd risen to such prominence in her profession as to bear golden references from the powerful Lady Caire at such a young age, but truthfully, her new housekeeper intimidated her.

Just a little.

"Yes." Megs nodded. "That will be quite satisfactory."

"Just so, my lady." Mrs. Crumb inclined her head. "I've taken the liberty of sending 'round to the Bird in Hand inn for a roast goose, bread, a half-dozen pies, and assorted boiled vegetables for supper, as well as provisions for the servants."

"Oh, wonderful!" Megs smiled at this efficiency. She hadn't been looking forward to a supper of boiled eggs—assuming there were any eggs left—and roast goose was one of her favorites. But was it one of Godric's favorites? She simply hadn't any idea—he'd never mentioned food in his letters, and from the paucity of his kitchen, what he ate obviously wasn't high on his list of important needs. Well, that was just silly. A pleasant meal made everything so much more enjoyable. She'd have to find out what he liked as soon as she could.

If Mrs. Crumb noticed her distraction, she gave no sign. "With your permission, my lady, supper will be served in here at eight of the clock."

Megs glanced at the clock over the mantel and saw that it was already half past seven. "Then I suppose I ought to go freshen myself."

Mrs. Crumb curtsied. "Yes, my lady. I'll go see that everything is ready."

And she marched from the room.

Megs blew out her breath and hurried to her bedroom. Normally she didn't bother dressing for dinner at home, but tonight was special.

"The scarlet silk, please, Daniels," she instructed her little lady's maid and then stood impatiently as she was dressed.

The scarlet was over four years old—from before her retirement to the country. What social events she'd attended in Upper Hornsfield had been far less formal than London. It'd seemed a waste to have new dresses made when what she had already outshone the local gentry.

Megs winced now as her bodice was drawn perilously tight over her bosom. Abundant country meals seemed to have led to growth in that portion of her figure. She made a mental note to visit a London modiste as soon as possible.

Still, the scarlet set off her dark hair and creamy pale complexion quite well. Megs leaned toward the cloudy mirror over the ancient dresser in her room and shoved a lock of hair back in place. She ought to have Daniels take the whole thing down and start over, but she hadn't the time—it was already five past eight.

Rushing from her room, Megs nearly cannoned into the back—the rather broad back, now that she looked at it—of her husband.

"Oh!"

He turned around at her involuntary exclamation, and she had to tilt her head back to see his eyes. He was close, his chest nearly brushing her bodice.

He glanced down swiftly, almost imperceptibly, at her bosom, and then up at her face. His expression didn't change at all. He might've just glanced at a side of beef.

"Your pardon, my lady."

"Not at all." She *wasn't* a side of beef, damn it! Inhaling, she smiled sweetly up at him and slipped her hand through his arm. "You're just in time to escort me down to dinner."

He inclined his head politely enough, but she felt him stiffen just a bit against her.

Well, she'd never been a quitter. She might've had to retire to the country for a bit to recover from the loss of Roger and their baby, but that didn't mean she was going to lie down without a fight now.

She wanted a baby.

So Megs pressed close to Godric, ignoring his rigid posture, and linked her hands, effectively tethering him to her. "We quite missed you today."

He'd left the ladies to organizing Saint House immediately after they'd all returned from St. Giles. Presumably he'd spent the day in some type of male pursuit.

His swift glance down at her was incredulous.

Megs cleared her throat. "Sarah and I did come to London to visit."

"I was under the impression that it was shopping you and my sister were after." His tone was as dry as the dust the maids had battled all day. "That and upending my house. You travel with a veritable village."

She felt the heat rise up her neck. "Sarah is your sister and a good friend and we need all the servants."

"Including the gardener?" Despite his remote countenance, he was careful to match his stride to hers.

"I'm sure your garden will need renovation," she said earnestly, "if the state I found your country grounds in two years ago is any indication."

"Hmm. And Great-Aunt Elvina? She rarely seems pleased with anything—including you."

They were descending the stairs now to the dining room and Megs lowered her voice. Great-Aunt Elvina had proved on more than one occasion that her hearing could sometimes miraculously return. "She's a bit starchy, but underneath she's as soft as pudding, really."

He only looked down at her and arched a disbelieving eyebrow.

Megs sighed. "She does get very lonely. I didn't want to leave her by herself at Laurelwood."

"She lives with you?"

"Yes." Megs bit her lip. "Actually, Great-Aunt Elvina has made the rounds of all my relatives."

His mouth quirked. "Ah. And you're the last resort, I'm guessing."

"Well, yes. It's just that she has a tendency to speak her mind rather bluntly, I'm afraid." She winced. "She told my second cousin Arabella that her baby daughter had the nose of a pig, which she does, unfortunately, but really it was too bad of Great-Aunt Elvina to mention it."

Godric snorted. "And yet you take this harridan into your bosom."

"Someone has to." Megs took a deep breath and peeked up at his face. It had lightened...a bit. She decided to grasp what encouragement she could. "I had hoped to use this trip to get to know you better, G-Godric."

Try as she might, the first use of his Christian name still stuttered on her lips.

His glance was sardonic. "An admirable goal, Margaret, but I think we've muddled along together well enough until now."

"*We* haven't done *anything* together," Megs muttered as they made the main floor. She caught herself and remembered what she was trying to do. She began stroking his forearm with one finger. "We've lived entirely separate lives. And please. Call me Megs."

He stared down at her finger, now drawing circles on the sleeve of his coat. "I was under the impression that you were happy."

He hadn't used her name.

"I was happy. Or at least content." Megs wrinkled her nose. Why was he making this so hard? "But that doesn't mean that we can't change things, even make them better.

I'm sure if we tried, we could find something...*enjoyable* to do together."

His dark brows drew together over his eyes, and she had the distinct impression that he didn't at all agree with her.

But they'd reached the small receiving room adjacent to the dining room now, and Sarah and Great-Aunt Elvina were already waiting for them.

"We've received word that we'll have a real dinner tonight," Sarah said at the sight of them.

Godric raised his brows, glancing at Megs as they joined the others. "Then you succeeded in hiring a new cook?"

"No, actually, we have someone much better." Megs smiled up at him, despite his solemn expression. "Apparently, I've hired London's most accomplished housekeeper, Mrs. Crumb."

Behind them came a snort. Megs turned to see a transformed Moulder. His wig was freshly powdered, his shoes were shined, and his coat looked sponged and pressed. "That woman is a termagant, she is."

"Moulder." Was that a flash of amusement on Godric's face? "You're looking quite...butlerly."

Moulder grunted and held open the door to the dining room. They entered and Megs was glad to note the transformation from last night. Gone were the spiderwebs overhead. The hearth had been swept and a fire crackled there now. The big table in the center of the room had been polished with beeswax until it gleamed.

Godric stopped short, his eyebrows raised. "Your housekeeper is indeed a gem to have changed this room in such little time."

"Let's hope her promise of dinner is equally as impressive," Great-Aunt Elvina boomed.

As it turned out, Mrs. Crumb was simply a paragon of housekeeperly virtue. A beaming Oliver and Johnny soon laid the dinner before them, and Megs was eagerly cutting her portion of goose.

She sighed with contentment over the mouthful of juicy meat and glanced up just in time to meet her husband's enigmatic gaze.

Hastily she swallowed and tried to appear more ladylike and less like a starving urchin. "It's quite good, isn't it?"

He peered down at his plate dispassionately. "Yes, if you like goose."

"I do." Her heart sank. "Don't you?"

He shrugged. "I find goose greasy."

"Grisly?" Great-Aunt Elvina asked, her brow wrinkled in confusion.

"Greasy," Godric repeated, louder. "The goose is greasy."

"Goose is supposed to be greasy," Great-Aunt Elvina boomed. "Keeps it from being dry." She picked up a piece from her plate and fed it to Her Grace without bothering to hide the motion.

Megs smiled. "If you don't like goose, what do you like?"

Her husband shrugged. "Whatever you see fit to serve will do well enough."

Megs tried very, very hard to keep her smile in place. "But I want to know what you like to eat."

"And I have told you that it does not matter."

Her cheeks were beginning to ache. "Gammon? Beef? Fish?"

"Margaret—"

"Eel?" Her eyes narrowed. "Tripe? Brains?"

"*Not* brains," he snapped, his voice so low it sounded as if it were scraping gravel.

She beamed. "Not brains! I shall make a note of it."

Sarah coughed into her napkin.

Great-Aunt Elvina fed Her Grace another scrap as she murmured, "*I* like brains fried in butter."

Godric cleared his throat and took a sip of wine before setting the wineglass down precisely. "I have a fondness for pigeon pie."

"Do you?" Megs leaned forward eagerly. She felt as excited as if she'd won a prize at a fair. "I'll be sure and ask Mrs. Crumb to tell the new cook."

He inclined his head, the corner of his mouth tilting up. "Thank you."

She caught a fond smile on Sarah's face as her sister-in-law looked between the two of them. Megs felt the heat rise in her face. "What did you do today while we worked on the house?"

Godric's gaze slid away as he took a sip of wine—almost as if he were avoiding her question. "I usually frequent Basham's Coffeehouse."

Great-Aunt Elvina frowned and Megs had an awful premonition—her aunt held quite strong opinions. "Nasty things, coffeehouses. Full of scandal sheets, women of low repute, and tobacco."

"As well as coffee, of course," Godric said with an entirely straight face.

"Well, naturally coffee, but—" Great-Aunt Elvina began.

"How is Her Grace feeling this evening?" Megs cut in hastily. From across the table, her husband shot her an ironic look that she chose to ignore. "I notice she seems to be eating well."

"Her Grace spent the entire day abed, panting quite dreadfully. That child overexerted her, chasing Her Grace about." Great-Aunt Elvina stabbed her fork meditatively into a carrot. "Babies are adorable, naturally, but so messy. Perhaps if there was a way of containing them, especially around sensitive creatures such as Her Grace..."

"Like a small cage, you mean?" Sarah asked innocently.

"Or a tether, set into the ground," Godric said.

Everyone looked at him.

Sarah's lips were trembling. "But what about indoors?"

He raised his brows, his expression grave. "Ill-advised, I'm afraid. Best to keep them outside in the fresh air. But if one did bring a baby indoors, I think a hook set into the wall with ties made to fit under the child's arms would suit."

Great-Aunt Elvina's brows had snapped together. She wasn't known for her sense of humor. "Mr. St. John!"

He turned to her attentively. "Ma'am?"

"I cannot believe you would suggest tying a child to the wall."

"Oh, no, ma'am," Godric said as he poured himself more wine. "You have me entirely wrong."

"Well, that's a relief—"

"I meant the child should hang *on* the wall." He looked kindly at the elderly woman. "Like a picture, as it were."

Megs had to cover her mouth with one hand to still the giggles bubbling up from inside. Who would've guessed that her somberly dry husband could say such outrageous things?

She glanced up and caught her breath. Godric was

watching her, his lips slightly curved as he sipped from his wineglass, and she had the oddest notion: that he'd teased Great-Aunt Elvina solely to amuse her.

"Godric," Sarah chided.

He turned toward his sister, and Megs blinked. She was reading too much into what was merely play between Godric and his sister.

Still.

It would've been nice to have some kind of connection to him. She was drawing closer to the point—the time when she would lie with this man. Perform a very intimate act, which she'd only done before with one man—a man she'd loved. To somehow seduce a near stranger into, well, *tupping* her was a daunting task. If there were any other way of accomplishing her mission, she'd take it and gladly. But there wasn't, of course. Bedding her husband was the only way to have her child.

Megs picked through the rest of the meal, her nervousness compounding as the hour grew later.

After supper, the four of them retired to the newly dusted library, where Sarah persuaded Godric to read aloud from a history of the monarchs of England while Great-Aunt Elvina nodded off in a wing chair. Sarah brought her needlework bag and was soon contentedly intent on her embroidery, but Megs had never been very adept at fine sewing. For several minutes she wandered the room, her husband's deep, husky voice making her nerves jangle, until Sarah complained that her "pacing" was distracting.

Megs sat and could only watch Godric as he read. The candle beside him sent a flickering light across his face, catching on high cheekbones and the hint of a dark beard along his jaw and upper lip. His eyes were downturned as he read, his eyelashes casting long shadows across his face. He seemed younger somehow, despite his habitual gray wig and the half-moon spectacles he used to read. While the thought should've reassured her, it only added to Megs's internal agitation.

He glanced up then, his eyes dark and hidden. She tried to smile, tried to look back at him alluringly, but her lips trembled imperceptibly. His gaze dropped to her mouth and stayed there, his face brooding. She caught her breath. She did not know this man. Not really.

At last the party adjourned for the night and Megs nearly fled up the stairs. Daniels was waiting in her room and helped her to undress and don her usual chemise for bed. Megs gazed at herself in the mirror as Daniels brushed out her hair and wished belatedly that she'd thought to buy a new chemise. Something in silk, perhaps. Something she could seduce a husband in. The one she wore wasn't old, but it was rather ordinary white lawn with only a bit of embroidery about the yoke.

"Thank you, Daniels," she said when Daniels had already brushed her hair for twice as long as she normally did.

The maid curtsied and retired.

Megs stood and faced the communal door to her husband's room. No more nerves, she chided herself. No more prevarications, no excuses, no dawdling. She clutched the doorknob and opened the door wide.

Only to find the room empty.

"AFTER HIM, MEN!"

The deep growl of the dragoon captain echoed off

the buildings as Godric swore and darted into a narrow alley, running flat out. This wasn't how he'd planned to spend the night in St. Giles. He'd hoped to question an old acquaintance about the lassie snatchers. Instead, almost the moment he'd stepped foot in St. Giles, he'd had the misfortune to run into the dragoons—and their near-maniacal commander.

The alley let out into a series of courtyards, but he didn't doubt the dragoons were circling to cut him off. Godric ducked into a well in the side of a building made by steps giving access to a basement.

Footsteps trotted up the alley.

Godric flattened himself against the near wall and prayed.

"We'll get the bastard tonight if God is on our side," came the voice of Captain James Trevillion from just above.

Godric rolled his eyes. The captain and his dragoons had been sent into St. Giles three years ago to quell the sale of gin and capture the Ghost of St. Giles. They'd achieved neither aim. Oh, the soldiers had rounded up plenty of gin sellers, but there were always more to take their place. Trevillion might as well be trying to empty the Thames with a tin cup. As to his search for the Ghost of St. Giles, despite being almost rabidly dedicated to his task, the captain had yet to lay hands on him.

And if Godric had anything to do with it, Trevillion's luck wouldn't change tonight.

He waited until the heavy boots of the soldiers had run past, then waited a bit more. When at last he ventured forth, the alley was empty.

Or at least it looked so. Trevillion was a wily hunter

and had been known to retrace his steps just when a quarry thought himself safe.

Tonight was not a good night for his Ghostly activities.

Godric made the mouth of the alley just in time. Trevillion had indeed sent some of his men to double back. There were three, only twenty yards away, when he emerged and Godric was forced to take to his heels, cursing under his breath.

Thirty long minutes later, he dropped into his own garden. Saint House had been built at a time when access to the river was of paramount importance to aristocrats, both as a sign of prestige and, more practically, as a means of transport. The garden ran from the back of the house to the old river gate—a grand crumbling arch that gave access to the private steps leading to the river. His ancestors might've enjoyed displaying their wealth with private pleasure barges on the Thames, but Godric liked Saint House's situation for more nefarious reasons: it was perfectly placed for a Ghost to come and go with no one the wiser.

Tonight he paused for a moment as he always did in the shadows of the garden, waiting, watching to make sure the way was clear. Nothing moved save the shadow of a cat strolling past, entirely unconcerned with his presence. Godric inhaled and crept up the garden path to his house. He carefully pushed open the door and entered his own study. He glanced around, noting that he was alone, and only then felt a measure of relief. Not that long ago he'd received a nasty surprise here.

Tonight, though, the fire was dead and the room dark. He felt his way to a certain panel by the fireplace and pressed the old wood. The panel popped out, revealing a cubbyhole in the wall and his nightclothes. Swiftly Godric stripped off his Ghostly costume and donned a nightshirt, banyan, and slippers.

Turning, he left the study and started for his own bedroom, feeling weariness sink into his bones. It'd been a long day. He still had no clear idea of how long Margaret planned to stay in town. Both his sister and the old tarter of an aunt had made vague references to the length of their trip—obviously they looked upon it as only a visit. But he couldn't shake the feeling that Margaret intended something more—a longer stay or, God help him, to take up permanent residence.

He was distracted by the thought, his defenses already lowered by the perceived safety of his own home. And as he entered his bedroom, he was attacked. Strong arms circled his neck, a body bore him back against the wall, and hands clutched at the back of his head. He smelled orange blossoms.

Then Margaret kissed him.

Chapter Four

But in the end, the Hellequin shrugged and looked away from the woman's face. He reached down and, thrusting his hand into the young man's chest, drew his soul from out of his body. The Hellequin wound a strand of spider's silk three times counterclockwise about the young man's soul to bind it, and then stuffed it into his sack made of raven's hides. He turned to go, but as he did, the young man's beloved cried aloud, "Stop!"…
—From *The Legend of the Hellequin*

Megs's first thought was that Godric was hard—much harder than she'd thought a man getting on in years would be. It was as if all of his muscles turned to stone the moment she touched him. She knew this because the momentum of her kiss had forced him back against the wall as she pressed herself into him. Chest, belly, arms, and thighs were unyieldingly obdurate against her much-softer body. She angled her head, opening her mouth, tasting wine on his cold lips—and nothing happened. She was trying all her wiles, which, granted, weren't all that sophisticated, but still…was the man made of rock?

The air burst from her lungs in a puff of frustration and she drew back a little to look into his face.

Which was a mistake.

His crystal gray eyes were narrowed, his mouth flattened, and his nostrils flared just a bit. All in all, *not* an encouraging expression.

"Margaret," he clipped out, using her full Christian name, "what are you doing?"

She winced. If he had to ask, her attempt at seduction must be truly lacking.

Baby. She must keep her purpose at the forefront of her mind.

She smiled, though the effort might've been a trifle strained. "I...I thought tonight would be a good time to become better acquainted."

"Acquainted." The word dropped, lifeless and heavy from his lips, and fell like a dead halibut between them.

She'd never liked fish. Megs inhaled to explain, but he set his hands on her waist, lifted her up and aside, and strolled past her to the fireplace.

Megs goggled. She'd never been one of those fairylike girls, the ones who lived on marzipan and the odd strawberry here and there. She was a bit over average height and had the figure of a woman with a fondness for hearty country food. Yet her husband—her *elderly* husband—had lifted her with as little effort as he would a fluffy kitten.

Megs squinted at Godric, now on one knee by the hearth, stirring up the fire that had died while she'd dozed waiting for his return. He'd left off his soft cap tonight, and she saw for the first time the shorn hair that lay close to his scalp. It was dark, nearly black, but there was a wide swath of gray at both temples.

"How old *are* you?" she demanded, truly without thinking.

He sighed, still efficiently prodding the fire into life. "Seven and thirty and, I'm afraid, well past the age of enjoying surprises."

He stood and turned, and somehow he seemed taller tonight, his shoulders broader. Without his gray wig, without the habitual half-moon reading spectacles, he seemed . . . well, not younger, precisely, but certainly more virile.

Megs shivered. Virile was good. Virile was what she most needed in the prospective father of her child.

Why, then, did Godric seem suddenly more *daunting* as well?

He gestured to one of the chairs before the fireplace. "Please. Sit down."

She sank into the chair, feeling a bit like she had the time her governess had caught her hoarding sugared almonds.

He leaned against the mantel and raised an eyebrow. "Well?"

"We've been married two years," she began, crossing her arms, then immediately uncrossing them. Best to try not to look like a schoolboy being called on the carpet by a particularly dreary schoolmaster.

"You seemed happy enough at Laurelwood Manor."

"I was. I am. . . ." She held her hands flat out and shook her head. "No." She wasn't making any sense, but the time had come to stop prevaricating. "No. I've been *content* enough, but not entirely happy."

His dark brows drew together as he stared at her. "I'm sorry to hear that."

She leaned forward urgently. "I'm not blaming you by any means. Laurelwood is a wonderful place to live. I love the gardens, Upper Hornsfield, the people, and your family."

One eyebrow arched. "But?"

"But it—*I'm*—missing something." She jumped to her feet, pacing restlessly around the chair, trying to think how to make him understand. At the last moment, she realized her direction was taking her to the bed. She stopped short and whirled, blurting, "I want—I desperately *need*—a child, Godric."

For a moment he simply stared at her as if stunned speechless. Then his gaze dropped to the fire. The light behind him silhouetted his profile, outlining a long brow and straight nose, and Megs thought rather irreverently that his lips from this angle looked so soft, almost feminine.

But not quite. "I see."

She shook her head, pacing again. "Do you?" *Not toward the bed.* "I was pregnant when we entered into this marriage. I know it was wrong of me, but I wanted that child—Roger's child. Even in the grief of his passing, it was something to hold on to—something of my very own." She stopped before his dresser, severely ordered, severely plain, only a washing basin, a pitcher, and a small dish on its surface all equidistant from each other. She reached out and picked up the dish. "A child. A baby. *My* baby."

"The urge toward motherhood is natural."

His voice had grown remote. She was losing him and she didn't even know why.

She faced him, her hands outstretched toward him, the little dish still in her hand. "Yes, it is. I want a baby, Godric. I know it's not part of our original bargain." She stopped, laughing bitterly. "Actually, I'm not sure what the original bargain you made with Griffin was."

He looked up at that, his face closed and detached. "Don't you? Didn't Griffin tell you?"

She glanced away, feeling too exposed. She'd been so shamed, so embarrassed, and so grief-stricken that she'd not even been able to look Griffin in the face when he'd told her. Asking any questions had been quite beyond her. And since then...

She realized now that she'd been avoiding her beloved older brother for years. She closed her eyes. "No."

His voice rasped low. "Consummating—or not consummating—the marriage wasn't mentioned."

Megs's eyes snapped open as she stared at him, this stranger who was her husband. *It hadn't been mentioned?* Belatedly—*very* belatedly—and for the first time, she wondered why, exactly, Godric had agreed to marry her. At the time she'd been near mad with grief and terrified of being pregnant out of wedlock. She'd only had the strength to follow Griffin's firm management. Now, though, she wondered...*why?* Had her baby survived, the child would've become Godric's heir. Hadn't he cared that he would've sheltered a cuckoo in his ancient familial nest? Money was the obvious answer—the Readings had enough to bribe a man to overlook the provenience of his heir. But Megs knew that Godric must not've been swayed by wealth. He had enough of it himself. Besides Laurelwood Manor—and its extensive property—he had land in both Oxfordshire and Essex, and although Saint House hadn't been in the best shape on her arrival, he hadn't blinked when she'd cited the sum needed to hire the new staff and redecorate. If anything, he'd seemed *bored* by the conversation.

Her eyes dropped to her hands, absently turning the

little dish over and over. He certainly hadn't agreed to marry her because of friendship for her brother—before the night Griffin had informed her of his arrangement, he'd never mentioned the name Godric St. John.

If Godric hadn't married her for money or friendship, then why?

"Margaret."

She glanced up from her puzzled musing to find him watching her.

He held her gaze as he came toward her and gently took the dish out of her hands. "You know, don't you, that I was married before?"

She swallowed. The tale of Clara St. John, both her devastating disease and her husband's unflinching fidelity, were well known in London society. "Yes."

He inclined his head and turned away, crossing to the dresser. He placed the dish back in its place—neither too far nor too close to the pitcher, and remained there, his back to her, as his long elegant fingers rested on the dish's edge. "I loved Clara very much. Our estates adjoined in Cheshire, you know. Her people are the Hamiltons. Her brother and his family live on the Hamilton estate now, I believe."

Megs nodded. She'd met Mr. and Mrs. Hamilton briefly at one of the ubiquitous country dinners, though she hadn't made the connection before now. The Hamiltons were solid country gentry.

"I knew her all her life," Godric said, and the thread of pain in his voice was all the more terrible for being so carefully repressed, "though I didn't really notice her until I returned from university. I attended a soiree and she was there with her friends, wearing a pale blue dress that made her hair shine. I took one look at her and knew—knew absolutely—that she was the woman I was meant to spend the rest of my life with."

He paused and the fire crackled in the silence, for of course he *hadn't* spent the rest of his life with poor Clara.

She knew about loss, knew about true love shattered. "Godric—"

His fingers let go of the dish and curled into a fist on the dresser. "Just...let me finish."

She nodded, though he couldn't see the small acknowledgment of his pain.

She saw his shoulders rise and fall as he took a deep breath. "When she became ill, I prayed to God—*begged him*. I offered hideous bargains. *Anything*, just so she wouldn't feel the pain. Had the Devil stood before me, I would've gladly sold my soul to exchange my body and life for hers."

She made a low sound of protest and he turned his head, almost but not quite looking at her.

Dear God. His face was etched, as if the agony of his wife's loss had touched him with acid.

He grimaced horribly. A single tear escaped from beneath his lashes, trailing down one lean cheek.

Then his countenance was still once more.

"I agreed to Griffin's mad plan," he rasped, his voice like gravel, "only because it was more than obvious that you would never have any interest in me or a real marriage."

"But—" she said, realizing suddenly how this was going to end. She took a step forward, her hands reaching for him, fruitlessly clutching empty air in front of her.

"No." The word was grimly final. "I haven't lain with

another woman since I married Clara, and I never intend to do so. I had my love. Anything else would be a parody of intimacy. So, no, Margaret, I am sorry, but I will not lie with you to make a baby."

GODRIC WATCHED THE door between his and Margaret's room close behind her. He shot the bolt, just to make sure, though no doubt it was rubbing salt in her wounds.

He ran both hands over his head, feeling his shorn hair beneath his palms. Dear Lord! How could he have guessed what she'd come to London for? He winced as he remembered again the hurt in her face as he'd rejected her.

"Damnation," he muttered under his breath, and crossed to the small table to pour himself a glass of wine.

He gulped a mouthful of the tart liquid and sighed. Why had she made these demands now? He'd thought her settled and provided for. He'd thought her happy.

His gaze strayed to the dresser. He tossed down the rest of the glass of wine and went to it. The key to unlock the top drawer hung on a silver chain about his neck—he'd trust Moulder with his life, but not with the things inside that drawer. The wood creaked as he opened it. Godric inhaled and looked inside. Clara's letters were wrapped neatly in a black ribbon. They'd seldom been parted once married, so the stack was sadly thin. Beside it was a small enameled box. Inside, he knew, were two locks of her hair. The first, taken when they'd been courting, was a lustrous dark brown, shot with gold. The second was a funerary memento, the hair thin, brittle, and streaked with gray.

Well.

He touched the hair at his temple. He was gray now,

too, unlike his too-young second wife. They were supposed to age together, he and Clara, step in step, man and wife, a lifetime of love and friendship.

Instead, she was in the ground and he was left with half a life at best.

A life that was now permanently entangled with Margaret's.

At the front of the drawer, directly beneath his fingers, was an untidy pile of letters. He hesitated, then picked one up, unfolding it. Scrawled inside—both horizontally and vertically—was a large, exuberant hand, as if Margaret had hardly been able to write fast enough to keep up with the flow of words from her brain. He tilted the sheet of paper and read.

18 September 1739

Dear Godric,

*   You will not credit it, but the population of stable cats has simply grown out of all proportions here at Laurelwood Manor! Both the gray tabby and the black-, orange-, and white-spotted were delivered of kittens this spring, and then the calico—that sly jade—fell pregnant again. Now whenever I go to visit Minerva (you remember the little bay mare I earlier wrote you I acquired of Squire Thompson?), I'm followed by a parade of cats. Black ones, gray tabbies, an abundance of spotted ones (invariably female, I'm assured by Toby, the lame stable boy), and even a single entirely orange miss, follow me about with inquiring, raised tails. Toby says I must quit feeding them the fatty bits left over from last*

night's joint, but I ask you, is that kind? After all, they've come to expect their little snack and—

He had to turn the paper to continue reading.

—if I quit now, I think they'll take an awful dislike to me and perhaps seek me out in the house!

Sarah is over her head cold, by the way, and has quit speaking in such a low, stuffy voice, which I find a pity (the voice, not the recovery!) because she did sound so very amusing when she spoke— rather like an aged intemperate uncle, if I had an uncle, which I do not.

Do you remember the leaky ceiling in the washroom? Last sennight it rained cats and dogs, and what do you think? The ceiling fell entirely in. Quite frightened Cook, I'm told (by Daniels) because it fell in the middle of the night and apparently Cook mistook the crash for the Second Coming. (A religious sort is Cook, everyone says so.) Anyway, Cook spent the rest of the night in prayer, which is why we had cold biscuits for breakfast that morning. Cook says it wasn't her fault. She'd been expecting the dead to rise, but only old Battlefield the butler greeted her at dawn. (Though I did hear Sarah mutter that Battlefield could easily be mistaken for the dead.)

Bother! I've run out of paper, so I must remain
Affectionately Yours,
Megs

A typical missive from her: quick, witty, full of the life she'd made for herself at his country estate.

Full of life itself.

Carefully, he folded the letter and placed it back with its brethren. He couldn't betray Clara and the memory of their love, but that didn't stop the fact that he was lying by omission to Margaret. The truth was that he'd not been unmoved by her embrace. Her kiss had been so essentially her: unplanned, reckless, without studied skill—and all the more erotic because of it.

She made something deep inside of him wake and stir as if he still lived and had hope for this life.

Godric closed the drawer and carefully locked it before pulling off his banyan and nightshirt. He blew out the candles and climbed into his cold bed nude, turning on his side to stare at the dying fire.

No matter how seductive Margaret's offer of life was, it was an illusion.

He'd died the night Clara last drew breath.

"THAT THERE TREE is dead, m'lady," Higgins the gardener said with absolute certainty the next morning. To emphasize his point, he spat into the decayed leaf litter that blanketed Saint House's garden.

Or what was left of its garden.

Megs regarded the tree. It was without a doubt one of the ugliest specimens she'd ever seen. At one point it had been some type of fruit tree, but age and neglect had twisted the heavy lower branches. At the same time, thin, whiplike water sprouts had shot up all over the limbs and suckers crowded the base.

"It might not be dead," she said with very little conviction. "It's been a cold spring."

Higgins grunted with patent disbelief.

The tree stood in the center of the garden. Without it, there would be no vertical interest.

She took a twig and bent it. It came off with a *snap* and she examined the center. Brown. The tree certainly *looked* dead.

Megs tossed aside the broken twig with a grimace. Dead. Well, she was tired of dead. Tired of a *certain someone* refusing to help her produce life. If she couldn't convince him—*yet*—to fall in with her plans, well then she'd occupy herself with other matters in the meantime.

"Cut away all these suckers and water sprouts," she ordered Higgins, ignoring the gardener's ominous throat clearing. Megs fingered a brown, twisting vine wrapped around the tree's trunk. "And cut away whatever this is."

"M'lady...," Higgins began.

"Please?" She glanced at him. "I know I'm being silly, but even if it's dead, we can grow a...a climbing rose up it. Or something similar. I just don't want to give up quite yet."

Higgins heaved a deep sigh. He was a bandy-legged man of fifty or so, his upper chest and shoulders heavy and slightly bent forward as if his lower half had trouble carrying the weight of the upper. Higgins had quite definite ideas of garden care—ideas that had meant he'd been let go from more than one position. In fact, he'd been without work when Upper Hornsfield's vicar had reluctantly given his name to Megs. She'd been looking for an experienced gardener to oversee the renovations at Laurelwood, and though she'd never once seen Higgins smile, she'd always been glad of the impulse that had made her hire him. He might be blunt, but he knew his plants.

"It's a fool idea, right enough, but I'll do it, m'lady," he muttered now.

"Thank you, Higgins." She smiled at him, feeling affectionate.

He couldn't help being an old curmudgeon, and she rather thought the fact that in a year and a half of employment he hadn't yet threatened to quit meant he must like her as well.

Or at least it was nice to think so.

"What about that bed there?" She pointed and soon Higgins was scratching his head and giving his blunt opinion of the rather scraggly looking boxwoods lining the garden.

Megs nodded and looked thoughtful as she half listened. The day was sunny and a bit brisk, and really, meandering around a tumbledown garden was a wonderful way to spend a morning. She'd suffered a setback with her baby plans last night, it was true, but that didn't mean she was finished by a long shot. Somehow she'd find a way to work around Godric's reluctance or—

Well, she could have an affair, she supposed. That was what some women in her position—assuming there *was* anyone else in a position like hers—would do.

But as soon as the notion entered her mind, she rejected it out of hand. No matter her great urge to have a child, she simply couldn't do that to Godric. It was one thing to marry because of an unwed pregnancy; it was *quite* another to deliberately cuckold a man she'd pledged herself to in front of friends and family. Even if that man was being quite pigheaded.

Megs's shoulders slumped. She was being unfair to Godric, she knew. The hard thing was that she understood. She, too, had loved someone desperately, had felt half dead when he'd died. For a moment, the thought brought her up short: Was she betraying Roger by wanting to create life without him? By wanting to do *that* with another man?

Except it was the *baby* she wanted, not the bedsport. If she could have one without the other, she would. Besides, she didn't expect to actually *enjoy* the physical act with Godric—how could she, after all? She'd loved Roger, not her dry older husband. In any case it didn't matter—the drive to have a child was simply too overwhelming to ignore.

But thoughts of Roger reminded her that she'd neglected what she'd owed him too long. She'd come to London not only to consummate her marriage, but also to find the Ghost of St. Giles and make him pay for his crime. If she'd been stymied at one goal, well then she could just pursue the other with more vigor. And as she watched Higgins uncover a yellow crocus and grunt with satisfaction, a thought occurred. Her first confrontation with the Ghost had not been exactly successful. Perhaps she should do a bit of information gathering before she tried again.

To that end, after she'd taken leave of her morose gardener, Megs went in search of Sarah.

"There you are," she exclaimed rather unoriginally when she tracked down her sister-in-law in a room nearly at the top of the house.

"Here I am," Sarah agreed, and then sneezed violently. With the help of two of the four girls from the home, she'd been taking down the curtains from the windows.

Mary Evening, a child of eleven or so with a freckled face and mouse-brown hair, giggled. Mary Little, the other girl, was rather more solemn with fine, flaxen hair.

Mary Little shot Mary Evening a chiding look before saying, "Bless you, miss."

"Thank you, Mary Little," Sarah gasped, then winked at Mary Evening. "Why don't you girls finish pulling down the curtains while I chat with Lady Margaret."

"Yes, miss!" The girls scampered over to the windows, apparently unperturbed by the quantity of dust.

"What is this room?" Megs asked, glancing around. It looked like a bedroom, but not one for a servant.

"I'm not entirely sure." Sarah hesitated, then said, "But in any case, it needs a good cleaning."

"That it does." Megs watched as one of the curtains fell to the floor in a billow of dust.

"You seemed to want to talk to me when you came up," Sarah prompted.

"Oh, yes." Megs remembered the matter that had sent her in search of her sister-in-law in the first place. "Didn't you say last night at dinner that we'd had a quantity of invitations?"

"Well, most of them were Godric's," Sarah said. "You wouldn't credit it, but I found a great stack going back at least a year piled on his desk. I really ought to get my brother a secretary."

"No doubt."

"But some were indeed for you and me and your aunt," Sarah continued, "and we've only been here two days! I'm not used to how fast word travels in London, I suppose."

"Mmm. Was there one from the Earl of Kershaw?"

Sarah's brows knit as she rubbed at a smudge of dust on the apron she'd pinned to her dress. "I believe so, but it was one of the invitations addressed to Godric. It was for a ball the earl and his countess are holding tonight."

"Perfect!" Megs beamed. Kershaw had been a friend of Roger's, and she'd heard in the awful months after Roger's death that the earl had searched for the Ghost in St. Giles. She'd go tonight and see if she could quiz the earl about the Ghost. "We can take one carriage, I think. I'd better go see if Great-Aunt Elvina would like to join us. She does like a ball, you know, and even if Her Grace is close to whelping, I think—"

"But..." Sarah's mouth had dropped open.

"What the hell are you doing?"

They both started and turned toward the quietly ominous voice.

Godric stood in the doorway, his face still—so still, in fact, that it took Megs a moment to realize he was white with rage. "I did not give you leave to enter this room."

Oh, dear.

One of the Marys dropped the curtain she was holding with a squeak.

Sarah cleared her throat. "Girls, please carry the curtains downstairs to Mrs. Crumb. She'll know how they should be properly cleaned."

Godric pivoted to the side to let the subdued maids past, but his gaze never left Megs's face. "You shouldn't be in this room. I don't want you in this room."

She felt her face heat and lifted her chin, holding his burning eyes. "Godric—"

He stepped closer to her, using his greater size to loom over her. "You may think me a puppet, madam, to be jerked about at your slightest whim, but I assure you I am not. I've been patient with your meddling in my home, but you go too far now."

Megs's eyes widened, her pulse heavy and fast at her

throat. She opened her mouth without any idea at all of what she would say.

But Sarah spoke before she could, her voice trembling. "I'm sorry. It's my fault entirely—Megs just came in. We were merely cleaning out all of the rooms. We haven't moved anything, although I can't fathom what this room is used for."

"It was Clara's," he said flatly. "And I don't need you messing about in it."

"Godric, I'm—"

But he'd already turned to leave. Megs took one look at Sarah's crumpling face and ran after her husband.

He was striding down the hall, completely oblivious to the hurt he'd caused his sister.

"Godric!"

He didn't even deign to break stride.

Megs darted around him, forcing him to stop short of the stairs and look down at her, and she saw...

God. She saw raw pain in his face.

Megs inhaled, suddenly on shaky ground. "She didn't know."

His lips compressed and he looked away.

"I'm sorry," she whispered, and reached out to touch the cuff of his coat. She almost expected him to shake her off.

Instead he merely stared down at her fingers. "Sarah should've asked first."

"Of course. We all should've asked before sending your house into such an upheaval. But, Godric..." She stepped closer, his cuff caught between her forefinger and thumb, her bodice nearly brushing the stiff wool of his coat. She angled her head to try to catch his eyes. "You wouldn't have consented had we asked, would you?"

He was silent.

"You're so self-sufficient." She puffed a small laugh. "It's daunting, because the rest of us aren't. Your sisters and mother aren't—"

"*Step*mother." His gaze slid toward hers, still unyielding, but at least he was listening.

"Stepmother, then," she compromised. "But I know Mrs. St. John and she's quite fond of you. All your family is. They hardly hear from you. Your letters are few and maddeningly uncommunicative. They worry for you."

He grimaced in irritation. "There's no need."

"Isn't there?"

He stared down at her, his face sagging into lines of weariness, and she abruptly understood that he'd learned to school his features into the mask of strict, unrelenting neutrality he usually wore.

"You know there is," she whispered. "You know that those who love you have real cause for concern."

"Margaret."

She straightened. "So you should go back and apologize to your sister."

He shot her a look of incredulous exasperation.

"She had no idea that was Clara's room, and even if she did"—she threw up her hands helplessly—"what do you intend to do, keep it the way it is as a shrine to her *death*?"

He was suddenly too close, his head bent down, shoved in her face, and she felt herself go quite still.

"You," he breathed very quietly, so close his lips almost brushed hers, "need to learn when not to overstep yourself."

She swallowed. "Do I?"

For a moment she couldn't breathe. He was too near,

his body tensed as if to do...something, and the tension seemed to communicate itself to her own body until she felt strung as tight as a violin string.

He muttered something foul under his breath and stepped back. "I'll apologize to my sister later."

And he spun and clattered down the stairs.

Megs inhaled and thoughtfully retraced her steps to Clara's room. One look at Sarah's face and Megs crossed to hug her. "Gentlemen can be so hardheaded."

"No." Sarah sniffed and pressed a lace handkerchief to her reddened nose. "Godric was quite correct—I ought to have asked him before rearranging this room."

Megs pulled back. "But you had no idea this was Clara's room."

"I had a notion." Sarah folded her handkerchief and gestured shakily to the massive bed in the center of the room. "Why else would that be there? Who else could've lived here?"

"Then why—"

"Because he can't just keep the room as some kind of macabre shrine to Clara."

"That's what I told him."

Sarah's eyes widened. "What did he say?"

Megs grimaced. "Well, he wasn't best pleased."

"Oh, Megs," Sarah cried, "I'm so sorry you got drawn into this, but...come here."

She darted away to one of the now-bare windows.

Megs followed more slowly. "What is it?"

"Look." Sarah pointed to iron bars running on the outside of the window. Iron bars meant to keep the occupants of the room safe. "This was the nursery once upon a time. And...and I know you don't have that kind of marriage with my brother, but I hoped with this trip to London, perhaps . . ." Sarah swallowed and grasped her hands together, whispering, "We've all worried for him so much."

Megs nodded. "I know. And to be truthful, I'd hoped to become closer to Godric too." She blushed but soldiered on. "It's just . . . I'm not sure how. I've tried, but he's stubborn. He loved Clara very much."

"Yes, he did," Sarah said, her voice grim. "But Clara's dead and *you're* here now. Don't give up on him, Megs, please?"

Megs nodded, but even as she tried to smile in reassurance at Sarah, she wondered, how was she to help a man who'd given up on himself?

Chapter Five

*Now, it's rare for a mortal to be able to see the Hellequin,
for being a thing of the night and death, he is usually
invisible to all. But the young man's beloved was a different
matter. Her name was Faith, and she'd been born with
the second sight. She knew who the Hellequin was—
and moreover, she knew where he was bound.
"My beloved has never hurt man nor beast in all his life,"
she cried. "You cannot take his soul down to Hell
to burn for eternity."...*
—From *The Legend of the Hellequin*

"She's going *where*?" Godric stopped in the act of pulling off his neck cloth that night and glanced at Moulder.

"A ball," Moulder repeated. "They're all going. Should've seen the maids running up and down the servants' stairs. Seems to take quite a bit to get a lady ready for a ball."

Why hadn't Megs mentioned that she intended to go out tonight? Of course, he realized with a wince, the last time they'd spoken they'd argued and he'd kept well away from the house since then. He'd returned only to ready himself to go out again to St. Giles. Which he was doing now. What his wife did in the evening wasn't any concern of his.

"*Whose* ball?" Godric demanded.

"Lord Kershaw's," Moulder replied promptly. "'Tis said to be one o' the biggest o' the season, what with him marrying that foreign heiress couple o' years back."

Godric stared at his manservant for a moment. When had Moulder become such a font of gossip? He must've been listening at doors all day. Godric shook his head. *Kershaw.* That was one of the names Winter Makepeace had given him. Perhaps his investigation into the lassie snatchers would be better served at a ball. He deliberately ignored the small, dry part of his intelligence that whispered it would mean spending the evening with his beautiful wife.

"Get out my good suit and then make sure the carriage waits for me."

"Wise o' you, if you don't mind me saying so," Moulder said as he did as instructed.

Godric pulled on a fresh white shirt. "What do you mean?"

"Well, no telling who she might meet there, is there?"

"What," he asked very slowly, "are you talking about?"

Moulder's eyes widened as it apparently belatedly occurred to him that he might've crossed a line. "Ah... nothing, nothing. I'll just go see to the carriage, shall I?"

"Do that," Godric bit out.

Moulder hurried from the room.

Godric grunted and threw on the rest of his suit, all the while conscious that he was being unreasonable. He'd told Margaret that he couldn't bed her. Rather dog in the manger, then, to care if she chose to go looking for a lover. He cursed and strode out the door. The thing was, he *did* care, and not just about the humiliation of Margaret possibly bearing another man's child. It was one thing for her to be pregnant by another man when he hardly knew her. Now that he'd spent over a year reading her letters, had sat across from her at dinner, had felt the sweet, urgent touch of her lips...

He stopped dead on the landing. *Damnation*. He didn't want Margaret taking another man to her bed; it was as simple as that.

The realization did not improve his mood.

He took a deep breath and descended the rest of the stairs more slowly. He had to keep his purpose in attending this ball at the forefront of his mind. He needed to find out if Kershaw knew anything about what his friend Seymour had been doing in St. Giles with the lassie snatchers. This was strictly a Ghostly matter.

Outside, the ladies had already settled in the carriage, but at least Moulder had kept it from leaving without him. Godric opened the door and jumped in, aware that the occupants were shooting him curious looks.

It was Margaret, of course, who spoke first, her eyes sparkling in the dim light of the carriage. "I didn't know you were interested in attending balls; otherwise I would've invited you along."

Godric schooled his face into what he hoped was a pleasant expression. "Naturally I shall escort you to evening entertainments."

"Naturally," Sarah said, just a bit drily. Her tone softened as she added, "I'm so glad you decided to come with us."

Was he really that inattentive? A trace of guilt shot through his chest. This was his sister, after all. With his father dead, he should be the head of the family, guiding and protecting his stepmother and sisters.

"I'm sorry," he said, and by the looks on both his wife's and sister's faces, he'd surprised them. Great-Aunt Elvina merely snorted, but he ignored the old harridan. "I shouldn't have snapped at you this afternoon."

"No." Sarah shook her head. "I'm the one who needs to apologize. I should never have moved things about in Clara's room."

"Do with it as you see fit," he said. "It's time, I suppose."

"You're sure?" Her eyes searched his.

He tried a smile and found it not that hard. "Yes."

Godric was mostly quiet then for the rest of the drive, letting the ladies' chatter flow about him. Twice he thought he saw Margaret examining him curiously in the dim carriage light, and he wished he could find some way of fulfilling her dreams without betraying Clara.

Kershaw lived in an old family town house that looked to be recently renovated. Godric remembered Moulder's gossip as he escorted the ladies inside, and wondered if it had been Kershaw's bride's dowry that had paid for the house's new façade.

The house opened to a grand receiving room, and Godric turned politely to help Great-Aunt Elvina out of her cloak. He gave the item to one of the waiting footmen and turned just in time to see Margaret's dress revealed.

For a moment he stumbled to a halt, there in the crowded hallway.

His wife wore a salmon-pink dress that was a perfect foil for her dark curls. Her hair had been arranged in a more complicated style than usual, and the jewels set in the locks sparkled and flashed under the chandeliers hung high above. The low round neckline of the dress revealed and displayed the soft mounds of her beautiful bosom, and as Margaret turned to laugh at something his sister said, he thought she looked like some goddess of gaiety come to life.

How very ironic that she was married to him, then.

He held out his arm to her. "You look lovely."

Her lashes fluttered in surprise as she took his arm. "Thank you."

Godric remembered himself then and paid similar compliments to Sarah and Great-Aunt Elvina, who arched an eyebrow with the first sign of humor he'd seen from her before taking his other elbow.

The ball was a mass of slowly shifting bodies.

"Goodness," Great-Aunt Elvina exclaimed. "I haven't been to such a crush since I was a girl."

"Look, there's your friend Lady Penelope, Megs," Sarah said.

"Oh, yes," Megs said absently. "I wonder where Lord Kershaw might be?"

Godric's eyes narrowed as he glanced at his wife.

But then Sarah was urging Megs and Great-Aunt Elvina toward Lady Penelope. Godric glanced in that direction. Lady Penelope was considered a beauty, but her looks had always been spoiled for Godric by the lady's silly personality.

"I'll go in search of refreshment," he said to the retreating backs of the ladies.

Margaret glanced back with a flashing smile, and then she was absorbed into the crowd.

Stupid to feel a sudden chill.

Godric shook off the feeling of loss and started making his way to the refreshments room. It was slow progress with the crowd, but Godric didn't mind. He kept an eye out for the earl. He'd met the man before and remembered him as genial and hearty. Hardly the description of a man running a slave workshop in St. Giles, but then Seymour hadn't been especially sinister either. Fifteen minutes later, he was before an enormous bowl of punch and wondering how he was supposed to carry three glasses.

"St. John," a deep voice rumbled at his elbow.

Godric turned to look into the pale eyes of his great friend Lazarus Huntington, Baron Caire.

He inclined his head. "Caire."

"Hadn't thought to see you here," Caire said, indicating to the footman that he wanted a glass of punch.

"Nor I, you."

Caire raised a sardonic eyebrow. "Strange how marriage can reform even the darkest reputation in the eyes of society."

"No doubt," Godric replied drily. "Here. Hold this for me."

Caire looked bemusedly down at the proffered cup of punch but accepted it docilely enough. "I take it you've come with your wife?"

"And my sister and my wife's aunt," Godric muttered, juggling glasses.

"A full house, then," Caire drawled.

Godric glanced at him, brows raised.

Caire's habitually bored expression had softened just a trifle. "I'm glad."

Godric looked away again. "Yes, well..."

"Come," the other man said. "You can introduce me to your wife properly. Temperance was all agog with the news of her arrival at the Ladies' Syndicate the other day."

Godric nodded and turned into the crowd, making his way without another word to Caire, but he felt the other man at his back just the same.

They'd made it halfway across the ballroom when Caire grunted behind him. "There's Temperance with a gaggle of ladies. Is that your wife there?"

And Godric looked up to see Margaret leaning close to laugh up at the dark face of Adam Rutledge, Viscount d'Arque—one of the most notorious rakes in London.

VISCOUNT D'ARQUE WAS really quite handsome, Megs thought, and he knew it too. His light gray eyes seemed to sparkle with sly, unspoken words: *Am I not the most beautiful man you've ever set eyes upon? Come, admire me!*

And Megs did—from his lean cheeks to the wickedly curving mouth with its pronounced Cupid's bow—although that wasn't the main reason she stood too close to him and laughed at his worldly witticisms. No, Lord d'Arque had been a close friend of Roger's. While Roger had been alive, Megs had always been a bit daunted by the viscount and his extravagant beauty. Too, he was considered a dangerous rake by society, and as an unmarried lady, it was in her reputation's best interest to stay well away from his path.

For a matron, though, it was an entirely different matter.

Marriage did have some advantages, Megs thought rather bitterly. She could flirt discreetly with rakes—when all she really wanted to do was continue her argument with Godric.

As if the thought had conjured her husband, Godric suddenly appeared in the crowd, making his way toward them, his face grim. Megs lifted her chin and deliberately turned to Lord d'Arque. "It's been an age since I've seen you, my lord."

"Any time away from such a lovely lady is an eternity," Lord d'Arque said gallantly, lowering his eyelashes and then glancing back up into her eyes.

Had he been looking down her bodice? The man really was deliciously terrible. She smiled. "I believe we have a mutual friend—or had one."

The cynical smile didn't leave his face, but his eyes seemed to grow wary. "Indeed?"

"Yes." Roger and she had kept their love affair secret. At the time it had seemed to make everything more magical. They'd just been on the point of announcing their engagement when Roger had...She inhaled, unable to keep her lips from drooping. "Roger Fraser-Burnsby."

Lord d'Arque's beautiful gray eyes sharpened.

"Punch," murmured Godric at her elbow, making her start ungracefully.

"Oh." Megs blinked, turning to see that her placid husband seemed to have acquired daggers for eyes—and they were aimed at Lord d'Arque. If looks could kill, Lord d'Arque would be a writhing, bloody mess on the earl's pink marble floor.

Well, this is interesting. She really ought to be contrite. Poor, darling Lord d'Arque hadn't done a thing besides act the rake he'd apparently been born. It wasn't his fault that she'd flirted outrageously with him, triggering his rakish instincts. But there was something terribly satisfying at seeing her husband mentally slaughter another man on her behalf.

She beamed at Godric as she accepted the cup of punch.

Godric narrowed his eyes at her before focusing his gaze on the viscount. "D'Arque."

The viscount's lips twitched, though it could hardly be called a smile. "St. John. I've just been…chatting with your exquisite wife. I must tell you that you have far more fortitude than I."

"Indeed? Why?"

Lord d'Arque widened his eyes innocently. "Oh, because I'd never be able to banish such a lovely lady so far away in the country. I'd want to keep her by my side—day and, especially, night."

Does he practice his silly words in front of a mirror? It was really too bad—both what d'Arque was implying and how much Megs was enjoying Godric's reaction. But she should stop this. She really should.

Megs opened her mouth.

Her husband was already speaking. "I'm surprised, sir. I would've thought that there'd be no room by your side at any time—but *especially* at night."

A deep chuckle came from beside Megs. She turned and saw a striking gentleman with silver hair clubbed back by a black bow.

He caught her eye and bowed even as Lord d'Arque made some retort to her husband involving celibacy. "Lady Margaret. I hope you don't think me bold to introduce myself. I am Caire."

Of course, Lord Caire. He'd once been almost as notorious as Lord d'Arque.

Megs sank into a curtsy. "It's an honor, Lord Caire. I count your wife as one of my very good friends."

"Hmm." A smile still played about Lord Caire's wide mouth as Godric made a comment about the pox to Lord d'Arque. "Temperance and I regretted not attending your wedding, but we understood it to be a small, family affair. St. John and I have known each other for years."

"Have you?" Megs darted a worried glance at Godric and the viscount. At least they hadn't come to blows yet. Although if they *did*, and over *her*, that would certainly make this ball very interesting.

Oh, she was wicked! "You must think me a terrible flirt."

"Not at all," Lord Caire murmured gently. "In fact, this is the most animated I've seen St. John in years." His eyes were a little sad, but then he caught her gaze and his lips quirked. "High choler is good for a man once in a while. I do hope you plan to stay in London."

Megs bit her lip at that, for she hadn't planned to stay past getting herself pregnant. The fact was that she loved Laurelwood. Country life suited her, she'd found, and the estate would be a perfect place to raise her child.

Lord Caire apparently read her face, his own becoming expressionless. "I see. A pity, but I am grateful for what time you can spend with my friend."

"I'd spend more time with him if there wasn't a ghost between us," Megs said, trying not to sound defensive. It was *Godric* who wanted her gone.

"Ah." Lord Caire nodded. "Clara."

Megs winced. "I don't mean to sound jealous. I know they truly had a wonderful love and were happy together."

"They loved each other deeply," Lord Caire agreed, looking thoughtful, "but whoever told you they were happy has lied, I'm afraid."

She blinked, sidling closer to him. "What do you mean?"

"She took ill very soon after they married. Within a year or so, at any rate, and after bringing in every doctor, both here and on the Continent, Godric realized that there was nothing he could do." Without turning his head, Lord Caire glanced to where Temperance was chatting with Sarah. "I can't begin to imagine what it would do to a man to watch the woman he loved die slowly and in pain."

Megs drew in a breath because while Lord Caire might put on a mask of world-weariness, she suddenly knew: He loved his wife deeply and without any reservations. She'd had that once—or at least the beginnings of it. She'd known Roger for only a little over three months, and while the flames of their passion had burned bright and hot, she acknowledged now that they'd only just begun. Love grown rich and golden over the years was what she really wanted.

What she'd never had.

She bit her lip. She hadn't had that with Roger, and she wasn't going to have that with Godric. He might be still trading jabs with Lord d'Arque, but that was a matter of pride, not care for her.

The thought made her frown.

"I'm sorry," Lord Caire said. "I didn't mean to cause you pain."

"No, it's nothing." Megs tried to smile and failed. She burst out, "I just wish…"

He waited and when she didn't—*couldn't*—finish the thought, he tilted his head down toward her. "Just because he felt love for Clara doesn't mean he can't feel it with you as well. Courage, my lady. Godric is a hard nut to crack, but I assure you, the man inside is worth it. And I feel that if any lady can do it, you are the one."

Megs watched as Godric glanced up at that moment and met her gaze. His eyes were dark, angry, and sad, and she wished—desperately—that she could believe Lord Caire's words.

ARTEMIS GREAVES WATCHED anxiously as Lord d'Arque smiled sweetly and said something truly atrocious to Mr. St. John. Lady Margaret's husband had always struck her as a staid, if very sad, gentleman, but even the most staid man could be provoked into—

"A duel!" Lady Penelope hissed delightedly and much too loudly. "Oh, I do hope this ends in a duel."

Artemis stared at her cousin in horror. She was very fond of Penelope most of the time—well, *sometimes*, at any rate—but really, she could be a ninny.

"I thought you liked Viscount d'Arque?" she asked with muted exasperation.

Penelope tossed her head in a gesture she must've been practicing in front of her vanity mirror, for it made the jeweled combs in her hair catch the light. There were three of them, and each had tiny ruby and pearl flowers on thin wires that shivered whenever Penelope moved. They probably cost more than Artemis's entire wardrobe, but they did perfectly complement her cousin's inky locks.

"I do like Lord d'Arque," Penelope drawled, "but he isn't a duke, is he?"

Artemis blinked, unable to follow her cousin's thought process, which was rather a recurring problem. "What does—"

A tall form cut through the crowd like a saber through an apple. He bore a faintly irritated expression on his face, and though he wore a sedate dark blue suit and waistcoat overworked in black, no one could mistake the command in his carriage. He bore down on d'Arque, while at the same time Lord Caire glided forward and murmured something in Mr. St. John's ear.

"A duke like *that* one," Penelope drawled with so much throaty satisfaction in her voice that Artemis's brows drew together in honest worry.

"Do you have a head cold?"

"No, silly," Penelope said with some irritation. She caught herself and smoothed her expression. Penelope had a fear of wrinkles setting on her face. "I've decided it's past time I marry, and naturally I shall wed a duke. *That* one, I think."

For of course the gentleman now causing Lord d'Arque's high cheekbones to darken was Maximus Batten, the Duke of Wakefield.

Artemis blinked. Penelope was the daughter of an earl—a fabulously wealthy earl. And while it was the way of the world that dukes often married fabulously wealthy, titled heiresses, would the Duke of Wakefield really want a wife so silly she insisted on putting ground pearls in her morning chocolate? Penelope claimed the pearl dust added a glow to her complexion. Artemis privately thought it made a good cup of chocolate gritty—besides being a waste of *pearls*.

Artemis knew her opinion mattered very little. If Penelope had made up her mind to marry a duke, she would no doubt be a duchess by this time next year.

But *Wakefield*?

Artemis glanced over now to where he'd straightened, his long face impatient. He was tall, but not overly so, his shoulders broad but lean, and the very sternness of his face kept one from calling him handsome. If she had to use only one word to describe the Duke of Wakefield, it would be *cold*.

Artemis shivered. From what she'd observed of the duke from countless balls spent in the shadows unseen, he didn't seem to have a trace of humor—or compassion. And one had to have both to live with Penelope.

"There are other eligible dukes," Artemis reminded her cousin. "The Duke of Scarborough, for instance. He's been widowed a year and has only daughters. No doubt he'll wish to marry again."

Penelope scoffed without taking her eyes from Wakefield. "He must be sixty if a day."

"True, but I've heard he's a very kind man," Artemis said gently. She sighed and tried another tack. "And what about the Duke of Montgomery?"

Penelope swung around to stare at her in horror at the name. "The man spends all of his time in the country or abroad. Have you ever seen him?"

Artemis wrinkled her nose. "Well, no . . ."

"And neither has anyone else." Penelope turned back to watch Wakefield with a calculating gleam in her eye. "No one has seen Montgomery in ages. For all we know, he's a hunchback or has a harelip, or *worse*"—Penelope shuddered—"is *mad*. I wouldn't want to marry into a family that had madness in it."

Artemis inhaled sharply and looked down. *No, no one wanted to marry into a family with madness.* She'd tried to immure herself against the pain in the last couple of years, but at times such as now, when something caught her off guard, it was simply impossible.

Fortunately, Penelope hadn't seemed to notice. "And

what if he has run through all his money traipsing about the Continent?"

"You're an *heiress*."

"Yes, and I want my money spent on *me*, not repairing some run-down castle."

Artemis knit her brows. "I presume that leaves out the Duke of Dyemore."

"It does indeed." Dyemore had at least three castles in need of repair. Penelope nodded in satisfaction. "No, there's only one duke for me."

Artemis turned to watch Wakefield's retreating back. Somehow he'd persuaded—or more likely threatened— Lord d'Arque into retiring with him. The duke might be a proud, cold man, but Artemis still felt a twinge of pity for him.

What Lady Penelope Chadwicke wanted, she got.

"I WOULD BE grateful if you stayed away from the Viscount d'Arque," Godric said as he led his wife onto the dance floor. He mentally winced at his own stiff tone, but in this matter he could not seem to see reason.

She was his wife and he'd damn well not take her straying lying down.

She cocked her head, looking more curious than outraged. "Is that an order?"

He immediately felt a fool. "No, of course not."

The music began, the movement of the dance drawing them apart before he could explain further. Godric inhaled deeply as he paced, trying to subdue the incredible wrath that had overtaken him at the sight of Margaret with d'Arque.

When the dance brought them together again, he murmured low so the other dancers could not overhear, "I know it's hard for you, wanting a child, but this isn't the way."

"What way do you mean?" she asked carefully. Too carefully.

Nonetheless, he could do naught but answer truthfully. "With d'Arque as your lover."

For a second her eyes flashed with wild hurt before she could shield the emotion, and he realized he'd just dug himself into a hole.

"You think I'm a whore," she said.

A very deep hole.

"No, of—"

But she whirled away, caught in the steps of the dance. This time he watched her anxiously, this wife he knew so little about. Had Clara ever thought she'd been so grievously insulted, she would've wept. Or perhaps stomped off. He truly didn't know because he never would've gotten into a discussion like this in the first place with Clara. The very idea was ludicrous.

Margaret in contrast held her head high, her cheeks flagged with a becoming rose color. She looked like a goddess enraged. A goddess who might, if they were alone, assault his person—the thought of which unaccountably aroused him.

When the dance brought them together again, they both opened their mouths at once.

"I never meant—" he began.

"You convict me without trial," she hissed over him, "and on pathetically thin evidence."

"You were flirting, madam."

"And if I was?" she asked, her eyes widening dramatically. "If every woman who flirted in a ballroom were deemed a slut, then all but nuns and babes would be thus branded. Do you truly think I meant to start an affair with the viscount?"

He hesitated a fraction of a breath too long.

Her beautiful brows snapped together. "You are the most maddening man."

They were drawing stares, but he couldn't let this bit of outrageousness pass.

"I? *I* am maddening? I assure you, my lady, that *you* are the maddening one. I've never caused a scene in a public venue before in my—"

"And now you're on your second," she flung back.

A childish retort, but also deeply annoying, as she managed to get it off just before they were forced to separate.

Which, naturally, gave her the last word.

He didn't even bother hiding his scowl as he followed her movements broodingly. A slightly plump matron took one look at his face and tripped over herself, bumping into the next couple.

His scowl deepened.

"Have I ever given you cause to doubt my fidelity?" she asked as soon as they came together once more.

"No, but—"

"And yet you accuse me of the worst thing a man can accuse a woman of."

"Margaret," he said helplessly, all his eloquence evaporated.

She inhaled and spoke quietly as he paced around her. "Why do you even care? You've made plain *your* disinterest. Why play the dog in the manger? *Why* did you marry me in the first place?"

His eyes slid away from her face, noting all those trying to hear their conversation without seeming to do so. "Your brother asked me—"

"Griffin hardly knew you."

He glanced back at her and saw the determined expression on her face. "This is not the place—"

"Why?"

"I had no choice!" he finally growled, and immediately regretted his words.

Oh, God, she looked so stricken.

"Margaret," he began, but she was already out of earshot, and he wasn't sure if he was glad or not. He should be disinterested. Whether she slept with another man or not should be no concern of his. He'd been willing to accept her child by another man before…and yet he simply could not now.

The thought astonished him. Everything had changed, it seemed, in only a matter of days. Ever since, in fact, he'd discovered his wife in St. Giles.

Damnation. What was Margaret doing to him?

He couldn't consider the matter now. They were on a dance floor with the better half of London's elite surrounding them. He needed to bring his wife under his control and try to retain some normalcy.

When at last they drew together again, he was ready, speaking low and steadily. "Despite your behavior earlier tonight and right now, Margaret, I have never held you in low regard. Rather, I wish to make sure you don't let your overpassionate nature lead you astray."

To which reasoned words she leaned in close and said, "I may be overpassionate, but at least I do not act as if I'm already *dead*. And I loathe the name Margaret!"

Whirling, she glided off the dance floor in high dungeon, the scent of orange blossoms trailing in her wake.

Which Godric couldn't help but admire, even though it left him alone in the middle of a dance like a prize ass.

A large form loomed on his right-hand side.

"Marriage certainly has effected a change in your personality," Caire drawled. "I've never seen you come so close to a duel—and to top that with a sparring match with your lady wife on the dance floor. Words fail me."

Godric closed his eyes. "I'm sorry—"

"You mistake me, man."

Godric opened his eyes to see Caire grinning at him. Caire, grinning! "Good God, St. John. I'd nearly given you up for dead."

"I'm not dead," Godric muttered.

"The whole of London knows that now," Caire said. "Come. I've an idea where our host keeps his brandy."

And Godric followed his old friend gratefully, because if this was life, it was much more complicated than he remembered.

Chapter Six

*The Hellequin opened his mouth and paused. How
long had it been since he'd spoken? Years? Decades?
Millenniums? When at last his voice emerged,
it was a creaky croak.
"It matters not how good the lad was in life.
He died unshriven."
Was the Hellequin's heart moved by Faith's sad face?
Even if it were so, he could do nothing, for the rules
were clear. So he turned the horse's head to go.
And as he did, Faith jumped upon his back....*
—From *The Legend of the Hellequin*

Megs stormed from the ballroom, uncaring of the scene
she was making. *How dare he?* How dare he think her
a loose woman when all she'd been doing was laughing
with Lord d'Arque? Trying to find out if the man had
heard any news about Roger's death.

She swiped at a hot tear coursing down her cheek and
ran down the stairs. She hadn't even been able to get as far
as questioning the viscount about the Ghost before Godric
had shown up and started insulting the man—and her.

"Megs!"

She stopped and turned on the landing.

Sarah was panting behind her and Megs realized that this wasn't the first time the other woman had called her name.

"Are you all right?" Sarah paused, looking worriedly into her face.

"I . . ." Megs tried for a calm, ladylike tone but in the end burst out, "Oh, Sarah, I just want to hit him sometimes!"

"Well, and I don't blame you," Sarah said loyally—or rather disloyally since she was taking Megs's side over her own brother's.

But Megs couldn't be anything but happy that Sarah was such a good friend. "I can't go back in there—not right now."

Sarah frowned. "Where will you go?"

"I need . . ." She needed to speak to Griffin. The thought bloomed in her mind fully formed, and she knew at once that it was the right thing to do. She had to ask Griffin several long-overdue questions.

Megs focused on Sarah. "I have to leave. Actually, there's something important I need to talk to my brother Griffin about. Can you make my apologies to the earl and countess?"

"Of course." Sarah's eyes softened in sympathy—and a touch of curiosity. "But we only brought the one carriage."

"Oh." Megs felt her face fall.

But Sarah had already rallied. "Your great-aunt Elvina has been gossiping with Lady Bingham all evening. I'm sure she'll be amenable to giving us a ride home."

"You're an angel." Megs just took the time to press an affectionate kiss to her sister-in-law's cheek and then she was down the stairs.

Fifteen minutes later, she was the sole occupant of the carriage and on her way to Griffin and Hero's town house. Only now did it occur to her that her brother might not be home at this hour. But considering the matter as her carriage clattered through the dark streets of London, she decided there was a good chance that he'd be in tonight. She knew from Hero's letters that her brother, once one of the wildest rakes in society, now spent most of his evenings at home with his wife and small son.

Megs decided that she wouldn't be jealous of her brother.

Twenty minutes later, her carriage was pulling up in front of a neat town house. On marriage, her brother had given up the house he'd spent his bachelor days in and moved here to a much better neighborhood.

Megs mounted the front steps, her heart dipping as she realized that although there were two bright lamps burning out front, the house itself was dark. For a moment she hesitated, but the matter really couldn't wait: she wouldn't face her husband again without clearing up this mystery.

She raised the knocker and let it fall twice.

There was a long pause and then a butler answered the door. It took a bit of wrangling to convince the manservant that she really was Lord Griffin's sister come to visit him at a terribly inconvenient hour, but soon she'd been ushered into a pretty little sitting room. A sleepy maid had just got done stirring the dying fire and left when Griffin burst into the room.

Her brother strode across the sitting room and took her by the shoulders, examining her with piercing green eyes. "What is it, Megs? Are you all right?"

Oh, dear, she hadn't meant to alarm him. "Yes, yes, I'm fine. I just wanted to ... uh ... talk to you."

Griffin blinked and stepped back. "Talk to me? At"— his gaze went to a brass clock on the mantelpiece—"half past midnight? Megs, you've been avoiding me for years."

She gulped. "You noticed."

He rolled his eyes. "That my favorite sister corresponds more often with my wife than with me? That she's declined half a dozen invitations to come visit? That when you came after William's birth you hardly spoke two words to me? I'm not stupid, Megs."

"Oh." She didn't quite know what to say to that. All she could seem to do was stare at her fingers as she plucked at a loose thread on her gown.

Griffin cleared his throat. "Hero said I should give you time. Was she wrong?"

"No." Megs took a breath and lifted her head. She was being a craven coward and it simply wouldn't do. "Hero is almost maddeningly wise."

He smiled crookedly. "Yes."

"I'm sorry I've been such a widgeon," she said softly.

"The only time you've been a widgeon is right now," he said almost irritably. "There's no need to apologize to me."

She caught her breath, feeling her eyes go all hot and liquidy, but really it was Griffin's own fault for being such a sweetheart. Why had she ever stayed away from him?

She beamed through her tears and sat on a delicate primrose settee. "Come talk to me."

He looked suddenly suspicious. "Megs?"

She patted the empty place beside her.

Griffin narrowed his eyes and picked up a wing chair, placing it in front of her before lowering himself to the chair. He'd obviously come from bed. He wore a dark blue banyan, edged in black and gold, and slippers on his feet, but in contrast to her husband, there was no soft hat on his bare head. Griffin, like most men who wore a wig, kept his hair cropped close to the skull.

"So," he drawled, "what is so urgent you must drag me from my bed? My very *warm* bed?"

She blushed, for although most couples at their level of society kept separate rooms, she had the sudden strong impression that Griffin and Hero did not.

Megs inhaled. "I want to know why Godric married me."

Griffin's face went entirely blank, but before he could say a word, Hero appeared at the door, a pale green wrapper held close at her throat, her beautiful red hair a curling mass over one shoulder.

"Megs? What has happened?"

Griffin rose at once, crossing to Hero. He bent over her, murmuring something quietly and with one hand touching her cheek in a tender gesture that declared louder than any embrace what he felt for his wife.

Megs bit her lip, feeling again that miserly twinge of envy. It wasn't that she didn't wish Griffin all the marital happiness in the world. It was just... well. She'd never have that with Godric, would she?

She winced in something very like pain at the thought. She had friends, family that cared for her, wealth and privilege. Maybe, if she could change Godric's mind, she might even have a baby.

Couldn't she be happy just with those things?

Hero nodded at whatever Griffin said to her and then smiled at Megs and gave a little wave.

Megs mouthed, *"Sorry."*

Hero nodded and retired from the room, closing the door behind her.

"Now, then," Griffin said, lowering himself once more to the wing chair. "What has Godric done to make you ask?"

And Megs realized that Griffin had used the brief interruption to marshal his thoughts.

Well, she certainly wasn't going to tell her brother that her husband refused to consummate their marriage. Besides, she saw now, Griffin was probably throwing the question back at her in an effort to get her off the topic.

"Godric hasn't done anything," she said coolly, and when he frowned suspiciously, she sighed. "He's been a perfect gentleman. That's not why I'm here. I want to know what you did to him to make him marry me."

His eyebrows flew up. "*Make* him?"

"He said he had no choice but to marry me, Griffin." She gripped her hands in her lap, remembering again the stab of foolish pain at her husband's words. "Why?"

Griffin took a breath, his head tipped back and his eyes closed. For a moment, Megs was afraid he wouldn't speak at all.

Then his eyes opened and they were filled with brotherly love for her. "You were so broken, Meggie. So grief-stricken, it was like you'd lost part of your mind." A muscle tightened in his jaw. "And then there was the fact that you were with child."

She flushed, looking away from her brother, the embarrassment and shame so strong she nearly didn't hear his next words.

"If your lover hadn't been dead, I would've killed him myself."

She stared at him, her mouth falling open. "Griffin! Roger was a good man, a man I *loved*, a man who loved *me*—"

"He seduced my baby sister and got her with child." Griffin's green eyes flashed. "I understand you loved him,

Megs, but don't expect me to wax poetic on the man. He should've never touched you."

"We would've married had he lived," she said with dignity, and then more pragmatically, "and you shouldn't be throwing any stones."

Griffin's cheeks turned ruddy at her words. There had been rather a scandal when he'd married Hero—who had originally been betrothed to Thomas. "We stray from the point. You were in pain and you needed a husband. St. John had a spotless reputation, was from an old aristocratic family, and perhaps most importantly, the man has enough money to keep you happy for the rest of your life. I didn't have much time, but I made the best match I could under the circumstances."

"And I thank you for it," Megs said with real warmth. Without Griffin, she would've been banished forever from society, a family shame to be kept secret and hidden perhaps until the day of her death. "But that still doesn't answer my question. Why did Godric marry me? He loved his first wife dearly. I believe had he had his druthers, he wouldn't have married again at all."

"But he didn't have his druthers," Griffin said softly.

And it came to her in a sudden and rather unwelcome flash as she stared into her brother's too-intelligent features. "You *blackmailed* him?"

Griffin winced. "Now, Meggie…"

"Oh, my Lord, Griffin!" She stood, too appalled to sit. "No wonder he…" *Doesn't want to bed me.* She stopped abruptly, realizing she was about to say much too much to her perceptive brother. Megs inhaled instead. "What did you blackmail him with? It must be truly terrible for a man to marry when he never wanted to in the first place."

Griffin's eyes were narrowed suspiciously, but he replied, "It's not as terrible as you seem to be thinking."

"Then what is it?"

But he was already shaking his head as he rose in front of her. "That was part of the bargain: I'd keep his secret to the grave. I can't tell you, Megs. I suggest if you really want to know, you ask St. John yourself."

GODRIC PAUSED TO catch his breath across the street from Lord Griffin Reading's town house. Sarah hadn't told him until nearly fifteen minutes after Margaret had left the wretched ball that his darling wife intended to ask her bastard of a brother something of import. He'd wasted another ten minutes making sure Sarah and Great-Aunt Elvina had proper escort home, and then he'd left with a muttered and probably ill-believed excuse. He'd hailed a hack back home and then changed into his Ghost costume as a precaution. Who knew where Megs might lead him?

He'd done it badly, his abrupt exit from the ball, but it wasn't as if he'd had much choice in the matter.

He could think of no reason why Margaret would seek Reading's counsel so suddenly unless it was to inquire about the circumstances of their marriage.

Damn it. He'd known, deep in his gut, the night he'd found Reading waiting for him in his own study, that giving in to Reading's demands would come back to bite him in the arse. But what choice had he had? Reading *knew*. Knew that Godric was the Ghost of St. Giles. The ass had threatened to make public the knowledge, and though something in Godric wanted to tell him to publish and be damned, he'd held back at the thought of St. Giles.

He still ruled the night in St. Giles. There was still a tiny spark inside of him that *cared* about the people there and the help he could give them. A part that hadn't died with Clara.

So he'd submitted to the blackmail and married Margaret, and now he'd had the stupidity to all but dare Margaret to ask her brother why.

Did he want her to find out?

The thought brought him up short. Idiot idea. Of course he didn't.

And he hadn't a moment more to think on the matter. The front door of Reading's town house opened and Margaret emerged, briefly haloed by the door's lanterns. She turned to say something to her brother and then descended the steps, looking the same as ever: maddeningly inquisitive and beautiful in her salmon ball gown and a white and gold short cape tied close at her throat.

Apparently one couldn't tell just by looking if a woman had learned one's deepest secret.

Margaret climbed into the carriage and the driver touched the horses with his whip. The convenience rumbled off, but because of the nature of London's narrow streets, Godric could easily keep up. Jogging behind the carriage, staying in the shadows, he was mostly hidden from others on foot.

Well, except for the night-soil man, who gave a strangled shout and dropped one of his odiferous buckets.

Godric winced as he ran by.

He breathed a sigh of relief when the driver finally pulled the horses to a stop outside Saint House. He should run around back. Be sure to be in his study when she came inside—assuming she went looking for him.

Something made him pause, watching the carriage, waiting like a lovesick schoolboy for the sight of his wife again.

The footman descended the carriage and placed the step, opening the door for Margaret. But instead of her emerging, the footman leaned forward as if to catch murmured words from inside. He stepped back and called something to the driver, and then he was remounting the carriage.

Damn it! What was she about?

He watched helplessly as the driver turned the carriage around and rolled away from Saint House.

Godric cursed under his breath and followed, glad now that he was in his Ghost costume. If she were going to meet a lover...

His chest squeezed at the thought. He might be a dog in a manger, as she'd accused him, but he *couldn't* let her go to another man. He'd kill the bastard first.

The carriage rumbled through London, heading north and a bit to the west. Toward St. Giles, in fact.

Surely she wouldn't? Not after being accosted that first night?

God's *balls*. She would. The carriage turned into St. Giles like a calf fattened for market, all but bawling its vulnerability and rich, succulent meat.

Godric drew both swords and followed.

MEGS GAZED OUT the window of her carriage. St. Giles was dark and quiet—almost peaceful-looking, though she knew that was deceptive. This was the most violent area of London.

This was where Roger had been stabbed to death two years before. He'd lain here on a cold early spring night and his life had bled away into the filthy channel in the middle of the lane, his precious life's blood mingling with excrement and worse.

She blinked back the tears in her eyes and inhaled, opening the carriage door.

Oliver started to climb down from the footboard of the carriage, but Megs waved him back. "Stay here."

"Best ye take him, m'lady," Tom rumbled worriedly from the high driver's seat.

"I...I need a moment alone. Please."

Megs leaned back into the carriage and withdrew one of the pistols from underneath the seat. She hesitated a moment and then took out a small dagger and carefully shoved it up her sleeve. It was mostly ornamental, but it might deter a robber long enough to call Tom and Oliver.

Not that she intended to be waylaid. She wouldn't go far from the carriage, but she'd been honest with Tom.

She needed a moment alone...with her memories of Roger.

Perhaps it was all the male stubbornness she'd dealt with tonight: Griffin and Godric and even Lord d'Arque in a way—the man had been more interested in flirting with her than wondering why she'd sought him out in the first place. She felt blocked at every turn. Nothing she'd come to London for was working out as she'd hoped.

Especially, in a way, *this*.

She felt farther from Roger than she ever had before— even as she walked the streets where he'd lived his last moments.

She stopped and looked up and down the empty lane. It was darker than most London streets. The St. Giles merchants and residents either couldn't afford to light their homes, or they didn't care to. In either case, the area was dim and shadowed, tall buildings leaning ominously overhead. The sound of something breaking and the clatter of footfalls came from...somewhere. Megs shivered and drew her short cape closer, even though it wasn't especially cold out tonight. Sound was hard to estimate here. The buildings and small, crooked passageways seemed to echo back whispers and swallow shouts.

This place was haunted by more than Roger's memory.

Megs turned in a circle. Her carriage was only yards away, a lighted, reassuring presence, but she felt isolated nonetheless.

Why had Roger come here that night?

He didn't live nearby, hadn't, as far as she knew, anyone to visit. She had loved him and knew, deep in her heart, that he'd truly loved her in return, but she had no explanation for his last journey.

All she knew, in fact, was that he'd come to St. Giles—and that the Ghost of St. Giles had seen fit to murder him here.

Why? Why Roger of all people?

Megs tried to imagine Roger being held at sword point, deciding to fight back even if mismatched.

She shook her head. Her conjured image was blurry. She couldn't quite set his features right. When she'd first heard the news of his murder, she'd been sure that he wasn't the type of man to foolishly provoke a fight with a footpad. Now...

Now she'd lost part of his memory. Lost part of Roger himself. She wasn't sure she knew who he'd been anymore, and the thought sent panic racing in her chest.

Something moved in the shadows.

She had the pistol grasped in both hands and pointed even before the Ghost of St. Giles stepped from the doorway.

The rage hit her, hot and quick. How *dare* he? He was sullying ground sacred to her, ground sacred to her memory of Roger.

"You shouldn't be here, my—"

She fired the pistol...except nothing happened but a sputtering sound and a tiny spark.

Then he was on her, big and hard, wrenching the pistol from her hands and throwing it, clattering, onto the cobblestones, out of reach.

She opened her mouth to shriek her anger, but his hand clamped down on the lower half of her face, his other arm hugging her close, trapping her hands against her sides.

She went insane. *Men!* All telling her what to do, all unable to give her the simple courtesy of treating her like she *mattered*. She writhed, trying to elbow him, trying to stamp on his toes, her dancing slippers sliding harmlessly against his jackboots. She twisted, small sounds of frustration and rage pushing against his damned hand. He grunted and staggered, pulling her with him as he half fell into the shadows against a house wall. She tucked her chin into her neck and slammed the top of her head against him, missing his jaw and connecting painfully with his chest, shaking with fury.

"Damn it—" His growl was low.

He didn't seem affected at all, this murderer, this killer of all she'd ever held dear. She raised her head and glared at him over the top of his hand, daring him to do what he might.

He met her look and his eyes narrowed behind that stupid mask, and then his hand was moving from her mouth, but before she could draw breath, he was slamming his lips over hers and he was...

Kissing her?

Her world whirled sickeningly because he was angry and she was angry and his mouth wasn't at all gentle, but somehow, despite all of that, or maybe *because* all of that, she felt it: a stirring. A warmth down below where—

No! This wasn't right; this wasn't going to happen, not for this man of all men. She tried to arch her head away, but he had a hand on the back of her neck, holding her there as he opened his mouth against hers, sweetly hot, *wrongly* enticing, and she *bit* him. She clamped down on his lower lip, tasting blood, whimpering. She couldn't take much more of this, couldn't hold out, but he didn't pull away. He still held her close against his large, warm, masculine frame and she could feel that part of him now, hard and erect, pushing into her, even through her many skirts, and the feeling was supposed to repulse and scare her.

Instead it made her wet.

She gasped and he surged into her mouth in triumphant possession.

No. *Nonono.* She wasn't this person. She refused to be.

He wouldn't stop. He was going to make her betray herself, betray Roger, and she simply couldn't let that happen. It would destroy what she had left of her world. The Ghost was so intent on her mouth, on teaching her that apparently it didn't matter *who* pressed his tongue between her lips, licking so ... so ...

He'd let go of her arms.

She brought them up around his back, withdrew the dagger, and stabbed, with all her strength, with all her fear, with all her sorrow.

She felt the resistance of the wool, the solidity of the

muscle, felt how, disgustingly, it was like carving beef-steak. She dug the knife into his back as far as she could, until it scraped against something hard in him.

He lifted his head, finally, *finally* looking at her with shocked, hurt, gray eyes, and parted his bloodied lips.

"Oh, Megs."

Chapter Seven

*The horrible imps Despair, Grief, and Loss tried
to push Faith off, but she was stronger than she
looked and held on firmly.
The Hellequin didn't turn to look at her, but she could feel
the muscles of his shoulders flex and relax as they rode.
"What is your intention?" he rasped.
"I shall cling to you until I can persuade you to free my
beloved's soul," Faith said bravely.
The Hellequin merely nodded. "Prepare yourself, then, to
cross the River of Sorrow."...*
—From *The Legend of the Hellequin*

Only a fool lets his guard down in St. Giles.

The words rang in Godric's head, spoken in the ghostly
voice of his dead mentor, Sir Stanley Gilpin. Sir Stanley would've called him a damned idiot if he could see
Godric now, the hilt of his wife's puny knife sticking out
of his back.

"Godric!"

He blinked, focusing on Megs's face. She'd gone pale,
her eyes wide and stricken, the moment he'd whispered
her name. Of course that might change as soon as she
remembered that she believed he'd killed her lover.

The clatter of hoofbeats sounded nearby.

Godric reached over his shoulder and was just able to grasp the knife.

"Dear God, I've killed you." Actual tears stood in Megs's eyes.

Godric wished he'd time to admire them.

"Not quite." And he pulled the knife free with a dizzying wash of pain and a spurt of fresh hot blood. He shoved the thing into his boot and took Megs's elbow. "Come."

Nobody could afford horses in St. Giles. Hoofbeats meant only one thing.

"But your back," Megs wailed. "You should lie down. I'll get Oliver and Tom—"

"Quickly, sweeting," he said, and turned toward her carriage even as he pulled the mask and hat off. In the near dark, perhaps her coachman and footman wouldn't notice the pattern of his tunic. Or the fact that he was wearing a half-cape and jackboots.

Never mind. There were worse things to fear at the moment than her servants discovering his secret.

Fortunately she came freely enough. Godric wasn't sure if he were up to dragging a struggling Megs into the carriage at the moment. She was surprisingly vehement when she fought.

Tom craned around to watch when they entered the carriage but made no comment when Godric curtly ordered, "Home. Fast as you can."

He thrust Megs down onto a seat even as the carriage started forward. Fortunately she had a hidden compartment under the seats—he'd thought as much since that first night when she'd produced those pistols. He shoved up the empty seat and threw in his swords, cape, hat, and mask. Then he shut the seat and sat rather abruptly, possibly because the carriage was swinging around a corner.

Shouts from without.

Megs was suddenly beside him. "You're still bleeding. I can see the wet shining against your tunic."

He didn't say anything, simply drawing the tunic off his head. Underneath he wore a simple white shirt. "Come here."

They were running out of time.

She seemed to realize suddenly that there was more to his urgency than his trifling wound. "What is it?"

"We're about to be stopped by the dragoons," he said grimly as he pulled her into his lap, parting her legs beneath her skirts so that she straddled him. "If they discover I'm the Ghost, we're both ruined. Do you understand?"

She was both brave and intelligent, his wife. Her eyes widened, but she merely nodded once.

The carriage was already slowing, with the soldiers' horses right outside the window. They could hear the shouts of the men, the answering voice of their coachman.

"Good," he said. "Follow my lead."

He took the little knife from his boot and slit the front of her bodice open, cutting through stays and chemise as well. Any other woman would've screamed—the dress was silk, an expensive, frivolous thing—but Megs merely watched him with startled brown eyes.

He pulled the edges widely apart and the most beautiful breasts he'd ever seen popped into view, round and full with dark rose nipples. Had it just been his life, he might've taken the time to look his fill. But it was her life as well—or at least her reputation. If he were hanged as a murderer, she'd be shunned by all but her family.

He pulled her close and bent his head as hands scrabbled at the carriage door. Then his mouth was full of her sweet nipple and he suckled strongly, as the heady scent of woman and orange blossoms swirled about his head. He could see her pulse beating at her tender throat like a fluttering bird. Damn it, if his mouth hadn't been full, he might've chuckled.

He was as hard as a rock.

The door to the carriage was yanked open.

He felt her jerk, her strong young back arching in his hands, and she brushed her fingers through his cropped hair.

"What—" The voice was loud and commanding. The voice of a dragoon captain.

Godric raised his head, eyes narrowed in anger as he pulled her into his chest, shielding her nudity. Megs made a distressed, embarrassed sound and hid her face in his shoulder.

And just like that, his anger became real.

"What in God's name is the meaning of this?" he growled.

He doubted very much that Captain Trevillion was used to blushing, but damned if the man's cheeks didn't darken. "I...uh...I am Captain James Trevillion of the 4th Dragoons. I'm charged with capturing the Ghost of St. Giles. One of my men thought he saw the Ghost enter this carriage. If you—"

"I don't care if you're charged with capturing the Pretender himself," Godric whispered. "Get out of my carriage before I carve your eyes out and use—"

But Trevillion was already muttering an apology as he withdrew. The carriage door slammed.

Megs straightened.

"Wait," Godric murmured, stilling her with a hand on her soft, bare back.

Trevillion might be red-faced, but the man was nothing if not canny.

Only when the carriage started forward did he let Megs slip from his lap.

"That was clever," she whispered. "How is your back?"

"It's nothing," he said, equally low. No one could hear them over the carriage wheels, yet somehow it felt right to whisper. His eyes dropped to her gaping bodice. One nipple was reddened and still moist. He averted his eyes, swallowing. His erection, silly thing, didn't know the show was over. "I'm sorry about your dress."

"Don't be an idiot," she retorted, though he thought her cheeks had pinkened. Had she arched into his mouth of her own excitement...or because she was playacting? "Let me see your back."

He sighed and leaned forward, wincing. In the little time that he'd been sitting with his back pressed against the squabs, the blood had begun to dry. Movement reopened the wound, for he could feel the hot wash down his back.

She drew a sharp breath. "Your entire back is wet with blood."

Her voice was trembling.

"It's a small wound," he said soothingly. "Blood is often more dramatic, I've found, than the injury that produces it."

That earned him an odd look, equal parts worry, doubt, and curiosity.

Then she reached around his back, pressing something on the wound, making the pain flare. The movement pushed her breasts into his arm and for a moment he closed his eyes.

"Godric," she whispered urgently. "Godric!"

He opened his eyes to find her face only inches from his, and he had a mad urge to pull her back into his lap and make her arch under his mouth again.

He blinked and the carriage seemed to dip and sway.

"I'm so, so sorry," Megs was muttering in a distressed tone as she fumbled with his back. Whatever she was doing didn't seem to be stopping the bleeding. "We'll need a doctor. I can send for one as soon as we reach home."

"No doctor." He was shaking his head but had to stop when nausea closed his throat. "Moulder."

"What?" She glanced at him distractedly, her eyes dipping to his lips and back up again. "If I'd known the Ghost was you, I'd never have stabbed you."

"Sometimes he's not," Godric said, and could tell by her confused expression that she didn't understand him. His words were slurring, but he had a sudden intense urge to make her understand one thing. "I didn't kill Roger Fraser-Burnsby."

Her gaze slipped from his as she examined his back again. "I didn't think—"

He grasped her arm, making her turn. Her hair was mostly down, a wild, magnificent cloud of black curling locks framing the white skin of her wonderful breasts. If he died tonight, he'd give thanks that he'd seen her like this before he entered Hell.

"I was at d'Arque's ball," he gasped. "That night. I—"

She'd fallen before him at the news of Fraser-Burnsby's death—her lover's death, though Godric hadn't known that at the time. Godric had barely managed to catch her before her head would've hit the marble floor. He'd carried her limp form to a secluded room and there left her to the care of Isabel Beckinhall.

He blinked, focusing on her face, which was too flushed, her eyes too bright. "I wasn't in St. Giles."

"I know." She touched his cheek with one finger, apparently oblivious that her hand was covered in his blood. "I know."

GODRIC'S EYELIDS FLUTTERED and for a moment she thought he'd passed out.

"Godric!" Megs's heart skipped as his head sagged to the side.

But then, as if with a supreme effort of will, he straightened again, his gray eyes clear and piercing as he stared at her, even though his face had gone pasty white. "Do you trust your coachman? Your footman?"

"Yes, yes, of course," she said at once, and then realized: his very life might depend upon the discretion of Oliver and Tom. She swallowed and thought about it, but in the end said sincerely, "They both have always been loyal. All my servants are."

"Good. When the carriage stops, please send Oliver in to get Moulder. He'll know what to do." A thin white line incised itself around his mouth as he pressed his lips together. He must be in terrible pain.

"How many times have you done this before?" she whispered.

He shook his head slightly. "Enough to know this wound isn't fatal."

She stared at him, appalled. Only days before, she'd thought him a doddering old man. And now...even wounded, the breadth of his shoulders strained the white shirt he wore, his hands were elegant and strong, and his face hard and intelligent. He fairly vibrated with vitality.

How had his pretended senility ever deceived her?

She shivered. She was still all but bare to the waist because he'd *cut* the dress from her torso and bent his head to fasten those ridiculously sensuous lips onto her breast. The shock of it, after violence and, *yes*, sexual excitement, had nearly made her forget their danger. When the dragoon captain had opened the carriage door, she'd squeaked with real surprise.

Megs shook her head. She'd have to examine these troubling feelings later. Right now they were near-ing Saint House. She scrabbled for the edges of what remained of her bodice, pulling it over herself as best she could and then buttoning her half-cape all the way to her neck. If no one looked too closely, she could make it to her room without embarrassment.

The carriage shuddered to a stop and she remembered his directions. Quickly, she opened the door a crack and ordered Oliver to fetch Moulder. Lord knew what the foot-man and Tom thought of tonight's events. They must've caught glimpses of Godric's costume as he'd entered the carriage, and if that hadn't been enough, the dragoon cap-tain had shouted his suspicions.

Yet Godric hadn't been arrested.

Megs vowed to talk to both men and thank them for their discretion.

The carriage door opened again as Moulder said, "Got yourself into a fix again, have you? Told you that…" The servant's eyes widened, his words trailing away as he caught sight of Megs. "M'lady?"

"I have a knife wound in my back," Godric said calmly, even though his hands were trembling.

Moulder blinked and turned his attention to his master. "Best get you inside, then, hadn't we?"

"Yes, and discreetly." Godric looked at his servant and some unspoken communication seemed to pass between them.

"O' course." Moulder produced an old cape and threw it around Godric's shoulders, effectively hiding the Ghost's costume. In a louder voice he said, "Had a few too many, have we, sir?"

Godric rolled his eyes as Moulder wrapped his arms around his middle to help him descend the carriage. "Hate this particular subterfuge. Makes me look such an idiot."

"Only an idiot would let himself get stabbed in the back by some footpad," Moulder said far lower. He grunted as they made the cobblestones, and Godric staggered.

"Wasn't a footpad," Godric gasped.

"Oh? Then who?"

The two of them were weaving as if Godric really were intoxicated. Megs hastily got down from the carriage and ran to Godric's other side, taking his arm over her shoulder. "It was I."

Moulder's eyes widened at her for the second time that night. "Is that right? Would've liked to've seen that, I would."

"Bloodthirsty bastard," Godric hissed as they made the front door.

"I'm not proud of it," Megs whispered miserably.

Godric halted, swiveling his face to look at her, his gray eyes like crystals. "Not your fault."

Moulder muttered something under his breath and they

all paused for a moment on the landing. Godric's arm was like a lead weight across Megs's shoulders, and she would probably be sore on the morrow, but that wasn't what worried her. She could feel Godric trembling against her and, even more distressing, the seep of something wet against the side pressed to his.

He was still bleeding.

"Come on," she urged gently. "We'll rest once we get you to your room."

For a second, her gaze caught Moulder's and she knew they shared the same concern. If Godric collapsed on the stairs, they'd have to get the footmen to carry him up. The fewer servants who knew of this matter, the better.

As if Megs's thought had summoned her, Mrs. Crumb appeared at the bottom of the stairway. "May I be of assistance?"

Megs turned her head to look at the housekeeper. It must be well into the early hours of the morning, but Mrs. Crumb wore her starched black dress, the white apron and cap as crisp as ever, and she gazed up at them as calmly as if inquiring if they'd like tea served in the small sitting room.

"Hot water," Moulder said before Megs could gather her wits, and his next words confirmed her suspicion that he was quite used to emergencies of this nature. "A stack of clean cloths and the brandy from Mr. St. John's study, if you please, Mrs. Crumb."

Megs held her breath, waiting for the housekeeper's outrage. To be ordered about in front of their employers was a clear breach of servant etiquette.

But Mrs. Crumb merely paused a moment before saying, "At once, Mr. Moulder."

Her expression was as serene as ever as she turned to do the butler's orders.

Megs glanced at Moulder.

He looked nearly as surprised as she. "I'm beginning to almost like that woman."

The rest of their progress up the stairs was slow but uneventful. Strange that she'd spent years hating the Ghost, wishing only for his death—and now she wished just as much to get him safely to his bed. Megs bit her lip. In the morning she knew she would begin again, somehow start the search for Roger's murderer, but right now all she wanted was for Godric to be well.

When they finally made it to Godric's room, he was panting, a sheen of sweat lighting his pale brow. Megs watched as Moulder helped Godric sit on a wooden chair; then he disappeared into the dressing room. Godric plucked at his blood-streaked shirt and she roused herself, quickly crossing to the chair where he sat.

"Here, let me help," she murmured, unbuttoning the shirt.

It had stuck to his back and she knew it would hurt terribly when removed. She concentrated on her trembling fingers, unable to meet his eyes, his warm breath ruffling her hair.

"Megs," he whispered, and she realized dimly that he was finally using her nickname.

Tears suddenly blurred her vision. "I'm so, so sorry."

She felt him raise a hand as if to touch her cheek.

"Here we are, then," Moulder said far too cheerfully as he returned with a small wooden box.

At the same time a tap came at the door.

Megs hurried to it, surreptitiously wiping her eyes.

Outside, the ever-efficient Mrs. Crumb had a pile of

neatly folded snowy white cloths, a bottle of brandy, and a steaming kettle.

"Oh, thank you," Megs said, taking the items from the housekeeper.

"Is there anything else you need, my lady?" Mrs. Crumb asked.

"No, that will be all." Megs bit her lip. "I'd appreciate it if anything you saw tonight were not discussed in the servants' quarters."

Mrs. Crumb's left eyebrow arched imperceptibly. "Naturally, my lady," she said before curtsying and turning away.

Oh, dear. She'd obviously just insulted her wonderful new housekeeper. Megs sighed as she closed the door behind her. She'd have to somehow make it up to Mrs. Crumb in the morning.

When she turned, she saw that Moulder already had Godric's shirt off. Her husband had turned to straddle the chair, his back bared for Moulder, who was washing the blood from the wound in rather brisk movements.

Megs started forward, but her footsteps slowed as she neared the tableau. Godric's back...it wasn't anything like a middle-aged man—or at least what she thought a middle-aged man's back should look like. She blinked, feeling muddled. He'd laid his bare arms across the back of the chair, making his muscles bunch along his upper arms and shoulders. Strong, working muscles, the kind used to swing an ax—or a sword. A thin silver chain caught the light at the back of his neck as he bent his head. His spine was graceful in a particularly masculine way, indented and taut, leading down to a narrow waist and buttocks outlined by his tight leggings.

Good God. Megs forced herself to look away as she set the cloths, brandy, and kettle on a table. She felt as if she couldn't catch her breath. Couldn't piece together the Godric she'd thought she knew and the living, breathing man before her.

It was too much.

Godric half turned his head, presenting his strong nose, lips, and jaw in profile, as if he sensed her confusion. "Moulder will take care of this. I'm sure you're tired."

"But"—she gestured helplessly—"I'd like to help."

"No need, m'lady." Moulder turned to open the wooden box, revealing several sharp knives, scissors, needles, and thread. He took out a needle and examined the thread already on it. "'Tis a messy business you'll not like."

Well of course she wouldn't *like* seeing Godric sewn up, but she felt—she wanted—to stay and...and just *comfort* him.

"Megs," Godric said, his tone commanding. "Please. Go to bed."

He didn't say it, but she could tell: She was in the way. He didn't need her comfort.

"Very well, then," she said, trying to sound practical. "Good night."

And she made her feet cross to the door and enter her own room.

GODRIC CAME AWAKE slowly the next morning to the persistent ache of his back. For a moment he lay with his eyes closed, remembering the fading wisps of a dream about sunshine and a blooming tree. Megs had been sitting in the tree, her salmon-colored skirts bunched about her. She'd leaned down toward him, laughing, and her bodice had parted, spilling her sweet, round titties into his face. Godric realized both that he was no longer dreaming and that he'd woken with a stiff cock.

And that someone was in his room.

No. That *Megs* was in his room.

He lay there, trying to reason logically how he simply *knew* that it was Megs. But in the end he had to give up the effort without result. It seemed that the part of himself that recognized his wife's presence wasn't accessible from his intellect.

He opened his eyes and rolled to his back.

Or started to. The immediate stab of pain brought the events of last night flooding back. Sweet Megs with the bountiful breasts had stabbed him and she knew he was the Ghost of St. Giles. His life had just become a great deal more complicated.

Megs stood, clad in a fresh apple green and pink frock, puttering about near his dresser. He watched as she placed the pitcher in the washbasin, then picked up the small dish that he used for spare coins and turned it over, staring at the bottom. She wandered to the mantelpiece and, apparently without thinking, set the dish down on the corner where the slightest nudge would send it crashing to the tiles below.

He must've made some sound.

She turned, her face brightening. "You're awake."

He sat up, repressing a wince of pain. "It would seem so."

"Oh." She trailed her fingertips along the mantel, frowning at the jar of spills that stood at the opposite end from the dish. She plucked out a spill, twisting it between her fingers. "Are you better? You certainly *look* better. You were as white as a . . . well, a *ghost* last night."

He swallowed. "Megs..."

She tossed the spill onto the mantel and turned to face him, her shoulders square, her chin level. It was the exact same stance she'd taken that first night when she'd shot at him. "Griffin told me last night that he forced you to marry me."

That wasn't what he'd been expecting to hear from her. He cocked his head, considering her as he replied cautiously, "Yes, he did."

She nodded. "I'm sorry. He should've never done that."

"Shouldn't he have?" he asked, his voice sharp. "He's your brother, Megs, and you were in dire straits. I may not've particularly *liked* being blackmailed by Griffin, but I've never questioned his reasons for doing it."

"Oh." She scowled down at the toes of her slippers as if they'd somehow offended her. "But even understanding the whole mess, you must hate me anyway."

"Don't be ridiculous." His tone and words were more irritable than he wanted them to be, but his back was throbbing. "You know I'd never blame you for—"

"*Do* I?" She threw her head back, her dark eyes shining, her hair already beginning to struggle out of its confines as she started pacing in front of his fireplace. "Until yesterday evening I thought I knew you. I thought you were a staid, elderly scholar who lived by himself in a much too dusty mansion and once in a while for a bit of excitement went out to coffeehouses. And then"—she spun at the far end of the room, waving her hands as if battling birds were attacking her head—"*and then* I find that you're a notorious *madman* who runs about in a ridiculous mask and gets into fights with footpads in St. Giles, and, Godric, I really, truly *don't* think I know you *at all* now."

She stopped dead and glared at him, her breast heaving. Dear God, she was magnificent when she was in a rage.

He cleared his throat. "Elderly?"

"Elderly?" She mimicked him in a horribly high voice, which he privately thought was a bit unfair—he didn't sound at all like that. "That's all you can say? I saw you *kill* that footpad the first night I was in London."

"Yes, I did."

"How many?"

"What?"

Her lower lip was trembling, the sight much more troubling to him than her anger. Megs in a rage was wonderful. Megs fearful wasn't something he ever wanted to see. "How many have you killed, Godric?"

He looked away from that vulnerable mouth. "I don't know."

"How"—she stopped and inhaled, steadying her voice— "how can you not *know* how many people you've killed, Godric?"

He wasn't a coward, so he lifted his head and met her gaze, silently letting her see the answer in his eyes.

Her throat worked as she swallowed. "But they were all bad, weren't they?" She couldn't hide the uncertainty in her voice. She was trying to persuade herself—and failing. "All...all the people you killed, they were like the footpad—you saved others by killing them."

He could see in her eyes the desire to believe that he wasn't entirely a monster. So he made it easy for her, though he knew there was no clear line in St. Giles. No true black and white. Yes, there were murderers and thieves, those who preyed upon the weaker...but those same murderers and thieves often sought to feed themselves or others.

One never knew.

Not that that had ever stopped him.

"Yes," he said. "I've only ever killed those who I caught attacking the weak and vulnerable."

There was glad relief in her eyes, which was as it should be. Megs was a creature of light and joy. She had no business contemplating the darkness that he fought night after night in St. Giles.

"I'm so glad." She frowned for a moment, absently taking a dozen spills from the jar and stacking them messily on the mantel, but then she seemed to remember something and turned back to him, a few spills still in her hand. "That was what Griffin was blackmailing you over, wasn't it? He knew that you were the Ghost."

Godric's mouth twisted. "Yes."

"I see." She nodded to herself rather thoughtfully and tossed the remaining spills onto the chair before the fire. Several slid off to land on the small rug underneath. "Well, I'm glad I found out, truly. I think a wife, even one so strangely married as I, should know her husband's past, and now that it's behind you—behind *us*, rather—I think—"

"Megs," he whispered, in dawning horror.

But she didn't seem to hear. "We'll muddle on much better in the future. I can learn who you truly are and you..." She trailed off as she seemed to at last realize that something was wrong. "What is it?"

"I don't intend to give up being the Ghost of St. Giles."

She stared at him. "But... you must."

He raised his eyebrows. "Why?"

"Because"—she threw wide her hands, nearly knocking the dish from its perch on the mantel—"it's dangerous and...and you *killed* people. You just must stop."

He sighed, watching her. He could tell her about the widow he'd saved from rape last month, the robbers he'd chased away from an elderly flower seller a week later, the orphaned girls he'd rescued on the night he'd saved Megs herself. He could tell her horror stories and brag about bravado, but in the end it hardly mattered. He knew, deep inside his crippled soul, that even if he'd never save another life, his answer would still be the same.

"No, I won't stop."

Her eyes widened and for a moment he almost thought it was in betrayal.

Then she tilted her chin up and glared at him, her eyes blazing. "Very well. I suppose that is your choice after all."

He knew that she wasn't done, that whatever she said next he truly would not like.

Still it was a blow, a hit delivered directly to the belly, when she said, "Just as it is *my* choice to find Roger's murderer...and kill him."

Chapter Eight

Faith looked up and saw before them a black, swirling river that stretched in either direction as far as the eye could see. The Hellequin never hesitated but rode his great black horse directly into the river. Faith took a firmer grip on his shoulders and looked down as the horse began to swim. There in the inky water she saw strange, white wispy forms drifting past, and the longer she stared, the more they seemed nearly human....
—From *The Legend of the Hellequin*

The second time Godric woke that day it was to the sound of muffled giggles. He glanced at his window and from the angle of the light shining in estimated it to be late afternoon. Apparently, he'd slept the day away after his catastrophic argument with Megs. Remembering her avowal to traipse into St. Giles and attempt to kill the murderer of her damned dead lover made his head start to pound.

She was his wife.

It was his duty to protect her, to keep her from her own folly, and he would've done that even if he hadn't grown rather...fond of her in the last several days.

The stab of pain behind his left eye at that thought was quite awful.

Godric sighed and rose carefully. Moulder had patched him up the night before, muttering all the while that the wound was but a tiny thing, hardly worth the effort. It didn't feel tiny as all that today, though. He had trouble lifting his left arm to put on a shirt, and it took him awhile to don stockings, breeches, and shoes. Still, Godric acknowledged that he'd had much worse injuries in the past.

There'd been times when he'd not risen from bed for days.

He shrugged on his waistcoat, buttoned it, and left his toilet at that for the moment, crossing to the door that connected with his wife's room. Another husky laugh sparked his curiosity and he knocked once before opening the door.

Megs sat on the round carpet by her bed, her skirts a pool of apple green and pink about her. The four little maids recently apprenticed from the home squatted beside her like acolytes to a particularly pretty pagan priestess, and on her lap was the cause of their mirth: a squirming, fat, ratlike thing.

Megs looked up at his entrance, her face shining. For a moment he caught his breath—it was almost like a light radiated from within her, and he was very glad that she'd apparently decided not to hold their argument against him.

"Oh, Godric, come see! Her Grace has had her puppies."

And she held out the ratlike thing—which, apparently, was a pug puppy—like a peace offering.

Godric raised his brows, sinking into a chair. "It's quite . . . lovely?"

"Oh, pooh!" She retracted her arms, cuddling the tiny creature against her cheek. "Don't listen to Mr. St. John," she whispered to the puppy as if in confidence. "You're the most adorable thing I've ever seen."

All four maids giggled.

Godric raised an eyebrow, replying mildly, "I said it was lovely."

His wife's laughing brown eyes peeked at him over the soft fawn creature. "Yes, but your tone said the opposite."

He started to shrug, but the sudden bite at his shoulder made him regret the movement.

He thought he'd suppressed the wince, but Megs's eyes narrowed. "Thank you, girls. Mary Compassion, could you take the other Marys downstairs? I'm sure Mrs. Crumb has need of you now."

The girls looked a bit disappointed, but they rose obediently and left the bedroom, trailing the eldest.

Megs waited until the door closed behind them. "How are you?"

She held the puppy to her face almost like a shield against him, and he wished she'd put the animal down so he could see her expression.

"Well enough," he replied.

She nodded, meeting his gaze at last. Tears sparkled in her eyes and his chest tightened. "I'm so very, very sorry that I hurt you."

If she wished not to speak of their earlier argument, it was fine with him. "You've already apologized, and besides, there's no need. It wasn't your fault. I suppose you thought I was attacking you."

She looked away and he felt a sinking sensation. Had his kiss been that repulsive, then?

There was a short and, for him at least, very awkward silence.

Finally he gestured to the puppy in her arms. "Doesn't the mother want her offspring back?"

"Oh, yes," Megs murmured, and to Godric's astonishment she turned and lay on her belly to place the puppy under her bed.

A squeak and rustle came from the shadows there.

Megs straightened and turned.

Godric raised his brows.

"Her Grace is under there with her puppies—three of them," Megs answered his silent question. "We think she whelped sometime last evening, but I didn't notice until late this morning when I heard the puppies crying."

"Strange," Godric murmured as he watched her rise from the floor, "that the dog chose your room to give birth."

Megs shrugged, shaking out her skirts. "I'm just glad we found her. Great-Aunt Elvina was so worried when she realized Her Grace was missing from her room this morning."

He nodded absently. How was he to keep her safe? How was he to save her from her own gallant heart?

She inhaled as if bracing herself. "Godric?"

He watched her warily. "Yes?"

"Can you tell me how"—she waved her hands in a fluttering gesture between them—"how this happened? How you came to be the Ghost of St. Giles?"

He nodded. "Yes, of course."

PERHAPS IF SHE could understand why he did this dreadful thing, then she could somehow dissuade him, Megs thought.

Godric was still pale. Megs examined her husband while trying to hide her concern, but his gaze was steady, his body solid and strong in the chair. She took a moment to marvel again that at one time she'd thought this man almost infirm. She realized now that he might not be as tall or as bulky as some men, but he was *solid*, as if he were made of some durable, indestructible material. Granite, maybe. Or iron that would never rust. Something strong and muscular and . . . and *masculine*.

Megs glanced down at her hands in confusion at the thought of her husband's body and nearly missed his next words.

"Have you ever heard of Sir Stanley Gilpin?"

She looked up again. "No, I don't think so."

He nodded as if her reply was expected. "He was a distant relation of my father's, dead now for several years. A third cousin or some such. He was a wealthy man of business in the city, but he also had other interests."

"Such as?"

"Theater. He owned a theater at one time and even wrote some plays."

"Really?" She couldn't see what this had to do with the Ghost of St. Giles, but she forced herself to sink into a chair at right angles to his, laying her hands decorously one atop the other. Fidgeting was, sadly, a particular failing of hers. "What are their titles? Perhaps I've seen one."

"I very much doubt it." His look was wry. "I loved Sir Stanley like a father, but his playwriting skills were terrible. I'm not sure any of his plays saw a stage beyond the first one, *The Romance of the Porpoise and the Hedgehog.*"

Megs felt her eyebrows lift, interested despite herself. "The . . . porpoise?"

He nodded. "And the hedgehog. As I said, simply terrible, but I've gotten off track." He leaned forward, wincing a little, and set his elbows on his knees, staring at his hands clasped in front of him. "I don't know if you know this, but my mother died when I was ten."

She'd known his mother must be dead since Sarah's mother was his stepmother, but she hadn't realized how young he'd been when his mother died. Ten was such a delicate age. "I'm sorry."

He didn't look up. "I was close to her and took her death rather hard. Then, three years later, my father remarried. I did not react well."

His tone was dry, unemotional, but somehow she knew that he hadn't been nearly so stoic as a young boy. He must've suffered horrible inner turmoil. "What happened?"

"My father sent me away to school," he said, "and then at the vacation, Sir Stanley Gilpin offered to let me stay with him."

Her brows knit. "You didn't go home to see your family?"

"No." His lips pursed very slightly, drawing her eye. The rest of him might be hard, but his mouth, particularly the lower lip, looked soft.

Was soft. She remembered suddenly his mouth on her breast, the tug of his teeth, the brush of his lips. His lips had been gentle on her breast, but those same soft lips had been unyielding on her mouth.

Megs swallowed, beating down the image. What was happening to her? She plucked at a thread on her skirts. "That… that must've been hard, to be separated from your father."

"It was for the best," he said. "We fought often and it was my fault. I was unreasonable, blaming him for my mother's death, for his remarriage. I behaved atrociously to my stepmother."

"You were only thirteen," she said softly, her heart

contracting. "I'm sure she understood your grief, your confusion."

He frowned and shook his head, and she knew somehow that he didn't believe her. "In any case, that became the pattern for the next several years. When I wasn't at school, I lived with Sir Stanley. And while I lived with Sir Stanley, he taught me."

She frowned, inadvertently tugging hard on the thread. "Taught you what?"

"How to be the Ghost of St. Giles, I suppose." He spread his hands. "Although at the time I merely thought it was exercise. He had a kind of practice room set aside with sawdust dummies, targets, and the like. There he taught me tumbling, swordsmanship, and hand fighting."

"Tumbling? Like an acrobat at a traveling fair?" She leaned forward in delight, imagining Godric turning somersaults.

"Yes, like a comic actor." He glanced up at her, his eyes crinkled at the corners. "It sounds absurd, I know, but the movements are actually difficult to master, and for a boy with too much anger within himself..."

She bit her lip, thinking of that lost boy, cut off from his family, angry and alone. She had a sudden warm gratitude toward the late Sir Stanley Gilpin. He might've been an eccentric, but he also obviously knew much about young men and their needs.

His eyes drifted to her mouth and then down to his hands, again clasped between his knees. "We continued thus for several years. It wasn't until I was eighteen that we figured out, from signs and odd comings and goings, that Sir Stanley was the Ghost of St. Giles and—"

"What? Wait." Megs jerked up her hands, snapping the

thread on her dress, but she was too eager to care. "*Sir Stanley* was the original Ghost of St. Giles?"

"Yes. Well"—Godric's lips quirked and he tilted his head—"at least he's the only one I know about. The legend of the Ghost of St. Giles has been around for years, perhaps centuries. Who is to say that some other man in some other time didn't don the costume?"

Megs's lips parted slowly as she imagined a parade of men, year after year, pretending to be the Ghost of St. Giles. Who would do such a thing? She looked at Godric, the question on her lips, but she didn't want to forget another pressing question.

"Who is 'we'?"

"Ah." Godric straightened in his chair, his hand absently rising to his left shoulder before he apparently remembered and let it drop to his lap. "As to that..."

Why was he stalling? "Yes?"

He inhaled deeply and looked her in the eye. "There's more than me."

"More..." Her eyes widened. "Ghosts?" The incredulous word came out a squeak. "*At one time?*"

He nodded. "By the time I was eighteen, another boy had joined our practice sessions. He was younger than I, but just as angry as I had been at fourteen." His brows drew together. "More so, actually."

"Who?"

"I can't tell you," he said apologetically.

"What?" Megs straightened in indignation. "Why not?"

He shrugged. "It's not my secret to tell."

Well, she supposed that was terribly honorable of him—and quite, quite frustrating for her. "So there were two of you...."

He cleared his throat. "Three, actually. Another came after I left."

Her eyes widened, the questions charging about and bumping up against each other in her mind. *"Three? But—"*

He held up his hands, palms toward her. "I know you were told that Roger was killed by the Ghost of St. Giles, but that's simply not true. None of us would ever—could ever—kill a good man such as Roger."

She nodded, swallowing. Somehow something was wrong with the story of Roger's murder. Either the witness had been mistaken...

Or he had lied. She frowned at the thought.

"Megs."

She looked up, meeting his eyes. She would follow the trail of Roger's murder, but at the moment Godric needed to finish his tale. "How did there come to be three Ghosts?"

Godric sighed. "I think Sir Stanley saw it as a lark, dressing up as the Ghost of St. Giles. He had rather a mischievous sense of humor. But by the time I left for Oxford, he was definitely looking for a successor for his grand scheme. He'd fallen in love with the people of St. Giles and wanted to make sure they had a protector even after he became too old to play the Ghost himself."

More questions trembled on her lips, and Megs had to bite the inside of her cheek to keep her mouth shut and not interrupt. She nodded for him to continue.

"I went away, as I said," Godric said. "I had come to terms with my father by then, knew that I'd been acting like an immature fool. I determined to right my life and perhaps gain the respect of my father and stepmother. I could tell Sir Stanley was disappointed in my decision, but he was understanding as well. Too, by that point he had his second apprentice well in hand."

Megs actually had to dig her nails into the palms of her hands to keep herself from asking the questions. Who was the other apprentice? Had Godric wanted to become the Ghost of St. Giles at such a young age? Had his father known what Sir Stanley was training Godric to be?

But her husband was speaking again. "So I went off to Oxford, learned many things, grew into a man, and when I came home to Laurelwood, I met Clara at a country ball."

He closed his eyes. "I've told you how that went. We were happy—so very happy—for nearly a year. And then she became ill. We moved to London to be closer to the doctors. I hoped—I prayed—that we could find an elixir or treatment to cure her. I held out hope for a year and a half before I realized there was no cure for my Clara. That she would die from this disease and I could do nothing about it—nothing but watch." A corner of his lovely mouth lifted, curling into an ugly sneer of pain. "I watched as she grew thinner, as the agony began to claw at her from the inside."

He opened his clear gray eyes then, and she saw the remembered despair. It must've been truly hellish being helpless in the face of his love's suffering.

She could stand it no more. Megs reached out, taking his cold hand in hers.

Godric bent his head, staring at her fingers atop his, making no move to grasp hers but not shaking her off either.

She took comfort in that.

"I think I would've gone insane," he murmured to their

hands, "if Sir Stanley had not called upon me one day. He'd heard, from my father, about Clara's illness, and he had a simple offer: to come train with him again. He had by then the third of our small coterie, a young man, barely more than a lad. His second disciple, the one I had known, had broken away from Sir Stanley and had already become the Ghost of St. Giles. Sir Stanley made the excuse that his new pupil would need a sparring partner, but I knew. He offered salvation, a respite from the daily torment of watching Clara die. He offered the Ghost for me as well."

Megs stared. "I don't understand. If there was already a Ghost, how could you become one as well?"

"It wasn't just me," he said. "The third man took up the mask and swords soon after I did. Until two years ago, all three of us were the Ghost of St. Giles."

Megs's brow wrinkled. "Didn't you run into each other?"

A smile lit Godric's solemn crystal eyes. "Very rarely. You have to understand—I didn't go out every night and neither did the other Ghosts. If by some chance we were both active on the same night, it was merely whispered that the Ghost could be in two places at once, which," he said wryly, "he can."

"But three different men..." Megs shook her head. "Didn't people notice you weren't the same man?"

Godric shrugged. "No. We have similar physiques. Besides, if one is wearing an outlandish costume composed of a mask, cape, large hat, and a harlequin's livery, well, any witnesses rarely notice what the man beneath looks like."

Megs nodded thoughtfully. "I think your Sir Stanley must have been a very clever man."

"Oh, he was," Godric said softly. He bent his head, seeming to be lost in a memory. He'd turned his hand in hers, and now his thumb was moving in circles on the back of her hand.

It was a rather nice sensation, actually.

"Godric," Megs whispered carefully.

He glanced at her. "Hmm?"

She swallowed, loath to shatter this moment. But her curiosity had always been her downfall. "Clara died three years ago, didn't she?"

He stiffened at the mention of his first wife's name on her lips and dropped her hand. "Yes."

She felt strangely bereft, but she soldiered on, asking the question. "Then why are you still the Ghost of St. Giles?"

WHY WAS HE still the Ghost of St. Giles?

Godric snorted under his breath as he edged close to the corner of a crumbling brick building. He peered around it, making sure the dark alley beyond was free of soldiers before darting quickly around it. It was often easier—and safer—to travel by rooftop, but the wound to his back made that impossible tonight. Thus he was forced to make his way by foot, keeping watch for Trevillion and his soldiers all the while.

He paused at the end of the alley, listening, and remembered the look in Megs's eyes as she'd asked the question: puzzlement tinged with worry. Worry for him.

The memory made his lips quirk. When was the last time anyone had worried for him? Not since Clara had died, surely, and even before that it'd been him worrying for her, not the other way around. Clara had never known he was the Ghost, but even so, she'd trusted that he was strong enough, smart enough, *man* enough never to come to harm. He supposed that he should be insulted that Megs thought him so frail that she worried over him, but he couldn't muster any outrage.

Actually, her concern was rather endearing. His wife had a soft heart—but a strong mind. She'd been shocked that he hadn't agreed to quit his life as the Ghost. He'd known that he'd disappointed her, and there was a part of him that wished he could give her what she wanted.

Both things that she wanted.

Godric ran across the street, whirling into the shadows again as he heard approaching footfalls. Two men reeled into the moonlit street, half propping each other up, half pushing each other down. The taller of the two tripped over his own feet and sank to the cobblestones in the strangely boneless manner of the very drunk. His companion braced himself on his knees and howled with laughter, stopping only when Godric slipped from his hiding place and continued on his way. He glanced over his shoulder to see the upright drunkard gaping after him.

The two drunkards seemed a clownish duo, but Godric's blood froze in his veins as he considered what might have happened if Megs had encountered them. Very few in St. Giles—drunk or not—were benign when faced with the temptation of a rich, beautiful woman.

His jaw clenched at the thought. Any other woman would've stayed far away from this area of London after that first trip. Not Megs, though, and he hardly thought the events of last night would keep her away either. No, she'd declared that she would go back to St. Giles—and continue to do so until she found Fraser-Burnsby's killer.

It might possibly be bravado, but he didn't think so. His wife was setting a course of suicide.

Damnation. He wouldn't let her own stubbornness lead to her hurt—or worse. Somehow he needed to find a way to send her back to the country, and the sooner the better.

St. Giles in the Fields church loomed up ahead, the tall steeple bisecting the full moon. Godric crossed to the brick wall surrounding the little graveyard. There was a lock on the gate, but it hung open.

Carefully, he pushed open the gate.

The hinges had been oiled and he slipped inside the churchyard without sound. The wind picked up, bending the branches of a single, pathetic tree and moaning around the headstones. Some might find it eerie, but Godric knew there was far more to fear in St. Giles than where the dead slept.

A very human grunt came from near the opposite wall, and Godric smiled grimly: He hadn't come in vain tonight. He slid from shadow to shadow around the perimeter of the graveyard, not speaking until he was within feet of his quarry.

"Good evening, Digger."

Digger Jack, a small, hunched man who happened to be one of the most notorious resurrectionists in London, straightened with a gasp.

His companion, a brawny, lumbering lad, was less sanguine. "It's the Devil!"

The lad threw down his shovel and sprinted for the cemetery gate with impressive agility, given his size.

Digger Jack made one abortive move, but Godric laid a heavy hand on the other man's shoulder before he could run. "I need a word with you."

"Awww!" Digger moaned. "Now, why'd ye 'ave to go an' do that? Ye've scared off Jed. 'Ave ye any idea 'ow 'ard 'tis to find a lad wif a strong back in St. Giles? I'm gettin' on in years, I am, an' the lumbago's been botherin' me somethin' fierce. 'Ow'm I to do me work wifout 'is 'elp?"

Godric raised an eyebrow behind his mask. "Sad as your tale of woe is, Digger, I can't find it in myself to pity you when you're in the very act of exhuming some poor corpse."

Digger pulled himself up to his full height of something under five foot two. "Man's got to make a livin', Ghost. 'Sides," he continued, narrowing his eyes spitefully, "leastwise I'm not a murderer."

"Oh, let's not start a game of name-calling."

The other man made a rude noise.

"Digger," Godric said low, his patience at an end, "I'm not here for your opinion of me."

The grave robber licked his lips nervously, his eyes sliding away from Godric's. "What yer want, then?"

"What do you know about the lassie snatchers?"

Digger's bony shoulders lifted. "Just talk 'ere and there."

"Tell me."

Digger's hard little face contorted as the man thought. "Word is, they're back."

Godric sighed. "Yes, I know."

"Uh..." Digger toed absently at the edge of his half-excavated grave. Clods of earth tumbled down, making no sound. "Some say as 'ow they've taken near on two dozen girls."

Four and twenty girls missing? In any other corner of London, there would've been a public outcry. News sheets would've printed outraged articles, lords would've thundered their ire in Parliament. Here, no one had bothered to even *notice*, it seemed.

"Where are they taken to?"

"I dunno." Digger shook his head. "But it's not a regular bawdy house, like. Don't no one 'ear from 'em again."

Godric's eyes narrowed. Digger didn't appear to know that the girls were used in a workshop. The place must be well hidden. A secret kept very close.

"There's a wench, though," Digger said as if remembering, "'oo 'elps to catch the lassies."

"Do you know what she looks like?"

"I knows better'n that," Digger said with a hint of pride. "I knows 'er name."

Godric cocked his head, waiting.

"Mistress Cook is what she goes by—or so I've 'eard."

It wasn't much, but it was better than nothing. Godric produced a silver coin and pressed it into Digger's grimy palm. "Thank you."

Digger perked up at the sight of money, although his tone was still a bit surly when he answered, "Anytime."

Godric turned to go, but hesitated as a thought struck him. "One more thing."

The grave robber heaved a heavy sigh. "What?"

"Two years ago, an aristo was murdered in St. Giles. His name was Roger Fraser-Burnsby. Do you know anything about the matter?"

If Godric hadn't spent years questioning informants of dubious reputation, he'd have missed the slight stiffening of Digger's body.

"Never 'eard of 'im," Digger said carelessly. "Now, if'n ye don't mind, I 'as me work to finish afore sunup."

Godric leaned into the smaller man until the crooked nose of his black leather mask nearly touched Digger's face. "But I do mind."

Digger gulped, his eyes flaring wide in alarm. "I...I don't know nothin', 'onest!"

"Jack," Godric rasped quietly. "You're a liar."

"All right, all right." Digger held up his hands as if warding off a physical attack. "There was rumors about when it 'appened. Talk that it 'adn't been the Ghost at all 'oo killed that aristo."

Godric raised his brows. "Did you hear who the real murderer was?"

Digger glanced over his shoulder as if searching for eavesdroppers. "Word was, it were another toff."

"Anything else?"

The grave robber threw up his hands. "Ain't that enough? You could get me killed, if'n this is toff business and they 'ear I been flappin' me mouth."

"No one will hear," Godric said softly. "You won't tell and I certainly don't plan to."

Digger's only reply was a derisive snort.

Godric tipped his hat ironically to his informant and made his escape from the graveyard, loping on foot toward the river and Saint House. The thought of Megs seeking bloody revenge troubled him. She was a woman of light and laughter. She wasn't made for grim retribution and death.

That was his job.

He couldn't let her do it. Even if it were safe for a lady to seek a murderer in St. Giles, he couldn't let her risk dimming her light, tarnishing her laughter. That kind of revenge would scar her forever.

There was only one way he could think of to distract her from her mission immediately and get her out of London.

Twenty minutes later, Godric neared Saint House, and as he always did, he slowed and ducked into the shadows of a doorway to watch and make sure he was unobserved. In all his years of acting the role of the Ghost of St. Giles, he could count on one hand the times when someone had been outside his house in the middle of the night. The times when his caution paid off.

This was one of those times.

It took him less than a minute to find the dark figure lurking by the corner of his house. A shadow so immobile, so silent, that had Godric not long ago memorized the monotone lines of his home by moonlight, he would have never seen him.

Godric stilled. He could flush the watcher, challenge him, and run him off. Or he could wait and see who had such interest in Saint House. His left shoulder throbbed, but he made himself breathe, deep and even, for he had a feeling this might be a long vigil.

As it turned out, it was three hours. Three hours of standing still, leaning against the doorway. Three hours of wishing he were asleep in his own bed. But at the end of those three hours he knew who was keeping watch over his house.

As the first gray-pink light began to dawn in the east, Captain James Trevillion stepped from the shadows. Without a backward glance to the house he'd guarded all night, he walked calmly away.

Godric waited until he could no longer hear the dragoon officer's footfalls—and then he waited five minutes more.

Only then did he creep to the back of his house and into his study. Godric doffed his costume slowly, weariness and pain making him clumsy. His sword belt slipped from his fingers and clattered to the floor. He stood staring at it. His hasty subterfuge the night Megs had stabbed him must not have fooled the dragoon captain entirely. Trevillion suspected he was in truth the Ghost. Why else keep vigil all night but to catch him as he returned from his wanderings? Godric had the feeling the man wouldn't care overmuch for rank should he obtain clear proof that a member of the aristocracy were the Ghost. The captain was dogged, a man who appeared to have no life outside of the chase. A corner of Godric's mouth kicked up in sardonic amusement. Perhaps his nemesis was only truly alive when he was hunting.

If so, they had more in common than the dragoon would ever suspect. Godric had long ago made peace with the knowledge that what small part of himself had survived Clara's passing dwelt behind the mask.

He heaved a sigh. The captain must be dealt with, the lassie snatchers and Mistress Cook found, and Megs kept safe even against her will.

All this he must do, but right now he needed sleep.

Godric put away the accouterments of the Ghost and donned his nightshirt and banyan before leaving his study. As he climbed the stairs to his bedroom, he remembered once again Megs's question: *Why was he still the Ghost of St. Giles?* and the answer he'd not spoken:

It was the only way he had left to know he yet breathed.

Chapter Nine

*Despair grinned, showing needle-sharp yellow teeth
against his deep red skin. "The souls of those caught
between Heaven and Hell drown endlessly in the waters
below, waiting for time to run out and their release. Rejoice
that your beloved's soul is not condemned to these waters,
for those who are trapped here are suicides."
Faith shivered at the imp's words and watched as a soul
in the black water opened its mouth wide as if to scream.
No sound issued forth from the void....*
—From* The Legend of the Hellequin

Megs stood late the next morning in the garden of Saint
House, staring hard at the gnarled old fruit tree. It looked
exactly the same as the last time she'd seen it a couple of
days ago.

Dead.

Higgins wanted permission to cut it down, but Megs
couldn't find it in her heart to do so. Ugly and gnarled
as the tree was, it seemed a lonely thing out here in the
garden by itself. Silly, of course, to give human feelings to
a tree, but there it was. Megs pitied the old, twisted tree.

"That tree is dead," came a dark voice from behind her.

She turned, trying to still the fluttering in her breast.

Godric stood on the garden path, clad in his habitual somber suit—gray this morning. He regarded her with clear, crystal eyes, searching it seemed for something in her face.

Megs smiled. "That's what my gardener, Higgins, said as well."

"I can have it cut down for you."

"He also offered."

He looked at her oddly. "You won't have it cut down, though, will you?"

She wrinkled her nose and placed a hand protectively on the rough bark. "No."

"Naturally not," he murmured to himself.

She clasped her hands before her. "I'm glad to see you've risen. When I heard you were still abed this morning, I feared you'd suffered a setback."

His eyes flickered away from hers for a moment, and she had the oddest notion that he was about to tell her a falsehood, but all he said was, "I was tired and thought it best to sleep a little more before I rose."

She nodded absently, trying to think of something to say. How could this be the same man who had torn the clothes from her breasts and kissed her as if he would die if he couldn't taste her skin?

"We've been invited to attend a pleasure garden tonight," she said. "My sister-in-law, Lady Hero, is quite fond of Harte's Folly and wishes to go to the theater there tonight. Will you come?"

His lips thinned. "Your brother Griffin will be there as well?"

"Yes."

Megs half expected dissent, but Godric's mouth relaxed

into a rueful smile. "I suppose I'll have to see him sometime—after all, I am married to his sister."

She shouldn't feel this excited at the possibility of his attending a play with her, but she did. Just to make sure, she asked, "Then you'll come?"

He inclined his head gravely. "Yes."

She nodded absently, turning to run a finger down a crease in one of the old apple tree's branches. "Godric?"

"Yes?" He'd stepped closer. She had the feeling that if she turned, she might be in his arms.

Megs shivered and concentrated on tracing patterns in the bark. "How did my brother know you were the Ghost of St. Giles?"

He was silent and she could almost hear him thinking. "I was careless. He followed me back from St. Giles one night."

She knit her brows. "St. Giles? Whyever would Griffin have been in St. Giles at night?"

"You don't know?"

Well, no one could withstand *that* kind of line. She turned and found she *was* nearly in his arms. He was looking down at her with his now-familiar puzzled half-frown.

"Know what?" she asked, breathless. Silly, of course. He wouldn't tell her, would fob her off with some transparent excuse as gentlemen always did to the ladies in their care.

But he surprised her. "Your brother Griffin used to have a business in St. Giles."

She blinked, stunned by both his honesty and the information. "But...Griffin has never been in business. He's never had to..." She trailed off at the expression on Godric's face. "Has he?"

Her husband shrugged his shoulders uncomfortably. "I don't know the state of your brother's finances. I only know that before he married Lady Hero, he ran a business in St. Giles."

Her brows knit. "What type of business?"

He watched her for what seemed almost a minute, and she waited to see if he'd answer.

Finally, he sighed. "A gin still."

"What?"

Her mouth fell open. Of all the things for her brother—the son of a *marquess*—to be doing, running an illegal—and immoral—gin still was the last thing she'd guess. Why would he? Griffin had skirted the edge of impropriety before his marriage, had had rather a terrible reputation as a rake, but she knew him. Deep down he was a good man, a man who wouldn't be doing such a horrible thing unless he were truly hard up for money, and why would he be? Their family was landed, had plenty of funds—

Her thoughts abruptly ran aground because she realized that she didn't actually know the state of her family's finances. She was a lady. Ladies didn't inquire about such things—it was considered vulgar. When she'd wanted a dress, when she'd come out and needed an entirely new wardrobe, she'd never asked if they could afford it, because they could.

Couldn't they?

Except now she remembered small things. The time Mama had suggested the less expensive striped silk rather than the embroidered. Megs had liked the color of the stripe better anyway—a lovely rose—so she hadn't thought much about it at the time. And then there had been the time the modiste had become quite snippy, insisting she hadn't been paid yet. Mama had said it was a mistake, but what if it hadn't been?

What if her family had been in financial straits—secret financial straits—and she'd never even known enough to *ask*?

"Does he still have that business in St. Giles?" she asked Godric in a very small voice.

"No." He shook his head at once. "He closed it— actually it burned—just before he married Lady Hero."

She nodded, feeling deflated. "I'm glad. But if he needed money, how does he make it now?"

"I don't know," Godric said gently. "We haven't been exactly on speaking terms the last couple of years. However, I'm sure Lady Hero's dowry was more than adequate to see to their needs."

A sudden, horrible thought crossed Megs's mind. "And my dowry? Was it adequate?"

"Your brother didn't offer one."

Her eyes widened. "But—"

"It's all right." He held out his hands, forestalling her protest. "I have more than enough money. I never needed your dowry, Megs."

Well, she supposed she should be glad of that at least. Megs poked at the apple tree rather irritably before heaving a sigh. "I'm sorry I didn't know of this before. You must've been terribly angry when my brother made his demand."

She peeked at him from under her eyelashes.

He shrugged, his face gentle. "I've already told you: I was angry at him, yes, but never at you. It wasn't such a hardship to marry you, after all."

Faint praise was better than none, she supposed. Or at least she told herself that as she pressed a fingernail into the bark of the tree. "I still don't understand. Why did he never tell me what straits we were in?"

"I don't know." He shrugged. "I expect he was protecting you."

Megs had rather dark thoughts about gentlemen who believed it best to *protect* ladies by leaving them in ignorance. At least Godric had told her the truth about her brother and his still.

She sighed and pushed away from the tree. "I suppose I ought to go now and inquire of Daniels if my new gowns will be ready in time for the theater."

But as she made to walk past him, he forestalled her by the simple expedient of grasping her hand.

His fingers were cool as they wrapped around hers, and she froze, looking at him before he dropped her hand again as if her warmth had burned him.

He licked his lips, and if she didn't know better, she'd say that Godric was nervous. "I actually came out here to tell you something."

She tilted her head in inquiry. "Yes?"

"I've decided"—he focused those clear gray eyes on her face—"I'd like to consummate our marriage tonight."

SHE'D GOTTEN WHAT she'd wanted: Godric's agreement to come to her bed. Why, then, was she so nervous at the prospect?

A wave of laughter rose from the theater audience, and Megs focused on the stage where a pretty actress dressed as a young man was strutting about. The actress turned and threw a mischievous glance over her shoulder as she made some quip, and the audience roared again. Next to Megs, Hero was giggling and even Griffin wore a grin, but Godric wasn't even smiling.

Perhaps he was as nervous as she about tonight.

The four of them sat in an elegant box over the stage at Harte's Folly. Swaths of red velvet lined the interior of the box and gilt trimmed the rail. A small table of wine, tiny cakes, fruit, nuts, and cheeses sat to the side, and Megs couldn't help reflecting how expensive the theater box must be to rent. If Griffin had been in financial straits three years ago, he didn't appear to be so now.

But then he hadn't seemed to lack for funds before marrying Hero either.

Megs blew out a restless breath, wishing she could have fifteen minutes alone with her brother. Wishing she could forget that when she and Godric returned home tonight, he intended to bed her.

She glanced down and then sideways at him. He wore a coffee-colored suit tonight, the cuffs and pockets worked in dull gold thread. Underneath, a silvery blue waistcoat hugged his torso, emphasizing the flatness of his belly. She'd seen him—briefly—without a shirt and had been stunned by the image. What would he look like entirely nude?

He seemed to sense her regard. His chin moved infinitesimally and his eyes flicked to her face. She caught her breath. His eyelids were half lowered, nearly but not quite hiding the gleam of those intense clear gray eyes. He looked at her as if he were deciding how, exactly, to eat her. Without thought, her lips parted and his gaze dropped, his eyes brooding as his nostrils flared slightly. Then he raised them slowly again, staring into her eyes, and Megs forgot entirely how to breathe.

The audience broke into applause and Megs jerked at the sudden, thundering sound.

Griffin grunted. "Shall I fetch some ices before the second half begins?"

Hero smiled up at her husband. "Yes, please."

Griffin nodded before glancing at Godric, his expression wary. "Join me?"

Godric raised his brows but rose willingly.

Beside her, Hero stirred and held out her hand. "I see my brother across the way. Will you accompany me to greet him?"

"Yes, of course." Megs rose, staring worriedly at the retreating backs of her husband and brother.

"Don't fret." Hero drew her hand through her arm as they began strolling companionably toward the opposite side of the theater. The corridor behind the boxes was crowded as everyone took the opportunity during the interval to find acquaintances or to simply parade to show to best advantage their costumes. "Griffin and Godric will come to terms."

"I wish I were as certain as you."

Hero squeezed her hand reassuringly. "Griffin loves both you and me, and Godric is very fond of you, I know. They both have incentive to make up this little quarrel."

Megs slanted a glance at her sister-in-law, strolling serenely in a mist-green frock trimmed in blond lace. "Godric is fond of me? However can you tell?"

Hero looked at her, amused. "By the way he cares for you, silly. He made very sure you had the best seat when you arrived—next to me so we might gossip. He filled a plate for you with cakes and grapes—no walnuts, as he knows you aren't particularly fond of them—and the very fact he's come to the opera tonight... well. I half expected him to decline, I must tell you. He's been a veritable hermit these last couple of years. Hardly anyone has seen him about in society. No, everything he's done tonight, small matters as they are, has been for *you*, sister."

Megs blinked. Was it true? Did Godric have feelings, however small, for her? He had, after all, conceded to her wish to try to make a child. The mere reminder made her body flush with heat, but she felt a pang of disquiet as well. When she'd been back at Laurelwood, dreaming up this plan to come to London and seduce her husband, he had been a mere cardboard figure. She'd known him only from his infrequent, curt letters. Bedding a cardboard man had seemed straightforward enough.

Bedding *Godric* was an entirely different matter.

He was real, flesh and blood, a man with powerful feelings—though he did his best to hide them from the world. Only now, at this terribly late date, did it occur to her that her emotions might be endangered if she lay with Godric.

Megs bit her lip. Emotional entanglement was not something that she'd accounted for. Roger was the love of her life, his loss a pain she felt every day. She had no other way to make a child for herself but to lie with Godric, but to *feel* for him as well—that seemed like a betrayal of her love for Roger.

A betrayal of Roger himself.

Hero suddenly squeezed her hand. "There she is."

Megs blinked. "Who?"

"Hippolyta Royle," Hero murmured. "The lady there in that delicious shade of dark coffee brown and pink."

Megs followed the discreet incline of Hero's head.

A tall lady stood by herself, watching the crowd with hooded eyes. She couldn't be called beautiful, but with her tawny complexion, dark hair, and regal bearing, she was certainly striking.

"Who is she?" Megs wondered aloud.

Hero huffed softly beside her. "You'd know if you hadn't been hiding yourself away in the wilds of the countryside for two years. Miss Royle is a rather mysterious heiress. She appeared in London out of the blue a couple of months ago. Some say she was raised in Italy or even the East Indies. I've thought that she must be a very interesting person, but we've not been introduced yet."

They watched as Miss Royle turned and began strolling away.

"And it looks like I won't have the opportunity tonight either," Hero said ruefully. "I see no one to make the proper introductions. But here's Maximus's box. Shall we?"

Megs nodded as Hero led the way into the splendid box. It was directly opposite Griffin's rented box and so was over the other side of the stage from where they sat.

Inside, the box was as luxurious as Griffin's—perhaps more so. Two ladies sat by themselves, and the elder of the two held out her hand at their entrance.

"Hero, how lovely to see you, my dear." Miss Bathilda Picklewood had raised both Hero and her younger sister, Phoebe, after their parents' death. A plump lady who wore her soft gray hair in ringlets across her forehead, she held a small, elderly King Charles spaniel on her lap.

Hero stepped gracefully forward and kissed Miss Picklewood on the cheek. "How are you, Cousin Bathilda?"

"Quite well," Miss Picklewood said, "but I do declare it has been an age since you brought William 'round."

As if to emphasize her words, the spaniel gave one sharp bark.

Hero smiled. "I shall correct my error as soon as possible. Tomorrow afternoon, in fact."

"Splendid!"

"Who is that with you, Hero?" the second lady asked, and Megs felt a pang, for it was Lady Phoebe Batten.

Megs stepped closer, hoping the dim candlelight in the box would help. "It's me, Phoebe. Megs."

"Of course," Phoebe said in a confused flurry. Her eyes were focused on Megs's face now, but Megs had the sinking feeling that the other woman still couldn't see her properly. "Are you enjoying the play?"

"Oh, yes," Megs said, though she'd hardly paid attention. "It's been a while since I've been to one, so this is quite a treat."

"Robin Goodfellow is so clever," Miss Picklewood said, and Megs scrambled a bit before she remembered that was the name of the actress in man's clothing. "I believe I've enjoyed every play she's been in."

"Harte was very smart to lure Miss Goodfellow away from the Royal," a deep voice said behind them.

Both Megs and Hero turned to see Maximus Batten, the Duke of Wakefield, standing in the entrance to the box, two ices in his hands.

He quirked an eyebrow. "Had I known you'd join us, Hero, I would've gotten more ices."

"Griffin and Mr. St. John have gone to get them for us," Hero said. "You remember Lady Margaret?"

"Naturally." The duke executed a very elegant bow, considering he was holding an ice in each hand.

"Your Grace." Megs curtsied. She'd been acquainted

with the Duke of Wakefield for years—he was a political ally of her brother Thomas—but she didn't know him well. He'd always struck her as a rather daunting gentleman.

"You know Harte of Harte's Folly?" Hero asked her brother curiously. She took one of the ices and placed it in Phoebe's hands.

"Not personally, no," His Grace replied as he offered the remaining ice to Miss Picklewood. "Actually, I'm not even sure that 'Harte' is but one man—the backers of the pleasure garden could be a syndicate of businessmen—but in any case it's well known that Miss Goodfellow was lured away from her previous theater, probably for an outrageous sum of money. It was a smart business move by whoever runs Harte's Folly, though. The pleasure garden needed a renowned actress."

"And Miss Goodfellow is the most renowned breeches-role actress in London," Viscount d'Arque drawled as he strolled into the box. "Your Grace." He swept a graceful bow. "Ladies."

"D'Arque." The duke eyed him noncommittally.

The viscount's gaze swept over the ladies appreciatively before landing on Megs. He stepped forward and in a swift move had her fingers in his. "Lady Margaret, you're looking enchanting this evening."

Megs's eyes widened as he bent over her fingers.

Directly behind the viscount was Griffin…and Godric.

"THE INTERVAL MUST be nearly over," Artemis Greaves murmured. "Perhaps we should return to the box?"

"Oh, pish." Lady Penelope tossed her head, making the

jeweled pins in her dark locks sparkle. "Don't fret so. I haven't yet greeted the Duke of Wakefield."

Artemis sighed silently, shifting Bon Bon in her arms as they strolled the corridor behind the theater boxes. The fluffy white dog gave a groan before falling back to sleep. Artemis wished—not for the first time—that Penelope had even a pinch of sense. The little dog, while quite sweet and docile, was getting too old to be dragged everywhere. She'd yipped when Artemis had lifted her from the carriage, and Artemis suspected rheumatism in the dog's back legs.

"I don't see why everyone thinks her so fascinating," Penelope muttered now, drawing Artemis's attention.

"Who?"

"*Her*." Penelope waved an irritated hand to a tall lady disappearing into a box. "That Hippolyta Royle. Silliest name I've ever heard. She's as dark as a savage from Africa, nearly as tall as a man, and not even *titled*."

"She's also rumored to be fabulously wealthy," Artemis murmured before she could think.

Penelope turned to look at her, eyes narrowed.

Oh, dear.

"*I* am the wealthiest heiress in England," Penelope hissed. "Everyone knows this."

"Of course," Artemis murmured placatingly, stroking the sleeping Bon Bon.

Penelope huffed one more exasperated breath and then her tone smoothed as she said, "Oh, here we are."

And Artemis looked up to see they were at the door to the duke's box.

Penelope swept in—or at least attempted to. The box, as it turned out, was rather crowded. Artemis squeezed in behind her cousin and glanced around. Lady Hero was here with Lady Margaret as well as Lady Phoebe, Miss Picklewood, the duke himself, Lord Griffin, and Mr. St. John, who appeared to be in a staring contest with Viscount d'Arque.

Well, at least the evening wouldn't be boring.

Penelope was saying something—probably outrageous—to draw the gentlemen's attention. Artemis sidled over to Lady Phoebe and sat down next to her.

Phoebe turned her face, leaning close to discreetly inhale. "Artemis?"

"Yes." Artemis felt quite proud. She'd taken to wearing the same scent—lemons and bay leaf—when she realized that Lady Phoebe sometimes used smell to identify people. She suspected that the other woman could see very little at all when the light was dim—such as tonight at the theater. "I've brought Bon Bon, though she's feeling rather low. I think she has rheumatism."

"Oh, poor thing." Phoebe stroked gentle fingers through the little dog's white fur. "What is going on with the gentlemen? They seemed quite tense when Lord d'Arque entered."

Artemis tipped her head toward the younger woman until they nearly touched. "Lord d'Arque has been flirting with Lady Margaret, and her husband, Mr. St. John, has taken exception. They made rather a scene at the Kershaw ball."

"Really?" Phoebe raised her eyebrows, her hazel eyes dancing in her soft, round face. She might be Hero's sister, but the women were entirely different. Where Hero was tall and willowy, Phoebe was short and plump. "I'm sorry to hear that for Lady Margaret's sake, but... I do wish I had seen it." Her mouth curved rather sadly. Except for events where her family carefully guarded her, Lady Phoebe did not go out in society. "I hope you don't think the worse of me for it."

"Oh, no, darling." Artemis patted her knee. "If it weren't for gentlemen behaving terribly at balls, I would've died of boredom long before this."

Phoebe laughed softly. "What are they doing now?"

"Not much. Lady Penelope is dominating the conversation." Artemis sighed. "I'm afraid she's set her cap at your brother."

Phoebe cocked her head. "Has she?"

"Yes, though I don't suppose she has much chance."

Phoebe shrugged. "As much as any lady, I suppose. My brother must marry eventually, and Lady Penelope is a fabulous heiress. He might think it a great advantage."

"Really?" Artemis frowned, watching as the duke listened to Penelope's chatter with his head propped on his left hand. He shifted restlessly, the red stone in his gold signet ring catching the light. His expression verged on boredom. "He doesn't seem particularly enthralled by her."

"Maximus is enthralled only by politics and his war against the gin trade," Phoebe said, sounding much too wise for her years. "I don't think he has any heart left over to give to a lady."

Artemis shivered. "I wonder if Lady Penelope quite knows what she's trying to ensnare?"

Phoebe turned her head slightly toward Artemis, her hazel eyes a bit sad. "Would she care? She seeks my brother's title, not the man beneath."

"No, I suppose you're quite right," Artemis said slowly. The realization was rather sad.

Lady Penelope leaned forward with a seductive smile, touched the duke's sleeve lightly, and turned toward the box's door.

Artemis recognized Penelope's usual farewell to a handsome gentleman and began gathering Bon Bon. "I'm afraid we're leaving now, but it was so nice to chat with you, Phoebe."

The other woman smiled vaguely. "Enjoy the rest of the play."

Then Artemis was making her way to the door, trotting to try to catch up with Penelope.

"Did you see the way the duke hung upon my words?" Lady Penelope hissed when Artemis was abreast of her.

"Oh, yes," Artemis said, not entirely truthfully.

"I think that went *very* well," Penelope said with evident satisfaction.

"I am so glad." Penelope in a good mood might just be amenable to granting a favor. She cleared her throat delicately. "I wonder if I might have the morning off this Friday?"

Penelope's brows drew together in irritation. "Whatever for?"

Artemis swallowed. "It's visiting day."

"I've already told you that you need to simply forget him," Penelope scolded.

Artemis kept silent, for there wasn't anything she could say that would help her cause—she knew because she'd already tried in the past.

Her cousin heaved a long-suffering sigh. "Very well."

"Thank you—"

But Penelope's thoughts were already back with her own affairs. "I saw His Grace's gaze observe my décolletage at least once. *That*, in any case, is something that Miss Royle cannot compete with. She's as flat as a boy."

Artemis's brows drew together. "I wasn't aware Miss Royle *was* competing."

"Don't be naïve, Cousin," Penelope said as they made their box again. "Any lady with the possibility of success vies for the Duke of Wakefield's attention. Fortunately, that group is very small indeed."

Penelope sank into a red velvet chair just as the curtain rose again, and Artemis took the chair next to her. The first part of the play had been quite diverting—not to mention very risqué—and she was looking forward to watching Miss Goodfellow match wits with the male actors.

Penelope shifted next to her, glancing down at the floor and then to the table between the chairs. "Drat."

"What is it?" Artemis whispered. The orchestra had launched into a lively tune.

"I've misplaced my fan." She looked up, her brow furrowed. "I must've left it in the duke's box. Too bad, because if the play had not already started, I could go back and spend more time with the duke." She shrugged. "But you'll have to get it now."

"Of course." Artemis sighed silently.

She placed Bon Bon gently on her seat before leaving the box. No one was in the corridor now, and Artemis gathered her skirts to run lightly down the hall. She paused outside the duke's box to catch her breath and pat at her hair, and as she did so, she couldn't help but hear the voices within, for the door was not shut fully.

"...must belong to Lady Penelope. It's far too expensive to be Artemis's," Miss Picklewood was saying.

"Who?" came the duke's bored drawl.

"Artemis Greaves," Miss Picklewood said. "Come, Maximus, you must've noticed that Lady Penelope has a companion."

Artemis put her hand up to push the door open.

"You mean that invisible little woman who trails her everywhere like a pale wraith?"

The duke's deep, masculine voice seemed to cut straight through Artemis. In the back of her mind, she noticed absently that her fingers were trembling on the door. Quietly, she balled her fist and let it drop.

"Maximus!" Miss Picklewood's tone was shocked.

"You must admit it's an apt description," the duke replied impatiently. "And I don't think I can be faulted for not knowing the woman's name when she does everything she can to blend into the woodwork."

"Artemis is my friend," Phoebe said, her tone very firm for one so young.

Artemis took a deep breath and carefully, *silently*, backed away from the door. She had a sudden horrific image of the door opening by itself and those within finding her there, listening.

She whirled and ran back the way she came. Phoebe's kind words should've healed any hurt the duke had inflicted so carelessly. He didn't know her, didn't care to know her. What a man like him thought of a woman like her should make no difference at all to her.

But no matter how many times she repeated this to herself, the arrow of his words still stuck in her bleeding breast.

And she still quivered with rage.

*   *   *

FOR A MAN who prided himself on his intelligence, it had taken Godric a ridiculously long time to figure out why Megs really wanted to talk to d'Arque. It wasn't until they were in the duke's box and she leaned close to d'Arque when she thought Godric wasn't looking and said, "You must miss Roger Fraser-Burnsby terribly," that the light had dawned.

D'Arque had been Fraser-Burnsby's best friend. It was at the viscount's ball, in fact, that the news had been first brought that Fraser-Burnsby had been murdered. Megs wanted the man as an informant, not as a lover.

And with that realization, all his male jealousy had calmed, letting Godric think again. Not only was d'Arque Fraser-Burnsby's friend, but he was also one of the men mentioned by Winter Makepeace.

One of the men who might be behind the lassie snatchers.

So, as they'd all left Wakefield's box, Godric had turned to d'Arque and, ignoring Megs's expression of apprehension and Reading's narrowed eyes, invited the man back to their box.

He'd had the pleasure of seeing swiftly masked surprise on the viscount's face before the man had accepted the invitation.

Which was how Godric came to find himself sitting between the two men he liked least in the world.

The play began again and Megs and Lady Hero, sitting in front of the men, turned rapt faces toward the stage.

D'Arque waited a beat before murmuring under his breath, "Your courtesy astounds me, St. John. Should I beware a dagger 'tween my ribs?"

Godric turned his head very slightly toward the other

man, his face expressionless. He might understand that
Megs wanted nothing more than information from this
fop, but that didn't forgive the viscount's flirtation with
his wife. "Do you deserve one?"

On his other side, Griffin sighed heavily before muttering between his teeth, "No doubt he does, St. John, but
it might disturb the ladies should the box suddenly flood
with blood."

A wave of laughter rose through the theater as evi-
dently the actors did something amusing onstage.

Godric cleared his throat. "Actually, I wanted to know
what you've told my wife about Fraser-Burnsby."

D'Arque stiffened. "I told her the truth: Roger was a
very good friend of mine."

Godric nodded. "Do you know anything about his
death?"

The viscount's eyes narrowed. He was a notorious
rake, a man who seemed to spend his days—and nights—
chasing women, but Godric had never thought him stupid.
For a moment he waited for the question—why was he
asking about Fraser-Burnsby's death in the first place?—
then d'Arque shrugged. "All the world knows that the
Ghost of St. Giles killed my friend."

Godric felt Lord Griffin's swift glance. "But he didn't."

"And how do you know this?" The viscount's words
were scoffing, but his expression was reluctantly interested.

"I just do," Godric said low. "Someone murdered
Roger Fraser-Burnsby and blamed it on a convenient cul-
prit: the Ghost of St. Giles."

"Even if that was so," d'Arque whispered, "what has
that to do with your wife?"

Reading inhaled as if to interject something, but Godric

was faster. "She was fond of Fraser-Burnsby and has taken up the cause of finding his murderer, I'm afraid."

"What?" Reading's exclamation was overloud, and both the ladies in front moved as if to turn and see what the commotion was about. Fortunately, something happened onstage at that moment, eliciting a gasp from the audience.

Godric waited until he was certain that the ladies' attention was on the play. Then he sent a look to Reading. "I have no doubt you'd know this yourself had you asked your sister about her return to London."

A dull flush lit Reading's face. "My relationship with Megs is none of your business—"

"False," Godric clipped out. "You made certain of that the day you signed the marriage settlement."

"Fascinating as this discussion is, gentlemen," d'Arque broke in quietly, "I'm more interested in the death of my friend. Who killed Roger if not the Ghost?"

"I don't know," Godric said.

The viscount leaned back in his chair and rubbed a hand over his jaw. In the silence a feminine voice rose onstage in a bawdy song.

At last d'Arque looked at Godric. "If your assertion is true—which, I am not yet ready to entirely concede— then Roger's murder wasn't a mere robbery or matter of happenstance. Someone killed him and then attempted to cover up the crime."

Godric nodded.

"But that can't be," d'Arque said slowly as if talking to himself. "Roger had no enemies. Everyone liked him—they had ever since we were both schoolboys. He'd smile at the most misanthropic bully and suddenly they were a jolly bosom-bow. I truly can't think of anyone who would've wanted to kill him."

"There were no witnesses?" Reading asked.

D'Arque's eyes flicked to him. "There was a footman. He was the one who came to tell us of the news during a ball at my home."

"Did you question him?" Godric asked.

"Only briefly." The viscount hesitated. "His name was Harris. He disappeared in the weeks following Roger's death. I remember a note came later asking that his things be sent to the One Horned Goat in St. Giles."

"This footman, he was the one who reported that the Ghost was the murderer?" Reading asked.

D'Arque nodded.

"Perhaps he was bribed," Reading murmured.

Godric leaned forward. "Had he been with Fraser-Burnsby long?"

"No." D'Arque slowly shook his head, a muscle jumping in his jaw. "Roger had hired him only the month before."

All three men were silent, contemplating the obvious conclusion.

"Damn it!" d'Arque hissed low. "I spent months searching for Roger's killer, but it never occurred to me that it might not be the Ghost of St. Giles."

The viscount's outburst seemed genuine enough. But then Godric had seen beggars weep real tears for the pain of their crippled legs—just before stealing a purse and running away.

"What about your friend Seymour?" he asked the viscount. "Wasn't he killed in St. Giles as well?"

Reading started to say something, then closed his mouth.

D'Arque's eyes narrowed. "What has that to do with Roger's death?"

Godric shrugged, for he could not reveal what he knew of Seymour's death. The viscount sighed and leaned back in his chair, watching the stage, though Godric doubted he saw anything. "We were all friends, Kershaw, Seymour, Roger, and I. Kershaw and Seymour helped me search for the Ghost of St. Giles before...before Seymour was killed in such an untimely manner."

His eyelids flickered and Godric took note. He knew from Winter Makepeace that d'Arque had known about Seymour's involvement in the lassie snatchers, had in fact helped cover up the true nature of Seymour's death for the sake of his widow.

Makepeace seemed to think that d'Arque had not been involved with the illegal workshop and the lassie snatchers. Godric decided to reserve judgment. After all, if d'Arque had been the other partner in the workshop, it would've been smart of him to lie low for a bit, convince Makepeace that he had indeed cleared up the entire lassie snatcher evil.

And then when the coast was clear, he could start up operations again.

"Odd," Godric said softly, "that two of four friends should be killed in St. Giles."

D'Arque frowned as if considering. "Don't think that I hadn't thought of the matter before now, but that's just it. There was no link between the killings." He turned to meet Godric's eyes. "None at all."

The audience roared and rose to their feet, clapping. Godric's gaze jerked to his wife, her head together with Lady Hero's, whispering some feminine secret. The play was obviously over.

The viscount caught his arm.

Godric looked down at the hand on his sleeve.

D'Arque let go of his arm, his face darkening with something that might've been embarrassment. "I wish to continue this discussion."

"Don't worry." Godric stood, watching as Megs turned and beamed at him, all glorious, vibrant life. Everything he was not. Everything worth protecting. "We will."

Chapter Ten

*"Hold on tight," the Hellequin grunted as he guided the
great black horse toward the far shore.*
*"Do you care for my welfare, then?" Faith leaned forward
and asked in the Hellequin's ear.*
His eyes slid sideways as he gave her a sardonic glance.
" 'Twould not do for you to fall in the River of Sorrows."
"Why not?"
*He shrugged his massive shoulders. "The waters would
think you a suicide and then you, too, would spend the
rest of eternity drowning."*
*The great black horse lurched as it climbed out of the
inky waters, and as it did so, Faith pushed Despair
into the river....*
—From *The Legend of the Hellequin*

Megs plucked nervously at the ties to her wrapper. She
stood alone in her room—well, alone save for Her Grace
and her three puppies, sleeping under her bed. She and
Godric had returned home in near silence from Harte's
Folly. If she didn't know better, she might think her husband as filled with trepidation over their belated wedding
night as she.

But that was silly, wasn't it? He was a man. Even if he'd
initially turned her down because of the memory of his

late wife, he still must, by his very nature as a male, take the marriage act more cavalierly than a woman. Why else would he suddenly change his mind over the matter?

Megs bit her lip, fearing that she might be lying to herself. She hadn't seen Godric act cavalierly about *anything* since her arrival in London. He must have a reason—a deliberate reason—to acquiesce to her. Damnation! She should've questioned him more in the garden this afternoon instead of being so overwhelmed with excitement and joy that she'd all but lost the power of thought. She had the feeling that whatever his reasons, it was important that she understand them—understand *him*. After tonight he would be her husband in fact as well as in name. She owed him the courtesy of at least caring about his motives. She was determined not to feel guilt, though. He was her husband and this was the legal—*and natural*—consequence of marriage.

Even if he'd been coerced into the marriage in the first place.

She heaved a sigh and glanced again at the pink china clock on her dressing table. It was well past midnight—and nearly an hour since they'd returned home. Had he forgotten?

Had he fallen asleep?

Megs tiptoed toward the door that connected her room to Godric's. If he'd fallen asleep, she'd just have to wake him up again, damn it.

The door opened abruptly and Megs stopped in her tracks, blinking.

For a moment Godric looked equally startled at finding her just inside the door. He wore a banyan, beneath which she could see his nightshirt and those ridiculous embroidered slippers.

Megs stifled a horrible, overwhelming urge to giggle.

Godric shut the door behind him. "I thought..." He stopped and his brow wrinkled before he began again. "That is, I'd like to talk to you prior to..." He cleared his throat, a nearly subaudible sound like the distant rumble of thunder. "Come."

He held out his hand, his long fingers gracefully curved. Megs gulped. He hadn't changed his mind, had he?

"Megs." His eyes were clear and calm and his entire attention was focused on her.

She remembered the feel of his mouth, hot and demanding, on her nipple. Her face flamed and she placed her hand in his.

He tugged her gently, pulling her down to the chairs by the door.

She sat, her hands primly tucked together in her lap, and looked at him.

"If I do this..."

She frowned, fingers flexing on her skirts.

"*When* we do this," he corrected himself, "I want a promise from you."

"Anything," she said, quite recklessly.

His face was grave and serious, but she found herself so distracted by the long sweep of his dark eyelashes that for a moment she didn't hear his words. "Once you know you're with child, I'd like you to leave London. Return to Laurelwood Manor and live there."

Her mouth dropped open, and it was stupid really— she was using him as a... a *stud*, but she was unaccountably *wounded*. "You want me gone?"

"I want you safe."

"Why am I safer at Laurelwood?" Her eyes narrowed as soon as she said the words, for she understood all at once. "You don't want me finding Roger's murderer."

A muscle ticked in the side of his jaw. "No."

She straightened, glaring. "You can't make me stop."

His lips thinned. "Agreed. But I can certainly withhold myself from your bed if you refuse my terms."

A baby or justice for Roger...she didn't want to make that choice. She wanted—needed—both.

Megs stood abruptly, glancing wildly about the bedroom, trying to think how she could make him see reason. Godric was a man of logic, but she knew he felt deeply as well. His love for his first wife was testament to that. She looked back at him. "If it had been your Clara, would you give up until you'd found her murderer?"

His mouth flattened. "Of course not, but I am a man—"

"And I am a woman." She spread her arms wide, her fingers grasping to make her emotions concrete so he would understand. "Don't paint my love any less than yours because of my sex. I loved Roger with all of my heart. When he died, I thought I would die with him. I have the *right* to find his murderer. To make sure he is avenged. I'll not stop until that mission is accomplished. Please do not try and dissuade me, for on this subject I will remain adamant."

He looked at her, silent for so long that she feared he would simply leave her. At last he inhaled. "Very well. While you remain in London—while we try to make a baby between us—you will continue your search for Fraser-Burnsby's murderer."

She eyed him suspiciously. "But?"

"But the minute you know you carry a child—*my*

child—you will leave, whether or not you have found the murderer."

She bit her lip, thinking. It wasn't everything she wanted, but she was well aware that he could've simply refused her outright. It was a compromise.

She'd just have to work harder at finding Roger's murderer.

Megs lifted her chin and stuck out her hand. "Deal."

A corner of his mouth twitched upward as he took her hand in his and shook it solemnly. "Will you at least permit me to help you in your search? To go into St. Giles in your stead?"

She inhaled, suddenly feeling shaky. "Of course."

He inclined his head gravely, still holding her hand in a firm grip. "Very well, then. I shall help you to find Roger Fraser-Burnsby's murderer whilst you remain in London. I shall bed you every night. And *you* shall leave this house and London for the safety of my country estate when I get you with child. Fair?"

"Fair."

"But, Megs…"

"Hmm?" She'd become somewhat distracted, ever since he'd used the words *bed* and *every night*.

"I retain the right to revisit the discussion about your lover's murderer," he said softly. Firmly. "We may yet find another way more amenable to us both."

She should argue, for he wasn't exactly playing properly—they'd already shook on the terms. But his hand was warm and strong, his long, elegant fingers wrapped around her own, and the *bed* was right there.

She'd been waiting for this since she'd come to London.

So she nodded jerkily. "Very well, if you insist."

"I do," he whispered, and stood as he pulled her up in front of him.

She was too close suddenly, staring at the pulse that beat at the side of his throat. She swallowed, opening her mouth—

And he bent his head and kissed her. It wasn't like the kiss in St. Giles. That had been wild and angry and passionate. This was a soft kiss, nearly chaste, as if he questioned with his lips: *Is this what you want? Am I* who *you want?* For a moment her thoughts stuttered. He wasn't who she wanted. She wanted Roger—*he* was the love of her life. The one to whom she'd given her virginity in happy bliss. The one she'd nearly died mourning for.

But Godric's lips were slow. Persuasive. Moving over hers almost curiously, as if she were a new, unknown creature. Something foreign and precious. His hands rose, drifting over her arms, skimming her shoulders, slipping up her neck to cradle her face as he angled his head, licking along her bottom lip. She gasped, a soft parting of her mouth, and he slid in, not intrusively, but almost playfully, touching her teeth, meeting her tongue in sweet greeting. It was suddenly too much.

She pulled back, staring wide-eyed at him, her chest rising and falling faster than it should've.

"What is it?" His voice was low, raspy.

She swallowed. "Nothing. It's just…" She bit her lip. "Do we have to kiss?"

His eyebrows winged up his forehead. "Not if you don't like it."

"It's not…" She shook her head, unable to find the words. She couldn't tell him that she didn't want to think about *him* while they did this. That she just wanted him to be a male body, not Godric the man.

His face had closed now, though, looking cold and nearly remote. "We don't have to do this tonight."

"No," she said shakily. "I mean..."

She inhaled, desperately trying to find equilibrium. She'd destroyed something just now, she could feel it, but if she let him walk through that door again, they might never do this.

She opened her eyes, looking at him imploringly. "Please. I want this now."

He watched her a moment more, his eyes unreadable, then inclined his head. "Very well."

He indicated the bed and she drew off her wrapper self-consciously before climbing in. She shivered as her bare legs slid along cold sheets.

Godric took off his banyan and slippers, standing in his nightshirt as he looked at her consideringly. "Would you like me to snuff the candles?"

She nodded gratefully. "Yes, please."

He didn't say anything as he snuffed the candelabra on the dresser and the one by the bed. The fire had already been banked for the night and the dull glow of the embers didn't give much light. Megs listened as Godric lifted the covers of her bed, felt the dip as his weight settled beside her.

She started to tense, and then she felt his touch, gentle but sure. The time to change her mind was past.

Megs tried to think of Roger, to summon his dear face to the front of her brain, but Godric was running his hand down her side, distracting her, making Roger vanish like a reflection in a pond disturbed. Godric leaned up on one elbow, his bulk a dark shape above her. It occurred to her that if it were any other man, she might fear him now.

But this was Godric.

She felt his breath on her face as he leaned closer, his hand on her hip. He paused to caress her through the fine lawn of her chemise; then he trailed his fingers down her legs, slowly, carefully. This lovemaking was sweet and gentle—and it *shouldn't* have aroused her.

Her breath was coming too fast. Perhaps she was a wanton, she thought rather wildly. Perhaps having tasted of fleshly delights, she'd become addicted without even knowing it, so that now even a near-impersonal touch had lit a forgotten fuse within her.

He didn't seem particularly affected. *His* breaths were even and calm. He'd reached the hem of her chemise now and pulled it upward, baring her knees, her thighs, her feminine triangle. He laid the skirt of her chemise on her stomach, quite circumspectly, and then his hand moved downward, back to her knee, naked now. He rested his hand there, warm and large, and she bit her lip to keep from making any noise.

His breath wasn't calm anymore—thank goodness for that. He traced lacy patterns on the inside of her knee with just his fingertips. Slowly, so slowly, working his way toward the juncture of her thighs. She parted her legs, offering him more room, inviting those fingers closer to her center, but he kept away, trailing along the crease that separated her leg from her belly.

He bent toward her then, and she had the idea that he meant to kiss her before he remembered and caught himself. Now she wanted to pull him close. To seal her lips to his and tell him that she'd been mistaken earlier. That she *did* want him to kiss her.

But that would let in thoughts, emotions, that she didn't

want to consider right now. This act was so she could have a baby. That and only that.

His fingers were stroking over her pubic hair, brushing lightly, drawing closer to the folds below. She tilted her head away, staring at the fireplace, trying to keep her equilibrium. She wanted to touch him, to feel the warmth, the beating heart attached to that seeking hand, but she'd already decided to make this impersonal. It wouldn't do to change her mind now when she wasn't thinking clearly.

And then he touched her there and all thought fled her mind. His fingers slid into her intimate recesses, where only she and Roger had ever been, and she should've felt invaded, but God help her she didn't.

She didn't.

The sob welled within her, unstoppable, unstiflable. She stuffed her fist into her mouth, afraid to make a sound and break apart this intimacy.

He brushed against that small bit of flesh and she jerked as if he'd stabbed her. She wanted . . . more. She wanted to grind herself against him, wanted to moan, loud and free, wanted to take his hand and make him touch her more firmly. But she did none of those things, for she was a lady who had asked of him an impossible price and if he was gentleman enough to accede to her wishes, the least she could do was bear it with composure.

Even if it might kill her.

He continued with those light, relentless brushes, and she felt herself begin to swell. To become engorged with a kind of liquid pleasure, heating, pulsing in her loins. She'd felt this before, knew what it led to.

She grabbed his wrist and the sound that emerged from her throat was perilously near a whimper.

"Shhh," he whispered. "It's all right. If you just let me—"

"No," she gasped. "Please, no."

"Megs," he sighed, his voice troubled.

She couldn't answer, could only tug on his wrist, mutely indicating what she needed.

He took pity on her, rolling atop her.

She let go of him then, spreading her legs to let his hips slide between them, a firm weight. He bunched up his nightshirt and then she felt the heat of his bare legs, the soft scrape of his body hair. So intimate. So close. She felt thin, cold metal fall between her breasts, some type of pendant he must wear on that chain about his neck. She wondered, absently, what it was—and then all thought fled her mind.

The head of his penis probed her entrance.

She grit her teeth, tensing uncontrollably.

He made a soothing sound and slid through her folds, wetting himself. Teasing her.

She wanted to tell him to just put it in her, damn it. Do the thing and get it over with so she might regain her balance. But he took his time, gliding against her, circling. She could hear the small, wet sounds, feel the spark every time he pressed her *there*. By the time he finally put the blunt tip in and began to push, she was trembling, trying to keep herself from falling off that ledge. He shoved into her agonizingly slowly. A subtle insertion and retreat, each time filling her a little more with his length. He was as solicitous as if she were a virgin.

And she was going to go insane if he kept it up.

This wasn't what she wanted, what she *needed*. She hadn't asked for careful, warm lovemaking.

She'd asked for his seed.

Just when she thought she could stand it no longer, he made one last thrust and she felt the stretch of her inner thighs as his hips met hers. He rested there a moment and his chest pushed against her breasts, unbound under her chemise, as he inhaled. He rocked, sliding against her without saying a word, his breath rough above her in the dark. She wondered what his face looked like, if this act transformed it, if he watched her even though he couldn't see her.

If he hated her for making him do this.

She couldn't touch him—she'd forbidden herself that luxury—so she fisted her hands by her head, torturing her pillow with her nails.

And still his hard penis invaded her, surging and retreating, demanding something without words. Demanding what she refused to let herself give.

When his breath caught, when his pace quickened, so that her hips sank beneath his into the soft mattress, she swallowed, straining her eyes to see in the dark. When he suddenly stilled, buried deep in her throbbing flesh, locked with her in animal intensity, she wanted...so much.

But all she received was what she'd asked for.

His seed.

GODRIC CAREFULLY DISENTANGLED himself from Megs, rolling aside as his softening cock slipped from her warm depths. He wanted to stay, to perhaps hold her, and if she let him, kiss her.

But she'd made it plain that she did this without affection and he was not a raw lad.

So he stood and pulled the covers back over her form and when she made a small, questioning noise, he only said, "Good night."

Turning, he scooped up his banyan and slippers by feel and exited her room.

He'd left a candle burning in his own bedroom and he was glad of the light now. It brought him out of the too-intimate darkness, made him remember who he was.

Who she was.

But even with the candlelight, he found himself at the dresser. His fingers didn't shake when he fitted the key in the lock and he was inordinately proud of that fact.

He opened the enameled box. The locks of hair lay there, the same as always, and he reached to touch them but found that he couldn't. His fingers were still damp from Megs's skin.

"Forgive me," he whispered to Clara.

At that moment he couldn't even remember her face, the sound of her laughter, or the sight of her warm eyes. He was speaking to empty air.

Godric gripped the edges of the drawer, the corners pressing painfully into his palms, but still he couldn't find Clara.

Somehow, he'd lost her.

He was alone.

He inhaled shakily and fished through the loose letters in the drawer with fingers that now trembled until he found the one he wanted.

2 November 1739

Dear Godric,
    Thank you for the monies you made available to me. I've had the roof repaired and already the east wing has nearly stopped dripping! There is just

one rather persistent leak in the tiny room just off the library. I'm not sure exactly what the room was used for. Battlefield informs me that a former lady of the house was locked in there after her husband became enamored of his (male!) steward, but you know how Battlefield likes his little jokes.

We ate the last raspberry out of the garden last week before cutting back the brambles. Everything aboveground has been killed by the frost, except for the kale, and I've never really liked kale. Have you? I confess I feel a strange kind of melancholy at this time of year. All the green things have gone to ground, pretending death, and I have nothing left but the frosted trees and the few remaining leaves, dead yet hanging on nonetheless.

But how dreary! I will not fault you if you grumble under your breath and fling aside my maudlin ramblings. I am not an entertaining correspondent, I fear.

Yesterday I went to tea at the vicarage, playing lady of the manor while being plied with very rich cakes and tea. You will not credit it, but we were served a kind of tart made from orange persimmons, quite pretty, but a bit bitter (I think the persimmons were under ripe) and, I am told, a specialty of the vicar's wife. (So I could do naught but swallow and smile bravely!) The vicar's youngest son, a babe of only forty days, was presented for my inspection and though he was a brave boy, my eyes watered for some odd reason and I was forced to laugh and pretend I had got a bit of dust in my eye.

I don't know why I tell you that.

And again! I've dribbled into quite boring territory. I shall endeavor to mend my ways and be only cheerful in my next missive, I promise. I remain—
                                        Affectionately Yours,
                                                    Megs

PS: Did you try the ginger, barley, and aniseed tisane recipe I sent you? I know it sounds quite revolting, but it will help your sore throat, truly!

Her postscript blurred before his eyes and he blinked hard, inhaling. This was who he'd done it for: Megs, who thought old crotchety butlers had any sense of humor, who ate bitter persimmon tarts to please the local vicar's wife, and who cried at the sight of a baby and couldn't admit even to herself why.

She deserved a baby of her own. She'd make a magnificent mother: kind, gentle, understanding.

He placed the letter back in the drawer, closed, and locked it.

He'd promised to give her that baby, and he would.

No matter the cost to himself.

MEGS WOKE TO the sound of Daniels rustling in her armoire. She squinted at the window, realizing it was rather late in the morning, and as she stretched, she made her second realization. Her thighs were sticky.

Godric had made love to her last night.

She knew her face was heating. She could feel the ache of the muscles between her legs, a twinge she hadn't felt in years, and she wished that she could've woken alone so that she might assimilate the changes to her life.

To her.

Fortunately, Daniels's mind was on other matters. "We have visitors, my lady."

Megs blinked. It couldn't be *that* late. Besides, they hadn't had any callers since coming to London. She wasn't even sure the sitting room had been cleaned yet. "We do?"

"Yes, my lady." Daniels frowned at a yellow brocade gown and placed it back in the armoire. "Three ladies."

"What?" Megs sat up hurriedly. "Who are they?"

"Relations of Mr. St. John, I believe."

"Good Lord." Megs scrambled from the bed, feeling a bit irritated. Why hadn't Godric told her that he'd expected family to visit? But then, knowing the state of Saint House when they'd arrived, she had the sudden idea that maybe he *hadn't* known.

Good Lord, indeed.

Megs made a hasty wash while Daniels's back was discreetly turned, using the warm water already brought up. Then she stood obediently as Daniels and one of the little maids from the home dressed her in a pink and black figured gown. It was several years old and Megs made a mental note—*again*—that she really needed to call upon a modiste while in London.

Daniels tutted despairingly as she dressed Megs's hair. Usually her lady's maid needed a good forty-five minutes to tame the springy locks. Today she was making do with ten.

"That's enough," Megs said, keeping her voice calm even though she wanted to run down the stairs before these relatives of Godric left in high dungeon at the state of the house. Good lady's maids were hard to find—particularly ones who would work in the country. "Thank you, Daniels."

Daniels sniffed and stood back, and Megs walked quickly out of her room.

The first floor was very quiet and Megs bit her lip as she descended. Had they left?

But as she made the lower level, she was greeted by Mrs. Crumb, looking as perfectly put together as always. "Good morning, my lady. You have guests waiting in the primrose sitting room."

Megs nearly gaped. Saint House had a primrose sitting room? "Er... which room might that be?"

"The third on the left, just past the library," Mrs. Crumb said sedately.

Megs's eyes widened. "The one with the ball of cobwebs in the corner of the ceiling?"

Mrs. Crumb's left eyebrow twitched. "The very same."

"Er..." Megs bit her lip, staring at the formidable housekeeper. "It doesn't still—"

Mrs. Crumb's left eyebrow slowly arched.

"No. No, of course not." Megs smiled in relief.

The housekeeper nodded solemnly. "I've taken the liberty of ordering tea and biscuits from Cook."

Megs nearly gaped again. "We have a cook?"

"Indeed, my lady. Since this morning at six."

"You're a paragon, Mrs. Crumb!"

The housekeeper's lips curved very, very slightly at the corners. "Thank you, my lady."

Megs took a breath and smoothed her skirts before gliding down the hallway at a sedate pace. She opened the door to the primrose sitting room, bracing herself for some aged relation of Godric's, but she immediately relaxed with relief when she saw the three ladies within.

"Oh, Mrs. St. John," Megs exclaimed as she hurried

forward. "Why didn't you tell us you were coming to London?"

Megs hugged the elder woman and then stood back. Godric's stepmother was nearing her fifty-fifth year. A short, somewhat stout woman, she had the flaxen hair that all her daughters had inherited, though hers was faded now to a vague pale color. Mrs. St. John's face had taken on a ruddy hue as she aged. She was a rather plain woman, physically, but one hardly noticed because of the vivaciousness of her expression. Megs knew from village gossip that Godric's father had been deeply in love with his second wife.

"We took a page from your notebook, Megs, and thought it best to simply arrive on Godric's doorstep." Mrs. St. John huffed as she sat down on a settee.

"Rather like one of those vagabond peddlers," Jane, eighteen and the youngest St. John sister, said. "The ones who won't leave the doorstep until you buy some ratty length of ribbon."

"That ribbon was *not* ratty." Charlotte, who was two years older than Jane, looked indignant. "I vow you're jealous because the peddler came around when you were out romping through the fields with Pat and Harriet."

"Pat and Harriet needed a good run." Jane pointed her nose in the air. "Besides, I wouldn't want a ribbon that ratty if it were *given* to me."

"Girls," Mrs. St. John said, and both sisters abruptly shut their mouths. "I'm sure Megs doesn't care to hear you bickering over fripperies and the dogs."

Megs didn't really mind. She found the St. John sisters' obvious affection for each other—when they weren't quarreling—rather refreshing, actually. She'd never been close to her own older sister, Caro. The St. John dower house was in the village of Upper Hornsfield, so she had the opportunity to observe the St. John sororal dynamics quite often.

"I can't think where Sarah is," she said diplomatically. "Or Godric, for that matter."

"We were told that Godric had already gone out," Jane informed her. "And no one could find Sarah."

"That's because I was out for a walk," Sarah said from the doorway. The two little maids were behind her, carefully holding trays full of tea things. "I only just returned."

Charlotte and Jane were up immediately, hugging and exclaiming over their sister as if they hadn't seen her in months rather than little more than a week.

Mrs. Crumb entered the room with the maids during the flurry and quietly directed setting everything out. She glanced inquiringly at Megs when the maids were done. When Megs thanked her, Mrs. Crumb nodded and ushered the maids out, closing the door behind her.

"Mama," Sarah said, leaning down to kiss her mother on the cheek. "What a surprise."

"That was the idea," Mrs. St. John said.

Sarah sat. "Why?"

"Well, I thought this estrangement had gone on long enough, and since Godric obviously won't do anything about it, I decided to. Thank you, dear." Mrs. St. John accepted a dish of tea from Megs, sweetened with several spoons of sugar, just the way Megs knew she liked it. "And," she added practically after taking a sip, "the girls and I are in need of new frocks, especially Jane since she'll have her coming-out this autumn. You as well, Sarah, dear."

"Oh, good," Megs murmured. "I've been meaning to visit a modiste. We can all go together."

"What fun!" Jane bounced in her seat. The door to the sitting room opened, but she continued, oblivious. "That sounds much more pleasant than having to visit grumpy old Godric."

"Jane!" Megs hissed, but it was far too late.

"I wasn't aware we were expecting visitors," Godric rasped from the doorway.

Megs bit her lip. He did not look pleased.

Chapter Eleven

*"Is this Hell?" Faith asked as she looked at the rocky shore.
"No," the Hellequin said. He'd either not noticed or not
cared that she'd pushed Despair off the great black horse.
"We still have a long journey ahead before we reach
Hell. Before us now is the Peak of Whispers." He pointed to
a range of black, jagged mountains that loomed across the
distant horizon. "Are you sure you wish to continue?"
"Yes," Faith said, and wrapped her arms about
the Hellequin's middle.
He merely nodded and spurred his horse on....*
—From *The Legend of the Hellequin*

Grumpy old Godric.

It was a fair assessment—though Godric doubted that
Jane had taken any time thinking the matter over. He *was*
grumpy—or at least morose. And as for old, well, he supposed he was that as well—in comparison to his half sisters, anyway. He was seven and thirty. Sarah was a mere
dozen years younger than he, but Charlotte was seventeen
years younger and Jane nineteen.

He was old enough to be her father.

It was an unspannable gap—always had been, always
would be.

"Godric," his stepmother said softly. She rose and crossed to him, and then surprised him by taking one of his hands in her own, small soft ones. "It's so good to see you."

There it was, the guilt and anxious resentfulness he felt every time he saw this woman. She made him into an awkward schoolboy, and he hated it.

"Madam," he said, aware that his tone was too stiff, too formal. "To what do I owe the pleasure of your visit?"

She looked up at him—the top of her head came only to his midchest—and her eyes seemed to search for something in his face.

"We wanted to see you," she said at last.

"And we need new frocks," Jane said from behind her mother. His half sister's tone was defiant, but her expression was uncertain.

He'd probably looked like that much of the time when he'd been her age.

Godric nodded, leading his stepmother over to where she'd been seated before. "How long do you intend to stay?"

"A fortnight," his stepmother said.

"Ah," Godric murmured, and felt Megs's look. For the first time he glanced at his wife.

His wife, whom he'd bedded just last night.

She wore a smart pink gown with black figures and trimmings, her hair dark and lustrous, and she sat very straight, watching him with a worried frown knit between her gracefully arched brows. He nearly stopped breathing. She was so lovely, Megs, his *wife*. Had his father's family not been here, he might've crossed to her, pulled her from her seat, and led her to their rooms where—

But, no.

She'd made quite plain that was not the type of arrangement she wanted with him. Even had his stepmother and sisters not been looking on curiously, he would've had to wait until tonight.

He was a stud, nothing more.

Godric took a breath, focusing once more on the conversation. "Would you like me to escort you to the shops?"

He saw Megs's look of surprise out of the corner of his eye.

Jane, predictably, opened her mouth first, but the glance her mother shot her made her close it again very quickly.

His stepmother smiled at him. "Yes, that would be lovely."

He nodded. Megs gave him a small, grateful grin and handed him a dish of tea—a drink he'd never particularly cared for. But he sipped it and let the women's chatter flow around him, observing.

It seemed his wife had formed an intimate bond with his father's family while she'd lived at Laurelwood. That wasn't so surprising, he supposed, since the dower house was nearby. She made a pretty picture with his sisters, her dark head in contrast with their lighter ones. All three had inherited their mother's coloring. Charlotte was the fairest, while Jane's tawny locks were the darkest. Sarah sat next to Megs, laughing at something, and Jane was nearly in Charlotte's lap, her arm draped companionably over her sister's neck, the skirts of their dresses frothing over each other. His stepmother looked on benignly and the circle was complete: a feminine sorority perfect and exclusive.

Godric glanced down at his tea.

It would be awkward with his father's family in the house. He still had to continue his Ghostly duties, find the lassie snatchers, and now Roger Fraser-Burnsby's murderer as well. Add to that Captain Trevillion watching him suspiciously, and his job had become *much* more difficult.

Not that obstacles would stop him.

"...if that's agreeable with you, Godric?" his stepmother inquired.

He looked up to find five pairs of feminine eyes focused on him. Godric cleared his throat. "I beg your pardon?"

Megs sighed, making him aware that he'd missed more than one or two sentences. "We've decided to visit the modiste directly after luncheon and then tonight we're to dine with Griffin and Hero. But"—she turned to his father's family—"I'm sure Hero will invite you as well, once she hears you're in town."

Jane's eyes rounded in awe. "She's the daughter of a *duke*, isn't she?"

Megs smiled. "And the sister of one. In fact, the duke may be there as well tonight."

For a moment, the girl was frozen in apparent awe. Then she burst into a flurry of excited movement, chattering all the while about dresses and shoes and *what would she wear?*

Godric sighed. This was going to be a long day. He caught Megs watching him with a small, approving tilt to her lips.

But perhaps it would be worth it.

THAT NIGHT, MEGS watched as the Duke of Wakefield frowned down at his nephew in ducal disapproval and said, "I don't understand why the boy cries every time he sees me."

"He's developing good taste," Griffin replied kindly as he picked up sweet William, who immediately quieted, leaning against his father's chest as he sucked on his forefinger.

Hero rolled her eyes discreetly—something she would never have done before marrying Griffin.

They were in the family sitting room where William had been brought down by his nurse before being put to bed. Great-Aunt Elvina leaned close to Hero, her hand behind her ear to hear whatever Hero was shouting at her. Jane sat ramrod straight, her eyes wide in awe as she watched every movement the Duke of Wakefield made. Beside her, her sisters and mother were more relaxed, obviously enjoying being in such exalted company. Knowing how the gossip mill worked in Upper Hornsfield, Megs knew they could dine upon this night for months. Godric stood near the mantel, watching. Megs frowned. Why was it that he always seemed so apart, even when in the midst of his own family?

William made a sound, drawing her eyes. A splotch of baby drool darkened Griffin's waistcoat and Megs couldn't help smirking. Her brother had been such a notorious rake before meeting Hero.

"May I?" she asked shyly, indicating William.

"Of course."

Griffin placed sweet William in her arms and then she was being examined by large, green eyes the exact shade of his sire. He was heavier than she'd expected, a solid, warm bundle, smelling faintly of milk and biscuits. William had reddish-brown, curling hair, plump cheeks, and his lips, pursed around his finger, were so rosy and sweet Megs couldn't help kissing him on his little forehead.

Soon, oh, please let it be soon.

William withdrew his finger from his mouth and patted her cheek wetly.

"Babies are terribly messy," Great-Aunt Elvina announced, then ruined her stern words by making clucking noises at William.

"He's teething again," Hero said beside Megs. "Do you want me to take him? He'll think nothing of ruining your dress."

"No, let me hold him a bit longer," Megs murmured. "He's quite beautiful."

"Yes, isn't he?" Hero's mouth curved in maternal love.

A pang of desperate longing went through Megs's breast. *This. This was what she wanted.*

She looked up and met Godric's watchful eyes. As if he'd heard her thoughts, he inclined his head almost like he was making a promise. Her breath caught. What other man would be so good to her? He was so protective, so *kind*. He'd spent the day escorting her and the St. John women about to shops, never once making a demure or seeming bored by frivolous feminine things. The day had been so enjoyable that she'd remembered only as she'd been dressing for dinner that he'd promised to look for Roger's murderer. And she knew she ought to ask him what his plans were, to press him on the point and make sure he wasn't going to conveniently forget his vow, but she simply wanted a small respite from the matter.

From death and grief and loss. If only—

"Ah, Mandeville," the duke drawled.

Megs turned to see that her other brother, Thomas

Reading, the Marquess of Mandeville, had arrived. Beside him was his vivacious wife, Lavinia, whose hair had grown if anything more brightly red since Megs had last seen her.

"You've got a spot on your waistcoat," Thomas said to Griffin.

"Yes, I know," Griffin replied through gritted teeth.

Megs sighed. Her brothers weren't the best of friends, but at least they now *spoke* to each other. For several weeks after Griffin's marriage, that hadn't been the case.

The gentlemen converged, speaking in low tones about politics before the butler interrupted with the call for supper.

Hero took sweet William from Megs's arms, bussing him on the cheek before giving him over to his nurse with a murmured word and a lingering look as they left the sitting room. She caught Megs's eye and smiled ruefully. "I usually put him to sleep myself. It's silly of me, I know, but I hate letting someone else do it."

"You can look in on him later," Griffin said tenderly, offering Hero his arm.

She took it, wrinkling her nose up at him. "You shouldn't indulge my sentimental quirks."

"But I *like* indulging you," he whispered into the auburn curls at her temple, and Megs blushed, rather thinking she wasn't meant to hear that last part.

"Shall we?" Godric was at her side.

"Of course." She laid her fingers on his forearm, realizing that they trembled slightly. There was something about being this close to him, a warmth that transmitted itself from his body to hers, a kind of vibration almost, so that her body seemed to tune itself to his. And she real-

ized with almost horror that even if he weren't the means
to give her a baby, she *wanted* him.

That isn't right, she thought shakily as he led her into
the dining room and pulled out her chair. She sank into
the seat without thought, her mind full of a confused
buzzing. Her body wasn't supposed to long for his. She'd
loved *Roger*, and although she was grateful to Godric
and had come to know him a little more, had, perhaps, a
kind of *admiration* for him, that wasn't love.

Her body shouldn't respond without love; it just shouldn't.

She realized that Charlotte sat to her left—the gentlemen were overmatched by the ladies—and, *oh dear*, to
her right was the duke. Megs mentally sighed. The Duke
of Wakefield was a rather daunting gentleman to make
dinner conversation with. The footmen brought out great
platters of fish and began serving as Megs searched her
mind for something to say to His Grace.

Instead it was he who turned to her. "I trust you enjoyed
the play at Harte's Folly last night, my lady?"

"Oh, yes, Your Grace," she murmured, watching as he
tore apart a crusty roll. "And you?"

"I confess that the theater doesn't entertain me," he
replied, his voice bored, but then something softened
about his eyes as he glanced at her. "But both Phoebe and
Cousin Bathilda like it very much."

For the first time, Megs felt a faint liking for the duke.
"Do you take them there often?"

He shrugged. "There or other theaters in London. They
also like the opera, particularly Phoebe. I think the music
partially compensates for the fact that she can't entirely
see the stage." He frowned down at his fish as if it had
offended him.

Megs felt a pang. "It's that bad, then?"

He merely nodded and seemed relieved when Thomas's voice rose farther down the table.

"The act hasn't been given enough time," he was telling Griffin. "When the gin sellers all have been arrested, then the drink must perforce be reduced in the streets of London."

"It's been two years," Griffin growled back, "and your gin act hasn't done much more than line the pockets of a few crooked informers. I could still buy gin at every fourth house in St. Giles were I wont."

Thomas's eyes narrowed as the footmen brought in the next course—a roasted joint and various vegetables—and he opened his mouth to retort.

But the duke intervened. "Griffin is right."

Both brothers turned to him, astonished. The duke was not a bosom-bow of Griffin's—he'd been determinedly against the younger brother's marrying his sister—and Megs knew Thomas considered him a friend and ally.

But the duke set his fork down and sat back. "The act has had two years to effect change and it hasn't. The only real good it's done is correct the faults of the '36 act, which"—the duke grimaced—"is faint praise indeed. We are at an impasse. London cannot continue with the loss of vigor and blood that gin sucks from it like some ungodly parasite."

"What do you suggest?" Thomas asked slowly.

The duke pinned him with his cold eyes. "We need a new act."

Griffin, Thomas, and the duke burst into furious political argument while Godric twirled his wineglass, his eyes intent as he followed the discussion. He wasn't a peer, so he didn't sit in Parliament, but every male seemed infected by the blight of gin these days and the discussion on what to do about it.

And, of course, the blight of gin affected everything in St. Giles.

Megs sighed and turned toward Charlotte on her other side. "Are you pleased with the gowns you selected today?"

"Yes, although I did want that sky-blue moiré."

Charlotte cast a disgruntled glance at Jane across the table. The sisters had nearly come to blows over the gorgeous fabric before Mrs. St. John had hushed them with the simple threat that *no one* would get the sky-blue moiré if the matter wasn't decided in the next second. Charlotte and Jane had looked at each other silently and Charlotte had huffed and conceded the silk to Jane. Ten minutes later, they were enjoying ices, elbows linked, bright blond heads together, and one would never have known the sisters had fought so adamantly just moments before.

Which didn't mean that Charlotte had entirely forgiven her sister, of course.

"You did get that lovely turquoise brocade," Megs reminded her diplomatically.

"Yes," Charlotte said, brightening, "and those delicious lace mitts." She sighed happily before turning to Megs. "That peachy-pink silk is going to look so pretty with your dark hair. I'm sure Godric will be smitten."

Megs smiled, but she couldn't help her gaze sliding away from her sister-in-law's. Did she want Godric smitten? She glanced up and saw that he was watching her now, his gray eyes heavily lidded, his long, elegant fingers still playing with the stem of his wineglass.

Twirling. Twirling. Twirling.

Her face heated for some reason and she looked hastily away again, taking a sip of her wine to calm herself.

"Megs?" Charlotte asked hesitantly.

Megs focused her attention on her sister-in-law. "Yes?"

Charlotte was pushing together a mound of creamed potatoes and parsnips, pressing the tines into the fluffy vegetables to make small, parallel furrows. She leaned close to Megs, her voice lowering. "Do you think Godric will ever…" She cleared her throat as if searching for the word, her forehead compressing into furrows that matched the ones on her plate. "Do you think he'll ever want to be *close* to us?"

"I don't know," Megs said honestly. Having heard Godric's recollections of his youth, she knew now the broad gulf between him and the rest of his family had started long before Clara's death had made him a near hermit. They were so very far apart. Could anything bridge a gap widened by both time and distance?

Megs bit her lip and sat back as the footmen cleared their plates and brought in individual glasses of syllabub.

"It's just…" Charlotte was still frowning, peering now at her dish of syllabub. She picked up her spoon and poked the quivering mass, then sighed and set her spoon down again. "I remember when I was very young. He seemed so tall and strong then. I thought he was a god, my elder brother. Mama says I used to follow him about like a chick when he visited, though that wasn't often. He must've found it very boring to be tagged by a girl child still in the nursery."

Megs rather wanted to hurl her own spoon at her husband at that moment.

"I doubt very much that he was bored by you," she said gently. "It's just that your mother married your father when Godric was at a difficult age for a boy. And, too, he'd lost his own mother. . . ." She trailed off, feeling inadequate. The fact was that Godric might've been hurt as a lad, but he was a *man* now. There was no reason for him to hold himself apart from his sisters.

"He's my brother," Charlotte whispered so low that Megs nearly didn't catch the words. "My *only* brother."

And even the delicious syllabub didn't make up for the sinking of Megs's heart at those words. She had to find a way to make Godric see that his sisters and stepmother were important. This might be his only chance. Once they were married and had families of their own, they'd have far less incentive to want to bring him into their fold.

He'd end up entirely alone.

Megs slowly lowered her spoon to her empty dish at the thought. She'd promised to leave London—leave *Godric*—once she was with child. She'd have the baby and all her friends and relations in the country. She lived a full and happy life there—one that wanted only a child of her own. But Godric . . .

Well, who did Godric have, really?

There was his friend, Lord Caire. But Lord Caire had his own family—one that would no doubt grow and demand more of his time. She had a vision of Godric, old and alone, surrounded by his books and little else. Someday he'd have to give up being the Ghost of St. Giles—always assuming he didn't die doing it—and then he'd have . . . nothing.

The thought was distressing. Megs looked over at Godric, who was now bending down to listen to something

Lavinia was saying. She might not love him, but he was her husband. Her *responsibility*. How had she not seen before that she *couldn't* leave him alone?

The gentlemen suddenly rose and Megs realized that she'd missed Hero inviting the ladies to the sitting room for tea. The duke held Mrs. St. John's chair for her and then Megs's—putting age before rank, and quite properly in Megs's opinion.

Mrs. St. John linked arms with Megs on one side and Charlotte on the other. "And what were you two whispering about so seriously during the dessert?"

"Godric." Charlotte sighed, and Mrs. St. John merely nodded because there wasn't much to say to that, was there?

In the sitting room, Hero was already serving tea while Sarah sat at the harpsichord, experimentally plunking the keys.

"Oh, do sing, girls," Mrs. St. John said as she took a cup of tea. "That old ballad you learned the other day."

So Jane and Charlotte linked arms and sang to Sarah's accompaniment, for as it turned out the ballad was to a tune Sarah already knew.

"Lovely, quite lovely," Great-Aunt Elvina murmured, tapping her fingers on the arm of her chair in time to the song.

Megs leaned back and listened with enjoyment. Her own voice would startle a crow, but she did like to hear others sing and the St. John girls, while not the most polished voices she'd ever heard, were very pleasant. If they stopped now and again to giggle and retry a phrasing, Megs didn't mind. They were singing to family, and she was rather pleased that they had become comfortable enough with Hero and Lavinia to include them in that designation.

After an hour, the gentlemen joined them and Megs saw the moment the St. John girls instinctively stiffened. She sighed. It was hard to be relaxed with either Thomas or the duke about. But Griffin was here now and she was determined to talk to him.

So she sidled up to her brother and in a low tone suggested he show her his new house—after all, she hadn't been given a proper tour before.

Griffin gave her an alert look, but he held out his arm readily enough, leading her out of the sitting room with a murmured word to Hero. Megs felt Godric's curious gaze even after they'd shut the door behind them. The house was quiet outside the sitting room, until the harpsichord started again and a beautiful baritone voice began singing. Megs knit her eyebrows. That was funny. Thomas had no more vocal talent than she, and she hadn't been aware that Godric could sing.

But Griffin was leading her to the grand staircase and muttering something about *skylights* and *pilasters* and *the Italian influence*. Megs squinted at him. Was he having her on?

"Oh, for goodness' sake, Griffin, do stop," she said at last.

He turned and grinned down at her mischievously. "Thought you didn't really want to tour the house. What is it, Megs?"

"You and gin distilling," she said bluntly, because she couldn't think of any way to get to the point delicately, and anyway, she hadn't the time.

"What about me and gin distilling?" he asked carelessly,

but his face had closed, which on Griffin was a dead giveaway.

She took a deep breath. "I heard that you used to support the family, even Thomas, by distilling gin in St. Giles."

"Goddamn St. John!" he exploded. "He had no right to tell you."

Megs raised her eyebrows. "I think he did have a right. I'm his *wife* and more importantly *your* sister. Griffin! Why ever didn't you tell us that we were in financial straits?"

"It wasn't your business."

"Wasn't our business?" She gaped at her older brother and not for the first time thought how much a good knock on the head might suit him. "Caro and I were spending money as if we hadn't a care in the world. I distinctly remember Thomas buying that terrible gilt-trimmed carriage after Papa died. Surely he wouldn't have done that had he known. *Of course* it was our business. We could've been more frugal. Could've minded our purchases."

"I didn't want you to mind your purchases." Griffin expelled a hard breath, stepping back from her. "Don't you see, Megs? That was my burden to bear. I was supposed to take care of you and Mater and Caro."

"And Thomas?" she asked softly, incredulously.

"He hasn't a head for money. Neither did Pater. There wasn't anyone else."

"Griffin," she said softly, laying her hand on his arm. "There was me. Maybe not when I was younger, but I've been past twenty for five years now. I had the right to provide mental support for you at the very least. I had the right to *know*."

Griffin grimaced and looked away. Megs expected him

to refute her right—the Griffin of three years ago, prior to marrying Hero, would've—but when he glanced back at her, his eyes had softened.

"Oh, Megs," he said. "You know I can't deny you anything." She arched her eyebrows pointedly, and he threw up his hands. "Fine. Yes. *Yes*, I should've told you, should've let you shoulder a bit of my burden."

"Thank you," she said, not without a hint of complacency. "I have one more question."

He looked a little hunted but nodded his head bravely enough.

"Is the family still in financial straits?" she asked. "Are *you* in financial straits?"

"No," he said immediately, with what sounded like relief. "I'm still in filthy business, of course, but it's respectable enough now. I've got sheep grazing on the family lands and a workshop here in London spinning the wool." He shrugged. "It's small now, but we're making a good profit and I'll be expanding soon. Not"—he added wryly—"that I'd ever say that aloud in society."

Having money was good, naturally. Actually *making* money was deeply frowned upon by society. Presumably a gentleman would rather starve than let his hands get dirty with commerce.

Megs was very grateful that Griffin had never cared particularly for society's rules.

She threaded her arm through his elbow. "I'm glad to hear it. But, Griffin?"

"Hmm?" He was strolling with her back toward the sitting room where the baritone was still singing.

"Promise me that if ever you run into straits again—financial or otherwise—you'll tell me."

"Oh, all right, Megs," he replied, rolling his eyes a bit.

She smiled to herself. He might balk, but it was important to her that Griffin was honest with her. A family should be honest. And they should share things—both good and bad.

She was reflecting on the subject and wondering how exactly she could push Godric in that direction with his own family when they entered the sitting room and she stopped short in surprise.

It seemed the Duke of Wakefield had a magnificent singing voice.

MEGS LAY IN her bed that night, surrounded by the cold darkness of her room, and tried not to anticipate Godric's arrival.

Tried not to long for him.

She lectured herself on the reasons why she was doing this, but the arguments had become muddled in her own mind and all she could hear was the drag of her breaths in and out of her body. She focused on the dinner at Griffin and Hero's house, the face of sweet William, the accord she'd found with Griffin, the astonishing sight of the rigid Duke of Wakefield singing like a stern archangel, but each image wavered and slipped through her mind's grasp. She even tried remembering the taste of the syllabub at dinner, the smooth texture of cream, the tart wine, but the phantom sweet dissolved in her mouth, and all she could taste on her tongue was Godric's mouth.

There in the darkness she might've moaned.

He came at last, moving like the ghost he was. She didn't even know he'd entered her room until she felt the dip of her bed, the warmth radiating off his body.

She trembled before he ever touched her.

Then his hands were gliding over her shoulders, sweeping down her chemise-covered sides, sliding up the slopes of her breasts while his head and shoulders hovered over her like a hawk shielding its prey.

Her breath caught. There was something dangerous about him. Perhaps there always had been and he'd simply damped it the night before. This was only their second joining and she nearly panicked at the thought. There would be many nights more. Nights when she lay in the dark and waited for him. Nights when she desperately tried to order her mind. Nights when she tried not to *feel*.

As she was trying not to feel now—trying and failing.

His hands moved, swift and sure, cupping her breasts, and she had no trouble at all remembering their pale, elegant length. Imagining what they would look like against her flesh.

She bit her lip, and his thumbs coasted over her nipples, catching, for they were already erect and pointed. Goose pimples shivered across her skin at his touch. When he brushed across her nipples again and then pinched both at once, it was all she could do not to arch into those beautiful hands.

Roger. She had to think of Roger.

His head descended with alarming swiftness and suddenly his mouth, hot and wet, was on her nipple. He tongued her through the thin fabric of her chemise and all thought scattered. She arched beneath him, whimpering. His hands clamped around her rib cage, holding her still. His pendant slid coolly across her belly as he suckled her nipple hard. He let go and drew back, blowing on her oversensitive skin, covered only by the wet fabric, and she shivered under the sudden chill. Then he was ministering to her other breast, thoroughly, intently. His focus entirely on her and her body. She hadn't time to recover, to regain control under his sexual siege.

She could only feel and yearn.

He lifted his head finally, when her breath was ragged and nearly broken, and began trailing his open mouth down her quivering belly. At first she had no idea of his intent—couldn't even think—but as his hand bunched up her chemise and moved lower still, she had a terrible premonition.

"No." It was the first word spoken between them since he'd entered her room, and it sounded overly harsh to her own ears.

Megs licked her lips, feeling her heart still beating too fast in her chest, the obscene dampness on both her nipples, and the still of the night.

He'd frozen at her word, but it wasn't in fear or apprehension. His stance, hovering over her, his arms on either side of her hips, seemed dangerous somehow. As if his will were held back by only a tiny thread. As if he might ignore her plea and place his mouth against her anyway.

Against her cunny.

That's where he had been moving. She was no virgin and she knew what his intent was: to disintegrate her composure. She wouldn't be able to take it. She'd succumb to that beautiful mouth, that quiet expertise, and she'd forget everything.

The last vestiges of Roger would dissolve and blow away from her mind.

So she inhaled slowly and reached tentatively for his shoulders. His muscles were bunched, hard and unyielding, and she couldn't move him if he did not wish it.

"Please," she whispered.

For a moment more he didn't move. Then he was shaking her hand off his shoulder, hauling up her chemise, settling between her thighs. She was already wet, but perhaps not quite enough. He rocked against her, his penis a hard prod, sliding in her moisture before catching and slowly beginning to invade.

She swallowed, arching her head back, trying to relax as he slid more and more of himself into her. Animals did this without thought. Why, then, couldn't people? She knew some did. But not her it seemed.

She thought—*felt*—far too much.

She gripped his arms as he shoved resolutely against her, seating himself fully. She looked up, trying to see something of him in the darkness. An expression, perhaps how he held his head.

But he was simply a large male shape.

And yet...she knew it was him. Would've known it blindfolded. Whether by scent or some more primitive means—perhaps an alchemy of souls—she felt him bone-deep.

Godric. Poised above her.

Godric. Withdrawing his cock in one long, pulling slide.

Godric. Flexing his hips back into her with a final twist at the end.

He was overpowering her senses, laying claim to her soul.

She struggled internally, resisting, closing her eyes, dropping her hands from his arms, trying to shut away her senses.

But that was impossible. How could it not be? *He was making love to her.*

She tried her best, she really did, and in the end she had one small victory: As his thrusts grew harder and closer to his point, she held herself together. He shook against her, rubbing into her, making her feel, but she was stubborn and strong, and when finally he shuddered, the dark shape of his head arching back, it was by himself.

She had no time to congratulate herself.

He leaned down in the dark and she thought he meant to kiss her. She turned her head aside and it was in her ear he whispered huskily, so close she could feel the brush of his lips.

"Who are you making love to, my lady? For I know it's not me."

Chapter Twelve

*Faith was hungry as she clung to the Hellequin's broad
back. She fished in a pocket of her dress and took out
a small apple. The Hellequin's nostril's flared as she
bit into the sweet-tart flesh.
Faith was abashed at her discourtesy. "Would
you like some?"
"I have not eaten the food of men for a millennium,"
the Hellequin rasped.
"Well, then," said Faith, "it's past time you did so."
She bit off a piece of the apple, and taking it from her own
mouth, held it to his....*
—From *The Legend of the Hellequin*

At his words Megs froze beneath him.

Rage was pumping through Godric's veins, corrosive
and hot, expanding, making him feel as if he'd explode
from inside if he didn't get out of here at once. He gingerly withdrew from her silky depths, moving carefully
so as not to hurt her.

He'd never in his life worried that he might harm a
woman in shear anger.

His movement shifted the covers, stirring the scent of
semen and sex and *her*. He couldn't think; his emotions
were overwhelming him.

"I didn't—" she started, foolish wench.

How dare she try to deny it?

"Quiet," he bit out, sliding from the bed.

"Godric."

"Will you leave it?" he hissed, turning on her in the dark. He had to leave before he said something—did something—he would regret.

But she was ever contrary. He felt her fingers wrap around his wrist, feminine and strong.

He stilled.

"Where are you going?" she whispered.

He could still smell her scent, and he realized to his horror that it was probably imprinted upon his skin. "Out."

"Where?"

He sneered, though she couldn't see it in the dark. "Where do you think? I go to St. Giles. To find your lover's murderer. To do my work as the Ghost."

"But…" Her voice lowered in the dark, a mere whisper. "But I don't want you to go, Godric. I think you lose a bit of your soul every time you go out as the Ghost of St. Giles."

"You should've thought of that before you made this bargain, my lady." He flexed his hand, his tendons moving within her grasp, but made no move to pull his wrist from her fingers. "You wanted me to investigate. Well, I do my investigating as the Ghost. Have you changed your mind? Do you want me to give up the hunt for Fraser-Burnsby's murderer?"

He could hear her inhale in the dark, imagined he could feel the brush of her hair against his arm. She hesitated, and in that still moment his heart seemed to stop, waiting—*hoping*—though he wasn't entirely sure for what.

At last her fingers slipped from his wrist, and with their loss the warmth seemed to drain from his body. "No."

"Then I shall fulfill my end of the bargain."

He didn't wait to see if she would say anything more. He fled the room.

Downstairs he quickly donned the costume of the Ghost, determinedly driving all thought from his mind, and drifted into the night.

Twenty minutes later, Godric strode down an alley in St. Giles. The One Horned Goat was a rather notorious tavern. The mere fact that Fraser-Burnsby's footman had been in any way connected to it should've made d'Arque suspicious of Harris's motives.

But then the viscount obviously didn't know St. Giles as well as he.

The One Horned Goat was on the ground floor of a brick and wood building perpetually listing ever so slightly to the side. The goat on the dark wooden sign swinging from the corner of the building had no horns at all—on its head. The eponymous "horn" of the tavern's name lay elsewhere on the animal's body. The place did a brisk trade in everything illicit to be had in St. Giles: gin, prostitution, and the trade of stolen items. More than one highwayman had used the One Horned Goat as his base of operations.

Godric slouched in the shadows until he saw the lad who worked about the place come out to empty slops into the channel.

"Boy."

The child was a product of St. Giles. His eyes widened,

but he didn't bother trying to run as Godric revealed himself. Neither did he come any closer.

Godric flipped a coin to the lad. "Tell Archer I'd like a word—and mind you inform him that I'll come in after him if he's not out in two minutes."

The boy pocketed the coin and ran back into the tavern without a sound.

Godric didn't have long to wait. A tall, thin man ducked his head to avoid braining himself on the lintel as he emerged from the One Horned Goat.

He straightened and looked cautiously around before sighting Godric and looking resentfully resigned. "What you want from me, Ghost?"

"I want to know about a man named Harris."

"Don't know no 'Arris." Archer looked shiftily away, but that didn't tell Godric anything. Archer always looked a bit shifty. His complexion was an unhealthy yellowish white, as pale as some cave-dwelling aquatic animal. His eyes were bulbous and colorless, his hair a strange, flat black, clinging greasily to the tavern keep's skull.

Godric arched a brow, leaning against the building, his arms crossed. "The footman who saw Roger Fraser-Burnsby murdered in St. Giles?"

"Lots o' murders in St. Giles." Archer shrugged.

"You're lying to me." Godric dropped his voice to a silky whisper. "Fraser-Burnsby was a toff. There was a manhunt immediately after his murder. All of St. Giles remembers it."

"And if'n I do?" the tavern keep asked gruffly. "What's it got to do wif me?"

"His possessions were sent here several weeks after the murder."

"An'?"

"Who picked them up?"

The tavern keep gave an odd wheezing sound that must've been his version of a laugh. "'Ow you expect me to remember that? It's been years, Ghost."

Godric uncrossed his arms.

Archer abruptly stopped wheezing. "'Onest, Ghost! I swears on my ma's grave, I do. I can't remember who might've taken 'Arris's stuff."

Godric took a step closer.

The tavern keep squealed and backed up, his hands raised. "Wait! Wait! I do know somethin' you might like."

Godric cocked his head. "And what's that?"

Archer licked his lips nervously. "Word is, 'Arris is dead."

"When?"

Archer shook his head. "I don't know, but a long time ago. Maybe afore 'is things were ever sent for."

Godric studied the tavern owner for a minute. Archer was a born liar, but Godric thought he might actually be telling the truth now. He could threaten and intimidate the man more, but he had the feeling that it would be a waste of time.

The One Horned Goat's door crashed open and three soldiers staggered out, obviously the worse for drink.

"You learn anything more and I want to know about it." Godric flipped a coin at the man and turned away to duck into an alley, swiftly gliding away.

The moon was a mocking oval above, her light pale and sickly. Behind him, he could hear wild laughter and the crash of barrels being knocked down. He didn't turn.

He could sense someone following him and his heart

sang with gladness. Suddenly the rage from earlier tonight was back, as fresh and raw as ever.

How dare she?

He'd given up his home, his solitude, his peace of mind, and his goddamned *body* for her, and *this* was how she repaid him? By imagining he was another man while he had his cock in her? He'd been suspicious the first time but dismissed the notion. But tonight, there'd been something—the way she'd held herself, the refusal to meet his eyes, the very fact that she wouldn't let him *make love* to her properly, damn it—that had roused all of his doubts. And then it had hit him: He wasn't the man she was fucking at all. He didn't know if she dreamed of Fraser-Burnsby or d'Arque or some man he'd never met, but it hardly mattered.

He wasn't going to be used as a blasted proxy.

They came from around the corner up ahead, riding two abreast, and he was so distracted that he didn't realize they were even there until they were almost on him.

Godric didn't know who was more surprised: him or the dragoons.

The man on the right recovered first, drawing his saber and kicking his horse into a charge. He couldn't outrun a galloping horse and the alley was narrow. Godric flattened himself against the grimy bricks at his back. The first dragoon charged past, the horse nearly brushing Godric's tunic, but the second, slower dragoon was smarter. The soldier kneed his horse until the great beast was hemming him in, threatening to either crush him against the bricks or, more likely, run him through with the sharp point of a saber. There was no room to dodge around the sweating, snorting horse. He looked up and saw the sagging wooden balcony, tacked on the building he was pressed against like an afterthought. It might not hold his weight, but he had no choice now.

Godric stretched his arms overhead and jumped, grasping one of the supporting rails of the balcony. He curled his legs up, his left shoulder aching as he felt the stitches pop from the wound. His legs were suddenly near the horse's head and the animal was startled at his movement. The dragoon pulled hard on the reins, trying to control the beast, and the horse reared.

Godric swung and dropped in back of the horse, rolling away as he hit the hard cobblestones and rising with his long sword out and up.

But the first dragoon had wheeled his horse around by now, trapping Godric between the two mounted men. The only thing he could be glad of was that the dragoons seemed to be by themselves, a mounted patrol of two.

"Surrender!" the second dragoon shouted, his hand reaching for the pistol holstered in his saddle.

Damn it! Godric leaped for the man, catching his arm before he could lay hand on the pistol, and yanked hard. The dragoon half fell over the side of the saddle. His horse shied violently at the shift in weight, and the man tumbled to the ground.

Godric turned to the first dragoon in time to parry a sword thrust aimed at his head. He was at a disadvantage on the ground, but he was in no mood to retreat. He swung at the mounted man, missed, and only just in time saw the flicker of the other man's eyes.

Or perhaps it wasn't *quite* in time.

The blow from behind knocked him to his knees. His head spun dizzily, but his mood was foul. Godric twisted and embraced his attacker's legs, toppling the dragoon. He swarmed up the other man's supine form, straddling him, and—

God *fucking* damn!

The dragoon really shouldn't have kneed him in the bollocks.

Godric sucked in a pained breath, reared over the soldier, and slammed his fist into the man's face. Over and over again. The *smack* of bare flesh on flesh savagely satisfying in the dark alley. Behind him, the other dragoon was shouting something and the horse's hooves were clattering dangerously close to where they were sprawled, but Godric just didn't give a damn.

Only the sound of more horses nearing made Godric stop. He stared at the man beneath him. The dragoon's eyes were swollen and his lips split and bleeding, but he was alive and still struggling.

Thank God.

He was up and running in less than a second, the horses close behind him. A barrel at the corner of a house gave him a leg up and then he was climbing the side of the house, toes and fingertips straining for holds before he reached the rooftop.

A shout came from below, but he didn't take the time to look back, simply fleeing over the roof, loose tiles sliding and crashing to the street below. He ran, the blood pumping in his chest, and didn't stop until he was nearly a half-mile away.

Only then, as he leaned panting against a chimney, did he realize he was still being followed.

Godric drew his short sword, watching as the slim shape cautiously made the ridge of the roof and nimbly began climbing down. He waited until the lad came abreast of him. Godric grabbed him by the collar, arching his head back, laying the short sword on the bared neck.

"Why are you following me?"

Quick, intelligent eyes flashed to his, but the boy made no move to free himself. "Digger Jack said as 'ow you'd be wantin' information 'bout the lassie snatchers."

"And?"

The wide mouth curved without mirth. "I'm one o' 'em."

Twenty minutes later Godric watched as the boy stuffed his face with tea and lavishly buttered bread. He'd revised his estimation of the former lassie snatcher's age downward. When he'd first seen the boy, Godric had thought him a young man, but that was because he had the height of a grown man. Now, sitting in the kitchens of the Home for Unfortunate Infants and Foundling Children, he saw the boy's soft cheeks, the slim neck, and gentle lines of his jaw. He couldn't be older than fifteen at the most.

His brown hair was clubbed back with a ragged bit of string, strands falling out and around his oval face. He wore a greasy waistcoat and a coat several sizes too big for him and a floppy hat pulled low over his brow, which he hadn't bothered removing even when inside. His wrists were thin and rather delicate and the nails on both hands were rimmed with grime.

The boy caught him staring and jerked his chin up defiantly, the corners of his mouth wet with milky tea. "Wha'?"

Winter Makepeace, sitting beside Godric, stirred. "What is your name?"

The boy shrugged and, apparently sensing no immediate threat, turned his attention to the plate of bread before him. "Alf."

He spooned out a huge blob of strawberry jam from an earthen jar, plopping it on a slice of already buttered bread, and folded the bread around the gooey middle. Then he shoved half of the bread into his mouth.

Godric exchanged glances with Winter. It had taken quite a bit of persuasion—as well as a threat or two—before he'd been able to get Alf into the home. Godric daren't remain outside in St. Giles while the dragoons were abroad, and he certainly wasn't about to take a strange lad back to his own house.

Especially when the lad was an admitted lassie snatcher.

"How long have you been employed by the lassie snatchers?" Winter asked in his deep, calm voice.

Alf gulped and washed down his bread with a long drag of tea. "'Bout a month, but I don' work for them arse'oles no more."

Winter refilled his teacup without comment, but Godric was less forbearing. "You led me to believe you were a lassie snatcher *now*."

Alf stopped chewing and looked up, his eyes narrowed. "An' I'm the best yer gonna get. Ain't none o' them 'oo's lassie snatchers *now* gonna talk to yer. Best settle for me."

Winter caught Godric's eye and shook his head slightly.

Godric sighed. He was finding it difficult to quiz this youth while keeping his own voice to a whisper so it might not be recognized in the future. Besides, Winter had far more experience with boys.

Even difficult ones.

"How did you become a lassie snatcher?" Winter asked now. He reached for the loaf of bread and sawed off two more slices.

Godric raised his eyebrows. Alf had already eaten half the loaf.

"Word gets 'round," Alf said as he started smearing large lumps of butter on his bread. "They like to work in teams, like, a bloke an' a lad. Knew one o' their snatcher lads 'oo got run over by a dray cart. Busted 'is 'ead an' were dead in a day. So there were an openin' like. Pay was good." He paused to take a slurping gulp of tea before covering the bread with jam. "Job was fine."

"Then why are you no longer employed as a lassie snatcher?" Winter asked neutrally.

Alf's bread was all ready, jam running out of the pinched sides, but he just stared at it. "It were one o' the young ones, name o' Hannah. 'Ad ginger 'air, she did. Not more'n five or so. Chattered a lot, like, wasn't afraid o' me or nothin', even though 'er auntie 'ad sold 'er to us. Me an' Sam took 'er to the workshop and she seemed fine enough. . . ."

"Fine?" Godric growled low. "They *work* those girls, beat them, and hardly feed them."

"There're worse." Alf's words were defiant, but he wouldn't meet Godric's eyes. "Bawdy 'ouses, beggars what'll blind a babe to make 'er more pathetic."

Winter shot Godric a quelling look. "What happened to Hannah, Alf?"

"Just it, innit?" Alf dug his dirty fingers into the folded bread until red jam oozed out. "She weren't there next time I come by. They wouldn't tell me what 'ad 'appened to 'er. She were just . . . gone." Alf looked up then, his eyes angry and wet. "Stopped it then, didn't I? Ain't gonna be part o' 'urting wee little lassies."

"That was very brave of you," Winter said softly. "I would think the lassie snatchers would not be pleased by a defection."

Alf snorted, finally picking up his messy bread and jam. "Don't know 'xactly what *defection* is, but they'd be glad enough to see me put to bed wif a shovel."

"Tell us where they are, *who* they are, and we'll solve the problem for you," Godric growled.

"Ain't just one place," Alf said, speaking seriously. "There's *three* workshops I knows of, and prolly more'n that."

"Three?" Winter breathed. "How could we not have known?"

"Sly ones, ain't they?" Alf shoved the bread into his mouth and for a moment was mute as he chewed. Then he swallowed. "Best do it at night. They've guards, but everyone's sleepier at night. I can show you."

"We'll have to move fast," Godric said, looking at Winter and receiving a nod. "Can you show me tomorrow night?"

"Aye." Alf took the rest of the cut bread and shoved it into a pocket of his coat. "Best be off, then, 'adn't I, afore 'tis light out."

"You're more than welcome to stay here," Winter offered.

Alf shook his head. "Kind o' you, but I don't like staying in such a big place."

Godric frowned. "Will you be safe?"

Alf cocked his head, smiling cynically. "Worried I won't be back tomorrow? Nah, no one's can catch me if'n I don't want. Ta for the tea."

And he was gone out the kitchen door.

"Damn it, I should follow him," Godric muttered.

But Winter shook his head. "We don't want to scare him off. Besides, I saw the dragoons in the back alley earlier."

Godric swore. "They followed me." That would make getting home more difficult than usual. He looked at Winter. "Do you really think the boy's safe until tomorrow?"

Winter shrugged as he put away the bread. "It's out of our hands now."

And Godric supposed he'd have to be content with that knowledge until tomorrow night.

THE SOUND OF male voices outside her window woke Megs from a restless slumber. She blinked sleepily, glancing about her bedroom. It was light, but so early Daniels hadn't yet come to wake her and help dress her.

Megs rose and wandered to the window, parting the curtains to look down on the courtyard. Godric stood, wrapped in a cloak, talking to a man in a tricorne. Megs stared. There was something about the other man, something about the way Godric stood so stiffly that made her uneasy.

Then the man in the tricorne looked up at the house and Megs gasped.

It was Captain Trevillion.

As she watched, his hand shot out suddenly, wrenching Godric's cloak open.

She whirled and found her wrapper, pulling it on as she ran from the room and down the stairs, her heart in her throat. Would Godric's costume be enough for the dragoon captain to arrest him?

But when she tumbled breathlessly into the entry hall, her husband was closing the door behind him as serenely as if he'd just returned from a chat with the king.

"Godric!" she hissed.

He looked up and she froze.

It was subtle, but she could read the signs now—his mouth thin and tense, his eyes a little narrowed. He wasn't serene, not really. He looked both tired and angry.

She didn't remember descending the rest of the stairs, only her hands rising toward his face, wanting to give comfort.

His own hands blocked hers.

She blinked, focusing on his eyes, and saw that he stared at her blankly.

He hadn't forgiven her for the night before, then.

"What happened in St. Giles?" she asked in a small voice. She wanted so badly to touch him, to make sure he was whole and well. "Why did Captain Trevillion let you go?"

"Godric." Mrs. St. John's surprised voice came from the stairs and Megs turned to see that both she and all three of Godric's sisters stood there.

Moulder appeared from somewhere. "Sir?"

"Why is everyone up so early?" Godric muttered.

"Have you been out?" Sarah asked quietly.

"None of your business," her brother said flatly, walking toward the back of the house.

"But—" his stepmother started.

"Don't question me," he growled without looking back, and disappeared down the hall.

Mrs. St. John looked helplessly at Megs, her eyes shining with tears.

"I'll talk to him," Megs said with all the reassurance she could muster before hurrying after Godric.

If it weren't for her mother-in-law and those tears, she would never have dared beard him again this soon after the disaster of last night. She'd hurt him badly, and he'd already made it clear he didn't want her nearby.

Well, he'd just have to put up with her anyway.

She opened the door to his study without bothering to knock.

Inside, Godric was pouring himself a glass of brandy and talking to Moulder. "The usual place. Make sure you're not followed."

"Yes, sir." Moulder looked relieved to scurry from the room.

Megs closed the door behind him and cleared her throat.

"Go away," Godric growled at her, tossing back half his glass of liquid.

Megs winced. He truly was a bear bearded in his den.

She took a deep breath. "No. I'm your wife."

He cocked his head, his beautiful lips curled. "Are you?"

Her face flamed. "Yes."

Godric looked away then, as if losing interest in her. He shrugged off his cloak and coat, moving stiffly.

Megs blinked. Beneath the cloak Godric was wearing a sedate brown suit, not a trace of harlequin motley anywhere. He pressed his fingers against a panel next to the fireplace. The panel sprang open, revealing a hidden cupboard behind it. She watched as he took his short sword from an inner pocket in his cloak and stowed it in the secret cupboard.

She ventured a little farther into the room. "Did Captain Trevillion follow you?"

"Yes." He hissed under his breath as he gingerly pulled his shirt over his head and she inhaled. His wound had reopened, a sluggish trail of blood dripping down his broad back. "From St. Giles. He's very good, actually. Several times I wasn't sure he was even there behind me."

She picked up his shirt and started to tear a strip from the tail—it was ruined by the blood anyway. "I'm so glad you didn't wear your Ghost costume last night."

"But I did."

Her hands froze on his shirt, staring at his crystal gray eyes. "What do you mean?"

He shrugged and then winced. "I knew he was following me and would no doubt take the opportunity to confront me if I led him home. Fortunately I made provisions for just such an eventuality years ago. I left a set of clothes in the care of an old widow. It was only a moment to duck into her crowded tenement and exchange the Ghost's costume for my hidden clothes. Actually," he said thoughtfully as he stared into his glass, "it's rather a miracle Trevillion didn't lose my trail in the tenement. But then again, I did say he was good."

"I'm so glad you admire him." Megs tore a strip from his shirt with a rather violent motion. She wadded the linen and dipped it unceremoniously into his brandy glass.

"That's good French brandy," Godric said mildly.

"And your back is good English flesh," she retorted rather nonsensically before pressing the wet cloth against the cut.

He grunted.

"Oh, Godric." She dabbed with tender care at his hot skin, her fingers trembling. "What happened last night?"

He shot a look over his shoulder at her, his eyes glittering, and for a moment she thought he'd say something they'd both regret. "I questioned the owner of a tavern on your behalf."

"And?"

His jaw tightened. "I learned very little, I'm afraid. The footman who reported Fraser-Burnsby's death is thought to be dead himself."

Her hand stilled on him. "Killed?"

He shook his head. "Perhaps. I simply don't know. But it's certainly suspicious that the only witness disappeared and then presumably met his death soon after Fraser-Burnsby was murdered."

His wound had ceased bleeding and the blood was cleaned from his back. Still she pressed the cloth carefully to his skin, loath, somehow, to stop touching him. "Where do we go from here?"

"The footman must have family or friends." Godric frowned. "If nothing else, I can ask d'Arque again about Fraser-Burnsby."

"But I can do that—"

"No." He stepped away from her.

She blinked at the fierce growl, her hand still raised foolishly in the air.

He grimaced and looked away from her, grabbing a banyan that had been lying over the back of a chair. "If the footman was deliberately killed, Megs, then there is at least one man out there willing to murder to hide his crime. I don't want you poking at this."

"Godric—"

"We made a pact." Godric pulled on the banyan, buttoning it up. "I upheld my part."

She held his gaze a moment longer before throwing the

bloody bit of linen down. They'd have to burn it later so the servants wouldn't see. "Very well."

His shoulders visibly relaxed.

She pressed her useless hands together. "You said earlier that you had your own Ghostly business to attend to in St. Giles. Can I ask what it was?"

His eyes narrowed and for a moment she thought he wouldn't answer her. "I was on the trail of a group who steal little girls and work them near to death making silk stockings, of all things. They're called the lassie snatchers."

Megs's mouth sagged with horror. She thought of the girls at the home, the little maids they'd so recently hired. The idea of someone abusing children just like them made her stomach roll.

"Oh," she said weakly.

He nodded curtly. "Now if your curiosity is assuaged...?"

It was a dismissal, but her curiosity *wasn't* satisfied. "What about your back? You've pulled the stitches out."

"Don't fuss. I'll have Moulder bandage it later," Godric said curtly. "It'll just pull out again when—" He glanced at her and closed his lips.

She felt an awful premonition. "When what, Godric?"

The corner of his beautiful mouth curled down. "When I return to St. Giles tonight."

Chapter Thirteen

*The air became brisk as the Hellequin's great black horse
climbed into the Peak of Whispers. Faith shivered and
huddled against the Hellequin until he reached into one
of his saddlebags and drew out a cloak.
"Wrap this about you, lass," he said gruffly, and Faith took
the cloak with a grateful word of thanks.
Tall pines, gloomy and black, rose around them now, and
as the wind whistled through their branches, Faith seemed
to hear faint cries and murmurs. As she looked, she saw
small, trailing wisps, floating in the wind....*
—From *The Legend of the Hellequin*

Artemis Greaves slipped through the crowded London
street, her pace fast and determined that morning. She
had only a couple of hours to herself before Penelope
would wake and want her company to chat and ana-
lyze every detail of the previous evening's ball. Artemis
sighed—albeit fondly. If she'd thought Penelope feath-
erheaded before, it was nothing to what her cousin was
like when she was determined to marry a duke. There
were angled invitations, plotted chance meetings, and the
near-constant jealousy over Miss Royle, who, Artemis
suspected, didn't even know she was engaged in a fierce
rivalry with Penelope.

All of it would be a quiet source of amusement were it not for the object of Penelope's obsession: His Grace, the Duke of Wakefield. Artemis didn't like the man, doubted very much that he would, in the end, make her cousin happy. And if they ever did marry...

She stopped and was nearly run down by a porter carrying two geese on his back.

"Watch out, luv," the man flung over his shoulder, not unkindly, as he stepped around her.

Artemis swallowed and started forward again, moving easily in the stream of shuffling, stomping, running, strolling, limping, and tripping people. London's streets were like a great river of people, constantly flowing and ebbing, joining into greater rushing courses, parting into side streams, getting caught in whirlpools of milling humanity.

One swam or ran the risk of drowning.

If Penelope married the Duke of Wakefield, in the best case Artemis would join her in her new home, a constant, pale wraith, as His Grace had put it. Continuing to be Penelope's handmaiden, eventually perhaps, the kind aunt to their children. In the worst case, Penelope would decide that she no longer needed a companion.

Artemis inhaled shakily. But those worries were for the future. She had more immediate problems to deal with.

Twenty minutes later, she at last neared her destination: a small jeweler's shop in a not very fashionable area of London. It had taken Artemis months of carefully worded questions among the ladies of her acquaintance to get the address of a suitable shop. Her queries could've caused comment and started gossip if she'd taken a more direct route.

Artemis glanced around cautiously and then pushed open the door to the little shop. The interior was very dim and almost bare. An elderly man sat behind a high counter with a few rings, bracelets, and necklaces displayed. She was the only patron in the shop.

The shopkeeper looked up at her entrance. He was a small, stooped man with an overlarge nose and leathery, wrinkled skin. He wore a worn gray wig and red waistcoat and coat. His gaze seemed to appraise her clothing: not rich. Artemis stopped the urge to lower her head.

"Good morning," he said.

"Good morning," she replied, taking her courage in her hands. She *needed* to do this—there was no other way. "I am told that you sometimes buy items of jewelry."

He blinked and said cautiously, "Yes?"

She approached his counter and withdrew a small silk bag from her pocket. The strings were knotted and it took her a minute to untangle them, tears pricking at her eyes. It was her most treasured possession.

But need outweighed sentimentality.

The strings finally gave up their struggle and she pulled open the little bag, sliding out the treasure within. Green and gold sparkled, even within the dimness of the shop, belying the necklace's true worth: she knew the stone was really paste, the gold merely painted gilt.

Still, she gazed with as much awe upon the little pendant as she had when it had first lain in her hands, nearly thirteen years ago on her fifteenth birthday. His dear eyes had gleamed with eager anticipation as he'd given the silk bag to her, and she'd never asked how he'd come by the necklace, almost afraid to.

She watched now as the jeweler fixed spectacles over

his eyes, pulled a lamp closer, and bent forward, a magnifying glass in his hand. The delicate gilt filigree around the green stone glittered in the light. The pendant was in the shape of a teardrop, the chain it hung from much cheaper and duller.

The jeweler stiffened and bent closer, then abruptly looked at her. "Where did you get this?" His tone was stern.

She smiled uncertainly. "It was a gift."

The elderly man's eyes, sharp and clear, lingered on her admittedly pedestrian clothes. "I doubt that."

She blinked at his rudeness. "I beg your pardon?"

"Young lady," the jeweler said, sitting back and gesturing to the necklace still lying on the counter. "This is a flawless emerald set in what I suspect is nearly pure gold. Either you are selling this for your mistress or you stole it."

Artemis acted without thought. She snatched up the necklace and, clutching her skirts, ran from the little shop, ignoring the shopkeeper's shouts. Her heart was beating like a deer in flight as she darted down the street, dodging carts and chairmen, expecting any moment to hear shouts of pursuit from behind her. She didn't stop running until the breath caught in her throat and she was forced to walk.

She hadn't left her name with the jeweler. He didn't know who she was and thus couldn't send a thief catcher after her. She shuddered at the thought, and then surreptitiously glanced at the emerald still in her hand.

It winked slyly at her, a fortune she'd never wanted, a treasure she couldn't sell precisely *because* it was much too dear. Artemis laughed bitterly. The necklace had been a gift, but she had no proof.

Dear Lord, *where* had Apollo gotten the necklace?

*   *   *

DUSK WAS FALLING when Megs went into the garden for a walk after an early supper. Higgins had cleared the paths and laid down fine gravel, weeded the beds and neatly edged them. A few faltering daffodils trailed bravely near the house, planted and then forgotten by some ancestor of Godric's.

Megs paced and thought. Gardens were such peaceful spots, even half-naked ones such as this. But soon she and Higgins would be able to add roses and irises, peonies and Michaelmas daisies.

If Godric let her stay that long.

She frowned. He'd shut himself in his room since his early morning appearance, ignoring both luncheon and the dinner summons, although she'd noticed that trays of food had been brought up to him. At least he wasn't starving in there.

She paused by the old fruit tree and laid her hand on the rough bark, somehow soothed by its presence. The light was nearly gone, but she peered closer at the low branches, her heart beginning to speed. There were buds on the twigs that lined the branches, she could swear. Maybe—

"Megs."

His voice was low but carried easily through the garden, steady and commanding.

She turned and saw Godric, standing in the open doorway to Saint House, the light behind him casting a long, black shadow into the garden. For a second she shivered at the image, the dark stranger come to invade her peaceful garden, but then she shook herself. This was Godric, and whatever else he might be, he was no longer a stranger.

He was her husband.

She walked toward him, and as she neared, he held out his hand to her. She took it, lifting her head to peer at him as she'd peered at the fruit tree, looking for signs of life.

"Come," he said, and pulled her gently into the house.

He led her through the hall and ascended the stairs, her hand still locked in his, and with every step her pulse beat faster until she was nearly panting when he opened the door to his room.

The room within shone with candlelight and Megs blinked and looked at Godric.

He watched her with eyes from which he'd dropped the shutters. The intent that blazed from within was daunting. She nearly took a step back.

He still held her hand.

"I made a promise to you," he said. "And I will keep it—but not as we did before."

She suddenly knew he was talking of their lovemaking the previous night.

"I...I'm sorry," she stuttered. "I didn't mean to give you the impression that I was pretending you were Roger. I wasn't. It's just that what we did seemed like a betrayal of him. I didn't want to lose him any more."

Her lips parted, but nothing more emerged because it had finally dawned on her whom she'd actually been betraying.

"Don't you think I might've felt the same way about Clara?" he asked low. "Don't you think I had to sacrifice something to give you what you wanted?"

She bowed her head, for she felt ashamed. "I'm sorry, Godric."

He cupped her face in his hands and lifted it so she could

see his clear gray eyes. "It no longer matters. What matters is how I—*we*—intend to go forth. Starting with *this*."

He lowered his mouth toward her, slowly, so that she could see what he would do. Her eyes widened before she let them fall, surrendering.

It was the least she could do to make amends.

His kiss wasn't like the gentle embraces of before. This was a seal, a promise of purpose, a pact of understanding. His thumb pressed against her chin, opening her for him, letting him lick inside, claiming her. Her doubts rushed to the surface, making her stiffen, but he wouldn't let her pull away. He held her and bit down on her lower lip, waiting until she stilled again.

She opened her eyes and saw that he watched her, assessing her even as he let go of her lip, laving it slowly with his hot tongue. She snapped her eyes shut again. This was too close, too personal.

He'd paused at the corner of her mouth, licking it almost pensively, until she yielded with a shudder, parting her lips wider, inviting him in. He made a low, pleased rumble at the back of his throat, and then he was inside her again and she caught his tongue, suckling in atonement. His hands drifted to splay over her neck, arching her head back so that she was entirely open, entirely vulnerable to him, her mouth a sacrifice.

His hands slid from her neck, down her bodice to her waist, and then he was lifting her, walking with her across the room, his mouth on hers, his tongue between her lips. He set her down by the bed and only then lifted his head. While her chest felt tight—her lungs laboring to draw breath—only the dampness of his mouth, the heaviness of his eyelids gave any indication of what they did.

"Take off your clothes," he ordered.

Megs's eyes widened.

He tilted his head down, looking her in the eye. "Now."

Her lips parted, swollen and oversensitive, and she touched them gently with her tongue, exploring. "Will you help me?"

"I'll undo any hooks or laces you can't reach."

She bowed her head then, fumbling with her bodice. It was no small thing for a lady to undress. Usually she had the help of Daniels and two maids. It would take time. It would not be graceful.

And in the end she would be exposed.

But he stood before her, only inches away, and demanded it, so she complied.

First came the bodice, unhooked and pulled apart. When she'd gotten it off, she moved to put it on a chair or table, but he took it from her before she could and tossed it on the floor nearby.

She bit her lip and didn't say anything, merely working on the ties at her waist. Her skirts fell in a pool at her feet and she stepped from them, kicking them gently aside. She toed off her slippers and then bent to lift her chemise and roll down her stockings. He didn't move and her head was nearly touching his thigh. The position made her gasp.

At least she thought it was the position.

She straightened, barefoot, and began on the horrible laces to her stays. They always tangled when she tried to undo them herself. Her fingers shook and she made a frustrated sound as the knot tightened. Godric seemed uninterested, breathing slow and deep in front of her. But then her eyes glanced down and she saw—

Well. He wasn't *entirely* uninterested.

The laces finally loosened and she began to draw them through the eyelets, her chest expanding, her breasts falling free. She glanced up at him and held those crystalline eyes as she drew the stays over her head.

He didn't react other than to glance down her body. She still wore the chemise.

His gaze rose to meet hers again. "Everything."

She knew it would come down to this, knew he was determined to impress upon her that tonight was different from their previous nights. She would do it, no matter that her neck and face felt aflame, except the reason *why* she was doing it had become confused in all the heat and emotions. Because while she still wanted a baby—very, very much—there might be a more immediate want.

And he was standing right in front of her, waiting for her to finish stripping for him.

She reached for the hem of her chemise and threw it off before she could think, and then she just froze, standing there naked before him.

He took the final step that made their bodies meet—her nude nipples against the fine wool of his coat, for he was still entirely dressed. He flattened his palms over her shoulders before delicately running his fingers down to her breasts. He circled her fullness, trailing his fingers up to her nipples and running his blunt fingernails around the very edge where rose skin met pale.

She gasped, but before she could say anything, he bent in one swift move and picked her up as if she were as light as a feather, which she most definitely was not.

He placed her on the bed before she could fully understand the fact that he was carrying her. She lay there watching as he toed off his shoes and removed his coat and waistcoat. He doffed his wig and laid it on his dressing table, and then turned back to her. She expected him to continue disrobing, but instead he knelt on the bed, crawling until he was braced over her supine form, close but not actually touching her. He stared at her with severe gray eyes until she lifted a hand and touched the side of his face.

He closed his eyes, almost as if she'd pained him with her touch. "Say my name."

She swallowed before she could make her tongue work. "Godric."

His eyes opened and they no longer seemed quite as cold. "Megs."

He bent his head and touched his lips to hers, brushing, once, twice, until his mouth settled on hers, demanding entrance. She let him in, teasing his tongue with hers, learning the taste of his mouth, the feel of his lips. He broke their kiss and stared at her once more, his eyes demanding something of her.

"Godric," she said obediently.

And it seemed to appease him. He tongued his way down her throat, making her arch, making her wonder how very different he was from Roger. They'd met in trysts, Roger and she, and thus, perhaps by the very nature of their meetings, their joinings had been hurried—the flare of passion fast, nearly out of control, and over again much too quickly.

Godric, in contrast, seemed to enjoy simply exploring her. Taking his time as if he wanted to wring something from her. Something more than mere passion.

The thought made her uneasy.

He lifted his head suddenly as if he were aware her attention had wandered, his eyebrows drawn together over stormy gray eyes. "Say my name."

"Godric," she whispered.

He lowered his mouth to her right breast, licking around the sensitive nipple before abruptly drawing her into his mouth.

She gasped, her hands flying instinctively to his shorn hair, grasping uselessly at the too-short locks. He suckled strongly, his tongue working against the underside of the nipple, his fingers petting her other breast. That one point of pleasure was so intense, making her mouth open soundlessly.

He moved to her other breast, laving it before sucking for many long minutes. Her legs moved restlessly, her thighs clenching.

He raised his head above her, his eyes on her breasts, red and wet now. "My name."

"G-Godric."

He thumbed her nipples—in reward or punishment, she wasn't sure—as he began mouthing over her ribs and down her belly. He was heading in the same direction as he had the night before and she instinctively tensed.

He placed both hands flat against her hip bones and took the time to kiss her lower belly, just above where the springy hair began.

Then he looked at her face.

She licked her lips before parting them. "Godric."

He watched her as his hands grasped her thighs and slowly parted them, pushing until her legs were spread wide.

Then he looked down.

Instinctively she tried to bring her legs together again, but his hands were hard and firm. Not even Roger had examined her so closely. So intimately. The rooms they had trysted in had been dim. Even when he'd kissed her there, it had been only a fleeting touch. She'd been so embarrassed...

Was so embarrassed.

She knew—*knew*—she was wet there, her curls moist, and she couldn't possibly be pretty. Why would he want to do such a thing? Stare at her so long without moving? She looked wildly at all the candles lit around the room. Would he put them out if she asked?

"Say my name." His voice, even lower, even more gravelly than usual, interrupted her frantic thoughts.

"G-Godric."

It was as if his name on her lips put spur to him. He lowered his head so fast she hadn't the time to react, to try to pull him back, and once he'd found his goal...

She didn't want to.

She'd never felt such a wicked thing. He was licking her. Licking into her folds, lapping at that hard pebble at the apex of her slit, tonguing his way in deeper, circling and probing. She caught her breath and then couldn't exhale, her body shivering, her soul quaking. How was she supposed to endure this? How was she supposed to survive it? There were *sounds*—moist, intimate sounds. The sound of him pleasuring her in an act that felt like a primitive branding. How did he know? Where had he learned such monstrous, *awful*, excruciatingly wonderful things?

He opened his mouth, placed it over her clitoris, and sucked, and then she completely lost her mind.

It went flying out the window as she arched under him and moaned, low and embarrassingly loud—well, it would've been embarrassing if she'd still had her mind, which she did not. Because he was doing something so deliciously sinful that she was actually pushing against him with her hips, whining under her breath, wanting more. And he just kept doing it. Sucking and licking and— oh!—thrusting a finger inside of her until she exploded. She felt the combustion, the tremors, the roaring in her ears, and then the wonderful, languorous warmth. It snuck through her limbs, turning her muscles to pudding, her bones to ginger biscuits, utterly weak and sweet and open.

Megs giggled. Perhaps she *had* lost her mind.

She opened her eyes to see Godric sitting up beside her, watching her, his lips curved gently and his gray eyes almost warm.

"Godric," she whispered, and held out her hand to him.

He took her hand, spreading her fingers and kissing each one.

She caught her breath, her eyes blurring. He touched her as if he cherished her. As if what they were doing here was more than a simple physical act. He was standing beside the bed now, stripping off his breeches and stockings and pulling his shirt over his head. She watched him and saw that his pendant was a small key around his neck on a silver chain. Then she was distracted by the sight of his bare chest, and here in the light from all the candles she could see the scars: a twisted white line along his rib cage, a raised welt on one shoulder and an indent on his left forearm as if a chunk of his flesh had been ripped away sometime in the past. And yet, despite the scars— maybe even *because* of them—she found him beautiful.

His chest was wide, the curves of his upper arms and shoulders well delineated. He had a diamond of body hair centered between his dark nipples, and his belly was taut and lean. His waist tapered gracefully into his hips, and—

He lowered his smallclothes and she stared. He rose ruddy and proud, the round crown of his penis shining with liquid and his balls drawn up tight underneath. She'd never seen Roger completely nude. Never seen any other man completely nude. It was a glorious sight. She was glad, suddenly, that he was her husband. That she could be selfish in this one thing: no one else could ever see him like this. He was hers.

Even if it was only for a time.

Her eyes rose to his and she saw that he stood watching as she looked her fill at him.

She blushed. "Godric."

And he smiled, tight, approving, and predatory in a wholly masculine way.

He placed a knee on the bed and leaned over her. "Now. Now I take you, just you and me, Megs."

There was still a twinge of doubt in her, a fearful shiver that she was betraying Roger. But she'd hurt Godric, she knew that, and he'd never done more than offer her kindness.

So she smiled back tremulously. "Just you and me."

He lowered himself over her, settling between her spread thighs, and she could feel the heavy, slick weight of his cock, sliding from her thigh to wedge in her cleft.

She inhaled. She'd just come, lovely and hard, and her flesh was sensitive to his heat, his weight, his intimate dominance of her. He framed her face with his hands and lowered his head toward her. The kiss was gentle, almost reverent, and tears sprang to her eyes. This wasn't what she'd wanted, what she'd thought she'd *needed*. He was weaving a web of intimacy, strand by intangible strand that, knotted together, would become an unbreakable net, holding her tight until she no longer even considered escape.

Her thoughts scattered as he lifted his hips a fraction and his erection dragged through her valley.

Her breath hitched.

He was rubbing, their mingled dampness making the glide so slick, so sweet. She smiled at him in invitation and saw as he raised his head that his lips were curved as well.

"Now."

He notched the tip of his penis in her and began to push. Inexorably, relentless in his strength. In his determination. He watched her, locking eyes as he breached her entrance, as he made a place for himself within her, as he joined their bodies together.

She was open beneath him, her body, her cunny, her mouth, her face, everything. Open, splayed wide, absolutely vulnerable.

Then he began to move.

Just a little, hardly retreating at all, as if he couldn't bear to leave the welcoming warmth of her body. Hard little shoves that jolted her each time.

She arched her neck, her head tilted back against the pillows, her eyelids half lowered, but her gaze still locked with his. She widened her legs even more, receiving him like the offering, the promise this was.

And he seemed to know what she was doing. His expression didn't change, but his breath caught, his eyelids lowering just a fraction as he hitched his elbows under her knees and drew her legs up even farther. He held the upper half of his body up off her now, putting pressure on that one point of contact between them as he ground and ground and ground against her.

It caught her by surprise when it came, no slow buildup, no warmth diffusing through her body. This was fast and hard, a fire sweeping through limbs already weakened by the previous orgasm. She was dimly aware of her hands scrabbling at his sides, his shoulders, as she tried to urge him to do *something*. She was going to expire, to *die*, if he didn't pick up his pace, didn't take his cock and ram it into her.

And whether because he could sense her extremity or because he was there himself, he did it. He let her legs fall and braced himself on his strong, straight arms and slammed his hips into her, making violent, urgent, *blissful* contact with her. The bed rocked, the headboard banging rhythmically against the wall, and any other time she would have been mortified, but right now . . . right now she was in paradise. White light obscured her vision as bliss flooded her being, seizing her, shaking her, giving her life.

She could fly like this, perhaps live eternally.

She came down from the heights with her limbs liquid, just in time to see Godric. His head was arched, his eyes closed, his chest shining with sweat, and his lips drawn back over his teeth as if he were in extremis. He was beautiful like this, a god made mortal in his physical delight, and she stared in awe. At the last minute, his eyes snapped open, staring at her, gray and fervent, and she gasped.

It was as if he let her see into his soul.

He dropped then, his head falling forward limply, his body collapsing down. He rolled to the side as if he feared crushing her, and she had a moment's disappointment: she wanted to feel his weight.

She lay there, catching her breath, feeling her skin grow chill. She turned her head to look at him, her husband. He lay, his expression more relaxed than she'd ever seen it before, the lines smoothed from his face, one arm thrown over his head, those elegant fingers lax and curling. A single drop of perspiration trembled at his temple and she wanted to touch it, to rub it into his skin and feel the man beneath the armor he wore. She reached out a hand, but he was moving now, rolling from the bed, getting up without a word.

She stared, drawing the coverlet over herself. "What are you doing?"

He didn't look at her. "I need to go."

"Where?" she whispered, feeling lost, abandoned.

"St. Giles."

Chapter Fourteen

"Over there," Alf said later that night. He whispered so close to Godric's ear that he could feel the boy's panting breaths. Alf was scared, though he hid it well. "In that cellar across the way. Do y'see?"

"Aye."

This was the second—and biggest—workshop of the night. He'd already freed six girls from a shed in the back of a foul courtyard—a relatively easy operation, as there had been only two guards, one of them drunk.

Now both Godric and Alf lay prone on a roof catty-corner from the cellar he'd indicated. "Is there another way in?"

Alf shook his head decisively. "Not that I ever saw."

Godric grunted, analyzing. The lassie snatchers had chosen a good spot for the workshop. The cellar door lay within a narrow well—any attackers would be exposed from behind and perforce would have to enter single file.

Of course, he'd always planned to enter by himself, so the point was moot.

Winter had argued in favor of bringing in more men for this second workshop when Godric had delivered the first six shivering girls to him. Godric was loath to trust anyone else, though, both with possible exposure of his identity and with the attack itself. He was used to working alone. This way he didn't have to rely on another's skill and dependability.

No one could fail him if he only had himself.

"There's two guards." Alf's whisper was barely audible even this close.

Godric glanced at him, and for a moment his eyes were caught by the delicacy of his profile. Something twinged at the back of his mind—something that bothered him about the boy.

Alf jerked his chin forward, distracting him. "See? One by the door, one at the entrance o' the alley."

"And another one on the roof," Godric replied.

Alf started, his gaze swinging in that direction. "Sharp eyes," he said grudgingly. "What'll you do? There's only one o' you."

"Let me worry about that," Godric whispered, rising to his haunches. "You stay here and don't get involved. I don't want to have to worry about you as well as them."

Mutiny flashed in Alf's eyes and Godric respected the scamp more for it.

Then the boy looked at the three toughs guarding the workshop and nodded. "Luck, then."

Godric smiled at him. "Thank you."

He was off, running silently across the roof in a crouch. He leaped *away* from the building housing the cellar, moving in a wide circle as he jumped from rooftop to rooftop. He was careful about it, taking a good fifteen minutes to work his way around until he was in back of the guard on the roof over the cellar. Then it was a simple matter of stealth and quiet. Killing the guard wasn't hard: a firm, quick grasp on the guard's hair, a vicious tug to bare his neck, and a lightning-strike cut across his throat. The difficulty came in making sure the guard made no sound before he died.

But he didn't. Godric had more than enough experience to make sure it was so.

The man at the end of the alley was next; the fact that he stood in the open made it a bit more complicated. When the man turned at the last moment as Godric rushed him, Godric was forced to jab him hard in the throat before he could kill him. The man fell, wheezing quietly—the vulnerable hollow of his neck was crushed; he'd suffocate before too long.

Godric's dagger thrust was quick and merciful.

He couldn't waste a second after that. It was only a matter of time before the third guard noticed that his compatriot no longer stood at the end of the alley and gave the alarm. Godric scaled the building again, his chest heaving silently, his arms and shoulders burning as he hauled himself up. He ran over the rooftop, pausing only to see where the guard stood below, and leaped into space.

He landed square atop the guard and the man fell, smashing his head against the cobblestones. He didn't move again.

But as Godric landed on the guard, he tumbled to the side, instinctively bracing himself on his left hand. Pain, white hot and blinding, flashed through his wrist. For a moment, nausea boiled in his throat and he feared he'd lose his stomach.

He stood, staggering a little.

Godric ran down the cellar stairs and kicked in the door.

The interior was black. A figure came rushing at him, but Godric was ready for the attack. He used his left shoulder to deflect the man's body and then thrust his sword into his belly. The interior guard slumped, his eyes wide as he looked down at his bloody stomach. Godric withdrew his sword with a heave that made him swallow convulsively and looked around.

A second man dropped his pistol and backed, hands raised. "Mercy! Don't kill me!"

"Bob," the bleeding man moaned. "Bob."

"Where are they?" Godric rasped. Sweat drenched his brow and he had to grit his teeth to stay upright. "The girls."

"In back," Bob said.

"I'm hurt bad," the bleeding man said.

"You're dead is what you are," Bob replied flatly.

He couldn't tie the man with only one working hand. Godric hit him in the temple with the hilt of his sword. Bob fell without a sound next to his dying fellow guard. Blackness threatened Godric's vision and he shook his head hard, stepping over the guards. The room was small with a second door at the far wall. Godric took a breath, aware that saliva was flooding his mouth, and kicked it in as well, his sword raised in preparation for a fight.

But there wasn't one. Only the eyes of children—girls—stared back at him from the cramped little room. And Godric finally realized what bothered him about Alf, about the delicacy of the boy's features.

Alf was a girl.

Godric celebrated the realization by vomiting.

MEGS WAS AWOKEN from a deep sleep by someone shaking her shoulder.

"M'lady. M'lady, please wake up!"

"Moulder?" She blinked groggily at the butler's form in the light from the candle he held. He stood by the bed, half turned away, his eyes averted from her, despite the fact that every line of his body screamed urgency.

Oh. She was nude. Megs tucked the covers around herself as she sat up. "What is it? Where is Godric?"

"He's . . ." The butler looked honestly distressed, nearly panicked. "I don't know. He's hurt. Mr. Makepeace sent word from the home. They need you to go there an' fetch him home."

"Turn your back." Megs was already scrambling from the bed, searching for her chemise, thinking about what she could put on by herself. "Have you called the carriage?"

"Yes, m'lady." Moulder had turned his back as requested, but she could tell he was shifting from one foot to the other. "Shall I call a doctor? He doesn't like doctors, says they talk too much, but if he's truly hurt, it may be beyond my abilities."

Megs didn't even have to think. "Yes, please, send for a physician."

She was searching on hands and knees now, looking for the slippers she'd worn earlier. Her eyes were blurring with stupid tears and something awful was beating at her chest, trying to get in. The slippers had fallen under Godric's bed. She was still in his room and needed to go to her own to find a wrap. Which made her think of something else.

"Make sure to put his cloak and a change of clothing in the carriage. And I'll need at least two footmen to accompany me."

"Yes, m'lady."

"What is it?"

Megs looked up and met Mrs. St. John's wide eyes. Moulder slipped from the room without the older woman even glancing at him.

Her mother-in-law stood in the doorway, her graying hair loose about her shoulders, a purple silk wrapper clutched at her throat. "Megs? Where's Godric?"

"He's..." Her mind went entirely blank. She couldn't think of a lie, something to put the older woman at ease and make her go back to bed.

Suddenly it was too much. Her eyes overflowed, the tears coursing down her cheeks.

"Megs?" Mrs. St. John stepped forward, pulling Megs close and framing her face with her palms. "What has happened? You must tell me."

"Godric is in St. Giles. I've been sent word to go to him. He's hurt."

For a moment her mother-in-law simply looked at her, and Megs saw each and every line that had folded itself into the older woman's face. All the sorrows she'd borne. All the disappointments.

Then Mrs. St. John nodded decisively and turned quickly to the door. "I'll just be three minutes. Nothing more. Wait for me."

Megs blinked, bewildered. "What are you doing?"

Mrs. St. John glanced over her shoulder, her face firm and strong. "I'm his mother. I'm coming with you."

And she was gone.

Megs blinked, but she was far too worried to contend with trying to talk Mrs. St. John out of going to St. Giles. If Godric found fault with his stepmother discovering the truth about his secret life, then Megs would deal with the problem later.

Pray she had a problem to deal with later. Pray he wasn't dying at this very moment.

Megs dashed at the tears on her cheeks and scuffed on her slippers. She hadn't time for this. Every particle of her body was urging her forward, spurring her to go to Godric's side. She wasn't sure she could wait for Mrs. St. John.

But when she made the hallway below, her mother-in-law stood by the door, already waiting. The older woman was pale, her face sagging as if she braced herself for some terrible news, but she straightened and nodded as Megs came down the stairs.

There didn't seem to be anything to say. They stepped into the chill dark, walking briskly to the carriage. It was so early there was no light in the sky, not even the hint of dawn's welcome succor from the blackness of night.

She was glad to see both Oliver and Johnny standing on the running board behind the carriage, and then Megs climbed in with Mrs. St. John and the fear crowded close. What would she do if he were unconscious? If he'd sustained permanent injury?

She recognized then the awful thing trying to burrow itself into her chest: the same hopeless regret she'd felt on the night of Roger's death. Her breast tightened and blackness swam before her eyes. She couldn't do this again. Couldn't lose another so close to her. He wasn't Roger, she tried to tell herself. He wasn't her true love. But her heart didn't seem able to tell the difference. The panic was real—maroon edged with mud-green—twisting, twisting inside of her, making her feel nauseous.

I can't. I can't.

"You will survive." Mrs. St. John's voice was sharper than Megs had ever heard it.

The black receded enough to let Megs see her mother-in-law's face. Mrs. St. John was stern, the comfortable softness taking on a strength she'd never guessed was in the older woman. And she remembered: Mrs. St. John had lost a beloved husband. Had known sorrow and still lived.

"Listen to me," her mother-in-law said in a no-nonsense voice. "Whatever we find, you must be like iron. He will need you and you must not let him down."

"Yes." Megs nodded shakily. "Yes, of course."

Mrs. St. John gave her one more sharp look as if judging her mettle, and then nodded and sat back. They made the rest of the hellishly long drive in silence.

The lane in front of the home was narrow, and thus they were forced to halt the carriage at the far end. Megs clutched the soft bag holding Godric's clothes and descended with Mrs. St. John. She was comforted when

Oliver and Johnny came to stand beside them, each of the footmen holding a pistol.

She glanced up at Tom. "Will you be all right by yourself?"

"Aye," the coachman said grimly. He brandished a pair of pistols. "Doubt anyone will bother me."

Megs nodded and turned, hurrying down Maiden Lane to the home. Two lanterns hung to either side of the home's front door and she was so focused on their beckoning light that she never even noticed the tall man who separated himself from the shadows until Oliver gave a warning cry.

Captain James Trevillion raised his hands with insulting indifference. "Surely you'll not have your man shoot a soldier of the Crown, my lady?"

"Of course not," Megs said, eyes narrowing. What was the dragoon doing lurking outside the home? She glanced at her mother-in-law and was relieved to see that the older woman was watching her warily but was smart enough not to say anything. "But you must admit it's not wise to startle an armed guard in St. Giles."

"Naturally one can't be too cautious." A corner of the dragoon captain's rather cruel mouth twitched in something that definitely *wasn't* a smile. "Especially when the Ghost of St. Giles was seen this very night."

"That's none of my business."

"Isn't it?" Captain Trevillion stepped closer, despite Oliver's growl. "The Ghost went to ground near here." The captain turned and looked speculatively at the home.

Megs sucked in a breath, tilting her chin. "Let us pass."

Something darkened in the dragoon captain's pale blue eyes. "You are well esteemed, my lady, by everyone who knows you. Had I not seen it myself, I would not credit that you would shield a murderer such as your husband."

Megs heard the sharp gasp her mother-in-law made beside her. She couldn't turn to give the older woman a warning look—she was too busy staring the dragoon captain down. He'd come right out and accused Godric of being the Ghost of St. Giles. She shouldn't show fear, shouldn't show any emotion at all.

"I don't know what you're talking about," she said, half surprised that her voice emerged evenly.

"Don't you?" The captain's thin lips twisted. "Your husband may be an aristocrat, but he isn't a peer, my lady. Sooner or later I'll catch him in disguise as the Ghost, and when I do, I'll see him kicking up his heels at Tyburn."

Her chin jerked at his blunt words.

The dragoon spread his hands in a conciliatory gesture. "Please, my lady. Much better for you to disown Mr. St. John before his disgrace. You can retire quietly to the country and never be witness to the shame of having married a murderer."

She couldn't help but flinch at the last, awful word. He was right. Godric had murdered—had confessed he didn't even know how many he'd killed—and she hated it. But that didn't mean that she hated the man himself.

"You are mistaken," she said with commendable levelness.

He arched a brow. "Am I?"

Megs started forward, sweeping past the awful man, but then suddenly rage, pure and blinding, overtook good sense. This man had no right to say such things about Godric!

She whirled, marching right up to the dragoon captain

and stabbing her forefinger into his chest. "I would never desert my husband, Captain Trevillion, and if you think I'd ever feel *shame* for being married to Godric St. John, you understand neither him nor me. My husband is the most honorable man I know. He's a good man—the *best* man I've ever known in my life—and if you don't understand that, well, then you're an addlepated *ass*."

She thought she saw a fleeting look of surprise on the dragoon captain's face as she whirled to stalk away, but she was too agitated to spare a second glance.

"My lady," he called behind her.

She ignored the horrible man, climbing the home's steps and lifting the knocker. A fine tremor was making her hands shake. She wanted only to get inside, to find Godric and make sure he was safe and well.

The best man she'd ever known. She'd said it in the heat of anger, but it was true. She might've loved Roger with all her heart, but *Godric* was the one who risked his life to save complete strangers. He might deal in violence, but he also dealt in deliverance.

Even if it meant risking his soul.

The door opened to reveal the concerned face of Isabel Makepeace. She took one look at Megs and then her eyes flickered over Megs's shoulder. Immediately a serene social smile was pasted on her face. "Oh, do come inside, my lady," Mrs. Makepeace said loudly as if Megs were making an unremarkable predawn visit to the home. "Captain Trevillion? Is that you? Oh, sir, your sense of duty is to be commended, but I do feel that you may rest well at your own home now that the day is upon us. Besides"—Isabel's smile widened until her white teeth shone—"I don't think a single man, even one so brave as yourself, is much good against the many ruffians of St. Giles."

Megs turned inside the hall as Mrs. St. John and the footmen crowded beside her and Isabel shut the door. "Did he go?"

"No." Isabel shook her head, her social smile slipping now they were all out of sight of the dragoon captain. "Captain Trevillion has the most inconvenient stubborn streak. But please don't let it worry you. He's been hunting the Ghost of St. Giles for over two years and has yet to lay hands on the man. It's enough to make even the most serene of gentlemen become bullheaded."

Isabel's tone was light, but Megs wasn't reassured. The dragoon captain knew who Godric was—and as Isabel had noted, he was bullheaded. She shivered. He didn't seem the type to give up his hunt.

"Where is Godric?" Mrs. St. John interrupted her gloomy thoughts.

"Upstairs." Isabel immediately turned to lead the way.

Megs followed, afraid to look at her mother-in-law. What must the other woman think? There was no way she could've missed the captain's accusations.

But that worry fled when Isabel tapped at a door at the end of the upstairs corridor. She opened it and Megs saw Godric sitting on the side of the bed, in shirtsleeves and his Ghost leggings. His face was pale and he held his left arm cradled in his lap, but otherwise he seemed alert and unharmed.

Megs felt relief sweep through her.

An elderly woman rose from where she'd been sitting on a nearby chair.

"Thank you, Mistress Medina," Isabel said as she followed the elderly woman from the room.

The door shut gently behind them.

Megs started toward Godric but was stopped by the harshness of his voice.

"Why," Godric rasped, "did you bring *her* here?"

THE PAIN FROM his wrist was nearly overwhelming— sharp, jabbing, even now making the bile back up into his throat. Still, Godric knew his words had been overly harsh. Megs flinched, withdrawing the hand she'd stretched out to him, her beautiful mouth crimping with hurt.

But it was his stepmother who replied. "Please don't chastise Megs. I insisted on coming here, Godric. You're hurt and I care for you very much."

He opened his mouth, pain and irritation driving hot words to his lips, but then he looked at her. She stood before him, this little plump woman, as bravely as a martyr before Roman lions, her chin raised, her warm brown eyes steady but sad at the same time. He couldn't do it. Couldn't crush the flicker of hope he saw in her face.

Perhaps he simply was too weary.

She took advantage of his weakness, pressing forward. "Let us help you, Godric."

He pressed his lips together, but the pain flared again in his forearm and he suddenly cared less for argument. He wasn't sure he could recover from this injury. He'd known men made crippled by breaks in their bones that never healed properly. What, in that context, did any of this matter?

"Very well," he said warily, rising. His eyes met Megs's gaze and he thought he saw relief there.

"We'll need a bonesetter," she murmured. "I'll consult Isabel to see if she knows anyone discreet. In the meantime I've brought you a change of clothes in case we run into Captain Trevillion again."

Megs set a bag on the bed and then bustled from the room, leaving him with his stepmother.

"Do you need help to dress?" she asked.

"Makepeace will assist me if I need it," he said and stood, ready to go find the home's manager.

She moved next to him, putting her shoulder under his good arm. "Lean on me."

"That's unnecessary," he said stiffly.

She glanced up at him, her eyes sharp. "Then do it for me. Let me care for you, Godric."

So he did because it was easier than arguing further. She was stronger than she looked, his stepmother, and he stared down at her, puzzled. Why was she doing this?

Her gaze met his, and for a moment she seemed to read his thoughts, rolling her eyes. "Don't worry yourself over it. You always were such a sensitive boy, reading too much into every little thing and making yourself sick over all possible ramifications. For now just accept that I'm helping you to make your way to the hallway."

He laughed at that, a soft puff of air. "Very well."

Outside the home's sickroom, they found Winter Makepeace leaning against the wall. His dark eyes flicked to Godric's stepmother. "There are...matters we should discuss before you leave."

Godric glanced down at Mrs. St. John. "I'll join you downstairs, ma'am."

His stepmother pressed her lips together but merely nodded before turning away.

Godric looked at Winter. "My wife brought a change of clothes."

The home's manager followed him back inside the sickroom and watched as Godric began picking at the buttons on his leggings. "You rescued nearly thirty girls tonight. Six will need to stay abed for some days, but the rest are in fair condition, all things considered. They mostly appear to need decent food."

Godric grimaced at the thought of little girls deprived of enough sustenance, then remembered the main part of his worry. "Did Alf tell you where the third workshop is located?"

"He did." Winter frowned and helped him strip out of the leggings. "But I'm thinking they will have moved after your work this night. They'd be fools to stay and wait for your attack."

"True." Godric pulled on a pair of black breeches then looked down at his arm, already swollen. Perhaps if he braced it, there would still be time. "If I went out again tonight—"

"Don't even contemplate it," Winter said curtly. "You need to heal before you try again."

"I need to find those girls," Godric growled. The buttons of his fall were damnably difficult with only one hand.

"Yes, but becoming further injured—or killed—will do us no good." Winter hesitated. "There's one more thing."

Godric cocked his head impatiently.

"Alf left just after he brought you and the girls here," Winter said. "But he was agitated. Apparently Hannah, the ginger-haired lass he mentioned before, was not among the girls you rescued."

"Damnation." Godric glared at his arm. "Will she try to attack the third workshop on her own, do you think?"

"*She?*"

Godric nodded curtly. "Alf is a girl in disguise. I should never have brought her on tonight's mission."

"You—we—had no way of knowing." Winter looked thoughtful. "Aye, and now she might be off trying to free her ginger-haired friend by herself."

Godric had never felt so helpless. Well, that wasn't correct. The last time he'd felt this way was beside Clara's deathbed. He pushed the ugly memory away.

Winter looked disturbed. "I don't think Alf will act on her own," he said slowly. "She seemed quite respectful of the guards kept around the workshops. And remember: even if she did try something so foolish, the workshop has no doubt already moved."

Godric nodded, though the reminder was but small consolation. Alf might be careful to project a tough and pragmatic exterior, but she'd put herself at risk to inform on the workshops' whereabouts—and she'd been truly remorseful about delivering the ginger-haired little girl to one of them.

Pray she did nothing stupid.

He needed to heal. To get back to St. Giles and finish this business.

A soft scratch came at the door before it opened.

Megs peeked in. "The carriage is waiting and dawn is beginning to break."

Godric looked at her, his wife, hovering so hesitantly, not even venturing closer as if she feared rejection. She'd come for him when Winter had sent word, without demure or question. She'd lain beneath him earlier tonight and given him everything he'd demanded. She was so much and he felt so little—too broken, too old, too weary—to give her everything she needed. He should let her go, let her fly free to find a younger lover like her Roger.

He should do all those things, and maybe later, when he was healed and not in pain, he would, but right now he murmured his thanks to Makepeace, threw the cloak about his shoulders, and let her take his good arm. Let her draw it across her slender womanly shoulders. Let her take a small portion of his weight and guide him down the stairs.

His stepmother waited for them in the home's entry-way along with Megs's footmen. They bracketed him and the women as he made his slow, painful way to the carriage. Godric didn't miss Captain Trevillion, lurking in the shadows by the home, and he didn't miss the captain's deliberate nod. That nod was a warning, a challenge delayed. It meant, *I know who you are. Come again into St. Giles and I'll take you.*

Godric knew it as surely as if the dragoon captain had screamed the words. And yet he couldn't bring himself to care. Makepeace was right: now he needed to heal. But when he was strong again, he'd return to St. Giles, Trevillion or not, because those girls needed rescuing.

It wasn't until they were all settled in the carriage that his stepmother spoke again.

She waited until the door was closed, until the carriage jolted forward; then she looked at Godric and said, "How long have you been the Ghost of St. Giles?"

Chapter Fifteen

*Grief rolled down the Peak of Whispers, screeching his
rage all the way. The Hellequin made no comment, but one
corner of his stern mouth may've lifted up.
Now Faith grew thirsty, so reaching into her pocket,
she drew out a small skin of wine. She took a sip, and as
she did so, the Hellequin licked his lips.
She offered the skin to him. "Would you like a drink?"
"I have not drunk the wine of men for a millennium,"
he rasped.
"Then you must be very thirsty," she said as she held
the skin to his lips....*
—From *The Legend of the Hellequin*

The groan was muffled, as if Godric was doing his very
best not to make any sound at all, which only made it
worse for Megs—the knowledge that he must be in terrible pain to let the muted sounds slip past.

She stared at the closed door to his bedroom, wringing
her hands.

"Come sit, Megs," Mrs. St. John said from behind her.

Megs glanced at her distractedly, jumping when another
grunt came from the bedroom.

"Please." Her mother-in-law patted the seat beside her

on the settee. "You'll do him no good pacing like that. In fact, he'll be embarrassed if you see him afterward and you're distraught. He'll know you heard him. Gentlemen detest appearing weak."

Megs bit her lip, but she obediently sank into the settee cushions. "I don't think him weak. He's *hurt*. And I do so wish he'd let me stay with him when he's in such pain."

"Mmm," Mrs. St. John murmured in agreement. "But gentlemen are terribly stubborn and rather illogical when they're hurt, you see. Godric's father had the gout in his later years and he was an absolute *bear* about it. Wouldn't let anyone near him, including me." For a moment she looked wistful. Then she glanced down at her hands, folded in her lap, and said, "This is my fault, you know."

Megs blinked, confused. "What is?"

"That." Mrs. St. John waved a hand toward Godric's bedroom. "I knew he was alone after Clara died, knew he was hurting, but I let his stoicism keep me away." She grimaced. "He's always been so very self-sufficient, so *cold* when I made any overtures, that it's hard to remember he's a man like any other. That he needs the comfort of family as much as any other."

"I don't see how that's your fault," Megs said. "You *did* try, and if he rejected your attempts, then surely the fault lies with him, not you."

"No." Her mother-in-law shook her head. "I love him as surely as if I'd carried him within my own body. A mother never abandons her child, even when he seems to want it. It was—*is*—my duty to break through the barriers he surrounds himself with. I should have kept trying until he gave in." Her look softened as she watched Megs. "I thank God that you decided to seek him out, to make your marriage a true one. He needs you, Megs. You're the one who can save him."

Megs looked away, feeling ashamed. Mrs. St. John praised her falsely: She'd come to London, made their marriage "true" for purely selfish reasons. But she couldn't explain that to her mother-in-law.

Instead she focused on the last part of what Mrs. St. John said, uncertainty a tight band around her chest. "Can one save a man who seeks willful self-destruction?"

The older woman's brows arched. "You think that's why he goes into St. Giles?"

Megs looked at her with sorrow. "Why else?"

Mrs. St. John sighed. "You have to understand that it took years for Clara to die—years in which Godric could do no more than stand idle and watch. Perhaps his dressing as the Ghost is his way of *doing* something good after so long being unable to do anything at all."

"He does do good in St. Giles." Megs frowned as she fingered the tassel on one of the settee cushions. "But, ma'am, whatever good he does others must be balanced by the evil he does himself."

"What do you mean?"

"He may help people in St. Giles, but I think he does it at the expense of himself." She yanked overhard on the tassel and the thing came off in her hand. She stared at it, her lips trembling. "It can't be good for a man such as Godric—a sensitive, moral man—to deal in violence so often. It's as if he's chipping away at his own soul."

"Then you must find a way to stop him," Mrs. St. John said quietly.

Megs nodded, though she had no idea how to do that. She'd made a pact with him—a pact that forced him to

wear the Ghost's disguise. How could she have everything she wanted and save Godric as well?

The door to Godric's room opened behind her.

"We are done, my lady." The doctor was an odd, bent
fellow with an Italian—or maybe French?—name. Isabel
Makepeace had said that he was a refugee of some type
and could be trusted not to talk about Godric's injury.

Megs stood. "Will his arm heal cleanly?"

"I have done all that I can. The rest is in the good
Lord's hands." The doctor made a very foreign-looking
moue and shrugged elaborately. "Mr. St. John will need
bed rest for at least a week, preferably more. A simple diet
of fish or chicken, fine, soft bread, clear broth, and wine
will suffice, I think. A few vegetables such as turnips or
carrots and the like. No onions or garlic, naturally, nor
any overspiced foods."

"Of course." Megs nodded before looking up anxiously. "May I see him?"

"If you wish, my lady, but please make your visit a
short—"

She was already past the doctor, not waiting for him
to finish his sentence. Godric lay in the big bed, his left
arm atop the covers. Two flat wooden boards had been
strapped on either side of his forearm so that he could not
move his hand independently of his arm.

She tiptoed to his bed and stared down at him. His face
still shone with sweat, his short hair plastered to his head.
He'd not shaved and his beard was dark against the pallor
of his face.

"Megs." He didn't open his eyes, but his right hand
moved, reaching for hers.

"Oh, Godric," she murmured, tears filling her eyes as she placed her hand in his.

He tugged on her hand. "Come lay beside me for a while."

She resisted even as he pulled her closer. "The doctor said you mustn't be disturbed."

"Damn that French quack." A corner of his mouth twitched wearily. "You don't disturb me, Meggie mine. Besides, I'll rest easier with you beside me."

Carefully she crept onto the bed, fully clothed, and lay beside him. He shifted until her head was on his right shoulder, his arm wrapped securely around her, and then he sighed.

In a few minutes he was asleep.

And in a minute more so was she.

TWO WEEKS LATER, Godric peered bemusedly over his half-moon spectacles as Her Grace trotted into his bedroom with a curled puppy hanging from her mouth. The pug glanced at him warily but seemed to dismiss him—rather insultingly—as no threat before she disappeared into the open door of his dressing room. After a pause of five minutes or so, she trotted out again, sans offspring.

Godric raised a brow as the pug bustled out of his room again. This didn't bode well.

He shrugged and went back to the political and philosophical pamphlets that Moulder had brought him. A week of enforced bed rest followed by a week more when all the females of his household seemed to have conspired to keep him homebound was making him damnably bored. True, each of his sisters, stepmother, and wife in turn had made a point of spending time with him, reading aloud or simply chatting. Even Great-Aunt Elvina had deigned to sit with him and had only disparaged him—halfheartedly—twice. He'd tempted Megs with a walk in Spring Gardens—one of the many public gardens in London. But not even the promise of gravel walks and exotic blooms had made her waver in her determination to keep him inside.

He hadn't fulfilled either of his parts of the bargain with Megs in those two weeks either. At first the pain from his broken wrist had been too debilitating for any physical exercise. Now he was nearly well enough to resume his Ghostly duties, he thought, and certainly able to bed her tonight—purely as his matrimonial duty, of course.

Godric frowned down at the political pamphlet that he'd read twice now without remembering a word. A gentleman should not let self-delusion control him. He wanted to bed his wife, true, but it wasn't *entirely* because of duty.

Or even partially.

Her Grace trotted purposely back into the room, a different puppy held in her jaws. This one was a glossy chocolate, and Godric wondered exactly who her paramour was. He could've sworn that Great-Aunt Elvina had said Her Grace had been bred to another fawn pug.

The bitch disappeared into his dressing room and Megs appeared in his doorway. She wore a rather frivolous pink and yellow confection that he'd not noticed on her before.

"There are puppies in my dressing room," Godric said, lowering the pamphlet to his desktop.

Megs sighed gustily but seemed unsurprised. "I was afraid of that. We keep putting Her Grace and her puppies in Great-Aunt Elvina's room, but she insists on moving them elsewhere. Last week Mrs. Crumb found them in the linen cupboard and was not at all pleased."

Her Grace emerged from the dressing room, detoured around Megs, and vanished into the outer hallway.

"I can understand Mrs. Crumb's consternation," Godric said gravely. "She seems a very orderly woman, and puppies in the clean linens is the antithesis of orderly."

"Mmm," Megs murmured distractedly, glancing into the hallway again. Was she looking for the pug?

Godric felt a pang at the thought of her leaving him again. "Is that a new frock?"

"Yes." Megs's cheeks warmed prettily. She looked down at her skirts, smoothing one hand over them. "We've received our order of new gowns from the modiste. Do you like it? I wasn't sure about the yellow. It so often makes one look jaundiced."

"Not you," he replied truthfully.

The spring colors made the peach of her cheeks glow against the dark mass of her hair. A lock was working itself free of her coiffure, slowly tumbling down her elegant neck, and oddly the sight made him want to pull the pins from her hair, tug the mass down, spread it with his fingers, and bury his face in the glossy waves.

He casually flipped the skirt of his coat over his lap. "You're beautiful."

"Oh," she said softly, glancing up and catching his intent gaze. "Oh, thank you."

Her Grace came into the room with her last puppy and headed directly to the dressing room.

Godric smiled. "You should shut the door to my bedroom so that she doesn't move them again."

Megs looked uncertainly at the bedroom door. "I suppose I should leave you to rest."

"I've rested quite enough these last weeks," he said

smoothly. "I could use the company. That is"—he made himself look bravely forlorn—"if you don't mind sitting with an invalid."

He may've been laying it on too thick. She gave him an odd glance before shutting the outer door. "I'll get a chair from my room."

"No need. You can sit on my bed."

She looked at the bed, her brows drawn together with dawning suspicion.

"In fact," he said, rising from the chair, "I might join you for a nap."

She transferred her suspicious look to him. "A nap?"

"Hmm." He sauntered toward her, careful not to make any sudden moves. "When one lies abed in the middle of the day and sleeps. Surely you've heard of it?"

"I'm not sure you're interested in sleep," she muttered.

"Perhaps not." He reached up with his good hand and gently worked loose a hairpin. The escaping lock of hair immediately slithered down her back. "Do you have any other ideas?"

"Godric," she whispered.

"Hmm?" Two more pins fell to the floor.

"You haven't recovered sufficiently." Her brows were knit in worry.

His gaze darted to hers and he smiled gently. "Then you'll have to do most of the work, won't you?"

Her sweet lips parted soundlessly, her eyes rounding.

He couldn't help but bend his head to hers, covering her mouth with his, tasting again the wild strawberry sweetness of her tongue. Something seemed to settle in his chest, relaxing from an anxiety he hadn't even known he'd felt.

Her hands rose, fluttering by his shoulders, but before they could alight, he broke away, circling to her back, drawing the rest of her pins from her hair. The entire dark mass came tumbling down, a glorious tangle, and he stroked his fingers through it, leaning down to inhale the scent of orange blossoms.

"Godric?" She stood stock-still, save for a fine tremble running through her shoulders.

"My love?" He lifted her hair in his hand, watching as the sunlight from the bedroom windows filtered through the locks.

"What..." There was an odd catch in her voice. "What kind of work do you want me to do?"

He smiled as he brought her hair to his lips. "You can help me undress, for one."

"Oh! Of course."

She turned and he let the locks slide through his fingers. He still wore the boards on his left wrist, which had necessitated both his shirt and coat being slit up the left sleeves. He stood still as Megs held the coat so he could slip his right hand from it before she eased the garment over his burdened left arm. She had an adorable frown between her brows and her lips were parted as she concentrated, the tip of her tongue curled up and touching her upper teeth.

The sight was too tempting and as she began unbuttoning his waistcoat, he bent and caught her lower lip in a teasing bite.

She blinked, her eyes widening as he straightened. "That's...that's very distracting."

"I apologize."

She snorted under her breath, her cheeks brightening

again as she took his waistcoat off. His neck cloth was next, easily tossed to a chair, and then he watched as she worked at the buttons of his shirt. The room was silent, the only sound the faint snuffling of the puppies in the other room and their own breaths. He was aware that he was breathing deeply, that he was already hard and pulsing, but he was in no hurry. He could spend hours thus, simply watching the constant flicker of changing emotions across her face. She was so *vibrant*, his Megs, so alive with hope and love and happiness. If she left him— *when* she left him—he didn't know how he would return to his old life.

It would be like living without sunlight.

He pushed the thought aside because he wanted to concentrate on this moment, remember it when he dwelt only in darkness again.

Godric lifted his arms, letting her draw off his shirt over his head, feeling the brush of fine linen against his abdomen, the finer brush of her curious fingers. The shirt fell forgotten to the floor and then both of her hands were on him, stroking up over his ribs, brushing through the hair on his chest.

"You're beautiful," she whispered, and his lips quirked in amusement.

He wasn't anything like beautiful, but if she wanted to call him so, he would let her.

Then her fingertips were on his nipples, circling, and the smile died on his lips. She bent forward and pressed her mouth to one, flattening her tongue against his flesh before licking him like a cat does cream. He couldn't help the groan that burst from his mouth.

He looked down and met wide brown eyes, watching him even as she kissed him softly. "Do you like that?"

Couldn't she tell? He nodded jerkily and she hummed to herself before moving to the other side, tonguing him even as she thumbed the wet nub she'd left.

He threw back his head at the sensation, his eyelids half lowering in pleasure. But she moved then, sinking to her knees to remove his stockings and shoes before unbuttoning the placket of his breeches. The position, the nearness of her innocent lips to his randy cock, made him swallow drily. She must have sensed his stillness, for she glanced up curiously at him, pausing a moment when she met his eyes. She froze, looking at him, her hands directly over his hard flesh; then she ducked her head and fumbled the placket open, stripping him of his breeches and smallclothes. His cock bobbed obscenely before her and he held his breath as she seemed to lean closer.

But she rose swiftly and he gave her an ironic glance before climbing awkwardly into the bed. He sat back against the tall, carved headboard and watched as she disrobed. It was perforce a slow process, but somehow the more erotic for that. First came off the gauzy fichu that had been wrapped around her shoulders and tucked into the low bodice of her gown. She sat and removed her slippers and then rolled down her stockings. He might've seen her entirely nude, but the sight of her pale, slender ankles, the swells of her bosom as she leaned forward made him catch his breath.

He palmed his cock, watching.

She stood, not looking at him, and began undoing the bodice of her gown. It was a simple day dress, so she was able to take it off herself, the skirts suddenly collapsing about her ankles. She untied her petticoats and stepped free, in just her stays and chemise now. The chemise was very fine and he could make out the shadowy curves of her legs and hips as she turned to pick up the skirts, the dark triangle cradled between her thighs as she straightened.

He groaned under his breath, passing his palm over the head of his cock to gather the liquid seeping there before he stroked firmly down.

She glanced up at him then and stilled, her eyes seemingly caught by his hand slowly gliding up his cock.

His flesh jerked under his fingers.

She blinked and ducked her head, studying her own hands as she began unlacing her stays. But he could see her slyly peeking now and again as she worked.

He bent his far knee and angled himself so that she could see better and was rewarded by her breath hitching softly. His hand made a slicking sound as he watched her slowly open her stays. She looked up again and drew the whole thing over her head, leaving her in the chemise, wrinkles pressed into the nearly transparent fabric from the stays. The top was tightened with a simple ribbon and she plucked the bow undone, gradually drawing it loose. He licked his lips, growling softly when he saw the smile she tried to hide. She was teasing him, enticing him with the slow unveiling of her body.

But then she bent and took off the chemise, throwing it aside, standing like a wild nymph startled by the hunter. Her breasts were full but proudly high, the tips flushed a deep cherry. Her creamy belly was soft, flowing into the sweet curves of her hips. He branded the image into his brain.

"Come here," he said, his voice degraded into a gravelly growl.

She stepped forward, her lips curved mysteriously,

cheeks flushed, but chin tilted confidently. She crawled onto the bed beside him, and then sat back on her knees.

"Here," he said, indicating his lap with his chin, lowering his bent leg.

She looked uncertain but straddled him, her soft thighs brushing against both his legs and the knuckles of his hand. He let go of himself and brought his damp fingers to her cheek. He should wipe them off on the sheets, they still held the liquid from his body, but some part of him relished the idea of marking her with his scent.

He curved his hand around her neck and brought her lips to his. She opened sweetly for him, accepting his tongue into her mouth as he licked into her, slanting his head to draw her closer. He could feel the tantalizing whisper of her nipples against his chest, the wetness of her cunny as she settled on his thighs just behind his cock. He nearly raised his left hand to grip her hip before remembering and cursing his infirmity.

In the end he had to break the kiss instead. "Slide forward."

She looked uncertain and he realized that her lover may never have taken her like this—they'd not had much time together.

He should not have felt glad at that thought.

She rose on her knees above him, looking down, and their fingers tangled on his cock. He watched and felt as she lowered herself, slowly sheathing herself on him, her soft pink folds parting and accepting him within herself. The fit was tight and good, and he had to resist the urge to buck up into her, to end this too soon.

She licked her lips, her eyes dark, and looked at him inquiringly.

He let his hand fall, answering the unspoken question. "Do as you wish."

Her eyes narrowed speculatively at his words and she cautiously rose. His cock slid deliciously partway from her body. She moved against him slowly like this for several minutes as if discovering and judging each new angle. It was sweet.

Sweetly torturing.

Finally he broke, fisting his good hand in the coverlet as she ground down against him once more, not fast enough, not hard enough. "More."

She glanced at his face and her lips curved in a secret smile as old as Eve's before she leaned down, the tips of her breasts brushing his chest, her hands braced on his shoulders. "Like this?"

And she rode him, like a goddess triumphant, her face shining, her cunny gripping him fast and wet. He stared at her, even as his muscles tensed, even as he felt his lips draw back in a grimace of sexual bliss. She was too controlled, too assessing, and he was nearing his edge.

He caught her hand, bringing it to where they joined, pressing her fingers to her softness as her hips shuddered and lost their rhythm. "Touch yourself."

He'd made it worse for himself; he knew it the moment her fingers curled into her pretty cunny. Her lips parted moistly, her head thrown back as she began to stroke herself, and it took everything he had to keep from spilling. To watch her pleasure herself as she rode his cock and not end this too soon.

"That's it, darling," he whispered low, coaching her, wanting to see her bring herself to fulfillment. "It's sweet, isn't it? Touching yourself, letting me watch. Do you like it? Do you enjoy putting on a show for me? Parting your pretty lips, letting me see how moist you've become, fucking yourself on me?"

The crudity seemed to jolt something within her. Her eyes widened, her back arched, and he felt the muscles of her sheath grip him tight, so tight.

Right before he lost control himself.

Chapter Sixteen

The great black horse came down off the Peak of Whispers
and Faith saw before them a vast, barren plain, stretching
as far as the eye could see.
"Is this Hell?" she murmured in the Hellequin's ear.
He shook his head. "This is the Plain of Madness. It will
take us two days to cross it."
She shivered and huddled closer to the Hellequin's big
form, for even with the cloak it was growing colder. And as
she did so, she looked down and saw white wisps swirling
aimlessly in the dust on the ground. . . .
—From *The Legend of the Hellequin*

"Sir."

Godric came fully awake in the darkness of his own
bedroom, aware that it'd been Moulder whispering.

He blinked at the manservant, raising his eyebrows
as the man merely tilted his head toward the hallway.
Moulder was dressed in a rather ornate orange banyan
and tasseled cap and held a single candlestick in his hand.

Godric pulled the coverlet more securely around
Megs's shoulders and slipped carefully from the bed. He
quickly donned breeches, shirt, and banyan and then pad-
ded out of the room after Moulder.

"What is it?" he asked once they had made the hallway without waking Megs.

"Mr. Makepeace," Moulder replied. "He's here and he insisted on speaking with you, despite the hour."

Godric could think of only one reason for the home's manager to call on him in the middle of the night. "Show me."

They descended the stairs silently to the ground floor.

Makepeace turned as they entered the study. "I'm sorry to disturb you, St. John." He eyed Moulder, standing beside the closed door, for a moment before raising his brows. "Perhaps we could speak privately?"

"No need." Godric gestured to one of the wing chairs in the room, waiting for his guest to seat himself before taking one. "Moulder is in my confidence."

"Ah." Makepeace nodded. "Then I shall come straight to the point. Alf told me not more than an hour ago that she had found the last workshop."

Godric was up at once, stripping off the banyan. "Moulder, give me a hand here. We'll have to take off the boards on my wrist."

"Is that wise?" Makepeace was looking worriedly at his immobilized arm.

"We can't wait—Alf might try to rescue her friend by herself." Godric arched an eyebrow. "Unless you think we can persuade the third one of us to come and rescue the girls?" At Makepeace's frown, he shook his head. "I'm our only choice. The wrist has healed well enough. If Moulder can fashion a smaller, softer brace—"

"Godric?"

All three men looked up at the sound of the study door opening. Megs stood there, her glorious hair tumbled about her shoulders, a hand at her throat holding her wrapper closed, and Godric immediately wondered if that was the only thing she wore.

But his lady wife had other matters on her mind. She came into the room and shut the door behind her. "What is happening, Godric?"

Moulder had found a sharp knife but was standing frozen. Godric took the knife and began awkwardly cutting the bindings holding the two boards on his left arm. "I have to go out."

"May I?" Makepeace was beside him and Godric nodded, handing the knife over so the other man could work more ably on the bindings.

"As the Ghost of St. Giles?" Megs whispered.

"Yes." Godric kept his eyes on the work that Makepeace was doing.

"You can't." He could feel her stepping closer; then her hand was on his shoulder. "Godric! This is madness. You've only begun to heal. You'll break your wrist again if you go out, and who knows if the doctor will be able to set it. You could be crippled for life—assuming you're not killed." He heard her huff of desperate exasperation and then she was addressing Makepeace. "Why are you making him do this?"

The home's manager widened his eyes. "I..."

"Because I'm the only one who can do this." Godric looked at her finally. Megs didn't know Makepeace had been a Ghost once, but it didn't matter: the man had sworn to his lady wife not to take up the swords again. "Megs, there are little girls in peril."

She closed her eyes at that, visibly fighting something within herself. "Can you promise that this will be the last time? That you won't be the Ghost of St. Giles anymore?"

He watched as the last strap was cut away, freeing his arm. The swelling had gone down, but there were nasty purple-black bruises around the wrist. He didn't dare try flexing it. Moulder brought forth an old pair of stays they'd previously cut down to fit from his knuckles to his elbow in preparation for his next trip to St. Giles. He began binding it onto Godric's arm.

"Godric?"

"No." He didn't dare look at her. "No, I cannot promise that."

"Then promise me you'll return alive and whole."

He couldn't do such a thing. She knew that. Yet he found himself saying, "I promise."

The door opened and shut quietly.

Makepeace cleared his throat. "Perhaps if I alerted the dragoons—"

"We've been over this. Trevillion would take hours to agree—if he could be persuaded at all—and then hours more to mobilize his men." He met the other man's gaze. "Are you willing to risk the workshop moving again—or the girls being killed to cover the evidence?"

Makepeace flinched. "No."

Godric looked down just as Moulder tied off the last binding. He swung the arm experimentally. If he made sure to favor it, it should do all right. "In that case, perhaps you can help me get ready?"

"Very well," the home's manager said. "And then we'll need to plan a way to get past the dragoon standing guard over your house."

"He's still there?"

"Oh, indeed," Makepeace said drily. "And he no doubt saw my arrival."

Godric contemplated that fact while Moulder finished dressing him in his Ghost costume. When he sheathed his sword five minutes later, he nodded to Makepeace. "Come with me."

Godric doused the candles in the study and crossed to the long doors that led out into Saint House's garden. He spent a full minute waiting for his eyes to adjust as he carefully peered out, but saw no one. If Trevillion was good enough to hide from him in his own garden, he deserved to be caught.

Cautiously, he opened the doors and stole out into the moonlight, Makepeace a silent shadow behind him. The home's manager might not have donned the mask of the Ghost for over two years, but it was obvious that he'd not lost any of his skill in that time. The old fruit tree made a macabre outline against the night sky, and as he passed it, Godric wondered how long before Megs gave up and conceded that the thing was dead.

Then he shoved any thoughts of his wife from his mind. He needed to concentrate if he was to survive this night. Past the garden was the old river wall, the sound of lapping water and the stink of the river rising from beyond. An ancient gate pierced the wall, a crumbling arch crowning it. Godric pushed open the gate, glad that he made Moulder oil it monthly.

He grinned in the dark as the other man followed him. "One of the few advantages to owning a very old London house."

They stood at the top of a set of bare stone steps, set flat into the river wall. Below was a small dock with a rowboat tied to a post. Godric led the way down, stepping carefully into the rowboat. He picked up one oar while

Makepeace settled into the boat; then with a practiced movement, he used it to shove away from the dock and began sculling quietly downriver, using only his right hand.

They hadn't far to go. At the next set of river stairs, Godric maneuvered the rowboat in and tied it up.

"You'll not be able to use that method again," Makepeace said as they climbed the steps. "Trevillion is smart. He'll figure out how you slipped past him when he hears about your activity tonight."

"Then I'd best make sure I need not return again." Godric shrugged and amended his statement, "At least not for a while."

He felt the other man's gaze upon him as they made their way into the warren of streets beyond the river. This area wasn't rich, but it was certainly respectable enough. Lanterns shown by nearly every door and they were forced to keep close to what shadows they could find.

"This life isn't best suited for a married man," Makepeace observed neutrally.

"I've been married nearly two years," Godric replied. He didn't want to think about Megs's reproachful face right now.

"But living apart."

They paused at the corner of a cobbler's shop as a night watchman went limping by.

Godric glanced at the other man and Makepeace raised his brows. "Your good wife only came to London recently, yes?"

"Yes." Godric shook his head irritably. "What of it?"

Makepeace shrugged. "Most would take the change as opportunity to quit this life."

"And leave those children to be worked to death? Is that what you're proposing?"

"No, but perhaps the dragoons could be of more use, especially," Makepeace said drily, "if we let Trevillion in on the information we sometimes get."

Godric snorted. "You think Captain Trevillion would bother himself with mundanities such as little girl slaves?"

"I think he's not so unreasonable as he appears."

Godric stared at the other man. "What makes you say that?"

A corner of Makepeace's mouth lifted. "A feeling?"

"A feeling." They were nearly in St. Giles now, walking fast. Godric drew his sword, ignoring the slight discomfort in his left wrist. He used his short sword as a defense weapon, and the knowledge that he was without it made him uneasy. "Pardon me if I do not put much trust in your 'feelings.'"

"As you wish," Makepeace said, easily matching his stride. "But please remember that not even Sir Stanley Gilpin expected us to do this for the rest of our lives."

Godric stopped short, whirling to face the other man. They *never* said that name to each other. In fact, until Winter had spoken to him about the lassie snatchers, they hadn't even acknowledged each other for *years*—since before Sir Stanley had died, he realized now.

Makepeace had stopped at his abrupt movement and was watching him with eyes that might have held sympathy. "I've been thinking recently about Sir Stanley."

Godric flinched at the name of the man who'd been more father to him than his own father. Something inside of him wanted to weep and he repressed it savagely. "What about him?"

Makepeace cocked his head, his eyes sliding contemplatively to the full moon, half hidden by the rooftops above. "I wonder what he would make of us now. Your near-suicidal drive, our compatriot's obsession, my own solitude until my dear wife drew me from it...somehow I don't think this is what he meant for us to be. Sir Stanley was so *playful* in everything he did—the theater, teaching us tumbling, even while practicing sword craft. It was all a great, amusing lark for him. Not something to be taken seriously. Not something to die for—or to forsake life for. I don't think he would've been proud of us for doing so."

"He created us," Godric said softly, "but we're thinking creations with our own motivations. He cannot have been surprised when we made our own use of his instructions."

"Perhaps." Makepeace looked at him. "But it's something to consider nonetheless."

Godric didn't bother answering that, merely breaking into a jog as they neared the home.

Five minutes later, they saw the familiar steps and lit front door. Godric slowed, peering cautiously around. "Alf?"

"She was to meet us here, but she wouldn't come inside the home," Makepeace muttered. He sighed. "I'll go see if she changed her mind."

But the moment he stepped from the shadows, Alf glided over, so quickly that Godric wasn't sure where she'd been hiding. "Is 'e 'ere?"

"Yes." Godric stepped out of the darkness.

The girl whirled, obviously having not noticed him before. She cocked her head when she saw that he bore only one sword. "Can you fight like that?"

Godric inclined his head in a curt nod.

"Good luck," Makepeace said grimly.

"Come on." The girl led the way, winding through the alleys of St. Giles. She didn't try to move up into the rooftops, which Godric was grateful for. He might be able to fight with one hand, but he didn't want to try climbing.

They were in a narrow tunnel, approaching a courtyard, when Alf stopped short. Godric could see movement in the courtyard beyond her, but only her cry made him realize what was happening.

"They're taking away the lassies!"

At once he pushed past her. If the girls were moved, they might never find them again.

A man, obviously a guard, stood by as a tall, thin woman dragged two girls from a low cellar. Two more waited dispiritedly at the other end of the courtyard.

Godric charged the guard silently, dodging a blow made too late as the guard realized his danger and then hitting the man in the temple with the butt of his sword.

The guard crumpled, immobile.

The woman screamed, high and shrill, and two more men emerged from the cellar. Fortunately the door was so narrow they could exit only one at a time. Godric ran one through and caught the other by the arm, swinging him hard into the wall. The man's head bounced off the brick with a wet sound.

He turned to the woman to see if she would attack, but she was already running out the far side of the courtyard. The girls were huddled together. One was crying, but the others were apparently too petrified to make a sound.

A scrape came from behind him, and Godric twisted around only just in time: a fourth man had already emerged.

And this one had a sword.

Godric parried the strike. The blades slid along each other, screeching, and then broke apart. Godric backed a pace, watching the swordsman advance. Only aristocrats were allowed by law to carry swords. He tried to catch a glimpse of the other man's face, but he wore a tricorne and had wound his neck cloth around the lower half of his face.

Then he had no more time to ponder his attacker's face. The man was on him, his sword flashing with compact, deadly intensity—*expert* intensity.

Godric knew if he backed any farther, he'd be cornered. He feinted left and ducked right, hearing the rip of his cloak as he just managed to pass the other man. He whirled to repel a savage thrust and then lunged for the other man's exposed flank. His opponent curved to the side, his arm outthrust. Godric felt the blade tip run a line up the entire length of his right arm, searing like a brand. His sleeve flapped open and warmth began to run down his arm, but the cut must not've been deep—he could still use the arm. Godric attacked again. He thrust into the other's face, making the man arch back. His blade was caught, but he jerked it free, circling as he did so, trying to yank the other's sword from his hand. But the man leaped back, recovering, his blade still in his grip. The swordsman's neck cloth slipped and for a moment Godric looked him full in the face.

Then the swordsman stabbed to Godric's right and too late Godric realized it was a feint. He wasn't quick enough to parry the sword thrust with his blade, but he brought his left arm up, catching the blow on his elbow.

His entire arm sang with agony.

His opponent turned and leaped away, running toward

the alley on the farther side of the courtyard. Godric instinctively lunged after the man, the need to give chase and bring down his prey driving strong. His left arm was throbbing hard, though, and he remembered the promise he'd made to Megs. He'd said he'd return unharmed and alive.

Well, at least he was alive.

He turned wearily back to the children in time to see Alf kneel in front of a small, grimy redheaded girl. Alf was scowling fiercely, perhaps in an attempt to keep from seeming like she cared as she tenderly wiped the child's tearstained face.

The sight almost made his heart lighten. He tried to tell himself that the girls were rescued and that was the main thing, but it didn't lift the leaden weight in his chest. He'd seen the face of his attacker, the man responsible for enslaving children in St. Giles, the man he'd let escape alive, and Godric knew that the man was near untouchable. He'd never be brought to justice.

For the swordsman had been the Earl of Kershaw.

THERE WAS BLOOD on Godric.

Megs couldn't think, couldn't *see* beyond that one stark fact. She stood stock-still for an awful, endless minute after he opened the door to his bedroom, simply staring at the long bandage on his right arm and the slit, bloody sleeve that hung, flapping. She'd been waiting there, awake and pacing, ever since he'd left, and the room was in a bit of a mess—not that she cared. Moulder was behind him and Godric was saying something, but she couldn't hear.

"Get out," she told the manservant, unable to even phrase the order politely.

Moulder took one look at her and fled.

Godric wasn't so smart. He was frowning slightly now and saying something about *a minor cut* and *looks worse than it is*, and *Moulder has already seen to it*, despite the fact that anyone could see he was holding his left arm stiffly as well, and she just wanted to *hit* him.

Instead she grabbed his face in both of her hands and stood on tiptoe to bring her mouth to his. She kissed him savagely, her lips wide, her tongue demanding wet access to his mouth, and it was a damned good thing he opened at once, because she would've bitten him if he hadn't. She heard him groan and then his arms started to wrap around her, but she wasn't having any of it.

She broke free to attack the falls of his Ghost costume. "You *lied* to me."

"I came back alive," he said in a soothing voice. At least he never pretended that he didn't know the reason for her anger.

"I said alive and *whole*," she snapped, finally wrenching two buttons off. "*That* is not whole."

"Megs," he started, no doubt to make some stupid *male* excuse, and she shoved him none too gently into the one straight-backed chair.

She wasn't strong enough to manhandle him—she knew that somewhere in the back of her maddened brain. He must be conceding to her anger, letting her push him about.

Perversely it only made her madder.

She dropped to her knees, roughly spreading his legs and shuffling forward between them.

His eyes widened, which, at any other time she might've taken pride in. The man had been the Ghost of

St. Giles for years—there mustn't be many things that could surprise him.

"What—"

She reached forward and yanked open his fall and the smallclothes beneath, watching in satisfaction as his cock bobbed out, ruddy and half hard.

She took his length gently between her hands, her arms resting on his thighs, and looked up into his face. "I'm very, *very* angry with you."

And she opened her mouth over him. She'd never done this—although she'd wanted to before. She'd always been too shy, too worried that he'd think her sluttish or not like what she did.

But here, *now*, she simply didn't care anymore.

She trailed a line of kisses down his length, marveling at the pulsing warmth within him, then licked up the strong tendon on the underside.

He muttered something and his hips jerked under her arms, half lifting her.

She wanted to tell him to never go back to St. Giles. That she'd find Roger's killer herself. That she couldn't bear anymore to see him hurt. But she'd already told him that before and it hadn't changed his mind. *She* couldn't change his mind. He wouldn't allow her that far in.

But he would allow this.

She mouthed around the thick head of his cock, tasting the tang of his skin. She pulled back to stare at him as he'd stared at her once. The tiny slit at the top of his penis was leaking, and she drew her thumb through the clear liquid, smearing it about the soft skin.

The strong length in her hands jumped.

She smiled when she felt that and leaned down to kiss

the very tip, the warm wetness smearing across her lips. She looked up and saw that the color was high across his cheekbones and his eyelids half shielded his glittering gray eyes. Still watching, she took the head of his cock into her mouth and suckled.

His nostrils flared and he bit his lip, but he did no more, staring back at her as she opened her mouth and licked slowly around the head. Later she would be embarrassed by her boldness.

Right now she reveled in the freedom he gave her.

But when she lightly scraped her teeth around the rim, he moved.

"Megs," he growled, and reached for her.

She didn't like that—she wasn't done playing. She half rose and scrambled backward, trying to dodge his hands, her anger rising again.

"Damn it, Megs!"

He lunged and she reacted instinctively, a thrill of alarm shooting through her. She got to her feet and made two abortive strides.

It wasn't fair of her—he was wounded. She should've been able to get away.

He slammed her against the bed, using his greater weight and height to hold her there.

She was wedged between him and the bed, panting, though their struggle had only been a matter of seconds. He was behind her, his body pressed against her back, his erection imprinted on her buttocks, his arms braced on either side of her.

She could feel his breath puffing against her ear. She waited, expecting him to turn her around to face him.

Instead he began gathering her wrapper and chemise.

She caught her breath.

He whispered a kiss behind her ear. "Hold still."

Her bottom was bare now, her skin cooling in the air, and she felt the hot slide of his cock across her hip.

He placed his hand between her shoulder blades and pushed her gently but firmly down, until her upper half lay across the bed and her lower half was canted up, waiting for his pleasure.

She felt him nudge her legs apart, and then his palm was on her hip and she felt it: the nudge of his cock against her entrance. He seemed somehow larger in this position and she heard him grunt as he began squeezing his way in. She was wet, but she felt each ridge of his penis as he pushed himself slowly into her.

Her hands clutched at the bedclothes.

He seemed to take forever, widening her, burrowing into her swollen tissues. Then he made a final shove and she felt the fabric of his leggings brush firmly against her bottom.

He held himself there and she could hear the sound of his rough breathing in the quiet of the room. She bit her lip, mirroring his earlier grimace. She couldn't seem to catch her breath—and he hadn't even started to move.

And then he did, a slick, hard slide that rubbed against something wonderful inside of her. She couldn't help the squeaking cry she gave, and as if her hips moved of their own accord, she began bumping back against him.

He huffed a rough laugh. "So impatient."

She turned her head to scowl at him—or at least she meant to, but he chose that moment to reverse his glide, thrusting back into her.

Her eyelids fluttered closed. "Oh."

"You like that?" he whispered.

She nodded, unable to speak. He was embedding himself into her over and over, his cock rubbing against her deliciously, and she couldn't help but tilt her bottom up in submissive invitation. She burrowed one hand underneath and found her nub as he filled her again and again, his hardness sliding against her wet fingers.

His breath caught and he swiveled his hips, grinding against her, leaning close over her, whispering low in her ear. "You're touching yourself, aren't you?"

She swallowed, closing her eyes in bliss. "Y-yes."

"*God*," he muttered, and she wondered if he'd finally lost the power of speech.

Perhaps he had, for he suddenly planted one hand over her shoulder and shoved hard into her, pressing her into the mattress. He was pushing her body up the bed with quick, forceful jabs that spread her apart, made her see a starburst behind her closed lids.

A spike of near-painful pleasure bloomed between her legs, flowing and expanding through her, a river of sweet completion. She moaned, loud and low.

He stiffened behind her, his hips still working, even as his hot seed filled her, as if he didn't want to stop. And then he fell against her, his heat surrounding and cradling her. She felt his chest pressing into her back as he fought to catch his breath.

She should feel squashed beneath him, but instead she felt protected and oddly cherished.

She watched out of the corner of her eye as he moved his right arm—the one with the white bandage—and twined his fingers with hers, squeezing gently.

Were it up to her, they would stay this way forever.

Chapter Seventeen

"Do you see these things trapped in the sand of the Plain of Madness?" Loss hissed at Faith. He'd seen the fate of his imp comrades, so he was cautious of Faith, but he couldn't pass up the chance to wallow in her horror.
"What are they?" Faith whispered, filled with dread.
"They are the souls of those who died insane," Loss said with glee. "They meander aimlessly now, flowing with the shifting dust, and will remain so until men no longer walk the earth." ...
—From *The Legend of the Hellequin*

If Hell existed on earth, Artemis Greaves was walking into it. Her shoes crunched on fine gravel in a huge, nearly empty courtyard. Behind her were the tall iron gates. Before her, the baroque façade of a magnificent, beautiful building. White Corinthian columns marched in paired rows along the front, crowned by a central dome with a clock, the Roman numerals picked out in gold. The gilding was repeated on the top of the dome, a spinet with the figure of a veiled woman.

Artemis shivered and glanced at the front doors.

Hell might have a gorgeous shell, but it still roasted the damned within.

She passed the porter and paid him her precious penny, though she wasn't here to sightsee. Under the dome was an echoing hall with two long galleries leading off to her left and her right. It was early yet and the visitors were few, but that didn't mean the inhabitants of Hell weren't awake. They moaned or babbled, if they could make utterance, except for the few who simply howled.

Artemis ignored the galleries, walking straight on. Beyond the dome, two staircases curved away into space. She mounted the one to the left, holding her covered basket carefully. It wouldn't do to spill her few, meager offerings.

At the top of the stairs, a man sat on a wooden stool, looking bored. He was tall and thin and Artemis had amused herself—rather morbidly—on previous visits by noting his resemblance to Charon.

She paid Charon his due—a tuppence—and watched as he took out his key and unlocked the depths of Hell.

The stink hit her first, a thing so solid it was like wading into filth. Artemis held the handkerchief on which she'd sprinkled lavender water up to her nose as she made her way. The inhabitants here were always chained, and many could not or did not make it to their chamber pots. To either side were small, open rooms, almost like stable stalls, though most stables smelled better and were cleaner than this place. Each room held a denizen of Hell, and she tried to avoid looking in as she passed.

She'd had nightmares in the past from what she'd seen.

It was actually quieter up here than the vast galleries below, whether because the inhabitants were fewer or because they'd long since given up hope. Still there was a low droning of something that once might've been song and a high giggling that stopped and started fitfully. She knew to skip swiftly past a cell on her right, dodging the foul missile that flew out, hitting the wall opposite.

The last chamber on the left was where she found him. He squatted on filthy straw like Samson restrained: manacles on both ankles and a new one—she saw to her horror—about his neck. The heavy iron ring encircling his neck chained him to the wall with not enough slack to let him lie down fully. He was forced to crouch, leaning against the wall if he wanted to rest, and she wondered what would happen if he slept and fell forward. Would he strangle himself in the night without anyone knowing?

He looked up as she hesitated in the entrance to the chamber, and a broad smile lit his face. "Artemis."

She went immediately to him. "What have they done to you, my heart?"

She knelt before him and took his face in her hands. There was a lump over one hairy eyebrow, a scabbed graze high on his right cheekbone, and a cut on his too-broad nose. It looked broken.

But then it always had.

He shrugged massive shoulders covered only in a filthy shirt and coarse waistcoat. "It's a new beauty regime. All the court ladies are following it, I hear."

She swallowed a lump in her throat but tried to smile for him. "Silly. You mustn't taunt them just for fun. You're rather handicapped by these chains."

He cocked his head, his thick lips curling. "Only makes the playing field even, doesn't it?"

She shook her head and dug into her basket. "I...I haven't much, I'm afraid, but Penelope's cook kindly gave me some meat pies." She offered one on a napkin.

He took it and bit into the pie, chewing slowly as if to make the repast last. She examined him covertly as she unpacked the rest of the basket. His face was leaner and if she wasn't mistaken, he'd lost weight. Again. He was naturally something of a giant, with the shoulders and chest to fit, and he required large amounts of food. They weren't feeding him and she hadn't been able to sell the necklace for money to bribe the guards so they'd look after him.

Her brows knit worriedly as she came to the last thing in her basket.

"What's that?" he asked, leaning as far as he could to look.

She grinned at him, her mood lightening. "This is my prize, and I hope you're properly appreciative of the efforts I've made to procure it."

She drew out a fabulously quilted gentleman's banyan in dark red.

He blinked at it a moment and then threw back his head, roaring with laughter. "I'll look like a veritable Indian prince in that thing."

She pursed her lips, trying to look stern. "It's a castoff from Uncle and it'll keep you warm at night. Here, try it on."

Artemis helped him into the banyan and was pleased to see that while it was a tight fit across the shoulders, he was able to nearly pull it closed in front. He leaned back against the grimy stone of the chamber walls, and he did indeed look like an Indian prince.

If Indian princes had bruised faces and sat on straw.

After that, he insisted on sharing some of the food she'd brought, so they had something of a picnic. And if the sounds of shouted swearing filled the air at one point, counterbalanced by loud weeping, well, they both made a show of ignoring it.

All too soon, she knew she must leave. Penelope wanted to go shopping today, and Artemis would be needed to carry parcels and keep track of where they went and what her cousin bought.

She was quiet as she fussed with her basket, hating to leave him alone in this place.

"Come," he said softly as her lip began to tremble. "Don't carry on so. You know how I hate to see you sad."

So she smiled for him and gave him a hug that lasted just a bit too long and then she left that horrible chamber without another word. Both she and he knew that she'd come again when she could—most probably not until another sennight had passed.

When she made the outer hallway, she paused by Charon and gave him all the money she had within her purse—an embarrassingly paltry amount, but it would have to do. Hopefully it would be enough for the guards to remember to feed him, to empty his slops, and to not beat him to death when his wit became too much for them to bear.

She glanced over Charon's head at the sign that hung above the locked door at his back: *Incurable*.

Every time she saw it, her heart beat with equal parts rage and fear. *Incurable*. It might as well be a death sentence for her beloved twin brother, Apollo: the incurably insane never left Bethlem Royal Hospital.

Otherwise known as Bedlam.

WHEN THE DOCTOR arrived two hours after their love-making, Megs insisted on staying in the room while he examined Godric. The men seemed to find this an odd behavior. Godric exchanged a wary look with Moulder, while the doctor tutted under his breath, muttering in French. Megs wanted to roll her eyes. None of the *ladies* of the house thought her strange to stay with her injured husband to see if he'd ever use his left arm again. She nearly choked on another wave of fear, grief, and *anger*, and had to turn away from the sight of the doctor probing at Godric's arm. He'd already taken apart the original bandage on Godric's right arm, prodded the long, shallow cut, pronounced it trifling, and rebandaged the arm.

Megs glared when Godric shot her a triumphant glance.

She went to the window now and stared blindly out at the late-morning sun. Stupid men. Stupid, brave, *foolhardy* men who thought nothing of risking their lives by going into the worst part of St. Giles and seeking out danger. She raised her fisted hand to her mouth and bit down hard on her knuckle.

Sometimes losing their lives.

She couldn't bear another man lost to her. She'd go mad.

The doctor gave a loud grunt behind her. "Very illadvised, sir, to take the splint from your arm so soon. I cannot tell you how lucky you are not to have broken the wrist again."

Megs turned to find the doctor standing over a stoic-faced Godric, carefully rebinding his arm.

"It's not rebroken?" she asked.

"No," the doctor muttered. "But there will be swelling from where Mr. St. John...er...*fell* on it." That had been the tale they'd told the man—despite the ridiculousness of that long cut coming from anything but a sword.

She blew a breath out in relief. "And will it heal properly?"

He gave a Gallic shrug. "Perhaps. Certainly not if Mr. St. John abuses it further."

"I shall make certain he does not, then," Megs said determinedly, ignoring the wry look Godric sent her.

The doctor fussed for another five minutes, by which time Godric was leaning back in his bed, obviously quite tired. Megs saw the doctor to the bedroom door and then returned to the bed where she was exasperated to find Godric struggling upright.

"What are you doing?"

He glanced up, his brows drawn together. "Rising."

"No," she said, placing a hand on his chest and pushing down, "you are not. The doctor specified *rest* if that wrist is to heal."

He blinked up at her, a faint trace of amusement flashing in his eyes. She hadn't exactly let him rest when he'd first returned home. Heat rose in her cheeks.

But he replied gently, "Yes, my lady."

She eyed him suspiciously, but he had lain back down, his body relaxed. He really did look quite exhausted.

Her heart contracted painfully.

"Go to sleep," she whispered, softly touching the bandages on his right arm. When had he come to mean so much to her?

He closed his eyes, turned his head, and kissed her finger.

She swallowed down the lump in her throat. The only chair in the room was the one by the desk, so she took it and moved it closer to the bed, ignoring Moulder's look. Then she sat and watched Godric sleep.

It may've been minutes or hours later when a gentle tap came at the bedroom door. It had been left cracked so that Her Grace could come and go as she pleased. Megs looked up to see Mrs. Crumb beckoning her.

She glanced back at the bed, but Godric lay in deep slumber, so she rose and followed the housekeeper out of the room.

"Pardon me, my lady," Mrs. Crumb said in a low voice, "but there is a caller and he insists on speaking to either you or Mr. St. John."

Megs's brows rose. "Who is it?"

"Lord d'Arque."

For a moment she blinked, confused, before realization flooded her: He must've come about Roger and his murder. She followed the housekeeper down the stairs, feeling an odd sort of guilt at leaving Godric. But this was part of the reason why she'd come all the way to London, wasn't it? If she could find out more about Roger's murder, then she'd be that much closer to avenging him.

And leaving Godric.

The thought made her nearly stumble.

It wasn't until they made the first-floor hallway and the housekeeper indicated that Lord d'Arque was waiting in the library that she remembered Godric's dislike of the viscount. Even if her husband had been polite to the other man at the theater, it didn't mean he would approve of a private tête-à-tête with the man.

She looked at the housekeeper. "Will you ask Miss Sarah St. John to come here, please?"

"Yes, my lady."

She waited while Mrs. Crumb mounted the stairs, waited a moment more, took a deep breath, and entered the library.

Lord d'Arque was examining a bookcase on the far side of the room, but he turned at her entrance and crossed to her.

"My lady." He bent over her hand but didn't touch it with his lips. When he straightened, she saw that he was grave.

Strange. She didn't know him at all well, but whenever she'd seen him previously, he'd almost always been smiling wickedly.

Almost as if his smile were his armor.

"My lord," she replied. "What brings you to my home?"

He looked doubtfully at her. "I had hoped to speak to your husband."

"I fear he is indisposed."

He blinked, appearing to consider the matter before saying, "I came about Roger Fraser-Burnsby."

She nodded, having braced herself for the name.

Behind her, the door to the library opened again and Sarah came in. "Megs?"

"Oh, there you are," Megs said lightly. "I can't remember. Have you met Lord d'Arque?"

"I don't believe so," Sarah said, coming nearer.

"A terrible oversight on my part," Lord d'Arque drawled.

Megs turned. Ah, there it was. His crooked smirk was in place. Beside her, Megs felt Sarah stiffen. Her sister-in-law had decided opinions on rakes.

"My lord, may I introduce my dear sister-in-law, Miss

Sarah St. John?" Megs said formally. "Sarah, this is Viscount d'Arque."

"I am entirely enchanted to meet you, Miss St. John," the viscount said with smooth charm. "I confess your exquisite beauty dazzles my eyes."

"That sounds inconvenient," Sarah murmured as Lord d'Arque straightened. "Let's hope you can see well enough not to bump into the furniture."

Lord d'Arque arched an amused brow, but before he could say something awful, Megs broke in.

"Shall we adjourn to the garden?" That would be quite proper. She should be able to talk to Lord d'Arque out of earshot of Sarah but still be within sight. "We've made several new plantings and I'm sure you'll be pleased, my lord, to see them."

She had no idea if the viscount was at all interested in gardening, but he murmured an assent.

Sarah arched a brow but merely said, "That sounds lovely. Shall I fetch our hats?"

Megs smiled at her. "Please."

When she turned back around, Lord d'Arque was solemn again, but he didn't mention Roger. They talked of inconsequential things until Sarah once again returned, a wide straw hat on her head and one in her hand. Megs thanked her and they all three proceeded to the garden. They strolled for a bit with Megs babbling about crocuses and forget-me-nots before Sarah cast her an odd look and declared that she wished to sit for a while. She sank onto one of the marble benches near the house—recently cleaned by the little maids—and gazed discreetly toward the river wall.

"Perhaps you can give me an opinion on my fruit

tree," Megs said as she and the viscount strolled in that direction.

Lord d'Arque glanced disinterestedly at the tree. "It looks dead." He stopped. "My lady, you once asked about my friend Roger Fraser-Burnsby."

"Yes." She focused on the tree, searching out the tiny buds. It wasn't dead—quite the contrary.

"I think," the viscount said, "that you may have had a...close friendship with Roger."

She looked at him. He was watching her frankly, and she could see a deep pain in his eyes. She made an impulsive decision. "I loved him and he loved me."

He bowed his head. "I'm glad he found you before his death."

Her eyes pricked and she blinked rapidly. "Thank you."

He nodded. "I've been thinking the matter over since I talked to your husband at the theater. I wonder if perhaps we pooled our knowledge of his last movements, we might, between us, discover how he came to be killed—and who did it."

She took a deep breath, once again looking at the tree. "The last time I saw him, Roger had proposed to me."

His head jerked in surprise. "You were engaged?"

"Yes."

"But why didn't you tell anyone?"

She ran a finger over the gnarled branch of the old tree. "It was a secret—he hadn't yet asked my elder brother for my hand. Roger wanted to prove himself, I think. He talked about a business proposition, one that would make enough money that he could ask for my hand properly."

Lord d'Arque made a quiet exclamation.

She glanced at him curiously. "What is it?"

"About six months before Roger died, I was asked by a friend of ours if I wanted to take part in a business venture. One that he assured me would make lots of money."

Megs frowned. "What was the business?"

"I don't know." Lord d'Arque shrugged. "I find that business propositions that promise cornucopias of money generally end up with the investor losing all but his small-clothes. I avoid them when possible. Since I turned down the proposition at once, I never found out what the business was."

"Who was the friend who made the offer, then?"

Lord d'Arque hesitated only a moment. "The Earl of Kershaw."

Godric opened his eyes to the sight of Megs sitting on a chair next to his bed. He glanced at the window and was surprised to see the light dimming. He must've slept all day. For a moment he watched her. She sat with her head bowed, staring at her hands as she idly twined her fingers together. She looked deep in thought, and the spark that lit in his chest just from her presence was . . . warming.

"Have you been there since morning?" he asked his wife softly.

She started and looked up. "No, I went down for luncheon, and we had a visitor this morning."

"Oh?" He yawned, stretching lazily, a twinge from his left arm reminding him why he'd been abed to begin with. All things considered, he felt much better. Perhaps he could lure Megs into coming to bed with him for a repeat of this morning's activities.

"Lord d'Arque came to call."

He stilled. "Why?"

She bit her lip, looking a little lost. "He wanted to talk about Roger."

She told him of the conversation she'd had with d'Arque, and by the time she was telling him that Kershaw had once asked the viscount to invest in a mysterious business, he'd closed his eyes in horror.

"What is it, Godric?"

How could he tell her? He opened his eyes, a fierce sense of protectiveness flooding him. He never wanted her hurt. The knowledge he now had would bring no relief from her sorrow. But she wasn't a child. He hadn't the right to decide what information to give her and what to keep from her.

He took a breath. "Two years ago, the Ghost of St. Giles—a different Ghost than me—killed Charles Seymour." His eyes flicked up at her. "Seymour had been enslaving girls—small girls, most younger than twelve—to make fancy ladies' stockings."

"Like the workshops you told me about." She nodded. "What does that have to do with Roger?"

"We thought the stocking workshops had been shut down with the death of Seymour. But they started again in St. Giles, not long ago. Last night I found the last one—and freed eleven little girls. I got this"—he raised his injured left arm—"when I was attacked by a gentleman."

She simply looked at him, the question in her eyes.

He sighed. "It was Kershaw."

Her lips parted slowly, her brows drawing together. "Lord d'Arque said that the Earl of Kershaw offered him an investment opportunity but didn't say what it was. If Roger was made a similar offer by the earl..." She stood suddenly as if she could no longer sit still, pacing agitatedly in front of the bed. "He wanted to improve his funds before offering for my hand. If he accepted the business deal without inquiring what kind of business it was..." She stopped, staring at him, her eyes wide. "If he went to St. Giles and was presented with a workshop with enslaved little *girls*...dear God, Godric! Roger was a good man. He would've *never* condoned such horror."

Godric inclined his head. "They would've had to murder him so he wouldn't tell others."

"This is the answer, then," Megs whispered. "We must tell the authorities. We must—"

"No."

She jerked, her eyes wounded. "What?"

He sat up, leaning forward. "He's an *earl*, Megs, and we have no proof of anything, really, merely guesses. For all we know, Seymour killed Roger. Or someone else. Unlikely that an earl would do such stuff himself."

Her hands became tight fists. "He's still responsible, even if it was his partner or someone he hired. He helped kill Roger."

"We don't even know that," Godric said tiredly. "This is all speculation."

"If I told Lord d'Arque—"

"If you told the viscount—and he believed you—what do you think would happen?" he asked hard. "D'Arque would be forced to call Kershaw out."

She blinked and opened her mouth as if to protest, then closed it. Dueling was illegal. Even if d'Arque survived a duel—and Godric wouldn't put it past Kershaw to cheat—he would be banished from the country.

"Give me some time," he said gently. "I'll investigate and learn more."

She bit her lip and whispered, "I can't stand the thought of him walking free when Roger is in his grave."

"I'm sorry." He held out his hands. "Come here."

She came with slow steps like a reluctant child.

He took her hands, pulling her down to the bed with him, and he felt her slight resistance. "Shhh. I just want to lie with you, nothing more."

He was afraid she would make an excuse and pull away. He wasn't hurt and they weren't about to have sex. There was no practical reason for her to lie with him.

But she did anyway, a soft weight against his side, smelling of orange blossoms and life. He couldn't help but feel glad when she laid her hand on his chest and her breathing grew slow.

Still, he stared at the ceiling of his bedroom for long minutes, planning, calculating, trying to find a way to bring down an earl.

Chapter Eighteen

"Poor, poor souls!" Faith cried, and a single tear fell
from her eye.
Her unhappiness so enchanted Loss that he forgot himself,
letting go of the horse and clapping his tiny red hands.
Swifter than the blink of an eye, Faith pushed the imp from
the horse. He fell with a shriek and was trampled beneath
the big black horse's hooves.
The Hellequin chuckled under his breath. "Those demon
imps have been my sole companions for an eternity, yet
you've rid me of them in one day." ...
—From *The Legend of the Hellequin*

Late the next morning, Megs stared down at her figures and did the calculation again. For the third time. Both because she always got a bit muddled when it came to numbers and because, well, they couldn't be correct.

Yet the result was the same: She'd missed one of her courses and was late for the second. How was that possible? She tried to scowl at the numbers on the scrap of paper, but a gleeful grin kept taking over instead. She was trying very hard to be *practical*, to ignore the rising tide of elation within her breast. It was much too soon, she chided herself. If she got her hopes up, she'd be terribly disappointed to find brown stains on her linen tomorrow.

But what if she *didn't*? Have her courses again, that is. What if she were really, truly with child?

She giggled aloud.

The thought had her jumping up, too restless with possibility to sit still. She crossed into Godric's room almost without thought—and then was disappointed to see he was not there.

Megs wrinkled her nose, looking around. She tiptoed to his dressing room and peeked in.

Her Grace lay on a man's shirt—Megs truly hoped it was a castoff of Godric's—nursing her puppies. The dog raised her head and looked inquiringly at Megs.

"It's quite all right," Megs whispered. "I didn't mean to disturb you."

She watched for a minute more because the puppies were making quite adorable snuffling sounds, and the chocolate one kept trying to push his paw in his sibling's face. After a while she turned back to Godric's room, meaning to return to her own. Something about his dresser caught her eye, though. The top drawer was pulled out, the key still inserted in the lock.

She went to look—it was a quite irresistible urge.

The key was a small one on a silver chain, and she realized, looking at it, that it was the same key that Godric wore around his neck. She touched it with one finger, making the silver chain swing gently.

Then she looked in the drawer.

At the front was a messy pile of letters. Behind it was a much neater, thin stack of letters bound in black, and in the corner of the drawer was a pretty blue and white enameled box. She picked it up and opened the hinged lid. Inside were two locks of fine hair, one brown and the other the same shade of brown but with gray mingled in the threads as well. They must've been Clara's, and it struck her how long he'd known his first wife—long enough for her hair to start to gray. The thought made her melancholy. He'd had *years* of living and loving Clara while she—

But that didn't matter, did it? She hadn't come to London for Godric's love.

She frowned and slowly replaced the enameled box.

Megs looked closer at the two stacks of letters. The one bound in black was obviously from Clara, but the loose pile...

Her heart began beating faster.

She recognized her own sprawling writing on the top. She riffled through the letters and found that they were all from her. She stared. Godric had saved every letter she'd written him. The thought made her back prickle. All those missives hastily scrawled off without any forethought, all those ramblings about Laurelwood and Upper Hornsfield and her daily life and...and *kittens*. Why had he ever bothered to save them?

She picked up one randomly from the pile and opened it, reading.

10 January 1740

Dear Godric,
What do you think? We have piles of snow here! I don't know where it came from. Battlefield has been mooning about all day muttering about how he's never seen such snow hereabouts in his lifetime, which, as you know, is extensive—some would say

overly *extensive—and Cook has had three revela-
tions of the Second Coming already today and we
haven't even had Luncheon yet. Despite the possible Apocalypse, I do hope the snow stays, for it
is quite lovely and ices every little tree branch and
window ledge. If it snowed every winter I might
come to quite like the dark season.*

*I've watched a wee robin all morning, hopping
along the branches of the hawthorn tree outside my
bedroom window and pausing now and again to
pick out some startled insect from beneath the bark
and gobble it up. Some of the stable lads and the
younger footmen spent the morning in a snowball
skirmish that only ended when Battlefield was acci-
dentally hit in the back of the neck (!) and a forcible
peace was enacted.*

*Bother! I haven't yet asked you the question I
meant to with this letter and now I'm nearly out of
paper, so here it is. Sarah mentioned this morning
how much you enjoyed Laurelwood when you were
younger, and it gave me a nasty start. Has my presence kept you from visiting? I do hope not! Please,
please,* please *do come visit if you have a mind to—
and despite the descriptions above, which, really,
would put any sane person off. Cook might be mad,
but she* does *make the most divine lemon tarts, and
Battlefield is Battlefield so we must all put up with
him, and I am scatterbrained, but I will make every
attempt to appear solemn and serious and… well, I
do wish you would visit.*

*Yours,
M.*

The last bit was written in a very cramped hand because she had run out of paper after all that. Megs smoothed the letter, remembering that day in winter and how happy everyone was and how she seemed to miss *something*. She'd already known she'd wanted a babe by that point, but there was something more that she'd needed when she'd written this letter.

The door to Godric's room opened.

She looked up, not bothering to hide the letter in her hands.

Godric paused on the threshold, arching his eyebrows mildly at finding her in his room going through his personal possessions. "Good morning."

"You kept them all," she blurted out.

"Your letters? Yes." He strolled in and closed the door to the room. He didn't seem put out by her riffling through his secrets.

Which made her feel guiltier, of course. She hadn't kept all of his letters—just the most recent ones, and those she'd tossed in a drawer at Laurelwood. "Why did you keep them?"

"I liked rereading them." His voice was deep, and she shivered as if it were rasping over her spine.

She looked away, concentrating as she carefully folded the letter and placed it with the others. "Do you think of Clara?"

The question was too personal, too intimate, but she waited, breath held, for his answer.

"Yes."

"Often?"

He slowly shook his head. "Not as often as I used to."

She bit her lip, closing her eyes. "Do you feel guilty when you make love to me?"

"No." She felt him come nearer, standing near enough that the warmth from his body reached out to her. "I loved Clara deeply and I will never forget her, but she's gone. I've learned, I think, in these last weeks, to set aside what I felt for her so that I can feel something else with you."

She inhaled, her heart beating wildly, not entirely sure she wanted to hear this. "How...how can you reconcile it, though? The love you felt? It was real, wasn't it? Strong and true?"

"Yes, it was very real." She felt the press of his hands on her shoulders. They were warm and steadfast. "I think had you not come into my life I would've stayed a celibate hermit. But that didn't happen. You did come," he said simply, a statement of fact.

She opened her eyes, twisting to face him. "Do you regret it? Do you hate me for forcing you to give up your memories of Clara?"

A corner of his mouth tipped up. "You didn't force me to do anything." He looked at her, his dark eyes grave. "Do you feel you've betrayed Roger?"

"I don't know," she said, because it was the truth—her feelings for Roger were in a muddle. She saw the wince that Godric tried to hide and she felt an answering pain at having caused him hurt. But she soldiered on because he'd asked and he deserved the truth. "I want—wanted— a baby so terribly and I think he would've understood that. He was a joyful man and I think—I hope—he would've wanted me to be joyful even after he died. But I haven't brought his murderer to justice." She gazed up at him, trying to convey her confused emotions.

"I told you I'll find a way to make Kershaw pay and I

will," he said, iron hard. "I promise I'll help you lay Roger to rest."

"I don't want you going back into St. Giles," she whispered, stroking one finger along his jaw. "I owe you too much already. Everything you've done for me. Everything you've given up for me."

"There is no debt between you and me." He smiled. "I voluntarily chose to move beyond my grief for Clara. Life is by necessity for the living."

She stared up into his dark eyes, something kindling and glowing in her breast, and she longed in that moment to tell him. Tell him that she suspected that she was carrying his child. Carrying life itself.

But she remembered with a shock what that would mean: she'd promised him that she would leave when she became pregnant.

She didn't want to leave Godric. Not yet. Maybe never.

His eyebrows had knit together while she'd remained silent as if he were trying to figure out what she was thinking. It made him look stern and rather solemn paired with his usual gray wig and the half-moon spectacles pushed absently to his forehead. She found the look rather irresistible, actually, and she raised herself on tiptoe to brush her lips across his.

When she pulled back, he had a bemused expression on his face, but she smiled at him and he smiled in return. "Come. If you remember, you wanted to visit Spring Gardens today."

She ducked her head, linking hands with him as he drew her from the room. Happiness trembled near her heart, but it was held back by the knowledge she would soon have to tell him and when she did, he would ask her to leave.

And if nothing else, she needed to put Roger to rest before she left London. Somehow.

SPRING GARDENS WAS a pleasant place, Godric thought, even if he wasn't much interested in flowers or plants. Megs was interested, and it seemed her enjoyment of the gardens made it enjoyable for him as well.

They walked along a gravel path, edged with short boxwood trimmed with surgical severity into angular shapes. The beds themselves were mostly barren and Godric privately thought they weren't any better than his own garden at Saint House, save for the fact that they were neater.

Megs, however, found much to exclaim over.

"Oh, look at those tiny white flowers," she said, nearly bending in half to peer closer. "Do you know what they are, Mrs. St. John?"

His stepmother, who had been walking behind, crowded close to his elbow to look. "Perhaps a type of crocus?"

"But they're on stems," Megs said, straightening and frowning down at the flower, which looked quite pedestrian to Godric. "I don't think I've ever seen a crocus on a stem."

"Or with green bits," Sarah said.

"Eh?" Great-Aunt Elvina cupped one hand around her ear.

"Green. Bits," Sarah repeated, loudly and clearly.

"I see no green bits," Great-Aunt Elvina pronounced.

"They're *right there*," Jane said, pointing, while at the same time Charlotte murmured that she saw no trace of green *either*.

There followed a lively discussion on whether or not the flower sported "green bits" and if crocuses ever could be found with long stems. Godric watched in amusement.

"I've never seen her so happy," his stepmother said in his ear. He turned his head to find that while he'd been watching the others, she'd been watching him. "Or you."

He blinked, looking away, unnerved.

"Godric," she said, taking his elbow and walking down the path a bit. "You are happy, aren't you?"

"Can one ever really say one is happy?" he asked wryly.

"I believe so," she replied, her round face grave. "I was very happy with your father."

"You made him happy as well," he murmured.

She nodded as if this wasn't news to her. "The only thing I regret about my marriage to your father is that it made you so very unhappy."

He felt heat rising in his face, the old shame of how he'd treated her coming to the surface. He inhaled and stopped to stare fixedly at a strange, drooping tree. "I was unhappy before you ever married Father. Your arrival only gave me a focus for my ire. I'm sorry. I treated you very badly."

"You were still a boy, Godric," she said softly. "I've forgiven you for it long ago. I only wish you could forgive yourself. Your sisters and I miss you."

He swallowed and at last looked at her. Her eyes were crinkled with worry for him. Love for him. He didn't understand it. She should by rights hate him. He'd been truly cruel to her for years. But if she could put the past behind them, the very least he could do for her was try to do the same.

He placed his hand over hers, lying soft and warm on

his arm, and squeezed gently, hoping she'd understand what he couldn't say.

"Oh, Godric." Tears glittered in her eyes, but he thought they were glad tears. "It's so good to have you back."

He bent to kiss her on the cheek, murmuring, "Thank you for waiting."

Behind them he could hear the rest of his family coming to meet him, still apparently arguing about green bits and stemmed crocuses. He turned and saw Jane and Charlotte, arm in arm, despite their passionate discussion. Behind them was Great-Aunt Elvina, making an overloud point to Sarah, who was attentive but had a small smile on her face. And bringing up the rear was his dear wife. Megs looked up just then, catching his eye, and he saw that her cheeks were a deep pink from the wind and the excitement. She grinned at him and something broke free in his chest, lightening, glowing, warming him internally.

He made a mental note: he'd have to bring Megs to the gardens at least once a week while she was in London, for she was truly in her element here and he found it rather a wonderful place himself.

He waited until the others had passed him and Mrs. St. John, and then offered his wife his left arm. She looked at it cautiously as if afraid to injure it again.

"Come on this side of Godric," his stepmother murmured, and she exchanged a glance with Megs, one of those mysterious feminine ones that seemed to relate all the news of the world. "I want to stroll a bit with Sarah."

Megs took his right arm, which had healed nicely, the bandage already off, and glanced up at him as Mrs. St. John walked ahead to catch up with the others. "I'm so glad you talked to your stepmother."

She smiled brilliantly and he wondered—not for the first time—how women managed to know these things without speaking.

He pushed the matter from his mind, though, and smiled down at his wife, for it really was a lovely day. They strolled slowly, the others drawing farther ahead until it seemed they walked in a garden all their own, Godric thought whimsically.

But every garden has its serpent.

They were approaching an intersection with another path, the corner screened by several trees just beginning to leaf. Godric could see another couple coming closer, but it wasn't until he and Megs were at the junction that he saw who it was: the Earl and Countess of Kershaw.

Chapter Nineteen

Faith yawned. "I'm so sleepy. Can we not rest for a bit?"
The Hellequin dismounted the big black horse readily
enough and lifted Faith off. She lay down in the dust of the
Plain of Madness and wrapped the Hellequin's
cloak about her. Yet still she shivered.
Holding out a hand, she said to the Hellequin,
"Will you not lie with me?"
So he lay beside her and curved his big body around hers
and as she drifted into slumber, she heard him say, "I have
not slept the sleep of men for a millennium."...
—From *The Legend of the Hellequin*

Megs froze. Lord Kershaw had been laughing at something, his round face thrown back to the sun's rays, his mouth wide, his eyes squinting with laughter. It felt like a knife wound to the soul. Roger had once laughed so uninhibitedly.

Had once walked in the sunlight.

"How dare you," she said low, without any forethought, but she wouldn't have been able to remain silent and still breathe. "How *dare* you?"

"Megs," Godric said beside her. His entire body had tightened as if preparing for battle, but his voice was soft, almost sad.

She couldn't look at him, not now. All she could see was Lord Kershaw's dying laugh, the way his eyes narrowed with calculation, the stare he pinned on her.

"You killed him," she said, the words righteous on her tongue. "You killed Roger Fraser-Burnsby. He was your friend and you murdered him."

Had he denied her accusation, had he blustered and flushed, backed away, shouted that she was insane, done any of those normal, conventional things, she might've rethought her taunt. Might've come to her senses and pleaded sun poisoning or too much drink or merely the stupidity of her feminine sex.

But he didn't.

Instead, Lord Kershaw leaned forward, his thick lips curving into a sweet smile, and said, "Prove it."

She went wild, she knew it in retrospect, but all she felt in the moment was the hot burn of grief flooding her veins, like acid in the blood. She surged at him, arms outstretched, fingers scrabbling, and only Godric's hard hands saved her from disgrace. He picked her up physically, carrying her even as she bucked and sobbed. Her family was around her now and she saw Sarah's wide eyes, the muted horror on Mrs. St. John's face, and she knew she should feel shame, but all she felt was sorrow.

Drowning, overwhelming sorrow.

She spent the carriage ride home burrowed into Godric's shoulder, trying to inhale his familiar scent, trying to remember all that she had rather than all she had lost.

When they reached Saint House, Godric climbed out of the carriage and then turned around and helped her down, as solicitous as if she were an invalid. She murmured a protest, but he didn't reply, simply tightening his arms about her as he led her in.

Megs heard Mrs. Crumb ask something as they passed her in the hallway and was glad when Sarah stopped to murmur to her. Godric hadn't even hesitated. He mounted the stairs, keeping his right arm around her shoulders, and it was only when they made the upper floor that she remembered his wrist.

She looked anxiously up at him. "Dear Lord, Godric, I must've hurt your wrist when we were in the garden—"

"No," he murmured as he led her into his bedroom. "Hush. It's nothing."

"I'm sorry," she said. "I never wanted to hurt you."

A hot flush rose in her chest, sweeping over her neck and face, and then she was weeping, the tears scalding. There was no relief in these tears, though, no relief while Lord Kershaw lived.

She must've said something as she sobbed—or perhaps Godric knew instinctively what she felt.

He wrapped her in his arms as he gently let down her hair, and it wasn't until her heaving breaths began to quiet that she heard what he was saying.

"He won't get away, Meggie mine, I won't let him. I promise on my soul that I'll take him down. I promise, Meggie, I promise."

His repetition soothed her hurt a little. Megs laid her cheek against his shoulder, limply letting him do as he wanted. He was drawing off her dress, unlacing her stays, freeing her from her clothing. When she was in only her chemise, he laid her gently on his bed and crossed to his dresser. She heard the splash of water and then he was back by her, a cool cloth pressed to her swollen cheeks.

It felt like a benediction, the touch of unconditional forgiveness, and she whispered without thinking. "I loved him."

"I know," he murmured in reply. "I know."

She closed her eyes, her fingers pressing against her stomach, flattened because she was lying down. There was no sign, no manifestation of the baby, but she believed on faith alone.

"I can't begin again," she whispered, "not when he hasn't been avenged. I can't have this baby with this undone, and I can't leave London."

She opened her eyes to see that his eyes had widened and were fixed upon her hands where they lay kneading her stomach. Slowly, his gaze rose to hers, and it burned, but she couldn't read the expression in his eyes.

She hadn't meant to tell him like this, but she couldn't order her brain.

"I can't leave London now," she repeated.

"No," he agreed. "Not now. Not yet."

He got up and went to the dresser and she closed her eyes, drifting.

She felt the dip of the bed when he returned. The cloth was placed on her forehead and she murmured with pleasure. It felt so good, so right.

"Sleep now," he said, and she could tell by his voice that he meant to leave her.

Her eyes popped open. "Stay with me."

He looked away, his mouth tense. "I have business to attend to."

What business? she wondered, but only said aloud, "Please."

He didn't answer, simply toed off his shoes and removed

his coat. He took off his wig and laid it on his dresser, and then he lay down beside her and drew her into his arms.

She lay there, drifting, listening to his deep breaths. He'd not berated her for her outburst in the garden. Anyone else would've been ashamed of her—certainly disapproving. Yet Godric had treated her tenderly even when she'd fought him to get to the Earl of Kershaw. She didn't deserve a man so patient, so good. She turned on her side, watching his profile as he lay on his back next to her. His eyes were closed, but she knew he wasn't asleep. What was he thinking? What did he plan to do? Perhaps it didn't matter right now. He'd agreed that she didn't have to leave London right away, and for that she was grateful. She wanted to stay for Roger—but more importantly she wanted to stay for Godric.

Godric.

His nose was straight in profile and rather elegant, which was a funny thing to think about a man's nose, but it was. The nostrils were slim and well defined, the bridge of his nose shadowed on either side. His mouth, too, had always been beautiful, his lips lighter than the surrounding skin, almost soft-looking. She raised a hand and touched. Lightly, tracing, feeling the slight scrape of his beard on one side, the smooth softness on the other.

His lips parted. "Megs."

His voice, too, had always enthralled her. So gruff and low, sounding as if he'd spent the day shouting angrily at someone.

Except he wasn't an angry man, not really, and certainly not with her.

He rolled toward her so that they were face-to-face. "You should sleep, Meggie mine."

"But I'm not sleepy."

He watched her, his gray eyes weary, saying nothing, simply waiting to see what she wished. It grieved her, what this strong, good man would do for her, and it made her uneasy too.

She fit her lips to his and whispered, "Make love to me, please."

And he complied as he had with every other thing she'd asked of him.

He ran his long, graceful fingers into her hair and grasped the back of her head, holding her, embracing her, making her feel cherished.

His tongue licked into her mouth, gently probing, gently tracing her teeth and the roof of her mouth. She caught his tongue and suckled, pressing her palm against his chest so she could feel his heat, the steadfast beat of his heart. His mouth opened against hers, slanting, nibbling at the corner of her lips. He slid over her cheek to her temple, kissing her tenderly there.

"Godric," she whispered, her voice catching.

There was something he intended to do, something involving Lord Kershaw, and she thought she should find out what it was, make him confess his secrets.

But then he caught the skirts of her chemise and flung it up over her hip and she forgot. He kissed her on the mouth and drew back, watching her as he took her upper leg and drew it over his own, opening her. His hand dropped again, and she felt as he delved between her thighs, gently stroking.

Her eyelids drooped, and her hand rose to his jaw, bringing him closer so she could kiss him again as his knuckle brushed against her clitoris. He pressed there, and she arched her hips into his hand, wanting more, until he withdrew his hand. She moaned in protest, hearing his breathless hush in reply, and then she felt his bare cock against her thigh.

She opened her eyes, staring into his.

"Come closer," he whispered.

She did, inching close, so close that her hips were against his and she felt him at her entrance.

He moved slowly, pressing inside, widening her, making his own place for himself in her body. She watched his face as he breached her. His eyebrows were slightly knit, his mouth curved down. There was something in his dark eyes, a kind of sorrowful well, and she leaned forward to kiss him again.

Then he was as far inside her as he could go. He rocked against her, the movement gentle but strong. She tightened her leg against his still-clad buttocks, rocking with him, and they moved together like a rolling wave.

He gasped a little, his mouth against hers, and she bit down on his lip, opening her eyes lazily, lost in bliss.

Tears stood in his eyes.

She drew back, growing still, shocked. But he blinked and hitched her leg higher, pressing his thumb just above the place where they were joined. And she forgot, leaning into him, wanting this to last a lifetime, this slow movement, this gradual swelling.

He shifted a little higher and she gasped. With every slow grind, he was drawing across that sensitive point, lighting sparks within her.

He kissed her again, his mouth almost wild in contrast to the movement of his hips. It was building now, that savage feeling, and she was making tiny noises in her throat. Noises she couldn't control. He splayed his hand against her cheek, his thumb between her lips. She licked his thumb and he thrust hard against her.

She clutched at him, so close, almost there, and then his hand was stroking, pressing, and the sparks burst into flames behind her eyes. She cried out, arching her neck, nearly breaking their kiss, but he followed her, hungrily feeding on her mouth.

He thrust one last time, powerfully, and she felt the flood of his semen within her.

There was something...something she wanted to know. Something she should ask of him, but her limbs were liquid soft, warm and languid, and she couldn't move, couldn't think.

She felt the brush of his lips against her brow and the whisper of three words, but she was already so close to sleep it might've been a dream.

GODRIC WAITED UNTIL Megs's breathing became deep and even, and then he waited longer. Much longer than he should've, but then she'd become his weakness. His Achilles' heel, the one person who had reached deep down inside him and grasped his heart, squeezing until it started beating again.

She'd brought him back to life.

And in return it was only fair that he gift her with a death.

By the time he finally moved, it was after dusk, which was just as well since it was his element. He huffed out a breath, nearly but not quite a laugh. Godric St. John: Lord of Darkness. He looked down at her as he eased from the bed. Why such a creature of light and love and life should have come to him, he could not fathom. But he was grateful.

Very grateful.

He wanted to kiss her one last time, to impress her beauty upon his mind and carry it with him on whatever journey this night brought him, but he feared to wake her.

In the end, he simply left his bedroom without touching her again.

He called Moulder and dressed swiftly in his Ghost costume, answering the manservant's questions curtly. He took both swords because he would need them, and further injury would be a moot point after tonight anyway. And then he stole into his element.

The darkness.

The night was chill, but not overly so, the hint of spring's awakening whispering on the soft breeze. Overhead, the moon veiled herself seductively with wispy clouds. Godric looked carefully but caught no sight of anyone lurking. Perhaps Captain Trevillion had finally conceded the need for sleep.

He loped west, toward the more fashionable parts of London where the aristocracy built their new houses.

Toward the Earl of Kershaw's house.

He'd made his promise to Megs and he intended to keep it. Had he the time, he might've researched his enemy, found his weaknesses and flaws and brought him down more subtly. But that plan had changed perforce with the scene in the garden. Kershaw was a threat to Megs now. He'd not missed the look of hatred the other man had shot his Meggie when she'd lunged at him. She wouldn't be quiet, wouldn't do the safe thing and leave him alone. A man such as Kershaw didn't leave such potential dangers living. Fraser-Burnsby was an obvious example.

Godric shuddered and stopped at a corner, leaning into

the rough brick building over a chandler's shop. The mere thought of Megs in danger, of Kershaw somehow finding a way to hurt her, made crimson flood his vision. He would not—*could* not—let the other man live while he was a threat to Megs and their child.

That thought—that she was carrying his babe—steadied him enough to start off again. It was a strange but not unwelcome feeling to know that she carried his child. That someday she would hold a babe against her pretty white breast and that the child would be part of him as well.

For the first time in a very long while, he yearned to see tomorrow. Tomorrow and the day after that and the year after that. There was a possibility that with Megs he might have a life to look forward to. And because of that, tonight he was going to hunt down a man and assassinate him in cold blood. This act would damn his very soul, but for Megs it was worth it.

For his Meggie he would walk the fires of Hell.

It took another half hour to reach Kershaw's London town house. It stood in a modern square, white stone town houses on all sides, elegant and reserved. The moon was waning now, coyly hiding behind her cloudy veils. Godric approached Kershaw's residence cautiously, sliding in and out of the shadows, searching for any sign of movement from the house.

He was surprised when the front door opened.

Godric stilled, half hidden in the shadows by the stairs leading to the front door of a house across the way. He watched as Kershaw appeared on his step. The earl stood there, looking around impatiently, and Godric felt his hands fist. A carriage rolled around the corner and Kershaw got in.

Godric frowned, considering his options. No matter what else happened, he had to kill Kershaw and fast, before the man had a chance to hurt Megs.

He decided to follow the carriage, trailing it as it moved east. The roads in London were narrow and sometimes crowded, even at night, so he hauled himself up the corner of a building, grunting at the twinge from his left wrist, and followed by rooftop. Still Godric lost the carriage twice and had to scramble over sliding tiles to keep up, cursing under his breath until he caught sight of the thing again. He considered the destination of his prey as he panted along. Was Kershaw going to a ball or the theater? If so, Godric would have to cool his heels waiting for the man. On the other hand, such events were often crowded with carriages jockeying to either deposit or pick up their occupants. Perhaps he could catch the man unawares in a crowd. This wouldn't be a noble duel.

If need be, Godric would stab the earl in the back.

But it soon became apparent that the carriage was making for St. Giles, which meant this certainly wasn't a social outing. Was the earl scouting new locations for his workshops? Godric shook his head. The man was engorged with hubris if he thought he could simply set up shop again in St. Giles.

Twenty minutes later, the carriage stopped outside a dingy building that was all but leaning against its neighbor. There was no sign to indicate a shop, but a single lantern lit the low doorway, almost as if Kershaw had been expected. Godric lowered himself carefully to the ground and paused in the jut of a low wall, watching as a woman emerged from the building. She was tall and bony, and when she turned, the lantern light fell upon her face and he recognized the slattern who'd been at the third work-shop. She stood, arms akimbo, and said something to Kershaw, still in the carriage. There was a pause and she threw up her hands, turning as if angered. At that, the carriage door flew open and Kershaw emerged to hit her across the face, nearly knocking her down. She steadied herself, though, and went back into the shop.

There were two footmen on the back of the carriage and they descended as well, spreading out on either side of Kershaw. He'd brought guards. For himself or something—or *someone*—else?

The door to the crumbling building opened again and the slattern came back out, grasping a little girl in each hand. But they weren't who the guards were there for. Behind her was a third tough, both hands gripping tightly a much smaller figure in front of him. She was slim and held herself defiantly, but her face was bruised and she'd lost her old hat.

Alf. They had Alf.

If he waited until they got her into the carriage, he might lose the carriage—and both her and the little girls. Alf had said that the lassie snatchers wanted her dead, and he was surprised that she was still alive. He would've thought they'd kill her on sight.

There was no other choice.

Godric charged the tableau.

The guard closest to him still had his back to Godric. A quick thrust with his short sword under the man's ribs dispatched him, though it sent agonizing shards of pain up Godric's wrist.

"You!" Godric looked up to see Kershaw, face inflamed with rage, shouting at him. "Kill him!"

The earl didn't wait to see if his orders would be obeyed. He drew his sword as Godric rushed him and brought it up, repelling Godric's initial thrust. Godric pivoted past him as their swords locked, making sure to keep his back away from Kershaw's guards.

Faintly he could hear the sounds of horses approaching.

Then Godric concentrated on killing Kershaw. He felt the jar to his shoulder as he pushed against the other man, making him fall back. He jabbed at the earl's middle, then his head, moving fast, not giving Kershaw time to gather himself to make his own attack. The earl's eyes were wide, his mouth open and panting, his lips wet. Kershaw feinted to Godric's left and then kicked viciously at his knee. Godric moved, taking the blow on his outer thigh instead. But the earl had expected him to go down. His thrust had gone past Godric, and for a second Kershaw was overextended, his long sword of no use. Godric brought up his short sword and pressed it into the soft skin just under the earl's right arm.

Kershaw froze, eyes widening.

A shot rang out.

Godric glanced over his shoulder and met Captain Trevillion's cold blue eyes. They were surrounded by dragoons on horseback, all of them aiming pistols at his head.

"Hold hard, Ghost."

MEGS WOKE GASPING in the dark, heart beating hard, breath strangled in her throat, and knew at once that something was wrong. Shreds of her nightmare still lingered, a haunting vision of Godric caught in a black oily pit, slowly being sucked down while she did nothing.

Did *nothing* while her husband's mouth and nostrils were covered in obsidian slime, his eyes staring back stoically at her even as he drowned.

Oh, God. She sat up in his big bed, glancing around wildly, even though she knew he wasn't here. *Where was he?* She needed to find him, needed to place her hands on his chest and feel for herself that his heart still beat, that he was well.

She rose, hurriedly throwing on his banyan and lighting a candle from the embers still glowing on the hearth.

She looked first in her own room, a quick glance as she hurried past. The next place was the downstairs library. Perhaps he'd woken in the night and been unable to sleep? Perhaps he was even now dozing in a chair before the fireplace, that silly, stupid tasseled hat on his dear, dear head. She sobbed and realized that she'd broken into a near-panicked run.

He wasn't in the library.

She sagged against the door, pressing the back of her hand to her weeping mouth.

He wasn't here. He wasn't here. He wasn't here.

She tried his study last because hope died hard and she had to see for herself before she acknowledged what she already knew.

The study was quiet, the door to his hidden closet ajar. She could see that his Ghost costume was gone and she knew, *knew* what she had done. Megs pressed a hand to her mouth to stifle a wail of horror.

She'd abandoned a living man for a dead one.

Chapter Twenty

When Faith opened her eyes the next morning, the first
sight she saw was the Hellequin. He held the sack made
of raven's hides, and as she watched, he took out her
beloved's soul and unwound the spider's silk from around
it. At once her beloved's soul drifted upward, free and
sparkling. Faith watched until she could no longer see him.
Then she looked at the Hellequin, her eyes shining.
"Will my beloved enter Heaven now?"
"Yes," the Hellequin said.
"And what will happen to you?"
But the Hellequin merely shook his head and mounted
the big black horse....
—From *The Legend of the Hellequin*

Godric felt his chest rising and falling as he tried to catch
his breath. His left arm ached, deep and compelling, and
his hand shook just a little as he pressed the short sword to
Kershaw's vulnerable armpit. He stared at Trevillion and
wanted to hiss. Wanted to spit and howl. He was fated to
be taken tonight, it seemed, but he would drag Kershaw
with him, clasping him to his bloody bosom as he went
down. Something flickered in Trevillion's eyes, perhaps
a premonition, as Godric's muscles tensed, preparing to

shove the sword tip through skin and muscle, tendon and bone.

"Nooooo!" It was Alf's voice, hoarse and loud. The girl wrenched herself away from her stunned guard, running to Godric. "You can't take the Ghost, you soddin' redcoats. This toff steals little girls. If'n you—"

But her words were cut off as Kershaw took advantage of the confusion. He grabbed Alf's hair, bending back her head, exposing a throat much too thin and tender and placed the blade of his sword against it.

Godric lunged, sinking his short sword into Kershaw, pushing until the hilt hit his coat.

Kershaw wheezed.

Alf screamed, high and feminine.

Godric twisted the blade, staring fiercely into Kershaw's muddy eyes as they dimmed and he dropped his sword. He yanked the bloody short sword from the body and Kershaw's corpse fell gracelessly to the cobblestones.

"Hold your fire!" Trevillion screamed. "Hold your blasted fire!"

For a moment everyone froze, the only sound the nervous stomping of the horses and the whimpering of the two girls.

One of the guards took off at a run.

Trevillion nodded in his direction and a mounted man cantered after him.

"Arrest them all," Trevillion growled, dismounting, "save for the Ghost. He's mine."

He unsheathed his sword.

Godric backed a step. He had no particular urge to kill the dragoon captain—the soldier was only doing his job, after all.

Captain Trevillion glared at the mounted dragoons behind Godric. "Did you not hear me, Stockard? I *said* the Ghost is mine."

The soldiers trotted to the side, leaving Godric and Trevillion alone in an open space. Godric gripped his sword, feeling the hilt under his sweaty palm. The night was thick with the stink of blood and horses and the natural miasma of St. Giles.

Trevillion moved forward slowly, forcing Godric back. He lunged, but his attack was oddly clumsy. Perhaps the dragoon hadn't much practice with his sword. Trevillion jabbed again and Godric easily knocked his sword aside, frowning now, trying to understand what the other man was doing. Was he herding him into a corner? But the space behind him was open.

Trevillion thrust again, this time engaging Godric a little more skillfully, still pushing him back because Godric really didn't want this fight.

Their swords locked, each man straining into the other, sweat running down Godric's back, and then Trevillion rolled his eyes and leaned close. "Run, you idiot."

Godric realized that they'd moved several yards away from the other dragoons, close to the crossroads where a dark alley led.

Trevillion shoved hard against him.

Godric spun and fled, expecting any minute to feel a bullet hit his back or the thunder of hooves trampling him down.

They never came. Instead, he caught a flash out of the corner of his eye as Alf scaled a tenement wall as nimbly as a monkey while the dragoons shouted helplessly below.

He ran flat out, his boots ringing on the cobblestones. He ran until the blood roared in his veins, until the breath sobbed in his lungs. He ran until the Home for Unfortunate Infants and Foundling Children came into sight, a familiar carriage at the end of the lane and a cloaked female figure just about to mount the steps.

He stopped, hands propped on knees, his chest heaving, and craned his neck to stare as the woman turned around.

The hood of her velvet cloak was pushed back, glossy, dark curls tumbling to her shoulders. Those shoulders were square, a pistol gripped firmly in her right hand, and determination shone in her pretty eyes.

Godric caught his breath in admiration as he straightened.

Megs's chin kicked up. "No need to thank me."

He blinked. "What?"

She gestured behind her. "I brought the carriage." Her face was composed, but he could see the tremble of her lips as she said gently, "Believe it or not, Ghosts have been known to be accosted by dragoons in this very spot."

His heart had slowed when he'd stopped running, but now it seemed to speed again as he recognized her words. She'd come to rescue him, his brave Meggie. No one had ever done such a thing for him before.

He was aware, suddenly, of the chill condensing clammily on his skin, the smell of damp cobblestones, of the very air flowing in and out of his lungs.

But most of all he was aware of the woman, this woman, *his* woman, standing so proudly, waiting patiently for him, only him.

He walked toward her and knew with every fiber of his being that he walked to life itself.

MEGS'S VISION BEGAN to blur as Godric, dear, brave, *reckless* Godric, walked toward her. She'd held herself rigidly composed as she'd woken servants and found her pistols, as she'd waited for the horses to be harnessed and sent for a doctor, as she'd given hurried instructions to Mrs. Crumb, Moulder, and Mrs. St. John, as she'd ridden over in the carriage and tried not to imagine finding him already dead. She'd been concise, authoritative, and focused, but now she'd found him and he was alive.

Alive. Alive. Alive.

She didn't even know how they made it inside the carriage, for she'd begun to shake, and once inside she simply let go and sobbed. Great, heaving, sloppy tears that held all the pain and fear she'd held back for the last several hours. He wrapped his arms around her and she gripped him tight because there was simply no way she was ever going to let him go again.

After a bit, she quieted enough to hear him murmuring as they rocked through the London night, "Hush, Meggie mine, hush. It's all right."

But his words only brought a new wave of grief. She squeezed her fingers into his shoulders until she knew she must be hurting him, but she couldn't let go.

"No." She shook her head against him. "It's *not* right. You left."

She felt his palm against her cheek, pressing as if he was trying to see her face, but she wouldn't move.

"What's not right, Megs? Why are you so upset?"

"Because I found you in your Ghost costume in St. Giles. You went after Lord Kershaw, didn't you?"

"Yes," he said, and even without seeing his eyes, she heard the hesitation in his voice.

"How could you, Godric?" Her left hand curled into the back of his neck, her nails gently scraping against the short hairs there. "What if you'd succeeded in finding him? What if you never returned? I couldn't bear it if—"

"I did find him," he broke into her half-hysterical words. "He's dead, Megs."

She did draw back at that, staring in horror at him, and moaned. "Oh, no!"

He frowned, looking very confused. He opened his mouth, shut it, and then finally opened it again to ask cautiously, "I thought you wanted him dead in revenge for the murder of Roger Fraser-Burnsby?"

"Not at the risk of you being hurt or killed!" she nearly shouted.

He blinked. "I'm sorry...what?"

"I wasn't thinking properly earlier. I should've made it clear that you mean more to me than revenging myself on the earl. I should've told you that it didn't matter anymore—which wouldn't have been strictly true, but really, Godric, it would've been better than you going off to get killed without even a *word* to me. If you'd gotten yourself killed tonight, I would've never, ever forgiven you and—"

She gave up at that point because he was looking even more bemused and obviously she hadn't communicated her main point.

So she simply thrust both hands into his short hair and yanked his head down to kiss him.

Ah, there. The tightness of her chest relaxed a bit at the touch of his lips. He might not understand her words, but he was enthusiastic about her kiss, immediately opening her mouth farther and thrusting his tongue in. She hummed contentedly, stroking through his shorn hair, caressing the rim of his ear. He shuddered a bit and she wondered idly if his ears were particularly sensitive. If so—

He pulled back, staring at her in the dim carriage, his brows still knit. "Megs?"

Oh, right. She still hadn't told him. Well, it was his own fault; his mouth was simply delicious.

"I love you," she said, speaking clearly so that there might be no confusion. "I love you utterly and completely. I love your elegant hands and the way you smile with only one side of your mouth—when you smile at all— and I love how grave your eyes are. I love that you let me invade your house with nearly my entire family and yours, and never even turned a hair. I love that you made love to me when I asked you, purely for politeness' sake, and I love that you got mad at me later and made me make love to *you*. I love that you let Her Grace and her puppies construct a nest out of your shirts in your dressing room. I love that you've spent years selflessly saving people in St. Giles—although I want you to stop *right now*. I love that you killed a man for me, even if I'm still mad at you about it. I love that you saved my letters before we even knew each other well, and I love the curt, overly serious letters you wrote to me in return."

She looked at him very seriously.

"I love you, Godric St. John, and now I'm breaking my word. I will not leave you. You may either come with me to Laurelwood or I'll stay here with you in your musty old house in London and drive you mad with all my talking and relatives and...and exotic sexual positions until you break down and love me back, for I'm warning you that I'm not giving up until you love me and we're a happy family with dozens of children."

She paused at that point because she'd run out of breath and looked at him.

His face had gone still and for a moment her heart sank and she had to fortify herself for a battle.

But then his mouth quirked *like that* and he said, "Exotic sexual positions?"

And she knew even before he said anything else that it was all going to be fine—more than fine. It was going to be *wonderful*.

Still she listened attentively when he said, "Much as I'd like you to convince me to fall in love with you by the use of exotic sexual positions, you don't need to. I've loved you, Meggie mine, since you sent that second letter."

He might've said more, but she had to interrupt him at that point to kiss him again.

Long moments later she drew back to frown as sternly as she could at him. "No more Ghost."

"No more Ghost," he agreed docilely, his hands busily shoving the velvet cloak off her shoulders. He laid his open mouth against her bare shoulder and she shivered, gasping.

"I have a confession to make," he whispered in her ear.

She just barely managed to open her eyes. "Yes?"

His eyes were dark and laughing. "I didn't agree to bed you for politeness' sake."

He bent back to her shoulder, and after that there was no more conversation, which was just as well.

She had other matters to concentrate on.

FOUR WEEKS LATER...

Godric watched as a small bird with a bright orange breast hopped along a branch and disappeared into a hole in the apple tree. In all his years of living at Saint House, he'd never seen a robin here...but that was before his Meggie came to live with him.

"I told you that apple tree wasn't dead."

He turned at the sound of her voice. She was wearing bright pink and apple green this morning and looked like the very embodiment of spring as she picked her way down the gravel path.

"Are you feeling better?"

An hour ago, she'd sat down to breakfast, picked up a piece of toast, and then hurriedly dropped it and rushed from the room. He'd gone to see what was the matter, of course, and had found her draped over a chamber pot.

She wrinkled her nose at him. "I can't believe you stayed and helped me whilst I was gruesomely sick. I've never been so mortified in my life."

"I love you, sick or not." He raised his brows, searching her face for any signs of lingering nausea, but her cheeks were their regular healthy pink now. "*Are* you better?"

"It's the oddest thing," she said, coming up to him and slipping her hand through his elbow. The scent of orange blossoms drifted to his nostrils, welcome and warm. "Now I'm so hungry I could eat an entire fish pie. In fact, I would very much like a fish pie...and perhaps some scones with gooseberry jam. Wouldn't that be lovely?"

"Lovely," he agreed, although privately he thought the combination of fish and sweet gooseberries might be... odd. "Have you told Cook?"

She shot him a look that privately he'd classified as "wifely"—he rather liked that look. "Godric, we can't just ask Cook to make fish pies and go in search of gooseberry jam on a whim."

"Why not?" he asked. "I pay her wages. If you want fish pie, you ought to have fish pie. And gooseberry jam."

"Silly." She shook her head and gazed at the apple tree again, softly murmuring, "Not dead at all."

He smiled wryly because she pointed out the old apple tree every time they walked in the garden—at least once a day and more often twice—as an example of her gardening acumen.

It was a rather spectacular sight.

The tree had covered itself in an embarrassment of pink and white blossoms, a fragrant, joyous cloud that drew the eye as soon as one stepped into the garden. He was never, ever going to hear the end of this from Meggie.

Not that he was complaining.

"Oh, look," Megs exclaimed. "A robin's nest. And I saw baby bunnies hopping about yesterday evening. I didn't know there was so much wildlife in the heart of London."

"There never was before a goddess came to live here," Godric muttered.

She glanced at him. "What?"

"Never mind."

He wrapped his arms about her, watching with her as the robin took flight. No doubt his garden would be infested with squirrels and badgers and baby hedgehogs soon. Her magic was quite potent, it seemed.

Thank God.

He leaned down to murmur in her ear, "Have I told you how glad I am you invaded my house and turned my life upside down?"

She turned her head so that her cheek brushed his lips. "Every day."

"Ah." He smiled against her soft skin. "You saved me, you know."

She shook her head again. "Silly."

"It's true," he said, because it was. "And now I'm going to save you by demanding Cook make you a fish pie."

She pursed her lips.

"Yes," he insisted, turning her until she faced him. "Nothing is too good for the mother of my child." Her cheeks deepened to rose and she bit her lip, though that didn't stop the smile she was trying to stifle. "You're sure now, aren't you? That's what this morning was about?"

"Yes," she whispered. "Yes, I'm certain."

The grin she gave him was brighter than the sun. It echoed the swell of happiness in his heart as he bent to capture her lips with his.

Together they turned to go into the house in search of fish pie and gooseberry jam.

Epilogue

"Wait!" Faith cried. "Where are you going?"

"To meet the Devil," the Hellequin said.

"Then I shall come with you," she replied.

He looked at her, and for a moment Faith thought she saw an emotion in his eyes: sorrow. Then he held out his hand to her.

Faith took his hand and he pulled her in one movement onto the back of the big black horse. She wrapped her arms around his middle and for a very long time they rode in silence through the Plain of Madness.

At last a towering stone arch appeared before them, jagged and black.

"Is this Hell?" Faith whispered.

"Yes," the Hellequin said, "this is the mouth of Hell. Remember: whatever the Devil says to you, he has no power over you, for you live and breathe. He rules only the dead."

Faith nodded and gripped the Hellequin tighter.

The Hellequin rode the big black horse through the Mouth of Hell and into utter darkness. Faith looked about her, but she could see nothing and hear nothing. It was a place so hollow and bleak and cold that had she been alone, she might've simply shriveled up and lost herself. But Faith still held the Hellequin, and as she laid her cheek against his broad back, she heard the steady thump of his heart.

A thing in the shape of a man appeared before them, and though he was pale and thin and not particularly tall, the

*utter void of humanity in his eyes made Faith shudder
and look away.*

*Even so, the Hellequin took her hand and dismounted,
leading her to stand with him before the thing.*

*"You've let loose the soul I sent you to collect," the Devil
said, for of course it was he.*

The Hellequin bowed his head.

*"You know," the Devil said quietly, "what forfeit
you must pay."*

*Faith's heart squeezed. "What is he talking about?" she
asked the Hellequin. "What is the forfeit?"*

*"My soul," the Hellequin replied. "The Devil demands a
soul and since I lost one, I must pay him back with my own."*

"No!" cried Faith.

*The Devil's thin, cold lips curved as if he were amused.
"The living are so passionate. Shall I chain you to a red-
hot rock and roast your flesh for a hundred years,
girl?"*

*Faith lifted her chin, and though it made her tremble to do
so, she met the Devil's pitiless gaze. "I live. You have no
power over me."*

*"Ah. The Hellequin has been speaking out of turn, I see."
The Devil shrugged. "Begone from my domain, then,
human."*

*"I shall go," Faith said, "but not without the Hellequin."
The Devil threw back his head and laughed—a sound
like a blade drawn along a whetstone. "Silly girl.
The Hellequin is not human and hasn't been for a
thousand years."*

*"He drinks like a human," Faith said.
The Devil's eyes narrowed.*

*"He eats and he sleeps like a human as well," she
continued bravely, hope rising in her chest. "How is he
not a human?"*

*"He does not draw breath like a human," the Devil
snapped.*

Faith's eyes widened and she saw that she had lost, for the Hellequin had never drawn breath the entire time she'd ridden with him.

Faith turned to the Hellequin, her eyes swimming in tears, and stood upon tiptoe to place her palms on either side of his black face. "I'm sorry," she whispered. "I'm sorry."

And she laid her mouth on his and with a kiss blew air from her lungs into his.

The Devil shrieked in rage and around Faith and the Hellequin a roaring wind began to spin. The wind rose, spinning higher and faster until all Faith could do was close her eyes and cling to the Hellequin.

Then the wind was gone and she opened her eyes to find that it was night and they both stood on the crossroads where her beloved had breathed his last breath.

The Hellequin was making an odd rasping sound. He clutched his side and fell to his knees.

Faith knelt beside him, alarmed. "What is wrong?"

"Nothing," he said. "It hurts to draw breath after a millennia of stillness."

He threw back his head and laughed—and unlike the Devil his laughter sounded warm and alive.

The Hellequin drew Faith into his arms. "Dearest, you have given me food, drink, and sleep. You have made my heart beat and breathed life into my dead lungs. You have outwitted the Devil and saved me from Hell, a thing I have never seen before. I am not a good man like your beloved, but if you will take me as husband, I will spend the rest of my mortal life learning how to make you love me."

Faith smiled. "I love you already, for you would have given your own immortal soul simply to free my beloved's—and to please me."

And she pulled his head down and gave him the first of many kisses as a mortal man.

—From *The Legend of the Hellequin*

THREE MONTHS LATER...

As Lady Penelope Chadwicke's companion, Artemis
had witnessed many ill-advised ideas. There had been
the time Penelope had decided to take over the Home for
Unfortunate Infants and Foundling Children—and had
been pelted with cherry pits. Once Penelope had tried
to start a fashionable craze by using a live swan as an
accessory—who knew how irritable swans were? Then
there had been the debacle involving the shepherdess costume and the sheep. A year later the scent of wet wool still
made Artemis flinch.

But—hissing swans notwithstanding—Penelope's ideas
weren't usually *dangerous*.

This one, however, might very well get them killed.

"We're in St. Giles and it's dark," Artemis pointed out
with what she hoped was a persuasive tone. The street
they were on was deserted, the tall houses on either side
looming in a rather sinister manner. "I do think that ful-
fills the letter of your wager with Lord Featherstone, don't
you? Why don't we go home and have some of those
lovely lemon curd tarts that Cook made this morning?"

"Oh, Artemis," Penelope said with that disparaging
tone that Artemis had really come to loathe, "the problem with you is that you have no sense of adventure. Lord
Featherstone won't hand over his jeweled snuffbox unless
I buy one of those awful tin cups of gin at precisely midnight and *drink* it in St. Giles, and so I shall!"

And she went tripping off down a dark lane in the most
violent section of London.

Artemis shivered and followed. She had the lantern,
after all—and while Penelope was a vain, silly ninny,

Artemis was rather fond of her. Perhaps if they found a gin shop very soon, this would all end happily and Artemis would have another amusing tale to tell Apollo when next she visited him.

This was all Miss Hippolyta Royle's fault, Artemis thought darkly as she glanced warily around the awful lane. Miss Royle had captured the imagination of most of aristocratic society—the *male* half, in fact—and for the first time in her life, Penelope had a rival. Her response—to Artemis's deep dismay—was to decide to become "dashing," hence this foolish wager with Lord Featherstone.

"That looks promising," Penelope called gaily, pointing to a wretched hovel at the end of the lane.

Artemis briefly wondered what Penelope considered promising.

Three large men reeled out of the hovel and started their way.

"Penelope," Artemis hissed. "Turn around. Turn around right *now*."

"Whyever should I turn—" Penelope began, but it was already too late.

One of the men raised his head, saw them, and stilled. Artemis had once watched an old tomcat freeze in the exact same way.

Right before the cat tore apart a sparrow.

The men started for them, shoulders bunched, strides bold.

The lane was closed. There were only two ways in or out, and the men advancing on them blocked one.

"Run!" Artemis muttered to her cousin, gesturing with an outstretched arm for Penelope to come with her. She couldn't leave Penelope alone. She simply couldn't.

Penelope screamed, loud and shrill.

The men were almost on them. Running would buy them only seconds.

Dear God, dear God, dear God.

Artemis began to reach for her boot.

And then salvation fell from above.

Salvation was a big, frightening man, who landed in a crouch. He stood, an easy, athletic uncoiling of muscle, and as he straightened she saw his mask: it was black, covering his face from upper lip to hairline, the nose horribly huge, lines of scars twisting along the cheeks. Dark eyes glittered behind the eyeholes, intelligent and alive.

Before her stood the Ghost of St. Giles.

Artemis Greaves did not like to think herself a cynical person, but when the masked figure dropped into the alley to confront the three toughs *already* menacing her and her cousin, she reached for the knife in her boot.

It seemed only prudent.

He was big and wore a harlequin's motley—black-and-red diamond leggings and tunic, black jackboots, a hat with a wide, floppy brim, and a black half-mask with a grotesquely outsized nose. Harlequins were meant to be clowns—a silly entertainment—but no one in the dark alley was laughing. The harlequin uncoiled from his crouch with a lethal movement so elegant Artemis's breath caught in her throat. He was like a jungle cat—wild and without a trace of compassion—and like a jungle cat his attack held no hesitation.

He launched himself at the three men.

Artemis stared, still kneeling, her hand gripping the little blade sheathed in her boot. She'd never seen anyone fight like this—with a kind of brutal grace, two swords flashing at once through the shadows, too swift for the human eye to follow. The first of the three men dropped, rolling to lie still and dazed. On the other side of the fight Artemis's cousin, Lady Penelope Chadwicke, whimpered, cringing away from the bleeding man. A second man lunged, but the harlequin ducked, sweeping his outstretched leg under his opponent's feet, kicking the man to the ground, and then kicking him once more— viciously—in the face. The masked man rose, already striking at the third man, hammering the butt of his sword against his opponent's temple.

The man collapsed with a squishy thud.

Artemis swallowed drily.

The lane was suddenly quiet, the crumbling buildings on either side seeming to loom with decrepit menace. The harlequin pivoted, not even breathing hard, his boot heels scraping on cobblestones, and glanced at Penelope. She still sobbed fearfully against the wall.

His head swiveled silently as he looked from Penelope to Artemis.

Artemis inhaled as she met the cold eyes glittering behind his sinister mask.

Once upon a time she had believed that most people were kind. She also believed that God watched over her and that if she were honest and good and always offered the last piece of raspberry pie to someone else first, then even though sad things might happen, in the end everything would work out for the best. That was before, though. Before she'd lost both her family and the man who'd professed to love her more than the sun itself. Before her beloved brother had been committed wrongly to Bedlam. Before she'd been so wretchedly desperate and alone that she'd wept tears of gratitude when she'd been offered the position of her silly cousin's lady's companion.

Before, Artemis would've fallen upon this grim harlequin with cries of thanks for having rescued them in the nick of time.

Now, Artemis narrowed her eyes at the masked man and wondered *why* he'd come to the aid of two lone women, wandering the dangerous streets of St. Giles at midnight.

She winced.

Perhaps she *had* grown a trifle cynical.

He strode to her in two lithe steps and stood over her. She saw those intense eyes move from the hand on her pathetic knife to her face. His wide mouth twitched—in amusement? Irritation? Pity? She doubted the last, but she simply couldn't *tell*—and bizarrely, she wanted to. It mattered, somehow, what this stranger thought of her—and, of course, what he intended to *do* to her.

Holding her gaze, he sheathed his short sword and pulled the gauntlet off his left hand with his teeth. He held out his bare hand to her.

She glanced at the proffered hand, noticing the dull glint of gold on the smallest finger, before laying her palm in his. Hot strength gripped her tightly as he pulled her upright before him, so close she would've had to move only inches to brush her lips across his throat. She watched the pulse of his blood beat there, strong and sure, before she lifted her gaze. His head was cocked almost as if he were examining her—searching for *something* in her face.

She drew in a breath, parting her lips to ask a question.

Which was when Penelope launched herself at his back. Penelope screamed, obviously nearly out of her mind with fear, as she beat at the harlequin's broad shoulders uselessly.

He reacted of course, turning, yanking his hand from Artemis's fingers as he lifted one arm to push Penelope aside. But Artemis tightened her hand on his. It must've been instinct, for she certainly wouldn't have done it had she thought. As his fingers left hers, something fell into her palm.

Then he was shoving Penelope aside and loping swiftly down the lane.

Penelope panted, her hair half down, a scratch across her face. "He might've killed us!"

"What?" Artemis asked absently, tearing her gaze away from the end of the lane where the masked man had disappeared.

"That was the Ghost of St. Giles," Penelope said. "Didn't you recognize him? They say he's a ravisher of maidens and a cold-blooded murderer!"

"He was rather helpful for a cold-blooded murderer," Artemis said as she bent to lift the lantern. She'd set it down when the toughs had appeared at the end of the alley. Fortunately, it had survived the fight without being knocked over.

She glanced up to see Penelope pouting.

"But you were very brave to defend me," Artemis added hastily.

Penelope brightened. "I was, wasn't I? This is much better than drinking a cup of gin at midnight in St. Giles. I'm sure Lord Featherstone will be very impressed."

Artemis rolled her eyes as she turned back the way

they'd come down the alley. Lord Featherstone was, at the moment, her least favorite person in the world. It was he who had teased Penelope into accepting a mad wager to come into St. Giles at midnight, buy a tin cup of gin, and drink it. Lord Featherstone had nearly gotten them killed—or worse.

He still might, in fact.

Artemis kept a wary eye out as she hurried out of the alley and into another narrow lane. The channel running down the middle of the street was clogged with something noxious and she made sure not to look as she walked swiftly by. Penelope had quieted, following almost docilely. A stooped figure came out of one of the sagging buildings. Artemis stiffened, preparing to run, but the man or woman hurried away at the sight of them.

Still, she didn't relax again until they turned the corner and saw Penelope's carriage, left standing in a wider street.

"Ah, here we are," Penelope said as if they were returning from a stroll along Bond Street. "That was quite exciting, wasn't it?"

Artemis glanced at her cousin incredulously—and a movement on the roof of the building across the way caught her eye. A figure crouched there, athletic and waiting. She stilled. As she looked, he raised a hand to the brim of his hat in mocking salute.

"Artemis?" Penelope had already mounted the steps to the carriage.

Artemis tore her gaze away from the watchful figure. "Coming, Cousin."

She climbed the carriage and sat tensely on the plush indigo squabs. He'd followed them, but why? To discover who they were? Or for a more benign reason—to make sure that they reached the carriage safely. *Silly*, she scolded herself—it did no good to indulge in flights of romantic fancy. She doubted that a creature such as the Ghost of St. Giles cared very much for the safety of two foolish ladies. No doubt he had reasons of his own for following them.

"Just wait until the Duke of Wakefield hears my tale," Penelope said, interrupting Artemis's thoughts. "He'll be terribly surprised, I'll wager."

"Mmm," Artemis murmured, noncommittally. Penelope was very beautiful, but would any man want a wife so hen-witted that she ventured into St. Giles at night on a wager and thought it a great lark? For a moment Artemis's heart twinged with pity for her cousin.

But then again, Penelope was one of the richest heiresses in England. Much could be overlooked for a veritable mountain of gold.

Artemis sighed silently and let her cousin's excited chatter wash over her. She ought to pay more attention. Her fate was inexorably tied to Penelope's, for Artemis would go to whatever house and family her cousin married into.

Unless Penelope decided she no longer needed a lady's companion after she wed.

Artemis's fingers tightened about the thing the Ghost of St. Giles had left in her hand. She'd had a glimpse of it in the carriage's lantern light before she entered. It was a gold signet ring set with a red stone. She rubbed her thumb absently over the worn stone. It felt ancient. Powerful. Which was quite interesting.

An aristocrat might wear such a ring

Turn the page and explore deeper
into Elizabeth Hoyt's enchanting
Maiden Lane series . . .

WICKED INTENTIONS

Infamous for his wild, sensual needs, Lord Caire is searching for a savage killer in St Giles, London's most notorious slum. Widowed Temperance Dews knows St Giles like the back of her hand – she's spent a lifetime caring for its inhabitants at the foundling home her family established. Now that home is at risk . . .

Caire makes a simple offer: in return for Temperance's help navigating the perilous alleys of St Giles, he will introduce her to London's high society so that she can find a benefactor for the home. But Temperance may not be the innocent she seems, and what begins as cold calculation soon falls prey to a passion that neither can control – one that may well destroy them both.

978-0-7499-5455-0

NOTORIOUS PLEASURES

Lady Hero Batten is perfect, well-mannered and beautiful with an impeccable pedigree. After years of waiting for a gentleman to sweep her off her feet, she has decided to do her duty and settle for a proper society marriage to Thomas Remmington, the Marquis of Mandeville. True, the Marquis is a trifle dull and lacks a sense of humour, but he is handsome and rich.

Griffin Remmington, the Marquis' younger brother, is not at all perfect. In fact, some have called him the most notorious rake in London. When Griffin meets Hero he thinks that she is much too intelligent for society, let alone his brother. Their duel of words soon sparks a fire in them both, despite the fact that Hero's marriage to Thomas is drawing ever nearer . . .

978-0-7499-5455-0

SCANDALOUS DESIRES

Widowed Silence Hollingbrook is impoverished, lovely and kind – and nine months ago she made a terrible mistake. She went to a river pirate for help in saving her husband and in the process made a bargain at the cost of her marriage. That night wounded her so terribly that Silence hides in the foundling home she runs with her brother. Except now that same river pirate is back . . . and he's asking for her help.

'Charming' Mickey O'Connor is the most ruthless river pirate in London. Devastatingly handsome and fearsomely intelligent, he clawed his way up through London's criminal underworld. Mickey has no use for tender emotions like compassion and love, and he sees people as pawns to be manipulated. And yet he's never been able to forget the naive captain's wife who came to him when she was most in need . . .

978-0-7499-5450-5

THIEF OF SHADOWS

When society widow Lady Isabel Beckinhall becomes
involved with the Home for Unfortunate Infants and
Foundling Children, she soon clashes with its manager,
Winter Makepeace, whom she finds severely monastic,
terribly solemn . . . and quite distractingly intriguing.
And Winter does have a secret: at night he transforms
into the masked avenger, the Ghost of St Giles.

After the infamous Ghost of St Giles is wounded
while rescuing a notorious pirate from the gallows,
Isabel has no choice but to hide him from a ravenous
mob, though doesn't discover his identity. Winter is
haunted by this glimpse of the tender – and sensuous –
side of Lady Beckinhall, though he knows that they
are too far apart socially to ever be together. But when
a relentless dragoon captain begins hunting the
Ghost of St Giles, Winter must decide if he can trust
his secret, his life and his *heart* to Isabel's hands.

978-0-7499-5814-5